THE INCREDIBLE RISE OF A

GORBALS GANGSTER

Colin Macfarlane

Contents

3

4

Foreword

During the 1970s I was a leading member of the notorious Gorbals Cumbie gang. Our battle cry was "Cumbie ya bass!" We feared no-one but many people feared us. It was a ten year odyssey of gang fights, square goes and madness. The main character in this book, Johnny McGrath, is based on a conglomeration of other wild members of the gang. One such member, also a guy named Johnny, was the gamest guy I had ever seen and often led the Cumbie into battle against other gangs like the Tongs. I can remember him vividly waving a sword during one such gang fight against the Tongs in the Glasgow Green. The guy, like Johnny McGrath, was also aged 21 and had style – Arthur Black handmade shirts and other gear that made many of his contemporaries look like tramps by comparison. Like the main character in this book, the real-life

Johnny had style and a gameness which really stood out amongst the other gang guys. Believe it or not, many stories in this book actually happened and the prominent characters involved actually existed. Those in the know will recognise them immediately.

Many of them are now dead but many are still around and for legal reasons I have had to change the names of the still living characters slightly. Sadly, during the course of writing this book over three years, my great friend and soulmate Pam Cadden passed away. Another inspiration was Mick Murray of Clydebank who is no longer with us. Being part of the final days of the old Gorbals, and a Cumbie gang member, was an amazing experience never to be repeated again. Oddly enough, now and again, I still have the urge to shout "Cumbie ya bass!" if only as a reminder of the old days in the Gorbals.

Many thanks to Philippa MacFarlane for editing the book, actor Steven Berkoff for providing the brilliant Gorbals photos, and design consultant Norman Faulkner. Also Helen John, an extraordinary proof reader - a great gang of people!

Colin MacFarlane.

colinmacuk@yahoo.com

In memory of Pam Cadden of Bury, Manchester. An incredible person.

The past is a foreign country; they do things differently there – L.P. Hartley.

Colin MacFarlane was brought up in Crown Street, Gorbals, during the late 1960s and 1970s. He is the best selling author of The Real Gorbals Story, No Mean Glasgow, and Gorbals Diehards.

Prologue

"Down these mean streets a man must go who is not himself mean, who is neither tarnished nor afraid. He is the hero; he is everything. He must be a complete man and a common man and yet an unusual man. He must be, to use a rather weathered phrase, a man of honour—by instinct, by inevitability, without thought of it, and certainly without saying it. He must be the best man in his world and a good enough man for any world. He will take no man's money dishonestly and no man's insolence without a due and dispassionate revenge. He is a lonely man and his pride is that you will treat him as a proud man or be very sorry you ever saw him. The story is this man's adventure in search of a hidden truth, and it would be no adventure if it did not happen to a man fit for adventure. If there were enough like him, the world would be a very safe place to live in, without becoming too dull to be worth living in."

— **Raymond Chandler**

Chapter 1

BIG PLAN

Standing on the corner on a Saturday night,
Up came some bams who wanted a fight
Ah pulled oot ma razor as quick as a flash
And shouted, Young Cumbie, Young Cumbie,
Young Cumbie ya bass!
Gang song

DOWNTOWN GORBALS 1970s

Johnny McGrath, 21, leader of The Gorbals Cumbie
razor gang had just got out of bed and glanced into the
mirror, by God he looked handsome. He lived at the
top of a three-story tenement in the heart of The
Gorbals, Crown Street, which had originally been built
for the toffs in Victorian times. This made him slightly
superior to the other tenement dwellers in the area.
Many of them lived in rat infested, damp slums, and
had to share a stairhead toilet. Johnny's family had the
luxury of a small inside toilet which was no more than a
glorified claustrophobic cubicle. But even this made
them feel a cut above the rest.

He combed his thick black hair and thought to himself
that he looked like a young Elvis Presley. He left the
top floor flat and walked down the stairs of the
tenement. On the second landing there was a
homeless drunk lying crumpled in a ball. The lobby

dosser lay there like a piece of discarded human rubbish. Johnny stepped over him and proceeded outside, there were children singing in the backcourt:

"Does your maw drink wine?
Does she drink it aw the time?
Does she get a funny feeling when her diddies hit the ceiling?"
As Johnny stepped out of the close, he realised that The Gorbals had come alive. It was thronging with people on this fine Saturday morning. Nearby there was a crowd of wee women, clad in floral headscarves exchanging gossip and banter. One of them, a fat lady in her 50s, was saying "Have ye heard about her up the road? She's a right jezabel, been carrying oan wi' that coalman fella while her man is in the army. When he finds oot, there'll be hell tae pay. He'll probably shoot the pair o' them wi' his big effing rifle." The other women tut-tutted and nodded in agreement.
The thing that kept the Gorbals alive was the seedy gossip among the women and patter among the guys. Outside a nearby bookies, a team of old guys, wearing bunnets, who seemed to have been there forever, were exchanging patter about the day's racing. Johnny addressed them in a friendly tone. "What's the tip today boys?" One old guy was quick to reply, "September Virgin, 7-1 running at Ayr". His pal chimed in "Ah've never met a virgin in September." His comrade laughed, "You've never met a good-looking woman in September or the rest of the year, you ugly bastard, ye."

The guy put on a comic grimace, took a draw of his Capstan Full Strength before replying, "Whit dae ye mean? In ma early days ah wis the Gorbals answer tae Errol Flynn. The birds thought ah wis a right Casanova, ah can tell ye."

"Aye, look at ye now, an ugly auld geezer without a pot tae pish in." His crony retorted, "Yir no' like young Johnny here. A good-looking fella who's got the world at his feet and aw the birds chasing him."

His pal agreed "Aye, yir right enough, he's almost as good looking as me when ah wis 21. And ah had aw the woman chasing me."

His mate laughed heartily. "The only time you had the woman chasing you was when you were a handbag snatcher." Johnny felt embarrassed at the compliments he was being given. He could feel his cheeks warming into a red colour. "Ach," he replied, "Ah suppose everybody is good looking at 21."

One of the old guys contradicted him. "Are you fucking joking? Ye should see that big fat cow o' a sister o' mine. She was pot ugly at 11, even uglier at 21 and now at 51 she would give the Hunchback of Notre Dame a run for his money."

"Hey, that's a bit cruel tae the Hunchback of Notre Dame. Mind you, ah did hear that yir sister has a job at the Glesga Green shows, on the ghost train frightening people."

Johnny felt uplifted by the patter of these cronies. He saw a reflection of himself in a nearby shop window. He looked immaculate, dressed in a casual sort of way. Tailor made Arthur Black shirt, braces, Levi Sta Prest trousers and Doc Marten boots. He was dressed to kill in more ways than one. In his trouser pocket he had concealed an open razor.

The pensioners looked at him with stares of admiration. One of them said, "Look at young Johnny here, he looks like a male model. Has his shirts made by Arthur Black in St Enoch Square. That is class compared ta aw the scruffy young mob ye see hanging aboot the street corners. They're like tramps."

The old guy was right, Arthur Black was known as the tailor who dressed all the young "game guys" of Glasgow. The "gallus" razor men who led the gangs in the City. Being the leader of the YYC – The Young Young Cumbie – the junior division of the gang – Johnny was a regular customer of Arthur Black with various demands for different styles of shirt which he designed himself.

The cream coloured shirt he was wearing certainly looked ostentatious by street standards. It had three pleats at the back, button down collar, with two front pockets.

To show a bit of class, Johnny had the initials J.M. embroidered in gold thread on one of the pockets.

The shirts were not cheap – around £10 at the time – some working men were only earning up to £20 a week but Johnny saw the shirts as worth every penny. They separated him from the other mugs who looked like vagabonds in comparison.

They heaped more praise on him. "Aye, look at Johnny's gear, that's what ah call smart." His mate agreed. "When ah wis your age Johnny ah wis a real man about town – ah had plenty of gear."

"Aye" his pal retorted, "The problem was it was aw… bunnets!"

Johnny felt mildly amused and moved away, waving his hand shouting "See you auld bastards later, there's six billion people oot there and ah'm gonnae meet some of them!"

He walked through the shopping throng in Crown Street turned into Clelland Street and then into Thistle Street. He saw a group of young boys playing and singing. "Bum tit tit, bum tit tit, play your hairy banjo." One of the young boys pulled out his small penis and began to strum it like a guitar. He must have been aged around 10 and was clad in the uniform of poverty, soiled jumper with snottery marks on the sleeves, wrinkled and stained short trousers, with his arse sticking out a hole the back. A couple of young lassies who were playing peevers nearby giggled at the sight of the boy's penis. One of them shouted to him "Put your wee sausage away." The young flasher ran off to kick a ball with his pals.

Johnny shook his head in amusement, what he saw on the streets of the Gorbals never failed to surprise him.

The whole thing seemed ludicrous, it was as if he was living in a huge, run down, crumbling asylum, and he was one of the inmates.

It was a fine day to walk. The sun was beating down and there was a slight Spring breeze in the air.

In the sunshine outside of a pub three young Cumbie gang members were drinking out of a bottle of strong Four Crown Wine. It was cheap but very potent. They were all around the same age as Johnny but not nearly as smartly dressed.

There was a sign of fear and respect in their eyes. One of the boys, Big Wullie, shouted to him,"Dae ye fancy a wee swally?" Johnny stopped and grinned. He had known Wullie since they had been at primary school together. They had other cultural reference points: Wullie's mother often went to the Palace Bingo Hall in Gorbals Street with Johnny's mother. "Aw pals at The Palace" as they would joke.

Johnny shook his head and declined the generous offer. "Nah, never touch that stuff at this time of day, ye' end up getting lifted by the polis."

Another boy, Fat Archie, laughed as he glugged the wine. "Aye you're right enough, we're easy meat for the polis drinking this stuff."

Johnny nodded and smiled in agreement but then a third guy, who he did not recognise and had never seen before, shouted with wine dripping from his mouth, "What's the matter man? Are ye scared of a bit o' wine, are you a poof?" Johnny reached into his trouser pocket and felt his cut throat razor. If anybody's throat needed cut it was this guy. Cheeky bastard!

He looked angrily at the fellow who had made the insolent remark and replied "Aye, I am a homosexual… ah like ma sex at home." He pulled out his open razor and waved it about, "Any more of that patter and your face will be a jigsaw puzzle." It was a worthy reply. Wullie came over all apologetic, he had seen the good and bad sides of Johnny and played it safe. "Sorry Johnny, he disnae know who you are. This is Joe McCoy, he's just moved in from Bridgeton. He's no' a bad fella really, but the wine gives him a big gob."

Wullie looked at McCoy and scolded him. "Aye keep your mouth shut McCoy, ye can get too cheeky wi' that electric juice going down your neck."

Johnny glared at McCoy and realised he had taken an instant dislike to him. McCoy gave a brief wine sodden smile perhaps sensing he had overstepped the mark. Johnny shrugged his shoulders and said, "See you bampots later, that's if the polis don't see you first."

As Johnny headed towards Gorbals Cross he felt angry and irritated that he had not set about, and even slashed the McCoy fella there and then.

But in reality, he would not have slashed him for showing disrespect. A head butt or "a kick in the baws" would have sufficed. He had an inkling though that it had been a mistake to let McCoy off so lightly. He had shown weakness when he should have shown strength. Gorbals lesson number one, never give a sucker an even break. Especially a sucker like McCoy. He instinctively thought that because of his apparent weakness McCoy would be a problem in the future.

Johnny arrived at Gorbals Cross, two policemen spotted him, and came towards him marching in synchronisation. The taller of two, a real teuchter with a West Highland accent and beady eyes, said to Johnny, "You're no' looking for trouble are you pal?" Johnny mocked the question with laughter, "You sound like Elvis – if you're looking for trouble, you've come to the right place! Nah just having a wee stroll, a gander, just like you two."

The shorter of the two policemen grinned, "McGrath we all know where your wee strolls end up – putting some poor bastard into hospital wi' a slashed face."

Johnny gave a laugh of disdain. He hated the police and he knew they in turn hated him. He mockingly said, "Can a man no go for a stroll around the Gorbals without a couple of bampots like you pestering him?"

The two policemen looked annoyed. The taller one said, "Bampots? That's breach of the peace patter. Any more of that and we'll have to arrest you."

Johnny sighed, how the hell did these two idiots become policemen? To him, they had the combined intelligence of a small goldfish. Suddenly, out of the corner of his eye, he caught sight of Cathy McGee standing on the other side of the street.

She looked beautiful, perhaps one of the most beautiful women in the Gorbals. A working class Venus.

She was the same age as Johnny, 21, 5'8", long red hair, perfectly formed breasts and lips, and wearing a floral skirt that accentuated her shapely legs. He had to get these two annoying policemen off his back and talk to her as soon as possible.

"Look, officers," he said in a mild, almost soothing voice, "I don't want any trouble. As Buddy Holly sings, you go your way and I'll go mine."

The policemen looked baffled at the quip. Johnny crossed the road and approached Cathy in a gallus manner. "How's it gaun?" he said in his most confident tone. She blushed and her blue eyes fluttered. It was clear she had a thing for Johnny but she was good at concealing her emotions. It was part of the Gorbals psyche.

"Aye, no bad, Johnny boy. But ah'm a wee bit fed up that ma mother hisnae been well recently."

"Sorry to hear that, Cathy." Johnny replied with true consideration in his voice. "What's the matter wi' her?"

"As you know, Johnny, she hisnae been herself for a while. Ah put it down tae aw the fags she smokes – twenty to thirty a day. "

Johnny grinned slightly, "Twenty to thirty fags a day! She should put a chimney on her head."

Although she had heard that pun a million times before, Cathy laughed and stared at Johnny. She knew she loved him more than she had loved anyone else.

Johnny suddenly felt shy. But he knew that he loved her. It was an unusual feeling. A tingling, a flush and part erection. He wanted to screw her there and then. But she was not that kind of girl. Besides, when he thought about it, he'd rather love her than screw her.

He'd rather court her, give her bunches of roses and kisses rather than a shag in a dirty back lane like the other birds he had been with since the age of 12. The promiscuous line up whores who were ten a penny, but Cathy was one in a million. At times he thought his chances with her were one in a million as well.

Cathy sort of flushed and said in a soft voice, "Where are you off to, Johnny?" He replied regaining his confident tone, "Off to see ma pals. A quick rendezvous and have a natter, nothing important. I'd rather talk to you all day." Johnny was the leader of a razor gang and supposed to be fearless but he could not summon up the courage to ask her out.

She wanted him to ask her out but he had not been forthcoming. She thought, perhaps, he did not fancy her after all. It was a romantic stalemate.

Cathy gave a beautiful smile, perhaps the most beautiful he had ever seen. "Ok John, maybe I'll bump into you sometime soon." Johnny loved the fact that she sometimes used the formal John instead of

Johnny. It gave him a hard on. He smiled, "Hopefully sooner, rather than later."

Cathy laughed, she sounded like a schoolgirl. "John McGrath, you are a patter merchant, you could charm the birds out of the trees with that patter. See ya!" She moved off, a beautiful form of womanhood.

Johnny sighed, for the first time in his life he felt alone. He realised without her, he was nothing.

He walked in the opposite direction and instinctively knew he was walking in the direction of trouble and drama. But he thought rather absurdly that drama, like love, gave his life meaning.

Johnny sauntered towards Eglinton Street passing Nicholson Street on the way. He looked at the decaying tenements there with its shabby inhabitants. He thought it was like a scene from a third world country.

Filthy looking people loafing about in the streets while their children played in the murky puddles. A woman in a grimy looking headscarf was shouting to her equally manky looking son, "Hey ah told ye no' tae be eating any rubbish fae the middens."

The boy had in his hand a rank-looking, dirty apple, rotten to the core.

"But mammy," the boy shouted back, "Ah'm hungry."

"Throw that filthy fruit away or I'll tan your arse," she bellowed.

The boy did what he was told and threw the rotten apple into a puddle. A young girl appeared, picked it out of the puddle and took a bite out of it.

Johnny moved on, a few minutes later he entered the Mally Arms in Eglinton Street. It was known as a rough pub, but what pub in the Gorbals wasn't?

He walked into the bar and put on his best nonchalant and superior face. In other words, in local parlance, he looked "as gallus as fuck."

The dingy bar had an assortment of characters, mostly numpties clad in what looked no better than rags. Losers to the core. Among the older drinkers there were some young guys. It seemed that the whole of the pub had cast their eyes on Johnny. Sure, he was a handsome, well dressed, game looking bastard to them and he had a reputation as a hard man to boot.

One of the older drinkers looked up from his dominoes on the table and shouted to him, "Awright man? How's it gaun?"

Johnny shrugged his shoulders, "Ach no bad, ah'm still a million quid away fae being a millionaire."

John the landlord was behind the bar, a thin scrawny guy with a beard. "What can ah get ye young man?" he said to Johnny.

"Pint of McEwans Export, John."

"Do ye no want a nice malt whisky as well?" the landlord enquired, "Ah've got a wee sale on today, good price for a hawf!"

Johnny declined the kind offer, "Nah, just a pint of heavy. The jails are full of whisky and wine drinkers."

Landlord John gave a weak smile, "Aye and when they get oot they tend to come in here. I've missed my vocation in life. I shouldn't be a pub landlord, mair like a social worker or a psychiatrist wi' aw the drunken bums that frequent this place."

Johnny agreed. "Too right, John, some people call this place Bampot Central. Have ye seen any of the boys? Any of my pals?" The landlord pointed to the lounge at the back, "They're in there."

He headed to the lounge. Sitting there was Mad Brian, Wee Peter, Irish Chris and Wee Alex. They were deep in conversation. Johnny shouted to them, "If only the Devil could cast his net now, he'd have a good catch. You guys look like you are planning something. All's you need is the brains, that's where I come in." They all looked up and laughed knowing full well that Johnny was telling the truth, he was the brains of the crew.

Brian had a pen in his hand with a piece of paper on the table that looked like a diagram or a plan. Johnny sat down with his pint, "What's the score then?" Brian whispered, "Got it all planned out."

"Oh aye?" Johnny retorted, "Got what all planned out?"

Brian replied, "The robbery."

Peter chimed in, "Aye it's a cinch."

Chris agreed, "Like taking candy from a baby."

Alex nodded his head. "The only thing is, it's no' a baby we're taking candy fae, it's from an auld fucking Jew."

Johnny was interested, someone planning a bank robbery in the Gorbals always sounded glamorous and exotic. A lengthy jail sentence less so.

Brian was quick to enlighten him, "There is this auld Jew who owns a wholesalers near Gorbals Cross. Dae ye know who ah'm talking about?"

Johnny nodded his head, "Know the fella, he's loaded, he farts ten pound notes."

Brian was pleased that Johnny knew the fellow. "Too right, he's got enough dough to choke a dozen donkeys."

Johnny had no option but to agree. "I get the message. So what's the plan and what the fuck has this got tae dae wi' me?"

Chris said, "It's a brilliant plan, let Brian explain."

Peter appeared enthusiastic," This could make us all very rich men."

Brian continued pointing to the paper. "The auld Jew leaves his shop every Friday afternoon with his week's taking in a bag. We're gonnae bump him for the lot. Every penny."

Johnny thought it sounded too good to true merely saying, "And?"

Brian explained, "Well we reckon he could be carrying as much as ten grand in that bag."

Johnny was still sceptical said, "How?"

Brian looked at the diagram on paper and explained further, "Simple, when he comes out of the shop, we snatch the bag from him.

Johnny took a sip of his piss-poor pint and tried to bring some logic to the proceedings. "Look, the guy is an auld Jew and they know the value of money. He's no gonnae hand the money over without a fight."

Brian agreed but added, "We're gonnae bring a guy in. He's got a gun, an ancient army revolver. He's gonnae fire it intae the air tae frighten the auld bastard."

Johnny shook his head in disdain just thinking that numpties and bank robberies, that included a gun, were not a good combination.

"A gun involved? If you get caught they'll lock you up and throw the key intae the Clyde."

Chris disagreed, "Nah, the gun is only a bluff."

Peter was quick to the point, "When he hears the gun going off he'll shite himself."

Alex was in the same frame of mind, "We widnae shoot the fucker. Just fire a warning shot."

The plan sounded half decent but Johnny asked, "Who's got the gun"

Brian explained, "A new kid on the block. He's just moved tae the Gorbals from Bridgeton."

Johnny could feel the hairs on his back rise, a shiver went down his spine. "What's the guy's name?"

Brian replied, "McCoy."

Johnny was quick to the point. "Met that McCoy idiot for the first time this morning. He looks like trouble. Ah widnae touch him wi' a barge pole. The only thing ah would touch him wi' is ma razor. In fact, he's lucky ah didnae slash him." Brian agreed reluctantly. "He is trouble but he is a game bastard, and he's got a gun." Johnny thought for a while, took another sip of his pint and contemplated the situation. He had only met McCoy for a few moments but he could sense the guy had something unlucky about him. He concluded there was no way he could get involved in this caper.

Brian looked him straight in the eyes and said, "So, Johnny, are you in or are you out?"

Johnny had no hesitation in replying, "Taking into consideration this piss poor pint and your piss poor plan, I'm out."

Brian asked, "Why?"

Johnny explained in further detail, using the most forceful voice he could muster, "I don't like that McCoy guy. He gives me the creeps. Besides if there is a gun involved you are looking at 15 years inside, at least. Ah like a bit of sunshine." Peter was more enthusiastic. "Ten grand for a few minutes work, it could set us up for life man!" Alex agreed, "We'll be living the high life soon like toffs, champagne, nae mair piss beer." Johnny rose from the table, "Nah boys, ah don't have a good feeling about this, when are you gonnae do it?" Brian looked at his plan on paper and replied, "Next Friday 2.15."

Johnny finished his pint and merely said, "Well, boys, ah wish ye all the best." As he headed towards the exit, the juke box began to play Engelbert Humperdinck's Please Release Me. It was not a good omen.

Chapter 2

ALIBI

"Are ye no' out your bed yet?" Johnny's mother shouted as he noticed on his alarm clock it was almost 9am. He had slept soundly all night and had mixed dreams, some good some bad. One was about him and Cathy as they danced through the clouds kissing each other. The other dreams were more like a nightmare. He was doing the robbery with the lads when suddenly a gun went off blowing him away. At this, he awoke briefly in a sweat and then went back to his slumber.

Johnny got up and went into the kitchen, his mother, Jenny scolded him, "Johnny you are a lazy swine, dae ye want some porridge?"

"Aye mammy," he replied half dozily before going to the kitchen sink and turned on a small electric hot water heater. By Gorbals standards this was a luxury as most people washed themselves in the freezing cold water from the tap in the sink.

He then got his facecloth and carbolic soap and washed himself in the sink. While he was washing, he looked out of the window to see the people below in Crown Street. There were quite a few inhabitants milling around, many heading to chapel in their Sunday best. Johnny's mother put a bowl of porridge on the table with a strong mug of tea – two sugars and a dash of milk. "It's about time ye went tae chapel for a change," Jenny scolded her son, "It might knock some

sense into you instead of running about wi' the gangs."
She was going to chapel later that morning as she did
without fail every Sunday.

She worked as a waitress "up the toon". Long hours,
low pay, but she was always proud of her menial job
and equally proud of her religion.

Johnny's father, John senior, was a steward in the
Merchant Navy and sailed the high seas for months at
a time coming back to regale his family with wild tales
of his exotic adventures abroad.

He also fetched back numerous trinkets from
overseas, like a China teapot he had picked up in
Hong Kong and a floral vase he had purchased in
Kuala Lumpur. The artefacts were never used and
stood proudly as ornaments in a glass china cabinet.
As he finished his porridge Jenny said to her son, "Dae
ye want tae come tae chapel wi' me, son?" Johnny
always avoided going to chapel but in his heart he
would have liked to have gone with her. His image of
being a Gorbals hardman forbade it. No respected
gang leader could be seen going to chapel with his
mother, people would have thought he had gone soft.

"Nah, mammy, ah've got something on but maybe
someday soon," Johnny said rather unconvincingly.
His mother scolded him, rather gently, again, "Ach,
you'll end up in Hell, wi' a big roaring fire."

Johnny laughed at his mother's tease, "At least it
would be warmer than living in a Gorbals tenement!"

Jenny tut-tutted again and left for chapel. Johnny looked out of the window and watched his mother cross the road, she looked proud and graceful. Jenny carried herself with dignity, 52 and still going strong. She had an iron will that would put many mothers to shame. A few minutes later he felt a shiver going through his spine.

He spotted McCoy crossing Crown Street with two guys he had never liked. They were laughing and joking with each other and Johnny imagined they were talking about him. Another few minutes passed and he then saw Cathy, as beautiful as ever. She and her sister were wearing floral dresses and heading to chapel.

The porridge had been great, full of salt, only the English took it with sugar, and the cup of strong Typhoo tea had perked him up. He had always thought that "a wee cup of cheer" was far better than beer, and of course less expensive. Tea gave him a high that beer could not.

He thought about Cathy, then McCoy, and then the robbery, which would take place on Friday and was bound to be a disaster, an accident waiting to happen. A wave of paranoia overtook him. The robbery would happen near Gorbals Cross and he had no doubt the auld Jew would put up a fight. The Jews had got fucked about in Germany and Poland, and they were fed up with all that carry on. Nobody was going to fuck them about in the Gorbals, gun or no gun.

Perversely the robbery could have implications for Johnny. All the boys involved, apart from McCoy, were all associates of his. The police would put two and two together and come up with three. They would think that Johnny had to be involved and may be the mastermind or ringleader behind the whole shebang. The two bastard cops he had met at Gorbals Cross would have no hesitation in fitting him up. Framed for a robbery he had no involvement with.

Fifteen to twenty years for the perjury of two polis making up the same story. He imagined their testimony in court, "We knew John McGrath was a bad 'un and had an inkling he was the brains behind the armed robbery. Low life like that never give up." In the High court a wigged judge would agree with their testimony all the way.

The jury would nod their heads before finding him guilty and send him away for a very long time. Fifteen years plus in the nick and he would never see the beautiful Cathy again. It was not worth thinking about, but then again maybe it was.

If he was going to get fitted up, he needed to have a rock solid alibi. At first, he thought, at the time of the robbery, he would hang around a pub like the Mally Arms in front of plenty of witnesses. But when he contemplated that scenario he came to the conclusion that the sort of characters who hung around such pubs were undesirables and degenerates. They were mostly jailbirds, drunks, thieves and liars, and no court, especially the High Court would believe their testimony. He began to sweat profusely. What was the answer?

Then it came to him – the local priest at St Lukes. Johnny knew the parish house he lived in was in need of repair and the father always welcomed men who offered their services to help decorate the place. The polis could not accuse a priest of lying… perfect!

The next day Johnny went to confession in the chapel. He knelt down in the confession box and said, "Bless me, father, for I have sinned, it is a month since my last confession." It had actually been longer, but a month sounded respectable enough.

The father said, "So, tell me, son. What sins do you confess to?"

Johnny gave a nervous cough and then replied, "Well, father, I have been masturbating now and again to cope with the pressures of life. I have also been involved with bad men who want me to do an armed robbery, but being a good Catholic I turned them down. "The priest chided him briefly about the masturbation confession but the robbery was more important. He said in a thick Irish brogue, "My son, try to cut back on the masturbation and find yourself a loving relationship, a good Catholic girl to marry, that should stop you abusing yourself.

"Also keep way from those evil men who want you to do a robbery and as the Bible says, 'Though shalt not steal.' Four Hail Mary's and four Our Father's. God be with you."

Johnny thought he had got off lightly. He had anticipated his wanking confession would have received a higher penance.

He left the booth and did his praying penance. Afterwards he felt ten times better, as if his soul had been given a polish, and saw a clear scenario develop in his mind.

The next day, he went round to the priest's parish house and knocked on the heavy Victorian door. The father appeared with a big grin on his face. "Can I be of help son?" he said.

Johnny replied cheerfully "Well, father, I thought I might be of help to you. I've got a free day all day Friday and can do odd jobs for you, free of charge of course."

The priest gave a chuckle of delight, "Great, son, I need a lot of painting done on the stairs and the living room. But it might take all day. Are you willing to give up your whole day for me, the Pope and the Catholic religion?"

Johnny replied immediately, "Of course, father. See you at 9am Friday morning prompt!"

The Irish priest shook his hand warmly and firmly, "I had a wee prayer that someone would turn up and help me with the painting and then you arrive at the front door. God works in mysterious ways! See you Friday morning."

Johnny felt relieved, his battle plan was indeed going according to plan. It would need a biblical miracle for the police to fit him up now.

He walked into Crown Street and all the Gorbals cronies in their bunnets were there as usual outside the bookies. Johnny shouted to them, "Any winners the day boys?" One of the old guys retorted, "No' really Johnny. Ah backed a horse at ten to one and it came in at quarter to three! "

Back in the house it was comparatively quiet. Johnny's younger brother Joseph, aged 13, was sitting reading a Superman comic.

Johnny said to him, "Awright? How's Superman faring? Is he still winning the battle against the super crooks like Lex Luthor?"

Like his brother Johnny had always been a Superman fan, in fact when he was leading his Cumbie mob into battle against rival razor gangs he often felt like a superman.

Joseph replied, "Aye, Superman is doing all right but there's one thing he can't beat."

"What's that?" Johnny enquired,

"Green kryptonite. When he faces that, it makes him weak and could even kill him," Joseph said in a matter of fact manner.

Johnny instantly thought of McCoy," Some people are like that. They can make you weak then kill you. The Gorbals is full of the bampots."

Joseph laughed, "You're right enough. Superman widnae last two minutes in the Gorbals. There's more baddies here than in any comic."

Friday morning soon came and Johnny turned up at the parish house at the agreed time of 9am. He was greeted at the door by the priest who said "a slight problem had arisen with an elderly widow" and Johnny should carry on with the painting while he had an audience

Johnny got on with the work in hand, painting the stairs. The priest went into the main living room with the elderly woman. While he painted, he could hear their conversation clearly.

The widow said to the priest, "Father, I just want to go to Heaven, but I need to better myself. What can I do?

The priest consoled her in a soft Irish accent, "Be a good Catholic and go to mass as much as you can. I am sure you will be ok, you look like Heaven material to me!" She giggled at the remark. But Johnny could tell it was the laugh of a nervous uncertain elderly woman. She replied, "Oh thanks, father, another step away from Hell. Mind you, the road to Hell is paved with good intentions!"

The priest consoled her further, sure he was a spiritual expert, "Just keep on the road to righteousness and you'll be fine. In fact, you will end up dancing in heaven with the angels."

In a way, Johnny had been a bit disappointed by the old widow's revelations he had hoped she had had some scandal or even a few masturbation tales to tell.

After she left, Johnny got stuck into the painting and found it quite exhilarating. It was as if he was painting his troubles away. He even began to sing some Irish Catholic songs, "Hail Gloria Saint Patrick, the saint of our isle…." He worked laboriously all day with two short breaks for tea and was finished at 5pm. The robbery would have been over by then and there is no way he could be connected to it.

When he finished painting the priest looked at his work and said, "That's a fine job you've done my boy, well done. I am proud of you, the Catholic Church is proud of you and the Pope, if he knew, would be proud of you." He then made a sign of the cross and blessed him.

Johnny headed along Ballater Street euphoric that he had been blessed, he needed all the luck he could get. Also, crucially, his alibi had been sorted, it was cast iron.

But what about the robbery? Had those numpties managed to pull it off, or had it unravelled like a ball of wool?

Chapter 3

ROBBERY

Johnny had checked the TV and local news for any mention of the robbery – nothing. Maybe it had not gone ahead and the numpties had backed out. He was just ready to head to kip at 10pm when suddenly a newsflash appeared on STV. The announcer had a grim solemn face – the kind of face they wear when royalty or a famous person has died. The newscaster was a pretty young woman aged about 25 with long black hair.

He was sure he had met her somewhere and perhaps even shagged her after visiting one of the more upmarket dancehalls in Glasgow.

Maybe it was the Barrowland Ballroom. As she talked in posh broadcaster tones he was convinced it was the little educated bird he had met at the Barrowland, a few years back, who told him she was studying English at Glasgow University.

After a few dances and a winching session they had sex in one of the dark lanes in the Gallowgate. It was a quick stand up shag and how she moaned in her middle class way!

On the telly she looked nervous and shuffled her papers in front of her as if she was dealing with a very important story. She continued, "A Jewish businessman was shot on the way to the bank in the Gorbals this afternoon. It is believed he fought off several attackers who tried to grab a bag of money. It is thought the bag contained a week's takings of around £10,000.

"The businessman, Mr Ivan Solomon, aged 70, is an ex concentration camp internee. He came to Glasgow in the early 1950s and started up a successful wholesale business in the Gorbals area of Glasgow.

"He is said to be in a serious condition and fighting for his life in the Southern General Hospital, Glasgow."

She was then handed another piece of paper and added, "News just in. Police have released a statement saying several men have been arrested in connection with the robbery. They are being held at South Portland Street police station in the Gorbals."

The camera panned in. It was definitely that wee bird from the Barrowland! But then the shock of the news sunk in. Four arrested. Who got done? Who got away? Johnny went over to the kitchen sink and threw some cold water over his face.

"Hey maw just going out tae get a Daily Record," Johnny said to his mother who had also been watching TV with his brother.

"Be careful what you're doing Johnny, there's a lot of dodgy people out there at this time of night in the Gorbals. Some of them have even got guns now according tae that report."

Johnny smiled and shrugged, "Maw, who would want tae shoot me? They'd probably miss anyway – ah'm too fast for those bampots!"

Johnny's wee brother Joseph laughed, "Aye, faster than Superman and a speeding bullet!"

Johnny left the top floor flat in Crown Street and hurried down the tenement stairs. Nearby, Peter the paper man sold the Daily Record from 10pm every night, Monday to Friday. In Glasgow you could buy an early edition of the next day's paper at that time.

Peter, a shabby looking man in his 60s, wearing a greatcoat and bunnet, stood there come rain or shine hawking the paper surrounded by his nightly cronies, mostly old men of a similar age. They loved to stand around, gossip, and argue the night away.

When Johnny approached Peter there were about 15 old men "the bunnet brigade" milling about. Johnny asked for the paper and Peter replied, "Terrible carry on at Gorbals Cross today. An auld Jewish guy got shot. It's even made the front page headlines."

Johnny looked at the headline: **JEWISH BUSINESSMAN FIGHTING FOR LIFE. SUSPECTS ARRESTED.**

Johnny shook his head in bemusement but feigned ignorance. "Aye, you're right Peter, terrible carry on. Any idea who the guys are?"

Peter nodded and gave Johnny one of his glares. He had a knack for knowing everything that was happening in the Gorbals. "A wee bird told me that a couple of your pals might be involved."

One of his bunnet brigade chimed in, "Ah heard on the grapevine that one of them got away. The polis are still looking for him."

Johnny kept up his pretence of ignorance, "This place is getting like Chicago."

Peter replied, "It's worse than Chicago, all the young guys here think they're Glasgow's answer to Al Capone, but they're just cardboard gangsters."

Johnny, clutching his paper, ran back up the tenement stairs with gusto. A thousand thoughts came into his head. But two questions lingered in his mind. Who got caught? Who got away?

He
on his bed and sighed. It was a sigh of relief that he had not joined the hapless gang of Gorbals robbers. He put his head on the pillow and he could hear violent shouting from drunks outside staggering along Crown Street. "Ya dirty swine ye. Ah'll kick yir baws."

In other parts of Scotland people listened to birds chirping in the trees or the sound of waves on the seashore. But in the Gorbals there was only the noise of drunks whose lives had gone down the drain.

Johnny closed his eyes and dreamed of better days.

The next morning, he was awoken abruptly by loud noises.

Bang! Bang! Bang! "Open up! Police!" Johnny at first thought it was a dream or part of a nightmare. His mother, looking distraught, shouted "Get ready quick son, the polis are banging at the door." Johnny leapt out of bed and quickly put his gear on. But then he could hear the door being kicked in and was faced in the lobby with six big policemen who rushed at him, bundling him to the floor.

"Fuck off, filth," he shouted and spat at them. It was quite a mighty spit. The yellow gob cascaded over several of the officers. "Bastard!" one of them shouted as he wiped the mucus from his face.

Another policeman shouted, "Johnny McGrath we are arresting you on suspicion of armed robbery." He then gave the usual polis patter of not having to say anything, blah, blah, blah. As he lay on the floor Johnny thought talk is cheap, but polis talk sounded cheaper.

For a few moments he felt frightened but this gave way to anger. He had been right, they were determined to fit him up. A fall guy for the numpties!

"Hey! Hey! Hey!" he shouted, "Ah've done nothing, you've got the wrong man."

They handcuffed him and marched him out of the flat

Johnny's mother was crying. She wailed, "Oh, what have ye done now son?" Joseph just stood there in his pyjamas grimacing; had seen worse things happen to Superman in one of his numerous DC comics.

Johnny was bundled down the tenement stairs.
Outside in Crown Street a big Black Maria was waiting
for him. Although it was early morning a large crowd
had formed. As he was being thrown into the police
van he heard a female shouting, "Johnny! Johnny!
Leave him alone, ya polis bastards!" He looked over
his shoulder, it was Cathy with tears and mascara
running down her cheeks.

For a few moments his anger subsided and a warm
feeling came over him. At last he knew that she really
loved him.

He was taken to Glasgow Central Police Station, near
Glasgow Cross, told to remove his belt and shoelaces
and put in a cell.

The cell was a depressing affair. A little concrete
bench, a rancid looking, stinking toilet bowl and a small
barred window that had meagre sunlight coming
through.

So, this was how innocent men ended up. Hung drawn
and quartered for doing fuck all!

A turnkey looked through the peep hole every 15
minutes to check on him. "Go and fuck yourself"
Johnny shouted," And get me a blanket, it's freezing in
here."

After about an hour in the psychological wilderness the
cell door opened and two plain clothed CID men came
in.

42

"Hi Johnny," the bigger of the two said in a friendly voice. Johnny thought he had the same patter as a Gorbals social worker. The other CID guy was smaller and seemed to have a twitch when he spoke in a harsh voice. Johnny knew the game they were playing. The tall guy was Mr Nice and the smaller fellow Mr Nasty.

Mr Nasty said in an aggressive tone, "Look, ya bastard, we know who you are, a chib man who takes liberties. But if you co-operate with us it will make your life a lot easier."

Johnny decided to play them at their own game." Awright, I'll co-operate with you. Ah've got nothing tae hide."

The CID men both said unison, "Good."

Johnny was led from the cell to a nearby interview room. He sat down at a table with Mr Nice and Mr Nasty facing him. There was a policewoman sitting nearby taking notes. It made Johnny feel important. A somebody in a land of nobodies.

The interview began with Mr Nice. "We have information you were the mastermind behind the robbery."

"The mastermind behind a robbery? Johnny replied, "The last robbery ah committed was when ah took two bob from ma brother's piggy bank."

Mr Nasty began twitching at the insolence, "We know you are the fucker behind it. We had an undercover officer watching you."

Johnny replied nonchalantly to wind Mr Nasty up further, "An undercover polis? What under the blankets in my bed?"

Mr Nasty began to twitch even more, "Don't be funny, ya c**t. We had a good eye on you when you met up with your gang in the Mally Arms planning the robbery. You were looking at the plans on a table in the lounge."

Johnny replied, "I popped in for a pint of piss, met the boys by chance in the lounge."

Mr Nice grunted but Mr Nasty got angrier, "Look, smart arse, we can do this the hard way or the easy way. Which way do you want?"

"A Milky Way," Johnny replied.

"What the hell does that mean?"

Johnny explained "Ah'm starving, nae breakfast. Pop out to the shops and get me a Milky Way.

This was the comment that broke the camel's back, Mr Nasty began to twitch at a tremendous rate and he made a fist as if he was going to strike Johnny. He would have done so but remembered the policewoman was in the room talking notes.

"I'll fucking Milky Way you, sonny boy," Mr Nasty exclaimed. Johnny knew he had gone too far and tried to diffuse the situation. "The bampots that you caught red handed are the guys you should be turning the pressure on, no' me. So, charge me or let me go, twitchy."

Mr Nice and Mr Nasty left the interview room and Johnny was taken back to his cell. A couple of hours later the turnkey opened the door and said, "You're free to go." No apologies, nothing.

Johnny walked out of the police station towards the Gorbals but he was surprised that Mr Nice and Mr Nasty had released him. When he got back to his house it all became clear.

His mother was there with a big smile on her face, "Awright, son, so you are a free man then?"

"Aye maw, ah can't understand why they let me go so easily."

His mother laughed, "I'll tell you why. I went round to the priest's house and we both went to the police station and said on the day of the robbery you had spent the whole day painting his parish house. We also had an elderly widow who said she saw you at the house at the time of the robbery."

"That's true maw," Johnny replied.

"It really is a miracle, backed up by the Pope's right-hand man in the Gorbals!" his mother joked. His quick release did seem like divine intervention, but in reality it was his Gorbals' street cunning and forward planning that had performed the miracle.

Outside in Crown Street, there was a large poster declaring "Help the police." Someone had written in a felt pen below it "Kick fuck out of yourself!"

Chapter 4

WANTED MAN

He needed to know the full story behind the robbery. And when you are out and about, you are in with a shout. As soon as he left his tenement there were a lot of familiar faces around. But none of them would be able to furnish the information he needed.

He turned the corner and coming out of Murray's newsagents in Old Rutherglen Road was Tam the Bam, a guy in his 40s, who was always in the know. "Hi Tam, what's the score wi' the robbery? Who was involved and who was lucky enough to get away?" Tam took a deep draw of his fag and said, "The usual suspects, Mad Brian, Alex, Peter and Irish Chris. There were two other guys, a fella I don't really know, Joe McCoy and a getaway driver called Sam McGlinchy. He's got a reputation for being a great car thief, he was the one that got away, and mind you he did have the title getaway driver!"

"The polis have been all over the Gorbals, day and night, searching his regular haunts, the pubs and bookies and aw that, but ah heard he was hiding out in Castlemilk."

Castlemilk was a huge sprawling estate, a few miles away, and would be an ideal place to hide if the police were after you. Johnny thought of Sam McGlinchy, he did not know him that well and they had only met a few times. Sam was a baby-faced guy in his 20s with fast patter who had built up a reputation from the age of 14 for stealing cars from all over the place.

He had once pulled up in a shiny new Volvo and asked Johnny and his pal if they fancied "A wee day trip to the Ayr races." Johnny had been game for it but his pal refused point blank saying he had something on and didn't have the time to go all the way to Ayr.

As he thought of this the two policemen who he had encountered before at Gorbals Cross approached. Their footsteps seemed once again to be in synchronisation. The taller of the two, the officer with the Highland accent, looked Johnny in the eye and said, "Ah heard you got lifted for the robbery of the auld Jew. But they let you go after your priest friend came on the scene."

Johnny laughed, "Aye, your bastard CID pals tried tae fit me up but ah had a rock solid alibi."

The other policeman joined in, "You must have known something about it, McGrath, because you're a right fly man."

Johnny winced, "Aye, too fly, too shrewd tae be fitted up by you people."

He walked off showing the policemen an air of contempt. He racked his brains, who the hell would know where McGlinchy was hiding?

Suddenly it came to him, McGlinchy's cousin, Rab Buchanan, who was a Corporation bus conductor. He lived in Eglinton Street, not far from the Laurieston pub. Johnny went to the tenement and knocked on the door. Buchanan's wife, a stout lady in a bathing robe and curlers, looked nervous, "Rab's no' here, he's on the buses all day, number 48 service. Wait around for a while at the bus stop outside the Coliseum Cinema and you might just catch him on one." She gave a nervous, cough before saying, "What dae ye want him for anyway?"

Johnny played it cool, "Oh nothing really, just tae catch up about the auld days."

She was suspicious, closing the door with a bang as he headed to the bus stop. Johnny did not really know her that well but one of his pals said that she had a kind face, the kind of face you would like to kick in.

There was something in her manner that made him suspicious, was she hiding something from him? Or was it just that time of the month?

Johnny had known Rab Buchanan for years. They had often played football in the backcourts of Thistle Street. Buchanan had been an excellent football player and even had trials for his beloved team Glasgow Celtic. But a knee injury at 17, and turning to lager, brought his aspiring career to an end. In fact when Buchanan went out, people often reminded him he could have been the next George Best. Johnny laughed to himself, "The next George Best, when it comes tae the bevvy!"

It wasn't a bad day to wait for a number 48 bus. At least it wasn't raining, it was a bit breezy and the sun was out. There was a 48 bus about every 20 minutes. Johnny waited patiently. The first bus, no sign of Buchanan. The second, no sign, the third, no sign. He was about to give up when he saw another 48 coming his way with the front declaring the destination as Househillwood. It was several miles away, a good half hour journey. Like Castlemilk, it was a huge sprawling council estate which accommodated the overspill of tenement dwellers from Glasgow.

Buchanan was on the bus, all done up in his conductor's gear. "Fares please! Fares please!" He was collecting the fares and sticking them into a bag which hung around his belt. Buchanan, as usual, looked like he had a hangover. He was a small rotund man, in his early thirties, with red receding hair. Johnny sat down on the upper deck.

Buchanan approached, "Fares please! Oh, it's you Johnny you can have this ride for nothing. You off to Househillwood?"

Johnny shook his head, "Nah, ah came on here tae have a wee word wi' you."

Buchanan, like his wife, looked nervous, beads of sweat fell from his head. "A wee word. What about?"

Johnny whispered, "Your cousin, Sam."

Buchanan fumbled with the change in his bag, as if stalling for time, and then said, "Ok look we cannae talk about it now, too many people around. Call up to ma house at 6pm tonight and we'll have a natter. Fares please! Fares Please!"

Johnny got off the bus, just up the road, at Eglinton Toll, he went into the Star Bar for a pint. He liked the place, it had a sort of 1940s décor which hadn't changed over the years. But like all Gorbals boozers it had an unpredictable atmosphere. Some elderly men were at table playing dominoes when suddenly one of the shouted, "Ya cheating bastard, ye," and overturned the table in a rage. Johnny sunk his pint quickly and decided to make a fast exit. He thought people in the Gorbals would fight about anything, even a daft wee game of dominoes.

Later he was at Buchanan's front door bang on 6pm. His obese wife once again answered, still dressed in her bathing robe and curlers. She shouted in a gruff voice, "Rab, that Johnny fella is here again."

Rab appeared, still chewing his dinner. "Come away in. What's the score? How can ah help you?" He looked well fed and confident but there was still an air of nervousness about him.

Johnny was straight to the point, "Ah just wanted a word wi' your cousin Sam. How can ah get hold of him?"

Buchanan looked even more nervous, "That's what the polis have been asking in aw the Gorbals pubs. Look if ah knew where he was, I'd tell you. Fancy a cuppa?"

Johnny accepted his offer, "Thanks Rab, milk and two sugars."

Buchanan put two mugs of tea on the kitchen table with a packet of Jammy Dodgers. The tea and biscuits seemed to cheer him up and eradicated the nervousness he had shown. They talked about irrelevant things like football and pubs then Buchanan's mood seemed to change.

"Dae ye really want to talk to ma cousin Sam?" Johnny took a sip of his tea and replied, "Sure do, Rab"

Buchanan rose from the table and said, "Follow me."

He led Johnny into the back bedroom where there was a large double bed. Johnny wondered what was going on, then Buchanan whispered in the direction of the bed, "Sam, come out. My old pal Johnny McGrath is here to see you."

Suddenly Sam McGlinchy appeared from under the bed. "What the hell are you doing here?" Johnny said in astonished bewilderment.

"What do you think? Ah'm hiding fae the polis. That robbery was a fuck up."

"Why? What happened?"

"Brian, Peter, Alex, Chris and a new guy, McCoy got me in as the getaway driver. I nicked a motor for the job. We turned up at Gorbals Cross as planned and the auld Jewish guy came out with his sack of money. The boys surrounded him and tried to grab the bag.

But the Jew was no mug and put up a fight. Next minute McCoy pulled out a revolver and shot the fucker. I never knew McCoy had a gun, nobody told me. Anyway, we left the auld Jew bleeding on the pavement and sped off with the money. But the polis were quick on the scene and chased us in a panda car all the way to Castlemilk. We bolted out the car and left the bag of cash in it. I had a place to hide, my auntie who lives in a council house nearby. But the rest of the boys weren't as lucky. After a couple of hours scouring the place, the polis arrested all of the boys except me."

Johnny was taken aback by the story, his instinct had been right about McCoy, "What about the gun?

"During the car chase McCoy threw it out the window intae undergrowth on the edge of Castlemilk. The polis got the money fae the car and ah've got no doubt they'll find the gun. It was a real shambles, ah would never have done the job if ah knew McCoy had a gun. I'm in this mess all because they offered me a measly hundred quid to be the getaway driver."

Johnny shook his head, "A hundred quid is that all?"

Sam nodded, "A hundred quid was promised once they shared the money out. Now ah've got fuck all and face years in jail."

Rab Buchanan knew it was a hopeless situation but made an attempt to lighten the matter, "Don't worry Sammy boy, we'll hide you until the coast is clear and the heat is off."

Johnny asked, "So what's you battle plan once the heat dies down?

Sam suddenly looked confident, "Ah've got an auntie an uncle in Donegal wi' a wee farm. I'll sneak over to Ireland on the ferry and hide out there for a while."

Johnny said he was glad Sam had an exit plan. He wished him luck, shook his hand, and left the flat.

As he did so Buchanan put his fingers to his lips and said, "Lips sealed, Johnny"

"Aye, nae problem Rab, your secret is safe wi' me," Johnny replied.

Johnny went into the fading sunlight of Eglinton Street and breathed in the fresh air. "Drama brings meaning to life" he said to himself as he walked towards Crown Street.

That night at 10pm, Johnny got the Daily Record from Peter. The front page headline was: **THE MOST WANTED MAN IN SCOTLAND.**

Underneath it was a large picture of Sam McGlinchy.

Chapter 5

FERRY

It wasn't a very lucky time for Sam McGlinchy and the rest of the boys. The old Jewish guy had died. The papers went full blast, "Ivan Solomon was a victim of Nazi persecution. He came to the Gorbals area of Glasgow in the early 1950s. He had spent five years in Nazi concentration camps. Friends knew him as a fighter who got through life with a great sense of humour. He often boasted that nothing could beat him, not even Hitler. He arrived in Glasgow with a few pounds in his pocket and built up a successful wholesale business in the Gorbals. Through his hard work he became a leading light in Scotland's Jewish community and a millionaire. He lived with his wife and two grown up children in the wealthy area of Giffnock, Glasgow.

"But tragically, this man who had survived the concentration camps had his life taken away by a gunman in the Gorbals, last Friday afternoon. Several local men have been arrested and police are hunting for another man, Sam McGlinchy in connection with the brutal murder and robbery."

The next bit was more worrying for Sam, "The Jewish community has put up a £10,000 reward for information leading to the arrest and conviction of McGlinchy. They have even hired private detectives in an attempt to capture the fugitive – known as Scotland's most wanted man.

Dave Cohen, a spokesman for the appeal said, "Our brother has been taken from us in a cold calculated criminal act. We will not rest until the suspect on the run has been arrested and convicted of Ivan's heinous murder.

"The Jewish community has been quick to raise the £10,000 reward and our team of private detectives are leaving no stone unturned to find this man."

Underneath the story was not one, but three pictures of Sam McGlinchy. Johnny read the paper and thought, "Sam has landed himself right in it. 10,000 quid and a team of private detectives after him. It sounds like something from a James Bond movie."

Dave Cohen also appeared on television and radio accentuating the appeal. Johnny had to admit the Jews were smart intelligent people and it was a folly to mess with them. They had the money, the power and connections to be a force to be reckoned with. The three things that Sam McGlinchy did not have and would never aspire to.

Johnny wondered when McGlinchy would make his dash for Ireland and thought he had to do it quickly as the Gorbals was swarming with police and private detectives.

He decided not to go back to Buchanan's flat as it might implicate him leading to years in jail as an accessory. The best plan was to wait and see. Stay well clear.

Rab Buchanan looked at the report, and the coverage on the telly, and gulped, he had to get Sam out of the way as soon as possible. He knew his house could be raided at any time and if it was he'd lose his job and his freedom.

He went into the bedroom and whispered "Sam, time tae make a move!" Sam came out from under the mattress and said, "What are we gonnae dae, Rab? They've got ten grand on ma head, and all those polis and private detectives are after me. Ah've got no chance."

Rab agreed, "The odds are no' good Sam but we'll find a way to get you out of town, pronto."

Sam looked desperate, "Get me the fuck out of here and get me on the boat to Ireland, I'll be ok there. I can hide and change my name and all that palaver."

Rab replied, "Easier said than done Sam, let me check out a few things."

He left the room and McGlinchy went back under the bed. About half an hour later Buchanan came into the room and sounded more optimistic, "Sam, ah've been doing a few checks and there is an early boat leaving Stranraer going to Larne in Ireland tomorrow morning. I'll get you there in my mini van"

In the early hours of the morning, it was pitch dark as both men climbed into the little van. Sammy had been instructed to wear a flat cap to hide part of his face. On the way there, Rab told him to lie in the back covered by a blanket. As the van took off there was not a soul about. Rab drove through the Gorbals to Stranraer.

When they got there Rab gave Sam £20 and said, "I think you should be ok. The polis and detectives will be aw over the Gorbals looking for you. But ah don't imagine that they'd think of you heading tae Ireland. But you never know, the polis and the Jews are fly bastards."

They shook hands and Sam went to the ticket counter. A little fat woman did not even blink as she took the money and gave Sam his ferry ticket.

Sam felt content, so far so good. It was deathly cold as he boarded the boat. He sat down on a bench on the deck looking at the ocean "Ireland here I come," he muttered. There was still half an hour to go before the boat sailed and more people got on board. Several families with noisy and screaming children and a group of Irishmen. The Irishmen were singing The Wild Rover and glugging from bottles of whiskey. One of them spotted Sam and shouted, "Hey fella, come and join us for a good auld Irish dram."

Sam quickly worked out that if he joined the gang of Irishmen he could merge in, be less conspicuous, and people would think he was one of them.

He went over to take part in their drinking session. One of them shouted, "Come on pal, have a wee drink on us, Irish hospitality!" He was then handed a bottle of Bushmill's whiskey and took a slug. He felt better straight away.

After hiding under a mattress, to this! It was Utopia.The whiskey had a beautiful affect on his demeanour.

The ferry still had 15 minutes to depart. Suddenly Sammy felt a wave of shock coming through his body. It came from his balls right up to his head. While the Irishmen were singing, a Jewish guy come on board and glanced around. He looked like a real Orthodox Jew with a beard. He was dressed in a big black hat, a black suit and white shirt, what the fuck was he doing on a boat going to Ireland?

But after a few minutes, and another slug of the whiskey, the Jewish guy had disappeared. Paranoia! Sam thought it was turning out to be a beautiful day. He loved the Irish. They certainly knew how to enjoy themselves and they did not give a damn about those who didn't.

He began to daydream, He would work hard on his relatives' farm in Donegal, meet an Irish girl, get married and settle down. Have a couple of kids and live a life which could never have achieved in the Gorbals.

Suddenly he heard footsteps coming towards him. There were six policemen. One of them said, "Sam McGlinchy?" Sam replied, "No you've got the wrong fella. My name is Sean McGrory." As he replied he put on a strong Irish accent he had perfected after being at school with so many Irish kids in the Gorbals.

"Who the fuck do you think you are kidding, McGlinchy?" the policeman shouted. "I am arresting you in connection with murder and robbery. You do not have to say anything…"

Sam was handcuffed and led off the boat. The drunken Irishmen shouted at the coppers, "Leave the boy alone, ya polis bastards. He's done fuck all wrong."

As the Black Maria trundled towards Glasgow, Sam felt strangely relieved. He felt a huge weight lift from his shoulders. He had got rid of the monkey on his back.

Later Johnny was in the Turf Bar in Hospital Street and having a conversation with an old fellow about a forthcoming Old Firm match. The fellow said, "Celtic will trounce those orange bastards, wait and see, a doddle for the Bhoys."

Johnny agreed but suddenly spat out the beer in his mouth. A picture of McGlinchy appeared on the television screen. It was the same wee bird presenter. She looked ravishing, "Scotland's most wanted man was arrested this morning on a ferry in Stranraer ready to sail to Larne in Ireland."

Johnny uttered, "For fuck's sake!"

The old Celtic supporter looked at him and said, "Dae ye know that boy?"

"Johnny replied, "Aye, kinda."

The old man shook his head, "I'll tell you what, they'll throw the book at that poor bastard." Johnny had no option but to agree.

The next morning Johnny received a letter from Alex in Barlinnie prison. It was short and straight to the point. It had to be. Alex wasn't daft enough to give anything away to the authorities who scanned such letters.

"Hi Johnny, on a wee holiday courtesy of the Queen. Can you come and visit me? I've arranged a pass for you."

Johnny laughed, wee Alex had a great sense of humour – most Gorbals people do in situations of adversity.

On the day of the visit Johnny got a Corporation bus to Barlinnie. As he walked up the road to the jail, and a huge Victorian door, a sense of dread came over him. He was searched and led into a side room where other people were waiting. There was a large gypsy-looking Irishman sitting with thick black hair who seemed to be brooding

To cut the ice, Johnny initiated the conversation. "It's a drag coming up here. Came tae see wan o' ma pals." The big fellow replied, "Oh aye, what's he in for?"

Johnny said," That auld Jew robbery."

The big fellow grimaced, "Same here. Ma boy is up on the same charge."

Johnny was intrigued, "What's his name?"

"Joe McCoy"

Johnny felt a shiver go through his spine. A prison guard shouted, "Right you can go in now, but no' discussing any cases."

He was led into a large room where about a dozen inmates were at tables. He saw Alex and sat at the other side of his table. He spotted McCoy at another table. McCoy gave a weak smile and nodded to Johnny. Johnny reciprocated with no great feeling either way.

He said to wee Alex, "What's the score man?"

Alex shrugged his shoulders, "Ah cannae really discuss it here, prison rules and aw that, but ah've been done up like a kipper."

There was a vigilant guard nearby, so Johnny whispered, "Ah know Alex but ye were mental to take part in the first place."

Alex screwed his face up in an almost comical manner. He whispered back, "Two witnesses. Find out who they are and sort it for me."

Johnny replied confidently, "Nae problem Alex, leave it tae me."

The meeting had been short but effective. Johnny would not let down wee Alex and the boys. Suddenly he was a man on a mission. A mission to defeat the scales of justice.

Chapter 6

FAVOUR

Johnny always maintained that his word was his bond. But how was he to find out who the two witnesses were? The police had kept them a closely guarded secret. It was then he had a lightbulb moment. Ping! Sure, there was his auntie, Agnes McAuley, a woman in her late 50s. They had not talked for years after his mother fell out with her at the bingo.

For the past ten years Agnes, a widow who lived alone, had been a cleaner at Glasgow Central Police Station. Johnny went to Agnes' house in Florence Street and knocked on the door. He knew that she was a secret drinker who never went to pubs but was often seen at the off licence buying a bottle of her favourite tipple – Lanliq wine. Johnny had secured a half bottle and when she opened the door her lonely eyes lit up when Johnny said, "Agnes, a quick social call, wi' a wee present for you." He noticed that Agnes' breath smelt of stale booze. "Well it's a surprise tae see you here. You've no' been in ma hoose since ye were a young boy. Ah'm sorry ah fell out wi' yir ma - ah cannae even remember why we fell out. Anyway, what are ye doing turning up at ma door after all these years?"

Johnny replied, "Ah wanted to ask ye a wee favour, darlin'."

Agnes was suspicious, "Oh aye, and what would this favour be?" She went over to the kitchen table and poured herself a glass of wine. Johnny noticed her hands were shaking, "Well ah want tae know who the two witnesses are in the auld Jew robbery."

He explained, "You work at the polis headquarters cleaning their offices. I just thought you might have heard something."

She smiled, "Son, ah'm a cleaner for goodness sake, no wan of the CID. But ah'll tell you what, ah'll keep my eyes and ears open for ye, that's the most ah can promise."

Johnny was pleased, "Agnes you've got a great heart. I'll tell ma maw tae try and square it up wi' you. This argument has been going on far too long."

Agnes drank some more of the wine, "Ok Johnny, see what ye can dae. And ah'll see what I can dae. You scratch ma back and I'll scratch yours!" He left the tenement flat feeling instinctively that Agnes would not let him down.

A couple of days later Johnny was in the Cleland Bar pondering the situation when a drunk young guy staggered over to him and shouted, "Who are you looking at? Dae ye want a picture, ya tube ye?" Johnny had never seen the guy before and replied, "You're too ugly tae take a picture, ya bampot."

The guy grabbed Johnny in a bear hug. He grappled with him but the fellow had a tight grip. Johnny reached over to a table with his free hand and whacked the guy over the head with a large glass ashtray.

The young guy fell to the floor and blood began to gush from his head like a fountain. An auld fellow said, "You'd better get tae fuck before the bizzies and ambulance arrive." Johnny heeded his advice but was annoyed the young guy's blood had splattered all over his newly designed Arthur Black shirt and Levi Sta-Prest trousers. He headed round to Gorbals Cross toilets, rinsed his shirt in a basin. Then he found a scrubbing brush in a mop bucket and scrubbed the trousers.

Half an hour later, as his designer clothes dried, he looked better, not perfect but better. He walked back around the corner and could see two police cars and an ambulance outside The Cleland. A group of old women who must have just come out of the Palace bingo hall stood watching. "What's happening, missus?" Johnny said to one of them.

"Some drunkard nearly got murdered in the pub." She replied in a matter of fact voice. Johnny laughed, "Nothing unusual then!" The old woman replied, "Nah, it's happening all the time there. They should shut that bloody place down." The other bingo-goers nodded in agreement.

Johnny made his way along Rutherglen Road and the place seemed to be swarming with drunken navvies who had blown their pay packets on a night of booze. As he turned into Crown Street, he heard a woman's voice shouting, "Johnny! Johnny!" He turned round and saw it was Agnes. She handled him a crumpled piece of paper.

"Found this in one of the bins at police headquarters, it's a copy of the original," she said before making off. Johnny unfurled the piece of paper. It said in bold type: "Witnesses for the prosecution in the Ivan Solomon case. (1) Agatha Morag McFadden, aged 67, 120 Hospital Street, Gorbals. (2) John Edward Driscoll, aged 71, 94 Thistle Street, Gorbals."

Johnny did not know the Agatha woman but the Driscoll name rang a bell. It then came back to him. Driscoll was a regular at Cha Pa Pa's fish and chip shop in Crown Street and he had sometimes seen him having his hair cut at Felix's the barbers nearby.

Johnny had been in the barber's queue and heard Eddie Driscoll talk about his life. He was a retired engineer with Glasgow Corporation Housing Department and had been a part time volunteer at a local youth club.

He had a reputation as being "a dirty auld bastard" who used to tickle the young boys, pretending it was fun.

After complaints from some of the boys' mothers, he had resigned abruptly, presumably before the police got involved. Johnny went round to Driscoll's house in Thistle Street and picked up a half brick.

He had a rubber band and attached a note to it saying, "Grass up the boys and you are a dead man, you fucking pervert."

Johnny stood in the back court and could see Driscoll standing near his kitchen window. He threw the brick full force and it smashed the window into a thousand pieces. He then ran off through the darkness of the backcourts to his house in Crown Street.

He was sure that Driscoll would not report the incident to the police as the word 'pervert' would have brought attention to his dubious past in the youth club and his tickling days.

Johnny slept well that night and even had a dream about winning the pools. When he awoke, he considered the woman witness, Agatha McFadden of Hospital Street.

He stood for more than an hour across the road from her close and about mid-day a little white-haired woman came out of the close with a Scottish terrier. She looked respectable, respectable enough to testify and send the boys away for a long time.

A neighbour shouted, "Hello Aggie. Lovely day!"

"Great day for a walk wi' ma wee dog in the Glasgow Green," she replied in a cheery voice. Johnny was confused what to do. A brick though her window and a threatening note would not suffice in this case. A different modus operandi was required. Then a name flashed up in his mind – Bella Macilroy. Bella was one of the roughest women in the Gorbals, known as a heavy drinker who had even had a reputation for knocking men out who had annoyed her. She was rough, tough and hard to bluff.

She owed Johnny a favour. He had once intervened when a drunk man appeared to be throttling her outside of a pub. Johnny had run over and head-butted the man before giving him a swift kick in the balls. Bella said afterwards, "Johnny, you saved my life. I owe you a favour, just say the word."

He bumped into Bella about half an hour after Agatha and her dog went for a walk in the Glasgow Green. He told Bella the score, that she needed to give Agatha "a sherikin," a fright, and ward her off from testifying. But Bella looked ill with her bulging red eyes and foul breath, alcohol poisoning he thought.

He took her into the Sou' Wester pub in Eglinton Street and ordered not one, but three large glasses of powerful South African wine. After the third glass was downed, Bella rose from her seat and said, "Right where is this auld cow?"

They waited in Hospital Street and the light began to fade. Suddenly, Agatha McFadden appeared with her dog. Bella ran over shouting and waving her arms wildly. "See you, ya fucking auld cow, if you grass up those boys in court, I'll kill ye wi' ma bare hands." She then grabbed Agatha by the throat and slapped her on the face. The little dog yelped, Bella kicked it. It yelped even louder. Agatha began screaming, "Help! Ah'm being attacked by a drunken lunatic!" But the street was empty and no-one came to her aid.

Bella made off around the corner shouting, "You grass those boys up and I'll be back, ah know where you live." The terrified woman and her dog disappeared up her close.

Johnny was at first worried that Bella had gone too far. But surmised that the police would take it as an attack by a drunken woman who was out of her mind, which was not uncommon in the Gorbals. Also, there were no witnesses to back up any claim of attack

The police were called and did go to Agatha's flat but for some reason or another the matter went no further. Johnny surmised that Agatha would have been too terrified to identify Bella, as her attacker knew her address.

Had Johnny's plan worked? Would the two witnesses still have their day in court to testify?

The High Court case was looming on the horizon.

Chapter 7

Jo Jo

When Johnny got back home, he put his key in the door and he could hear laughter straight away. He heard his father's voice and a feeling of relief came over him. Johnny snr, known as Jo Jo, had been away for the last three months on the QE2 ocean liner. He had joined the Merchant Navy at the age of 16, just like his father before him, and had walked up the Broomielaw on Clydeside, to sign up.

At the age of 48 he could look back on a career on the high seas that had involved everything from peeling potatoes in the kitchens, maintenance jobs, and now he was steward on one of the world's finest ships. If not the finest ship in the world. Johnny's mother, when marrying him, knew what she was getting herself in to. Jo Jo, his nickname from school, had always been a bit of a colourful character. He was a real patter merchant who, at times, looked like a Hollywood movie star with his sun-tanned features, bright smile and a charisma that could transform the atmosphere of any room.

"So, a penguin walks into a pub and says tae the barman, 'Has my brother been in?' And the barman says, 'What does he look like?'" There was more laughter. Johnny walked in and Jo Jo rose from his chair to shake his hand. "How's ma boy getting on? Keeping out of trouble ah hope," he said in a humorous voice.

Johnny's mother looked on with a big grin on her face, even after all these years she was amazed at how identical they looked. Both thin, athletic build, with the same thick jet black hair. Indeed, when they talked, they sounded the same. They were like identical twins although Jo Jo could give twenty odd years in that department.

Johnny explained to his father, "You know how things are in the Gorbals. Always a wee bit o' daft drama going on. Ah'll no' bore ye wi' the details." He did not mention the robbery.

Jo Jo laughed out loud, "Ah travel all over the world but there's no place like the Gorbals. It's wan o' the maddest places on the globe. But ah'll tell you what – ah widnae live anywhere else."

Johnny's mother made them all "a nice wee cup of tea." Jo Jo dunked his digestive biscuit into the tea and said, "No matter where I am in the world, Hong Kong, New York or Sydney, I always look forward tae having a cup o' tea wi' ma family." He looked adoringly at his wife, "As far I am concerned you make the best cuppa in the world, darlin'." Johnny's mother blushed, it was the blush of a schoolgirl, like when she and Jo Jo first met. She was obviously still deeply in love with him and had put up with his numerous indiscretions over the years.

Jo Jo was not only a man about town but a man around the world. There were rumours that he had a woman in every port and some even suspected another family somewhere abroad.

But Johnny and his mother discounted the rumours even when there was a slight inkling they might be true.

Besides what you don't know about, you don't worry about. His brother Joseph said to his father, "Hey da, did ye met anybody rich and famous on the last trip?"

"Of course, son," Jo Jo replied, "Plenty of millionaires, we even had Charlie Chaplin and Sean Connery on board."

Joseph said, "Sean Connery, 007! What was he like?"

Jo Jo explained, "Nice fella, a good tipper, same as Chaplin. Connery was having a bevvy one night and I opened up a nice bottle of Beaujolais for him and his missus. He asked where ah came from and ah said the Gorbals. He took a sip of his wine and replied in that incredible voice of his, 'The Gorbals? Even James Bond would be wary about going there!'"

They all laughed heartedly. Johnny was never sure if his father's outlandish tales were true or even partly true but they provided a great deal of entertainment in this crumbling Victorian tenement.

"Right" Jo Jo said, reaching into a large suitcase, "Ah've got ye's all a present fae ma trip overseas."

First of all, he gave Johnny's mother a sparkling ring he had picked up in Barcelona. Then he handed

Joseph a miniature copy of the Eiffel Tower that he had acquired for a few francs in Paris.

Finally, he said to Johnny, "I got this hand made in Hong Kong for you." He pulled out from the large suitcase, a beautiful looking cream coloured suit. Johnny caressed the cloth, "Hey da, this is good gear. It's very shiny, just like Frank Sinatra wears in Vegas."

Jo Jo smiled, "Aye. The Hong Kong tailor said he had seen the Rat Pack, Sinatra, Dean Martin and Sammy Davies in concert and decided tae get in some sharkskin cloth."

Joseph asked, "Sharkskin cloth?"

Jo Jo put him right, "That's what they call the material, it gives off a real shine."

Johnny was definitely impressed – the suit was a certainty to attract the birds, but then again it could make a few of the local bampots jealous. Fuck them!

Jo Jo explained further, "Ah had two suits made up identical for father and son! Let's try them on Johnny and we'll come back and give your mother and brother a fashion parade."

They went into the small bedroom next door and changed into the suits. Both already had white shirts, ties and black shoes in the wardrobe.

They walked back into the front room together and on seeing them, Johnny's mother let out a gasp, "My god, you look like twins!"

Johnny joked, "Twins? Nah ah'm better looking than ma da!"

"Aye, in your dreams!" Jo Jo replied.

Johnny looked in a mirror nearby. He and his father looked swell, maybe too swell for the Gorbals.

Jo Jo announced, "Right, me and Johnny boy are going on a pub crawl. When they see us in the pub, they'll think we've won the pools."

"Or robbed a bank," Joseph said.

Jo Jo was not a big drinker but did not mind going on the odd pub crawl when he was home. They hit the pubs, starting with the Wheatsheaf in Crown Street, The Mally, Sou' Wester and Laurieston in Eglinton Street and then the Cleland bar in Hospital Street.

One drinker in the Mally Arms said, "You two look like you've just stepped out of a gangster movie." Every pub they went into there were compliments galore, some of them very cheeky but not offensive.

Johnny could also tell that several good-looking young birds had taken a shine to him, or his shiny suit.

When they walked into the Cleland bar there was lots of loud music going on. The place was thronging with mini skirted women. There was a rock singer called Jamie on the small stage belting out all the old hits. He was singing at full blast Tom Jones' 'It's Not Unusual.' The crowd were loving it, singing and dancing along.

Johnny made his way through the crowded bar and ordered two pints. Jo Jo said to him supping his pint, "Great atmosphere, but it's the same auld story, you mark my words there will be trouble soon. Just wait and see."

Johnny nodded his head in agreement as Jamie leapt about on stage singing 'Whole Lotta Shakin'. Then suddenly somebody launched a pint glass into the dancing crowd, hitting a young lady on the head.

Jamie leapt from the stage and wrapped a towel around the young lady's head and helped her sit on a chair at a table. No one could identify the culprit who had thrown the glass. A few minutes later Jamie was back on stage singing 'Sweet Little Sixteen'.

Johnny handed his father his pint and headed to the toilet. There was a big aggressive drunk there pissing on the floor, missing the urinals by a mile. He looked at Johnny, "Ah suppose you think you are a big shot wi' yir flashy gangster suit. Ah bet you couldnae punch your way oot a paper bag."

Johnny zipped up his fly and retorted, "No but ah could punch the fuck out of you." He then landed an uppercut to the man's chin. The big fellow went crashing to the floor.

Johnny made his way through the crowd on the dance floor. To his surprise the injured woman was now doing the twist with a bloodied towel wrapped around her head.

Johnny said to his father, "Let's beat it" They finished their pints and left. On their way back to Crown Street they saw two drunk men having "a square go" and belting the hell out of each other. In the tenement close a homeless man, a lobby dosser, had already curled up for the night. As he slept on the landing two rats ran past Johnny and his father.

They went into the house and Jo Jo said, "Same auld Gorbals, same auld pish." They headed off to bed a bit disillusioned but agreed the Gorbals would look different in the cold light of day.

A week later Jo Jo left to sail the high seas again. The family were dismayed to see him go but that was where he earned his money and it was good money. He hoped that Johnny would join him one day.

Johnny said he would go on the boats but not yet. There were still a few matters to deal with. Still a few scores to settle. And what about the lovely Cathy? He could not leave her before coming to some sort of resolution. If he went away on the boats someone might snap her up. There was no way that was going to happen. People knew Cathy was destined for Johnny and if any guy thought otherwise he would have to face the repercussions of Johnny's ferocious temper, razor and all.

While Jo Jo had been home, he had heard something about "the auld Jew's murder" but it had not really registered. His mind was full of people and places in far more exotic locations than the Gorbals. He would often joke, "It's a small world but ah wouldn't like to paint it."

While Jo Jo was on the cruise liner interacting with millionaires and stars from the world of showbiz, his son would be mixing with the numpties of the Gorbals underworld.

Chapter 8

CATHY

Cathy was a beautiful person, not only in looks but in her inner soul. She emitted kindness and had a smile that brought sunshine to any occasion. Many young men fancied her, with her long flowing red hair and bright red lips that had a seductive look about them.

Her father, Bobby McGee, had been somewhat of a gangster who had been involved in several bank robberies but had the good fortune never to have been caught.

For a while he had led the high life in handmade suits and driving a Ford Zephyr which he used to cruise around the Gorbals in to show that he was a man of prestige and glamour. Bobby also had a side-line as a money lender, and his rates were fairly reasonable. He had a team of young enforcers – or 'neds' as they were known, who were sent to collect payments every Friday from punters when they got paid.

Bobby's psychology was he offered rates that were equitable with the big banks. The only difference was if you failed or defaulted on the payments the interest rate went up significantly. And if the punter defaulted yet again the punishment could be severe. He would unleash his neds on the debtor who constantly failed to repay. Loans ranged from a pound to a hundred pounds.

He would simply comment on his money lending business by saying, "Put it this way if you default on the payments, you could end up with a sore face. But ah'm, no like the banks, ah won't turn up at your house and take your furniture away. I loan people money on trust, if they break that trust they could end up with a broken jaw or worse."

Throughout the 1960s Bobby had done well. He had married a local girl, Betty, in the late 1940s and they had two daughters, the eldest Cathy who was born in 1950 and Elizabeth, who came along a year later.

Both girls went to St Lukes RC Primary School in Ballater Street and were bright enough to go to Holyrood Secondary, in Govanhill, a school for the brightest of the pupils from the Gorbals.

Because Cathy was so pretty and so bright she became the victim of bullying at school. A jealous group of girls had beat her up at secondary school and for a time she was afraid of turning up. But when her mother told Bobby, he merely asked for the names of the bullies. He found out who their fathers were and had "a word" with them. The message was passed on and the bullying stopped.

One father who remonstrated with Bobby that his daughter had "nothing tae do wi' the bullying" was beat up so badly he was off work for a month. A gang of youths set about him with clubs as he left a pub. No-one knew who the culprits were but everyone surmised it was Bobby's neds and the message was clear – a heavy price would be paid if anyone messed with his daughter.

Elizabeth was less of a problem, her plain looks and a lower intelligence than Cathy meant that she merged in more easily with the other, mostly plain looking girls.

Cathy was in a different league and her mother always imagined she would one day be a star, sure she had the beauty for it. She took up dancing lessons. Her parents thought this would be the ideal way for her to enter the limelight.

But during one frenetic dance session, a robust tango, she fell and broke her leg. The leg had healed but she no longer had the flexibility to become a professional dancer. At the age of 16 she got a got a job as a machinist at the Twomax garment factory in the Gorbals. If you stood outside there in the morning, before the shift started, you could see the prettiest women in Glasgow go in.

Indeed, some would argue that these young women were among the most beautiful women in Scotland. Cathy was certainly one of them.

One day she came out of work, after her shift, with two pals, and saw a handsome looking guy walking towards her in Rutherglen Road, near the Rose Garden, a little park nearby.

The handsome, gallus looking fellow, gave them a bright smile and nodded. "Awright girls?" Cathy said to one of her pals, "Who is that guy?" One of them giggled," Oh that's Johnny McGrath the leader of the Cumbie gang. He's a handsome bastard, but a wild fella as well. All the lassies fancy him, and he knows it."

"Is he going out with anybody?" Cathy asked. "Nah," her pal replied, "He's a bit of a man about town, don't think he has ever had a steady girlfriend." Cathy went home and dreamed that one day she would be his girlfriend and even his wife. From then on, she made it a point to bump into Johnny "accidently on purpose" when he was around. As a result, the two began to build up a regular repartee with lots of banter.

Cathy knew he fancied her and perhaps even loved her, but Johnny was like a poker player, you never knew what hand he was holding.

Meanwhile her father's illicit business was booming. The money lending was very lucrative as were the card schools he ran in the illegal drinking dens, shebeens, he had in some tenements. He sold wine, whisky and beer after the pubs shut. He also had another sideline as a street bookie.

Cathy McGee and her family lived in a nice flat in Queen Elizabeth Square, in one of the modern high rises that had been built in the middle of the 1960s. Bobby would sit in the kitchen of his flat counting out bundles of money. He had built up a nice nest egg over the years and his ambition was to buy a bungalow in a leafy area like Newton Mearns, and eventually get his family out of the Gorbals.

With the money building up, it was his plan to go straight, perhaps become a legitimate bookie or launch his own security company. Sure, he had enough enforcers to man such operations. But Bobby had made a big mistake and broke a cardinal rule for any Gorbals gangster. He looked and acted too affluent, with his big flashy car and equally flashy suits.

As he passed by in his Zephyr waving to some people on the street corners he made some of them jealous. To them he was flaunting his wealth and was an accident waiting to happen. But of course they would never say anything to his face, Bobby knew they gossiped about him and his wealth but just thought, "Fuck them, what can they do? My business is my business and they can take a running jump."

The problem was the police were also watching him and were working on plan to nail their man. His money lending business was going at full throttle. And since he had become a street bookie, he raked in even more money. The police knew he must have a weak point. It eventually came in the form of his shebeen business.

His shebeen was raided and a guy who owed Bobby £30 grassed him up and spilled the beans on his various illegal activities. Police had enough evidence to arrest him and Bobby was taken to the Sheriff Court and sentenced to three months in jail for running a drinking den.

The imprisonment hit takings on all sides of the business. While in Barlinnie prison he worked out a battle plan to take away his family from the Gorbals forever. "Another two years and then I'll pack it in. Move to Newton Mearns live in ma bungalow and start legit," he thought.

But when he came out almost three months later, he found that his power had faded. His enforcers had switched their allegiance to "Big Arthur" who was said to be the Godfather of Glasgow. The shebeen and card schools had been closed down and when he tried to resurrect his street bookie and money lending ventures, he found that Arthur had taken over them as well. When the cat's away the mice will play.

The Gorbals people could also detect weakness, they could smell it a mile off and he was no longer being treated with the respect he once had. Punters stopped paying their debts. With little or no money coming in, his savings were dwindling but he consoled himself at least he had his family behind him. His wife Betty, daughters Cathy and Elizabeth would stand by him no matter what.

He had to get back in the game again and regain control. He had only one option, to go to Arthur's place on the other side of Glasgow, Provanmill, and work something out. An agreement that would suit both of them. But the meeting could go either way.

He did not reveal his plan to anyone, not even his family. He met Cathy outside of the Twomax factory and said, "Got a little bit of business on. Look, there's a few grand hidden behind the wardrobe in my bedroom."

Cathy was puzzled and replied, "Da, why are you telling me this?"

Bobby was vague, "Well just in case, you know. Things can be unpredictable."

Cathy had a bemused look on her face as her father climbed into his white Zephyr and sped off in the direction of Arthur on the other side of the city.

It was a gamble he had to take, but was it a gamble that would cost his life?

Chapter 9

TRIAL

Johnny walked from the Gorbals over the Albert Bridge to the High Court in the Saltmarket. It was a bitterly cold day and he did not feel at all well. He looked at the Clyde, people come and go with their pathetic little lives but the Clyde kept flowing. He thought of the line, "I'm tired of living, but scared of dying, but that old man river just keeps on moving along." How short life was compared to the River Clyde! When would people realise that their lives were short and basically meaningless, an individual life was like a single grain of sand on the beach. He also thought of the boys in the High Court, why did they have to get themselves into situations like this? Then he thought of his familiar mantra – drama brings meaning to life.

He grinned at the seagulls who swooped over his head who seemed to be grinning as well. He had not slept well that night, terrible dreams or rather nightmares. One involved him being chased by giant metallic machines. He had woken up in a sweat shouting, "Help me, the machines are gonnae kill me!" His mother came into the room in the middle of the night to see what the commotion was all about.

She stroked Johnny's head and said, "Don't worry son, it's only a dream, there are nae machines trying tae kill you." He had fallen back asleep and then floated into another one where he and Cathy were dancing on a cloud but in the background, he could see McCoy leering at them.

As he left the Albert Bridge, he noticed a crowd assembled outside the High Court. The usual Gorbals mob. Housewives nattering, old men in bunnets, and youth gang members looking as gallus as fuck.

He put on his bravest face and walked towards them. Some of the crowd turned their heads and he heard one of them say, "There he is, Johnny boy, ah told you he'd turn up." He walked over to the crowd and got submerged into the conversation. A woman, who he recognised as Alex's mother, said, "What dae ye think Johnny, do ye think they've got a chance of getting away wi' it?"

He shrugged his shoulders, "Depends on the evidence and the witnesses. We'll see what happens." On the edge of the crowd he saw McCoy's father but he did not acknowledge him. He thought of a Chinese proverb he had heard, "The father of an enemy should be treated the same as the enemy."

Johnny had a far superior intellect than many of them there who he perceived as no more than a bunch of shabby vermin. Lowly educated slum people living in poverty. He looked across the road and saw "respectable people" taking their dogs into the Glasgow Green. If only he could become one of them instead of being involved in this tragic farce.

The doors of the High Court were opened and the crowd headed towards the public gallery. As he walked upstairs Johnny noticed the legal teams standing about, most in pin-striped suits, some with wigs on and some not, advocates and lawyers. They looked different from the Gorbals rabble he was with. The lawyers had rosy cheeks, well fed men who lived in big fancy houses, ate in the best restaurants drinking the finest wines.

But this is how they made their money, dealing with impoverished rabble who lived in decaying tenements on bread and margarine. And when they got into trouble, legal aid was always there to provide a wig to defend them

Before he went into the public gallery he glanced again back downstairs. He saw several policemen walking towards the lawyers. It was then he noticed they were escorting someone. With the policemen were two people, an old man and a grey haired lady. His heart sank, it was the two main prosecution witnesses Edward Driscoll and Agatha McFadden. Unlike the self-confident and pompous lawyers, they both looked nervous and kept looking over their shoulders.

Johnny had been sure that the brick through the window for Driscoll and the woman being set about by mad Bella would have done the trick. But there was no accounting for human nature. The public gallery was packed and one woman sitting next to Johnny looked excited said, "This is just like being at the pictures, all the goodies and baddies and all free."

The accused were led into the dock, they all looked like they had put on weight, that's prison food for you. Three square meals a day and a cup of cocoa at night before bed. In many ways people who went to jail were better fed than when they lived in the Gorbals, the Barlinnie diet! You could go in looking like an athlete and come out looking like a fat bastard.

As they sat down, Alex and Peter gave short waves to the public gallery as if they were showbiz stars ready for a performance. Chris looked nervous and had a sneezing fit for a few minutes.

Brian looked more insane than ever, he glanced around the courtroom briefly and Johnny thought, "The eyes of a psychopath."

McCoy was impassive, he had had his hair shaved in prison and looked even uglier than Johnny had previously imagined. McGlinchey was dressed in a pin striped suit and looked like an accountant.

For the first hour or so it was pretty boring. The lawyers droned on with their legal submissions. Johnny thought that it was almost as boring as the science classes he had been forced to attend at his secondary school, St Bonaventures.

The boredom evaporated when the submissions geared up a notch. The prosecutor was a large fat man, a QC, in a wig. He had the poshest Scottish accent Johnny had ever heard. He began to sweat profusely as he talked, beads of perspiration dripping from his head. His nose looked like a red lightbulb.

Johnny thought, a right bevvy merchant, probably been whacking intae the expensive posh wines last night."

The fat QC began his speech, "It is the prosecution's case that these men before you carried out a violent robbery culminating in the murder of Ivan Solomon, at the Gorbals Cross area of Glasgow. We will show that this was a premeditated robbery and murder, involving a gun which had been acquired with sole intention of carrying out this heinous crime. Indeed, a crime that has shocked the Scottish nation to it's core."

The speech went on and on and when Johnny looked down at the dock, he could see Peter and Alex yawning, as if they were back at the science lesson in school. Chris had stopped sneezing but had now taken to shaking his head erratically. Brian looked like a volcano ready to erupt. McCoy just sat there like a dummy, showing no connection to the other guys. Sam looked placid as if he had seen it all before.

Next came the speech from a defence counsel representing Chris. He was a young sharp guy in his early 30s, who was very quick and had a powerful, dramatic Glaswegian voice. He had probably missed his real vacation in life and would have made an excellent soap opera actor.

He addressed the court, "It is our case that my client has been unjustly arrested for these offences. He is a man of very good character and was nowhere near

Gorbals Cross when the robbery and murder took place."

Johnny was greatly impressed by the young lawyer. He reminded him of the sharp suited guy from the telly, Perry Mason. He may have been a lot younger than the fat QC and a lot less experienced but his legal talent shone through. There was light at the end of the tunnel after all! The other boys had different lawyers, more or less based on the same defence. The robbery was nothing to do with them and they had been unjustly arrested.

After the defence submissions had been completed, Brian jumped up from the dock and shouted, "Take these fucking handcuffs off me – they're hurting ma wrists." The court ushers and several policemen rushed to the dock. Brian promptly head butted an usher and bit a policeman on the nose.

"Order! Order! Order!" the judge shouted, "Take that man back to the cells and lock him up!" Brian struggled with several policemen before being led away to the cells downstairs

The case was abruptly adjourned until the next day. One of the women in the gallery said to him, "What a palaver! Mind you the boy has a good point, tight handcuffs. He's getting treated worse than an animal."

Johnny agreed, "Too right, ye cannae blame Brian. Mind you when he gets riled, he can be like a wild animal." He went outside and it was a beautiful day. He breathed in the fresh air and there was a nice fragrance. The grass in the Glasgow Green had just been mown.

He looked over the road to the park and saw something more beautiful. It was Cathy standing there waiting for the court to come out. He walked across the road. She grabbed him tightly and kissed him softy on the cheek. Johnny was taken aback by this show of emotion.

"What's the matter Cathy?" he asked.

She began to cry, "It's ma father,"

"What about him?" Johnny said.

"He's gone missing, disappeared into thin air," Cathy sobbed.

The two of them began to walk, mostly in silence, through the Glasgow Green and because it had turned out to be a fine day there were people rowing on the river. It looked a bit incongruous. Something you might imagine happening in Oxford rather than the Gorbals. They soaked in the atmosphere and in the background was Templeton's old carpet factory building. A teacher at school had told Johnny that is a replica of the Doge's Palace in Venice. Johnny and his pal had laughed at the very thought of someone coming up with such an idea. To put a copy of such a famous building, not far from the centre of the Gorbals, seemed a ludicrous situation.

The silence was broken, "So where do ye think he is?" Johnny asked. Cathy frowned, "We don't have a clue, but he did say to ma mother that the taxman was after him for 25 grand and the polis were investigating him further."

Johnny said, "How come? The dough he was making from the money lending, shebeen and card schools, was unofficial money."

Cathy replied, "That's the point, he had no official income to explain away running a big flashy car, having expensive suits, wi' a lifestyle tae match."

Johnny said, "Ah know what you mean but he should have signed on the dole and claimed other benefits tae cover his arse."

Cathy looked indignant gave out a weak laugh, "Dole? My father widnae have been seen dead signing on in a dole queue. He is too proud a guy for that. He was about to start up a legit business to explain his income away but he was too slow as far as the taxman and the polis were concerned."

They decided to go into the People's Palace museum to kill some time. They looked at the reconstruction of an old tenement flat with an old woman, a wax dummy sitting in front of the hearth. It summed up the image of Glasgow's slums and poverty in the old days. Cathy pointed to the female wax figure. "Would you look at her Johnny! How could people live like that in the old days?"

Johnny smirked, "In the old days! Ah could take you to a wee woman in Thistle Street who lives in worse conditions than that now." Cathy gave a brief giggle and a few minutes later made their way across the Glasgow Green over the small suspension bridge that led them back into the Gorbals.

"So, you've got no idea where your father is, none at all?" he said.

Cathy thought for a moment and said, "Well he did get drunk a few weeks ago he said that because the taxman was after him for a right few grand, he might have to disappear to Ireland. But we just thought it was the drink talking. He always talked rubbish when he was drunk."

"Ireland? Why Ireland? Has he got connections there?" Johnny asked.

Cathy replied, "Aye he's got a cousin in Dublin but he's no' seen him for donkey's years, so ah don't think he'd head there."

"One o' the boys tried to scram there recently but he was arrested on the ferry before it sailed. Your father's not a wanted man, is he?" he asked Cathy.

"Nah he is too fly for that but the night he was drunk he said that while he was in jail his businesses had been taken over by some Glasgow gangster called Big Arthur." she said.

Johnny felt alarm bells ringing in his head. It would have been absolute folly to mess with Big Arthur. He just hoped Bobby had made it in one piece to Ireland. They got to where Cathy lived in Queen Elizabeth

Square. She looked at him with her big blue eyes. She knew she could play Johnny like a violin.

"Oh, Johnny you know everybody, can you no' find out what's happened tae ma father?"

"Aye ah'll find oot for you, I've got an idea who might know," he said confidently. She sighed and then kissed Johnny on the cheek. It was a moist kiss, the sort of kiss you give someone who you are infatuated with. They parted ways. Johnny walked past the Rose Garden towards Crown Street. He knew exactly who to ask about Patrick's mysterious disappearance.

He had a lot on his mind, the court case, his enemy McCoy and now this. It never rains but it pours.

He felt a tingling sensation come over his body. If this was the feeling of love, he liked it. Liked it very much.

Chapter 10

HEADBANGER

The next morning, he awoke from his slumber and realised he was running late for his visit to the High Court. His brother had already headed off to school, in his blazer, to Holyrood Secondary. For a brief moment he thought of his brother, he was destined for success in the future; he did not hang about with the street rabble and concentrated on his homework. In other words, "a good wee boy". Joseph also read with great energy his Superman comics which gave him a knowledge that school would never provide and kept out of trouble, never getting into fights. In many ways Joseph was such snob compared to him.

Johnny realised with a shiver he had taken a different route to his brother and went to a more mediocre school with numpties. He has attended a poor school because of his loutish behaviour, not because of his intelligence. This lay in the fact that from an early age he had mixed with the Gorbals riff raff and built up a reputation for being a Gorbals hardman. But what good was this image? It had no real meaning, no purpose, he was on a road to nowhere. His only saving grace for the future was Cathy but that could not be 100 per cent relied on.

She might tire of him and his ways. And then what, after his looks faded? Work in a lowly job with an ugly wife and two equally ugly children who would probably follow his route on the way to alcoholism, poverty and eventually oblivion. The thoughts sent more shivers down his spine. He was scrubbing his face at the kitchen window and when he looked out, he saw a newsagent's placard declaring: "Maniac Goes Mental in Court!"

It cheered him up, Brian had made the headlines. He had always said over a pint, "One of these days ah'm gonnae be famous." And he had been right, Brian had got his 15 minutes of fame right enough.

Johnny rushed down the tenement stairs and regretted sleeping in on such a big day. But he was not the only one who had overslept. He could smell the stench of a lobby dosser. The homeless man was curled up in a great coat on the first floor landing. "Hey Jimmy," Johnny shouted, "Cock a doodle do! Time to get the fuck up!" (At that time every guy in Glasgow had the precursor 'Jimmy', before the more modern 'mate' took over) The shabby man rose to his feet and scratched his head before scratching his balls.

He rubbed his eyes, "What time is it?" he asked, and Johnny could smell the wine of the night before coming from his rancid breath. But he tried to be diplomatic and a little more Christian to the dosser. "Nearly ten pal, time to fuck off before the polis lift you for lobby dossing," he said.

"Awright son," the dosser replied, "Eh, you couldnae lend me a couple o' coppers for a cup of tea?"

Johnny decided to be sterner, the dosser was taking him for a mug. "Look pal the only coppers you'll be having is the ones that turn up here to arrest you."

Going down the tenement stairs he could hear shrieking from the back courts – two large rats were fighting. Surprisingly the smaller rat was getting the better of the larger one. Johnny thought many of the people in the Gorbals lived just like rats and fought the same.

He rushed out of the close, heading towards the Albert Bridge, in the direction of the High Court, when he saw a large aggressive looking man walking towards him. The man then stood before him blocking his way. "Hey," he shouted, "Are you no' that guy who stuck the nut on me in the Cleland pub toilets?"

Johnny was in a rush and really had no time to stand and fight. He replied in the best foreign accent he could muster, "Me no speak English. Me just arrived from Poland."

The man looked confused and moved out of Johnny's way, "Well you must have a fucking double," he shouted. Johnny laughed to himself, "Aye, a double whisky!" he thought. Bullshit baffles brains, especially when it is foreign sounding bullshit.

He rushed to the High Court and saw a group of policemen there, they were accompanied by the two main witnesses, Eddie Driscoll and Agatha McFadden. One officer was saying to them, "Terrible carry on yesterday, that nutcase went doolally, and put a couple of our officers in hospital."

"Complete head banger," said a fellow constable, "They should lock that lunatic up and throw away the key. Hanging is too good for animals like that."

Johnny looked at the two witnesses faces. Neither of them smiled and they had worry etched on their faces. They realised now they had made a major mistake: they were testifying against the biggest nutters in the Gorbals. And at the end of the day the police would not be able to save them from a fate not worth thinking about.

Johnny made his way to the packed public gallery where somebody had kept a seat for him. The fat prosecuting QC was addressing the judge, "As you know one of the accused, Brian McMaster, assaulted four police officers yesterday, two of them ended up in hospital. He also attacked two court ushers, who are not in court today because of their injuries. Brian McMaster was taken from here in an agitated state to Barlinnie Prison. I have been informed that he assaulted several prison officers there, forced into a strait jacket and placed in a padded cell."

There were gasps from the public gallery but Johnny smiled, he found it amusing that Brian had been put in a padded cell, he had predicted that years ago.

The fat QC continued, his face getting redder and redder by the minute and beads of sweat fell from his furrowed forehead.

"As a result of his actions Mr McMaster was transferred to a psychiatric ward at Carstairs Hospital where he is now under heavy sedation. I have now been informed that he is mentally unfit to stand trial."

Johnny thought back to a conversation with Brian, in pub, a few years back. Brian confessed over a pint, "Ah'm no mental, ah've got a certificate from the doctors to say so." They had both laughed then but there had been some truth in the punchline. Many a true word spoken in jest and all that. But at least with his mad ways Brian had avoided going on trial and might even get out of the loony bin in a few years, if the authorities ever considered him to be sane. Anyway, one down, five to go!

Johnny glanced down at the dock, the boys looked as though they had cheered up. Brian had escaped justice by acting daft and, as the Glaswegian saying goes, "Kid on you're daft and you'll get a hurrell (a ride) for nothing." The only person in the dock who seemed to be detached from the rest of the boys was McCoy, he stared right ahead like the dummy he was.

The case for the prosecution began, at first it was a bit slow moving. Six policemen in turn stood in the witness box and swore to tell the truth, the whole truth and nothing but the truth. Their stories were all the same. They had been alerted to a robbery at Gorbals Cross and rushed there to see a car speeding off as the shot businessman lay bleeding on the pavement.

Two of them stayed with the bleeding victim, trying to stop the flow of blood, while the others gave chase in a panda car towards Castlemilk. At one point they saw a gun being thrown from the car window into some bushes. When they got to Castlemilk, six men ran from the car into the labyrinths of the sprawling council estate.

After searching the area with more reinforcements, and police dogs, five of the six men were apprehended. Johnny noticed that not one policeman had witnessed the robbery, but what about identifying who was in the getaway car? The fat QC attempted to put that matter right in a series of questions. He asked one policeman, "How long did you pursue the getaway car to Castlemilk?" The policeman replied, "About 25 minutes at high speed."

QC, "Did you get a clear view of who was in the car?"

Policeman, "Yes, six men, two in the front, four in the back"

QC, "Do you see those men here?"

Policemen, "Yes, it was all those men in the dock."

QC, "Are you sure?"

Policeman, "100 per cent. When the car stopped in Castlemilk the men jumped out and ran off through the estate. We got on our walki-talkies and called for reinforcements. After a thorough search of the area we arrested five of the men. A sixth man was arrested sometime later on board a ferry which was planning to sail to Ireland."

QC, "And you have no doubt these were the men who committed the robbery and murder?"

Policeman, "No doubt at all sir."

The boys shuffled nervously in the dock, driver Sam McGlinchy's face took on a deathly pallor. But now it was the turn of the young counsel for the defence.

Counsel, "Officer you say you saw the men in the car. Did they all have their backs to you?"

Policeman, "Yes sir, we were chasing them in our panda car."

Counsel, "At what speed?"

Policeman, "Eh, around 70 miles per hour."

Counsel, "At 70mph it would have been nigh impossible to recognise anyone with their backs to you."

Policeman, "We were going pretty fast but even then, I was able to clock what they looked like."

Counsel, "What happened then?"

Policeman, "The car turned a corner, stopped at a grinding halt, and the men got out and ran into the housing estate. After an hour searching the estate with police dogs, we apprehended them."

Counsel, "And were you sure the men you arrested, were the same men who ran from the car?"

The policeman began to look nervous as if his confidence was eroding.

Policeman, "Aye, well it certainly looked like them."

Counsel, "I look like one of the accused, does that mean you would have arrested me, if I had taken a walk in Castlemilk that day?"

The policeman looked unnerved, "I might have if you looked like one of the robbers."

Counsel, "Ah, now it is becoming clear, so anyone you thought that looked like a robber you would have lifted, is that not the case?"

The policeman stuttered. He had been used to giving evidence in menial cases in the magistrates' courts but now he was playing in the first division.

Counsel, "So what you are saying is my client and the other men were arrested on guesswork?"

Policeman, "Not really, sir – we knew it was them."

Counsel, "You did not see the robbery and shooting taking place. You only saw the back of the men's heads in the speeding car and then maybe for a few seconds you saw the men dash from the car from some distance away. It just doesn't add up officer, does it?"

The policeman shook with rage, "Well ah think it does."

Counsel, "We are not interested in what you think officer, we are interested for the sake of justice in what you know. And as far as I am concerned you know nothing."

All the blood drained from the policeman's face. He shook even more. He had been made to look like a fool. Johnny thought he was a fool anyway and after years of testifying against people in the lower courts he had been found out at last. The scales of justice work in mysterious ways

But the young lawyer was not finished yet. "Officer what were the weather conditions that day?"

Policeman, "Eh, no' bad, a bit rainy and a wee bit downcast."

Counsel, "A wee bit down cast? Is that not an understatement? Is it not true that at the time of the robbery it was very cloudy and the light was fading? And by the time you arrested these men in Castlemilk it was almost dark?"

The policeman's Adam's apple seemed to go up and down. "Well as I say, it was a wee bit downcast and it did get darker gradually by the time we got to Castlemilk. The weather and visibility weren't perfect but we were sure we arrested the right men."

Counsel, "We argue that that visibility was too poor for you to accurately identify the men in the dock as the culprits."

Johnny and the rest of the public gallery thought that the young defence counsel had played an excellent ploy, there was a chance after all!

Five other policemen came and went giving much the same evidence and all agreed there had been poor visibility that day. But all were sure they had arrested the right men. None had seen the robbery taking place and could only testify about the car chase and subsequent arrest. The case was adjourned until the next day and the boys were taken back in handcuffs to Barlinnie.

Johnny left the High Court feeling elated. There was no doubt about it the young defence lawyer was brilliant. He was definitely going places, perhaps QC next, and then a judge.

The headline in the paper that night was: **POLICE UNSURE ABOUT JEWISH MURDER BECAUSE OF BAD WEATHER.**

Johnny's mind now focused on Cathy and her missing father, Bobby McGee. A clear-cut plan came into his head. He would track down one of his old school pals called Donny, who had once worked as an enforcer for Bobby but now worked for Big Arthur in Provanmill.

As expected, he found Donny having a pint in the Victoria Bar in Govanhill. Johnny walked up to Donny when he was at the bar and said, "How's it gaun pal? Fancy a wee bevvy for auld time's sake?"

Donny looked genuinely pleased to see him. "Nae problem Johnny boy, mine's a Mick Jagger."

Johnny got two pints of lager and they both sat down at a table. He needed to have a quiet chat with Donny but the juke box nearby was playing loud rock music. Johnny shouted to the young spotty faced barman, "Turn that fucking juke box down!"

The barman recognised Johnny and was aware of his reputation, he did not only turn the juke box down, he turned it off.

They had some chit chat for a while and then Johnny whispered to Donny, "Listen ah want tae ask ye something, do me favour, tell me what's happened tae Bobby McGee, your old boss." Donny spluttered, "Ah hivnae got a clue, honest Johnny."

Johnny knew he was lying, concealing the truth, he said cheerily,"Let's get the hawfs in then." He went to the bar and ordered two double Bell's whiskies. Johnny handed Donny the large glass of whisky and said, "Just like the old days, right down in one go!" They both sank the whiskies. Johnny went back to the bar and ordered another two. Johnny was not really a whisky drinker, but it gave him a warm glowing feeling and Donny felt the same. Both their faces flushed red, and were in a more agreeable mood.

Donny whispered to Johnny, "Awright, you've got me by the balls. Bobby went tae see Arthur in his pub in Provanmill and they fell out. I was there. Bobby began to utter threats to Arthur and vice versa. It was a dangerous situation. Ah made ma excuses and left. But rumour has it after the argument Bobby was given a concrete overcoat and is now part of the foundations of the Kingston Bridge. He's not been seen since that night"

Johnny thought of Cathy and her delicate nature, news like this could kill her. He had no real evidence that her father was dead but believed Donny and his concrete overcoat story.

He bade Donny farewell and headed to an Irish Club nearby. Sitting in the corner was a big burly Irish labourer called Sean who Johnny had known for years.

He knew Sean was always popping over to Donegal to see his elderly mother. Johnny asked Sean when he was going over again. He replied,"This weekend to see ma auld maw, she's no' been well."

Johnny was glad to hear the news, "Sean, can ye do me a big favour?"

Sean supped his Guinness and said, "What's that?"

Johnny was straight to the point, "Ah want you to send a telegram from Donegal with this message on it – 'Here for a wee vacation from the taxman and police. Be back when things die down. Bobby.'"

Sean looked at the message, handwritten on paper, and smiled, "That's a queer looking message but don't worry I'll send it when I get to the local post office in Donegal." Johnny gave him a fiver, "to cover expenses", and left.

When he left the club two drunken Irishmen, in their wellies, were battering hell out of each other in Allison Street. He smiled when he thought about what Sean had said to him a few years back, "A drunken Irishman could cause trouble in an empty house."

He walked quite a distance to St Luke's chapel in Ballater Street. He knelt down and said a prayer for Bobby. He also lit a candle for him.

As the candle flickered against the background of the altar, he thought that life was like that – we all flickered for a short period until time and circumstance blew out the candle forever.

Chapter 11

PUNT

When Johnny sauntered through the Gorbals in his handmade shirts and other fashionable gear, in many ways he looked like a prosperous young man with a well-paid job.

But the fact was Johnny had not worked for a year. The gossip was that he had been an enforcer and collector for Bobby McGee and had moved up a division to work for Arthur. But this was a fabrication of reality. After leaving school he had a number of dead-end jobs, delivery boy, kitchen porter, trainee chef and a labourer on various building sites.

An Irish pal got him a start on one site as a labourer and Johnny slogged his guts out, digging holes to an extent his arms could barely move at the end of a shift, all for a tenner a week. He was also made the tea boy and made pots of tea for the Irish labourers who toiled on the site. They liked Johnny as he made them tea they wanted: strong and dark with plenty of milk and sugar. He loved the job and the camaraderie was part of its attraction. The big Irish navvies would sit in a wooden hut drinking their tea and smoking fags while telling the most outlandish stories.

One morning when he was on a tea break in the hut with 20 other labourers he was asked by an old guy from Limerick if he wanted to join their pools syndicate and put "ten bob in the kitty". Johnny was sceptical about throwing away ten bob, 50p a week, as these guys had been trying to win the pools for years and came up with the centre of a donut – nothing. But when he read stories about pools winners coming into millions, he realised they were people just like him.

They had a punt every week hoping their lives would be changed by a big win. Besides as the cliché goes, you've got to be in it to win it.

Johnny joined the syndicate with ten other labourers and for five months he moaned every week to the other labourers that it looked like a waste of money and would have preferred to have spent his cash on beer. But one Irish labourer gave him confidence, shouting to him as they dug a deep hole, "Don't worry Johnny boy, our day will come. Just wait and see!"

A few weeks later he was about to give up on the pools syndicate when the foreman of the site rushed into the hut and shouted, "Boys we've won the jackpot! It's no' gonnae be millions or anything near that but it's a few bob for the lot of us!" In the event they had won £20,000, £2,000 each. Johnny threw his shovel to the ground and never went back to the building site again. "Fuck that for a lark," he thought.

He gave some of his pals a "bung", bought his mother some nice clothes and treated his brother to a pile of Superman comics. But overall, he was careful with his money and told very few people about the pools win. He placed his new-found wealth in The Royal Bank of Scotland near George Square. He would never have placed his winnings in the Gorbals branch in Crown Street as that would have let the cat out of the bag.

The win meant that he could lead a comparatively comfortable lifestyle without having to dig holes. But he was shrewd, he also signed on the dole, pretending to look for work and a giro cheque arrived at his door every two weeks – this was his beer money and stopped him delving into his savings.

When his giro money was spent, he would sneak in the city centre to make discreet withdrawals.

As he sat in the public gallery for yet another day of the High Court farce he thought the pools win had been lucky for him in more ways than one. It meant he secretly had enough money to avoid taking part in capers like the failed robbery. But when he looked at the poor bastards in the dock, he realised they did not have that choice. To him all the crime talk had been bullshit. Money talks, bullshit walks.

The fat QC announced, "I would like to call the next witness for the prosecution. Mr Edward Driscoll."

"Bastard!" Johnny murmured. Even a brick through the guy's window had not put him off being a grass. Driscoll appeared in the dock looking very much like a retired respectable businessman, grey suit, shirt and tie and was wearing intellectual looking glasses that made him look far more intelligent than he really was. The clothes did not fool the public gallery, people saw him for what he really was – a grass in a suit.

QC, "Mr Driscoll can you please describe the events to us what exactly happened on the day of the robbery?"

Driscoll, "Well I was walking past Gorbals Cross when I saw an old Jewish guy carrying a large bag. Next minute, a gang of four guys ran over and tried to take the bag from him. They were all wearing balaclavas and gloves. The old guy put up a fight and grabbed a couple of the robbers. Then one of them pulled out a revolver and shot him. They ran off and jumped into a speeding car."

QC "Do you see any of these men here?"

Driscoll looked over the dock and hesitated, "I can't say for certain as the robbers were wearing balaclavas and it was a dull day and my eyesight is no' what is was."

Johnny realised that Driscoll was being economical with the truth – he had initially told police he had "seen couple of faces" but now he was reversing the story. The QC and the police looked annoyed. Driscoll had changed his story at the last minute. It got even better, under further questioning he said because of his age he was having "memory lapses" and could barely remember the day of the robbery.

The young counsel made mincemeat of him and by the end of the questioning he looked like a shattered man.

Driscoll had realised at a late stage that by telling the truth he would have written his own suicide note. The brick through the window had worked!

Agatha McFadden was next up, she looked even more nervous and worried than Driscoll. She told the same story and said she could not verify that the men in the dock were the robbers.

QC, "You said in an initial police interview you would have no problem identifying the men. Why has this changed, have you been got at?"

Agatha McFadden never mentioned she had been attacked by big Bella and replied meekly, "No it's just that it seems a long time ago and at my age it is hard to recall things with clarity. I'm no spring chicken and my memory isn't as sharp as when I was younger." Buying big Bella a few large glasses of cheap wine had been a good investment.

But the prosecution had a surprise in store- another witnesses popped up without any warning. She was Betty Blogger, a 60-year-old woman from Govanhill who had been passing by Gorbals Cross when the robbery took place. She told then court she was on her way to visit her daughter, who lived in Thistle Street, when she saw the robbers.

QC "Tell me this Mrs Blogger. Can you see any of the men here today?"

"Aye," she replied, "when they jumped into the getaway car, I could see two faces. The face of the guy who had the gun and the face of the driver."

The QC gave a smile of delight, "Do you see these two men in the dock?"

At first, she pointed to Joe McCoy, "That fella was the gunman."

Next, she pointed to Sam McGlinchy, "And that fellow was the driver."

At this McCoy who had showed no emotion during the trial turned white, in turn Sam McGlinchy turned into (like the song) a whiter shade of pale.

But all was not lost when the young counsel took over. He argued that the day was so gloomy, dark and rainy, it would have been impossible to recognise somebody accurately.

He asked Mrs Blogger, "Would you say you have perfect eyesight?"

Mrs Blogger, "Well, I don't wear glasses but my eyesight is almost perfect. I can get a bit of eye strain now and again because I watch telly all the time. Especially Coronation Street."

The young counsel was amused, "Coronation Street? A fine soap opera. So, you know all the main characters?"

Mrs Blogger replied confidently, "Of course I do, I watch every episode without fail. It's my hobby"

Johnny, the public gallery, and the boys in the dock were confused. What the hell was the counsel doing talking about Coronation Street? Had he suddenly lost his marbles? The counsel asked the judge to "adjourn for half an hour" so he could pick up "vital new evidence".

He then rushed out of the High Court in the pouring rain, still wearing his wig and gown, and returned 20 minutes later, soaking wet, clutching a magazine.

The trial resumed. Mrs Blogger was back in the witness stand.

Counsel, "Mrs Blogger before the short adjournment you said you were an avid fan of Coronation Street and knew all the characters. Is that not true?"

Mrs Blogger, "Yes, I am a big fan"

Suddenly the young counsel, who was standing about 30 feet from her, ripped a page out of the magazine, which had a large picture on it and said, "Who is this?"

Mrs Blogger squinted her eyes, thought for a moment, and said, "It looks a bit like Ena Sharples."

The counsel gave out a bellowing laugh, "No Mrs Blogger, it is Elsie Tanner. I have grave doubts about your eyesight. No more questions." (At the time in Coronation Street, Elsie Tanner was a glamorous sex symbol and Ena Sharples was a grumpy old pensioner.)

The case was adjourned until the next day and things were looking up for the boys. Johnny left the court and once again Cathy was standing across the road, outside of the gate at the Glasgow Green but this time she was smiling and holding a piece of paper in her hand. They both walked through the park and the birds were whistling in the trees. She handed Johnny the piece of paper, it was the telegram from Donegal, "Here for a wee vacation…" Cathy said, "Oh Johnny ah'm so happy ma father is safe and sound in Donegal and he'll be back when the heat is off."

Johnny felt guilty but put on an air of confidence that would bolster her hopes for the future, "There's an old saying. Everything will be ok in the end. And if it's not ok… it's not the end."

Chapter 12

SLUMS

He was living in strange times. The Gorbals had stood for hundreds of years but the publication of No Mean City in 1935 had led to it being castigated all over the world for its poverty, slums, drunkenness and violence.

The international media would often descend on the place describing in lurid detail, in some stories, how thirteen people lived in one tiny single end and even had rats running through their houses. The razor gangs, the slums, were all part and parcel of the picture that was painted. The articles often described the Gorbals as hell on earth. It was the 1970s, man had landed on the moon in 1969, but it seemed local people lived like the inhabitants from the Victorian age or a third world country.

By the age of 21 Johnny had seen it all, the drunks, the razor gangs, the slums the poverty, but in his mind it had all been magnified out of proportion. Of course the Gorbals was not hell on earth but neither was it heaven. It was the only place he knew, the only place where he felt at home, the only place where he could communicate effectively with other people.

The Gorbals he experienced was different from the one portrayed in the media. Of course, there were the slums but there was also grand magnificent buildings as well, comparable with those in posh Edinburgh. As far as he saw it, there was poverty, crime and drunkenness but surely every city in Britain had these problems?

The difficulty was the Gorbals had become the star of the dystopian show. He thought of an old joke his father had told him: A guy dies and wakes up the looks around. There are crumbling tenements everywhere. He says," Ah never thought that Heaven would look like the Gorbals." And a loud voice replies, "Who said this was Heaven? This is hell!"

By the early 1970s the area was being torn apart with many slums being demolished. Local MP Frank McElhone, had stood in the Commons and described in a dramatic fashion, the horrors of living in such a place. The authorites had listened to such voices and decided to tear the place down, dispersing thousands of people from the tenement buildings to vast soulless housing estates like Castlemilk or Househillwood. The planning was dire for such neighbourhoods. Around 100,000 people were given new houses in Castlemilk, there was a lack of amenities and not even one pub. It was much the same story in Househillwod, a leafy green area with hardly any amenities.

Many displaced people felt conned, nothing would ever replicate the atmosphere and community that existed in the Gorbals. Of course, there were plenty of bad guys but there were plenty of good guys. Johnny thought of himself as a good guy, but he had no hesitation in becoming a bad guy, and use violence, if need be.

It was part of the Gorbals unwritten rule – some people only understand violence when it comes to putting them right. It was strange days, strange times for the Gorbals and its rapidly declining population. Johnny walked along Crown Street and saw an old woman and a priest coming in his direction. He recognised them straight away. It was Mrs Brenda McGinty and her priest son Tony. He had known them for years.

Tony had been at primary school with him and both had been altar boys. The father at the time encouraged Tony to become a priest, and he did so with great evangelical gusto. He was with a parish on the other side of Glasgow. Johnny secretly admired him and all the good charity work he had done. They had similar backgrounds but both had taken different paths through life. Tony the path of the church. Johnny the path of a gang leader and hardman.

Mrs McGinty was originally from Cork in Ireland, and even at the age of 80, she still had a strong Irish accent with a personality to match. The priest and his mother stopped to talk to Johnny and have a "blether". Mrs McGinty said sardonically, "Would ye look at what they are doing to the Gorbals, pulling some fine tenements down and shutting perfectly good businesses. This isnae redevelopment, its murder. "

Tony nodded his head in agreement, "I agree mother, but then again, all good things come to an end, don't they Johnny?"

Johnny felt a bit shy having to answer such a philosophical question but replied, "They should just do a lot of these old buildings up instead of demolishing them out of existence." The mother and son nodded in agreement saying they were "heading into the toon", the city centre, to do some shopping.

Johnny wished them all the best and watched as they walked off together. They were an incongruous duo, a little Irishwoman, clutching her handbag, and a priest by her side. It was a sight to behold. But all was not what it seemed. Like the Gorbals, the McGinty family had two sides, the good and the bad. Mrs McGinty was proud of Tony the priest, she even hoped and joked he might become the Pope one day, "A Pope from the Gorbals – now that would be an achievement!" she'd say with a hysterical laugh.

But she would never, ever mention her other son, Al McGinty. Al had been one of the biggest gangsters in Britain and had even served his apprenticeship with the Kray twins in London. In fact, rumour had it the Kray twins came to Glasgow to visit their pal to discuss "various business opportunities."

Al was a top-notch professional gangster; protection rackets, moneylending, illegal bookmaking, the whole shebang. But gang warfare between him and other criminals meant that he was languishing in Barlinnie on numerous charges including attempted murder, extortion, police assault and having a firearm without a license. The speculation on the street was he was facing a 20 year stretch at least.

Johnny heard through the grapevine that Al more or less controlled the fellow prisoners in Barlinnie. He had a team of henchmen inside who ran various rackets including supplying snout – illicit tobacco. It was very profitable.

Al had always been an entrepreneur. He was a businessman with a psychotic violent side. Only a few people knew about his Irish mother and his priest brother. He had kept them a hidden secret and vice versa, mother and brother never mentioned him. His criminal activities and gang warfare were best never to be talked about.

Johnny thought that the Gorbals had many secrets and this was a cracker! He walked the streets and saw an old pal, Walter, standing on a corner with a bandage on his head, two black eyes and a bruised nose.

Walter was about 17, a nice wee guy, who often did errands for Johnny's mother. He looked at him and said, "You been fighting again Walter? Looks like you've been in the wars"

Walter looked subdued, "Nah, a guy has been going to the demands for money from me and when ah widnae cough up, he beat me up."

"Beat you up! Who is this bampot?" Johnny asked.

Walter was quick to put him right, "He's just moved into the area fae Blackhill. Dave's his name, he says he's an ex wrestler and if ah didnae pay him protection money every week he was going to break every bone in ma body."

Johnny had known Walter all his life. He came from a poor Polish family, he had no father, and his mother had single-handedly brought him up in a crumbling Thistle Street tenement. Walter was a timid little guy and never got into trouble, never got into a fight. Yet he had been beaten up by a bully, an ex-wrestler to boot. Johnny loved it. It was a case right up his street.

Walter told Johnny where the guy lived, a few blocks away in Florence Street – just above a seedy run-down café called Knot's Restaurant. Johnny headed to his back court in Crown Street, went into the midden, and took a couple of bricks out from the wall. Concealed there was a razor, a hammer and a knife. He had considered these hidden items necessary armour in times of trouble and this was a time of trouble.

He headed towards Florence Street and entered the stinking tenement. There was a terrible stench in the air, the smell of shite, poverty and pish – so unlike his own close in Crown Street where his neighbours took pride in keeping it clean. How could people live like this?

He knocked on the flat's front door, no answer. He knocked again, no answer. He knocked even louder. He then heard footsteps and the door opened.

A big unshaven guy was there and he gave a violent stare. He looked every inch an ex wrestler. He was dressed in a grimy, manky-looking string vest. He shouted, "Stop knocking on ma door so loud. What the fuck dae ye want?"

"Is your name Dave?" Johnny asked.

"Aye, who wants tae know?" said the ex-wrestler.

His fingers were around the edge of the door. Johnny pulled out his hammer and hit him full force on the fingers.

The man screamed, "Ya bastard ye!" and doubled over with pain. Johnny then kicked him in the balls. As the ex-wrestler lay bleeding at the door, Johnny pulled out a razor and shouted, "If you fuck wi' Walter, you're fucking wi' me, ya tube. Ah'll be back to slash your face to ribbons if ah ever hear about you again. By the way, give your string vest a wash. It's so fucking manky you could make a pot of soup out of it!"

Johnny was to quick escape from the stench of the rancid tenement. He placed the hammer the waist of his trousers and emerged into the fresh air of the street.

A woman in curlers and headscarf, pushing a pram, was passing by.

"Lovely day," she said.

"Aye too right," Johnny replied with a smile, "Lovely day, but no' for some!"

He had administered his own form of justice and in his mind it had been successful. But what about the High Court?

Would the scales of justice work in the boys' favour, or against them? He would soon find out.

Chapter 13

MUGGER

The court case re-started with a bit of a whimper. The red nosed QC argued on a point of law regarding identification and the young counsel counter argued back. It all sounded Blah! Blah! Blah! To those in the public gallery.

When normality and clarity returned there was shocking news, although there had been a question over the men's identification, the one thing the police did have was fingerprints. This was crucial to the outcome of the case. The other members of the gang had been wise enough to wear gloves but Sam McGlinchy the driver had not. The police did not find any fingerprints on the discarded gun but McGlinchy's prints were all over the car.

As for the gang, all of the boys had alibis for being in Castlemilk that day and had been "wrongly apprehended." Alex and Peter said they were visiting relatives who verified their stories. Chris's sister testified he was visiting her before being arrested. McCoy's uncle told the court that he and "the boy" were having "a wee bevvy" in his house at the time of the robbery. McGlinchy's auntie said that he had been with her all day and had not left her house during the time of the robbery.

The problem was, the auntie, out of all the witnesses, was the most unconvincing – dull, poorly-educated, with no hint of any real intelligence or education. She had a dreadful, guttural Gorbals accent. The jury was instructed by the judge to consider the evidence and the case was adjourned until the next day.

When Johnny went for the Daily Record that night, he was surprised to read the headline: **PRIEST AND MOTHER IN VICIOUS STREET MUGGING.**

There were pictures of Mrs McGinty and her son. The story was they were walking through George Square when a man appeared and grabbed Mrs McGinty's handbag. She put up a fight and was beaten to the ground. Her priest son tried to intervene but was also beaten up.

The mugger, who police described as a 30-year-old, well known alcoholic and drug addict, was later arrested and after a brief appearance in court was remanded to Barlinnie prison. Johnny speculated what fate would await him there. Al McGinty and his jailbird mob would be preparing to take deadly revenge.

Peter the paperman knew the family fairly well. He laughed, "That imbecile beat up Al's mother and brother. They'll be waiting for him inside. I wonder what his nickname is – Lucky?" The bunnet brigade laughed uproariously, they loved a bit of schadenfreude.

The next day Johnny and his pals waited for ages at the High Court for a verdict to come in but got bored and ventured into Paddy's Market which was just behind the High Court.

Johnny hadn't been there for ages. There were dozens of people selling what looked like piles of rags, calling them clothing. Inside there were stalls selling everything from illicit tobacco, radios, televisions and even fur coats. To Johnny this was the epicentre of poverty. He thought of some of his poorer pals at primary school who had been mocked for wearing Paddy's Market clothes.

There was a dodgy-looking café near the stalls and Johnny ordered ham ribs, mashed potatoes and cabbage. His pal ordered "mince and tatties". Both meals cost next to nothing. Johnny and his pal thought the food was delicious, but they were almost put off when they saw an old man eating a bowl of lentil soup. He had a runny nose and it flowed into the soup as he ate.

Johnny's pal quipped, "Look at that auld dosser, he's got the never-ending bowl of soup!"

When they got back to the court the jury had returned with their verdicts. The foreman, an obese grey-haired man who looked like a retired schoolteacher, read the verdicts from a piece of paper.

Alex – not proven of murder and robbery.

Peter – not proven of murder and robbery.

Chris – not proven of murder and robbery.

McCoy – not proven of murder and robbery.

Johnny thought that was the beauty of the Scottish judicial system. Unlike England, you had two chances of getting off, not guilty and not proven.

The foreman hesitated before giving the last verdict and revealed:

Sam McGlinchy, guilty of murder and robbery.

McGlinchy's face went pure white and his mother fainted in the public gallery. The judge said the other men were free to go. McGlinchy stood in the dock as the judge told him, "You have been found guilty of these heinous crimes. I sentence you to life imprisonment."

All this trouble for £100 which he never got in the first place. The fingerprints had gone against him but it had been a stupid mistake not to have worn gloves. Johnny just thanked his lucky stars that he had not got involved. McGlinchy was only the driver, a cameo actor on the main stage but had taken all the blame.

He now had at least 15 years to ponder over his mistake. Act in haste, repent at leisure. Sam McGlinchy had plenty of time to repent.

Chapter 14

CLUB

The celebration do was at the Railway Club just off Cumberland Street. The club, an elongated single-story building, looked shabby and miserable from outside but was warm and inviting inside. It had a small bar at the back and a large function room at the front which could accommodate more than 200 people.

It was often used for weddings and funerals. More than 100 people turned up to celebrate the boys being freed. Alex was smartly dressed and had scrubbed up well. He was a good-looking kid aged 22, with handsome Mediterranean looks. Peter was 23, a small-town sort of guy who thought he was a big town sort of guy. He was not dressed as well as Alex but was smart enough for the occasion. Chris, 22, wore a bright white shirt and jeans. He had never been a man for smart gear. A donkey jacket or a parka was his usual attire.

There was no sign of McCoy, 25, not that it mattered. He was a newcomer, a rank outsider, who had never really been a real Gorbals guy. He was just a ship that had passed in the night.

The place was swarming with young women, a disco and buffet had been laid on. A few local "businessmen" had clubbed together to honour the boys, it was a smart thing to do. The boys had enhanced their reputation by being on a murder and robbery charge and this had accentuated their kudos in the Gorbals limelight.

Maybe they were on their way to becoming big time gangsters and the businessmen who sponsored the night, including a well-known publican, thought that it was better to have the boys inside the tent pissing out, than outside the tent pissing in.

Beautiful mini-skirted young women gyrated on the dancefloor, joined by grannies aunties and uncles. Most of the young guys looked on from the bar while getting drunk. It was a rare do.

The acquitted guys sat at a couple of tables near the dancefloor. Well-wishers came over with trays of drinks to pay homage to these men who they now considered to be local superstars. Sure, their names and photos had been all over the papers. They had even appeared on TV as they entered and left the High Court every day under heavy guard. They had also been mentioned on radio, albeit with some "expert" commenting on the high rise of crime rates in the Gorbals.

Alex, Peter and Chris were lapping up their celebrity status. Their tables were jam packed with drinks, mostly pints of lager, vodka and cokes, with a few whiskies thrown in.

Alex shouted above the disco din, "Ah love this lark, people are buying aw this bevvy and it's no' costing us a penny. Ma middle name is crime and crime don't pay!" Peter took a slug of his lager and agreed saying, "We beat those polis bastards!"

Chris toasted their victory, "Aye if it wisnae for that young lawyer we'd all be doing a 15 year stretch at this very moment." Suddenly they were joined by a dishevelled grey haired woman. It was Sam McGlinchey's mother. "It's awright for you boys, as free as a bird. But what aboot ma boy? Life imprisonment and he was only the driver."

She began to sob uncontrollably. Peter tapped her on the back and said, "Cheer up missus, he'll get off on appeal, you mark my words. Let's have a wee toast for our pal Sam. Cheers!"

Alex and Chris raised their glasses, "Cheers tae Sam!" The party and the drinks continued to flow. The disco was at full throttle and the beautiful young birds were coming over to the table asking the boys to dance with them. T-Rex came on with Ride a White Swan when Johnny walked in looking as handsome and gallus as expected.

The young birds eyed him up with lustful stares because to them he looked beautiful. He had arrived at the party wearing the shark skin suit his father had bought him in Hong Kong. Also, he had been to Felix the barbers to have a "Tony Curtis" haircut. There was no doubt about it, Johnny was a handsome bastard. Other guys glared at him with envy, many were jealous. If only they had his looks, charisma and fighting skills.

A drunk young woman, called Lorraine, 22, broke from the pack, dancing around their handbags, she said, "Dae ye fancy a dance Johnny?" He looked at her and thought she was quite alluring but decided to turn the invitation down, "Nah a bit early yet doll. Maybe later when ah get tanked up a bit."

Lorraine sighed and gave a beautiful smile saying, "Awright maybe later, do ye promise me?" Johnny smiled back, "It's a promise, ah'll definitely dance wi' you. Just wait a wee while."

She wandered over to her pals on the dancefloor and gave them the thumbs up sign. Johnny joined his pals at the table. He grinned and shook hands with them, "Good to see all you innocent men enjoying yourselves!" One of the boys went to the bar and got Johnny not only one pint of lager but two. Someone else handed him a double whisky. Alex said, "If it wisnae for you sorting out the two grasses, we would all be in the nick."

Chris agreed raising his pint, "You were brilliant Johnny, you did us a real good turn."

Johnny laughed, "Too right, a brick through a window and a mad wino setting aboot a wee woman can work wonders!"

He scanned the bar and dancefloor, "Nae McCoy then?"

Alex shook his head, "Nah, we didnae want him here anyway, he's a fucking oddball."

Chris agreed, "He was the eejit who brought the gun along. We didnae know it was loaded, we thought it was blanks."

Peter gave a half-bevvied, concerned look. "That wanker could have got us aw life in jail like poor Sam." Johnny was relieved that McCoy was not there as he had a razor in his pocket and planned to slash him. But McCoy's absence meant he had one less problem to deal with. He would deal with McCoy another day, when the time was right.

A patter merchant called Harry joined them, he was always good for a laugh, "You guys were lucky tae get cleared 'cause you're all guilty as fuck! You remind me of the big Irishman who was in the High Court. The judge said, 'We find you not guilty of assault and robbery.' And the Irish fella says, 'Does that mean I can keep the money then?'" The joke cheered the boys up, it certainly was not a million miles away from what they had experienced.

The young ladies, getting drunker by the minute, gave Johnny more lustful glares and smiles. Johnny gave them a wave and they giggled. The drunken Lorraine once again staggered over to Johnny and said, "Come on then big boy, how's about a wee shoogle?" He told her it was still too early and she staggered back to her envious pals on the dancefloor.

The quick consumption of the beer and whisky made Johnny feel funny. One minute he was happy and contented the next paranoid thoughts came over him.

They then mutated into murderous dark thoughts. The thoughts of a psychopath. "If only that bastard McCoy was here, I'd show him. Show him no' tae mess wi' me." He should have avoided mixing lager with whisky it usually gave him too many schizophrenic ideas.

Once, when he had been on the lager and whisky, he awoke in Craigie Street police station, covered in blood. It had been after a Celtic and Rangers game. Johnny, wearing a Celtic scarf, was in the Tollbooth Bar at Glasgow Cross when a guy wearing a Rangers jersey bumped into him on the way to the gents and called him "A dirty Fenian bastard." Johnny retaliated by calling him a "dob" – short for a "dirty orange bastard" - and things escalated from there.

Johnny, as leader of the Cumbie gang, summoned his troops to go on a full-frontal assault on the "dob" and his team of protestant pals. The result was tables and glasses went flying everywhere. During the melee several Rangers supporters – thought to be members of the Derry gang from Bridgeton – gave Johnny a kicking. The result? Several people ended up in hospital and several in the police cells. Johnny was one of the latter.

When he woke up in the cell, he could barely recollect what had happened. But the blood on his face and clothes gave him a reminder that he had not been for a stroll in the park. He was fined £25 for breach of the peace. He later reflected that mixing his drinks had landed him into trouble.

Also, the experience made him think deeply about this Celtic versus Rangers business. Both clubs were giant money-making machines who depended on bigotry and sectarianism to fill their cash registers. King Billy versus the Pope. When he thought about it, it all seemed to be a waste of time, energy and money. From then on, he vowed to cut back on going to Celtic games, especially when they faced Rangers – it just wasn't worth the bother, or the spilt blood.

Another time when he had mixed his drinks, this time strong wine – "biddy" – with whisky, he was well tanked up when he led some of his gang over the Clyde Suspension Bridge, to Clyde Street. As they made their way across, a drunk guy had made a cheeky remark to them. Johnny in his psychotic wine-and-whisky condition head butted the fellow – gave him a "Glasgow kiss" –before he and his gang pals threw him into the Clyde. The man splashed into the freezing cold water and floated off, his head bobbing up and down.

Johnny awoke with a hangover the next day and wondered if he had killed the man. He checked the papers, television and radio news, but nothing, the drunk had either been saved or drowned. So maybe there was still a body out there, lying at the bottom of the Clyde, but then again maybe not. Johnny consoled himself that the man had probably been saved by one of Glasgow's Humane Society who rowed along the Clyde in a little boat rescuing people who had fallen in.

The paranoid thoughts began to torment him then the rock song by Free, All Right Now came on. On hearing it he felt slightly better. He thought about the guy in the Clyde and imagined the song being played at the disco was a good omen – the fellow was all right now.

Still feeling a bit strange, and mildly sick, he headed to the gents for a pish. Then it came to him, perhaps someone had spiked his drinks. Some jealous, evil bastard who wanted to do him in. He went into a cubicle in the lavatory and sat on the pan. He thought that if someone was spiking his drinks the best things to do was avoid any alcohol being bought for him. From now on, he would drink from only bottles and keep them with him at all times.

When he was in the cubicle, he heard two men come in, it was Alex and Chris. They were unaware that he was there.

"Great to see Johnny turn up," Alex said.

"Aye," said Chris urinating heavily, "Good job we didnae mention that bastard McCoy to him and how he told the polis that Johnny was involved in the robbery. Johnny would slash him if he knew."

So that's why he had been arrested, the low life bastard McCoy had told the police that he was behind it all! As they left Alex said, "Best keep quiet at the moment, we've been in enough trouble. The last things we need is Johnny doin' in that no-good grass."

Johnny felt better after hearing the revelation and strangely the psychotic thoughts weakened. He sat in the cubicle for a few minutes longer, it was nice and peaceful there, an oasis away from the madness. Then he thought of Mrs McGinty and her priest son. When the mugger got to Barlinnie there was no doubt Al would have him bumped off.

But Al had to be careful. He could not implicate himself and his gang as they were in the shit already. They could do without a murder charge while incarcerated. Police and forensics would be all over the place. Besides the jail was full of grasses who would spill the beans to have their sentences reduced. Johnny analysed what Al would do. Members of the gang would go into the mugger's cell and give him an ultimatum – "Hang yourself or get stabbed to death. Hanging yourself is easier and much less painful." Johnny knew that Al had used this modus operandi several times before, in jail and out, and it had always worked, especially with weak people.

He left the toilets, bought a bottle of Newcastle Brown Ale from the bar and stood at the edge of the dancefloor. Lorraine seemed to have sobered up, probably because she had stuffed herself with sausage rolls and cheese sandwiches from the free buffet.

She approached him again and they began to dance to Chubby Checker's The Twist. They were fine dancers and people looked on in admiration. Lorraine was no doubt a sexy woman, with big breasts, clear, pale complexion and long dark hair. To accentuate her beauty, she was wearing a mini skirt and black stockings.

But she was not a woman of great sophistication. Lorraine cuddled into Johnny during a slow dance and whispered into his ear, "Johnny, ah want you to shag me." He could feel himself getting harder. He thought momentarily about Cathy, but a standing cock has no conscience.

They both left the club and went outside into the cold night air. Johnny led her behind the building where it was dark and poorly lit and began to shag her standing up. He was used to stand up sex because in the Gorbals that was the favoured position. Young couples with no place to go, regularly shagged at night standing up in the dark and dingy backcourts and closes.

"Oh, Johnny give it tae me. Give it tae me hard," Lorraine was moaning. Johnny felt himself come and a few minutes later they were back in the club. Lorraine took again to dancing and Johnny joined his pals. It was as if nothing had happened. As everyone got drunker and drunker, becoming louder and incoherent, Johnny decided to make a quiet exit, like a thief in the night. He got back to Crown Street and Peter was there as usual selling the Daily Record. On The front page the headline screamed out: **PRISONER ON PRIEST MUGGING CHARGE HANGS HIMSELF.**

Chapter 15

WOMAN

Johnny awoke in an exalted mood although he did feel slightly exhausted after yesterday's events. The boys being released, the party and of course the sexual encounter with the lovely Lorraine. The shagging behind the club had been great and it certainly put a spring back in his step. Previously, for several months, he felt as if he had lost his mojo, lost a sense of who he really was. He had even lost his sense of humour, unforgiveable for a Gorbals guy like him.

He thought back to Lorraine, her sensuous lips, her perfectly formed breasts, and unusual for a local woman, her French kissing, deep that it was. He smiled and got a hard on when he thought of it. A few years back he had attempted to French kiss a blonde after meeting her at the Portland dance hall. He led her into a dark lane nearby and had expected full sex. All was proceeding well until he stuck his tongue down her throat. She pushed him away shouting, "Get your tongue out ma throat, ya dirty bastard ye!"

She, like Lorraine, was obviously not a woman of great sophistication and had the most guttural Glaswegian accent he had ever heard. He was only 16 at the time and when they got back on the street, he asked to see her again. She took a draw of her fag and looked at Johnny in a menacing way. "Aye maybe, but you've got tae keep your tongue tae yourself. Ah like being kissed like a lady, no' a fucking whore in a line up."

He thought her accent was so rough and loud, like a foghorn, she would never get a job as a BBC newscaster.

But at the end of the day, she was a decent girl, who worked long and hard in the Templeton's carpet factory. She had been right, she was not another "line up merchant" who were known to have sex with up to a dozen boys in the dark back lanes.

Johnny remembered when he was number five in such a line up with a rather plump nymphomaniac from Nicholson Street. Two policemen raided the scene. The other boys ran off leaving several discarded condoms behind. On seeing this one of the policemen said to the girl, "Are you a saleswoman for Durex?"

He had been with quite a few line up merchants –they had given him a degree of sexual experience when he started at the age of 12.

He was full of himself as he got out of bed and he could hear his mother singing as she scrubbed the tenement stairs outside. As she did so she was singing, the old Scottish ballad, "Yir no awa' tae bide awa." As she did so he thought she had one of the most beautiful voices he had ever heard. Indeed, she had been talented at school and often sang at school concerts and the parties her parents would have. But like many Gorbals women, her dreams were only dreams. She had neglected her talent to become a tenement housewife while having Johnny and his brother.

Johnny thought of all the wasted talented women who were out there. Lovely looking women, who in another environment would have become models or actresses, musicians or singing stars. But they all had one thing in common, they had thrown their looks and talents away for a mediocre life in the rat-infested, decaying tenements.

It was then he thought of Cathy, a fine specimen of womanhood, a gentle creature full of love and passion who was clearly too good for this filthy, poverty ridden, environment. Maybe she was too good for him!

As he washed himself in the kitchen sink, he looked down to Crown Street and by coincidence he saw Cathy briefly before she turned the corner into Rutherglen Road. She looked stunning. Johnny's mood changed dramatically. It was a feeling of guilt. How could he have shagged that woman behind the club? The thought had at first pleased him but now it became a torture. What if one her pals had spotted him with Lorraine? What if they had told Cathy? She would not speak to him again, not even one single word. He began to shake; it was a fate worse than death.

His exasperated thoughts were interrupted by his mother who had finished scrubbing the stairs, "You are a handsome boy Johnny, time ye settled down and stopped all this gang nonsense."

Johnny put on a conciliatory tone, "Ah know ma, maybe one of these days."

"Ah'll believe it when ah see it," she said.

They both laughed, Johnny did look handsome. He had a new Arthur Black shirt on, black with white pearl buttons, two pockets at the front with one having the initials J.M. embroidered in white thread. He had also splashed out from his savings and bought a new pair of black coloured Levi Sta-Prest trousers and a pair of shiny Doc Marten boots.

His body was also in great condition with not an inch of fat. It was a different story 18 months ago. He had let himself go, too many pints, too many fish suppers. He then had a ghastly thought that one day he would end up looking like a sumo wrestler. Johnny called it his "fat Elvis" phase and vowed from then on to go on a diet and work out every day. The diet consisted of having one banana sandwich a day, cutting out the pints of lager, and "running like fuck" through the Glasgow Green. He also swam every day in the pool at the Gorbals bath house. When he was fat, he joked that the birds did not look at him anymore and "no' even the poofs" fancied him.

But now he was back in tip top condition. He had seen Elvis in the 1968 comeback special and he looked starved to perfection. He just thought – "What's good enough for Elvis, is good enough for me." Indeed, Johnny did at times look like a young Elvis and when someone would remark this he'd reply, "If only ah had his voice, ahuw!"

He walked along Crown Street with no particular place to go. Though at one point he thought he must see Cathy soon for peace of mind and also to paper over any cracks there might be. He went into Lombardi's ice cream parlour and ordered a cup of tea. He felt quite content there reading a copy of the Daily Record which had a brilliant story about Celtic and Rangers. Suddenly a man joined him at the table. It was Larry McGowan, a well know conman and thief. Larry, in his mid-40s, was not a fighter or hardman like Johnny, but people respected him because he always had a dodgy scheme on the go. "Awright Johnny boy?" Larry said, "What's the Hampden roar?" (The score.)

Johnny took a sip of his Typhoo tea, "Nothing really Larry, same auld shite, different day!" Larry bent over the table and whispered, "Got a wee thing on the go that might interest you."

"Interest me?" Johnny said, "If it involves spending money, count me out, ah've spent it all. No' got a pot tae pish in." It was a bluff and Larry knew it.

Larry laughed and whispered again, "Ah've got a cousin who works in a bank up the town and she says you're loaded."

Larry put a bag on the table and pulled out a bundle of forged one pound notes. Johnny looked around the cafe to make sure no-one was watching. He picked up some notes and studied them carefully, "They look like the real deal."

Larry nodded his head in agreement, "Ah've got plenty of the fuckers, you can have as many as you want."

Johnny sensed there was a transaction to be made. "How much?"

"Forty pence for every pound note, minimum purchase 500 notes," Larry explained.

It was an interesting proposition and Larry gave some advice, "The only thing is be careful where you spend them. Only buy small things, get the change and disappear. Ah've done 30 already today in places like Hillhead and Partick where they don't know me."

Johnny was impressed, "Forty pence for a pound sounds like a win-win situation to me. Ok, get me 500 tomorrow, same place, same time."

The next day they met again in the cafe and Johnny was handed a brown paper bag with 500 notes inside. Larry gave him one piece of advice, "Make sure you and your boys only have one pound note on you at any time. And if you do get done just say you got it in change from another shop."

The plan was unfolding. Johnny would get some of his pals to go into shops all over Glasgow and cash them. He'd then meet them in a local pub or café to replenish the scam. He would not change the counterfeit notes himself, he'd get his foot soldiers to do it on commission. For the next few days the plan worked beautifully. The big department stores were easy meat when it came to small purchases in a hurry.

Johnny put his profits into his bank account every day. Alex and Peter had been in on the scam and the money was flowing in. When it came to the weekend, they were all in the mood for a pub crawl to spend some of their ill-gotten gains and maybe have a dance later. They did the Mally, the Sou' Wester and The Laurieston pubs before heading to the notorious Portland dancehall. It was reputedly the roughest dance hall in Glasgow, full of drunken Irishmen and equally drunken gangsters.

Johnny scanned the dancefloor. It was packed with intoxicated eejits and a few female line up merchants. If Hell had a dancefloor, this would be it. An Irish band called Big Tom and The Mainliners were on stage singing a Country and Western song – 'Do the Hucklebuck'. Johnny was aware that the Irish were no mugs, they did not fear the gangsters. When he was 16, Johnny, well bevvied up on cheap wine, had made a cheeky remark to a big burly Irish navvy who promptly knocked him out for half an hour.

The women and men on the dancefloor looked rough, almost uncivilised. Johnny saw one man urinate near the stage and the bouncers bundled him out of the building. At the end of the night everyone had to stand up and sing the Irish National anthem – if any man did not do so he would get beaten up by the bouncers for disrespecting the Irish nation.

The place was run by Big John, who was known by his nickname "The Irishman." He was a tall lanky-looking fellow with black hair. He looked innocent enough. There was nothing in his demeanour to suggest he was in fact the leader of the IRA in Glasgow. Johnny had been told the Portland was being used to launder dirty IRA money, gun running and illicit booze trading. When Johnny looked around the bar downstairs at all the older Gorbals gangsters, they looked like they were afraid of nothing. But there was one thing they were afraid of – the IRA. Those fuckers would shoot you or blow you up without any hesitation.

Johnny found himself a quiet corner in the downstairs bar and spectated as lots of drunken men and women staggered about. Alex and Peter had gone upstairs to see if there was any talent on the dancefloor. He was sipping his pint of Tennent's lager when suddenly The Irishman, joined him, "Young Johnny, don't see you much these days. You been inside?"

Johnny put on his most confident voice, "Nah been keeping a low profile John. Steering away fae trouble and aw that."

The Irishman grinned, "Ah've been hearing good reports about you. You're a game Fenian boy. Maybe you'd like to join the cause. If ye fancy it, give me a call." He handed Johnny a piece of paper with his phone number on it.

Johnny suddenly felt elated, he felt like a schoolboy, who was good at football, being signed for Celtic. He had been asked to join the IRA- what an honour! "Up the IRA!" a drunk navvy shouted at the bar.

If he wanted, he could become one of them soon, but was that a future he wanted to contemplate? A short time later he left the dancehall, with Alex and Peter, as

Big Tom and The Mainliners were on stage singing Del Shannon's "Kelly and I" They walked away from the club along South Portland Street. Alex said, "Fuck's sake, look who's coming!" It was Joe McCoy and two other guys, they all looked half cut. Johnny walked towards McCoy and shouted, "Hey you, ya tube, you got Sam McGlinchy life in jail for that fucking gun."

McCoy showed no sign of fear, "What the fuck has that got tae dae wi' you, ya bampot?" He reached into his pocket and Johnny saw a razor coming out. But the bevvy had slowed McCoy down. Johnny launched himself at McCoy and both began punching and kicking like wild animals. They fell into a manky puddle in the street. "Fucking wanker," Johnny was shouting.

The guys who had been with McCoy made no attempt to intervene, neither did Alex or Peter. It was a Gorbals rule, a square go was always man to man. Johnny took a couple of blows to the face with McCoy shouting, "Come on ya bastard, you're no' a hardman, you're a fake." They rolled on the ground. There was a pile of building rubble a few inches away. Johnny leapt to his feet, grabbed a half brick, and hit McCoy over the head with it several times. Blood began to gush from McCoy's face and head. He was a bloody, defeated man. Johnny kicked him full force in the balls. McCoy fell silent, he was either dead or unconscious. Then they could hear the noise of police sirens. They all ran off just before the police arrived, leaving McCoy in a bloodied pulp.

A few blocks away Alex said, "You sorted him out proper Johnny, he looked like something you see in a butcher's shop window."

Peter laughed, "Ah've seen slaughtered pigs in a better condition than McCoy."

Johnny got back to his house, his mother and brother had gone to bed, oblivious to his actions. He looked into the mirror and his face and hands were covered in blood. What really annoyed him though was the fact that there was blood all over his Arthur Black shirt, Levi trousers and shoes.

He had a quick scrub in the sink until there was no sign of blood at all on his face and hands. He gave his boots a good scrub until the blood disappeared. Johnny changed into fresh clothes and put his bloodied ones into a bundle.

He walked across the Albert Bridge and threw them into the Clyde. He had to, if he had murdered McCoy the bloodied clothes could have convicted him. Johnny crept back into bed and thought rather oddly, "I'll bet Elvis disnae have to put up wi' shite like this."

He fell soundly asleep. At times living in the Gorbals could be a nightmare, any sweet dreams he got now would be a godsend.

Chapter 16

GANGSTERS

"John McGrath, you are charged with the murder of Joe McCoy. How do you plead?"

Johnny looked up to the public gallery and saw his mother there, crying into a big white hanky. His father was also there, dressed in his shiny suit from Hong Kong. On the left of them was McCoy's father who made a cut-throat sign to Johnny.

He could see his life slipping away. A life that could have been ten times better if only he had been studious like his wee brother and played the game of respectability instead of the low life game of being a gangster.

He just thought that this is how many of the so called Gorbals hardmen ended up – a drunken fight, a murder, and then life imprisonment. Prison was meant to rehabilitate people like him, but, in reality, they went to jail acting even harder. Hard talk, hard walk, hard look on the face, hard language full of threatening expletives. In jail of course, there would be square goes, the gang rivalry, the utter nonsense and futility of a life in a squalid existence. Being a hardman was 99 per cent to do with image. He thought of the phrase, if it walks like a duck, talks like a duck and looks like a duck, then it's a duck. Johnny certainly walked, talked and looked like a young gangster.

As he looked from the dock, he could see policemen grinning and whispering to each other. They gave sly grins that policemen give when they have snared their prey. He thought of the police and the job they had to do. Basically, it was sweeping up the rubbish of society and brushing it under the carpet, the carpet being a metaphor for jail. The police were a shower of bastards but as his father often said, "They might be a shower of bastards but you need them."

Johnny was asked again by the prosecutor, "Mr McGrath, I will ask you for a second time. How do you plead?" Johnny shouted, "Fucking insanity, your honour. Complete and utter insanity." The people in the public gallery began to laugh and then, all of a sudden, their faces began to change into the faces of rats. Big fucking dirty rats.

He awoke with beads of sweat on his fine head. It had all been a nasty dream or rather a nightmare, but it was a nightmare that could come true. He had a quick wash in the sink and headed down to Murray's newsagents to buy not one, but all the Scottish papers. He went through every paper but nothing – not a word about any murder in the Gorbals. Maybe it had missed the deadlines so he waited for the early editions of the Glasgow Evening Times and the Citizen to come out. But once again, nothing.

It was the same story with radio and TV, if he had murdered McCoy it would have been all over the shop. He was thankful in many ways. No news is good news.

It was late afternoon when he walked into the Wheatsheaf pub. He knew a gang of older criminals who met there every Saturday for a bit of craic. He needed to have a laugh and was never disappointed at the outlandish tales these old gangsters had.

In the corner having a bevvy was Freddy the bank robber, Bobby Mac, a retired razor king and Jimmy, an ex-safeblower. Johnny walked over to join their company at the table, He was greeted with friendly handshakes and smiles. These older men, in their late 60s and 70s, recognised that he was one of their kind. On entering the company, Johnny's first line was extremely gallus, "Have ah no' seen you three guys before? On wanted posters?"

The old gangsters laughed in mock agreement but now it was time for the storytelling to begin. Johnny listened as if he was a pupil at school.

Freddy took a sip of his beer and said, "There is no better job than robbing a bank, as long as ye don't get caught. Ye can do anything ye want, but never make the cardinal sin of getting caught. Only mugs get caught. Ah did thirteen robberies and loved every minute of it. Me and the boys would walk into the bank with our masks on. Mine was Mickey Mouse, and I'd shout, 'Get down on the fucking floor or I'll blow your head off!' I would wave the gun as if I was a fucking madman. The tellers would fill our bags full of notes. Always used ones so they couldnae be traced.

It was the biggest rush of adrenalin you could ever have, better than drink, drugs or sex. Ah got addicted to it."

Johnny asked, "Did ye ever shoot anybody?"

Freddy laughed and shook his head, "Nah, the gun wisnae a real one, it was a starting pistol. But when you fired it, it sounded so real, people were shiteing their trousers."

Johnny did not have the impertinence to ask Freddy where all the money had gone but he did know the old fellow had a nice detached bungalow in leafy Newton Mearns. Some of his pals had nicknamed it "Bank Bungalow." Freddy continued, "By the time of the 13th robbery ah was getting too confident. Ah was waving ma pistol in the Clydesdale Bank when my Micky Mouse mask fell off. One of the customers, who was lying on the floor, clocked ma dial. He knew my face. He had been at the same school years before. So that was it, ah ended up getting nicked "But the other masked guys, Donald Duck, Pluto and Minnie Mouse all got off. Ten years I got just because the elastic band on the mask slipped. After serving ma time I never did a bank job again, but at least I got ma bungalow out of it."

Bobby Mac was up next, "I loved razors when I was growing up and had my first one when I was 12. Stole it from the barbers. I slashed ma first guy when ah was 14 and after that it became a habit. I became the leader of the Bee Hive gang and we usually went to war wi' the San Toi fae the Gallowgate and the Billy Boys fae Bridgeton."

He pointed to a large scar down the left of his cheek. "One of the Billy Boys gave me that. To me it disnae look that ugly and it's a reminder of the old days when real men were real men. Sure, I ended up wi' a Mars Bar (scar) for life but I wear it like a badge. It shows people you are a fighter." They all nodded their heads in agreement.

Jimmy, who was in his 70s, was next up, "For years I did a lot of jobs blowing up safes all over Scotland. Wee jobs that just about covered your wages, £100 here, £200 there, and maybe a grand now and again. I had a team of three, somebody to help me enter the building and another guy who was a look out. When the going was good, it was good, but when the going was bad it was fucking terrible. I'd often spend hours trying to open a safe and then find out it was empty!

"We did one job in Helensburgh, a shoe shop, and after two hours I eventually cracked the safe. You know what was inside? A mouldy cheese sandwich! I was so fucking hungry ah ate it!

"We got a tip off about a jewellers in Oban. We went in the middle of the night and it was the easiest job we ever did. The Highland people are no' like the Glasgow businessmen. They left themselves wide open. I think it must be aw the fresh air and beautiful scenery that makes them a bit soft. No' like stinking Glasgow!

"Anyway, we made off wi' more than £2,000 in jewellery and watches, made a right few bob. But I made one mistake. I gave this lovely brooch to my girlfriend at the time. She was heading for the dancing one night and a copper spotted her wearing it. All the polis in Glasgow had been alerted wi' photos of the stolen gear.

"To cut a long story short, she sang like a canary and told them it was me who gave it to her and did not know it had been stolen. The polis arrested me that night. But I told them I had bought it fae a gypsy called Michael in a pub. They couldnae pin the robbery on me but I still got three years for handling stolen goods. Three years for a fucking brooch!"

Jimmy went for a pish and came back a few minutes later to continue his story, "I didnae waste my time in jail. I had a wee job in the prison library and started to read books on safe manufacturers, like Chubb etc. I studied them carefully, so became a bit of an expert in safes and how they worked. I did a few safes when ah came out but never as big as the Oban job. I also learned never to give some daft woman nicked jewellery who would parade about Glasgow wi' it, showing it off.

"To add insult to injury, she ran aff wi' another bloke, a taxi driver fae the Cowcaddens. That bird definitely had nae class, the brooch was too good for her. She had a lovely face but was thick as a bucket of shite."

Johnny felt compelled to tell them about his square go with McCoy and ask them for advice how to handle the matter. But he resisted. Better to keep it quiet, anyway he had got the advice he needed –do anything you want but don't get caught.

The jails were full of people who had made the mistake of getting caught. Johnny had no intention of getting caught but had a paranoid inclination that his nightmare could come true.

Chapter 17

POSHLAND

It was a beautiful Saturday morning. Johnny decided to get out of his slum and catch the underground to the West End. As he sat there trundling along, he was amazed that these old Victorian carriages still existed. Glasgow had a primitive but effective Underground that went from Bridge Street in the Gorbals to place like St Enoch's Square, Partick and leafy, prosperous Hillhead in the West End.

When he walked along Byres Road in the West End, he realised the people there lived completely different lives from the inhabitants of the Gorbals. This was poshland with articulate middle-class accents who were mostly well educated, in many ways the elite of Scotland. It was teeming with students from Glasgow University who would become (among other things) teachers, lawyers, accountants, dentists and media performers.

He looked at the beautiful young ladies as they paraded down Byres Road, some were hippy types with flowers in their hair and they glowed with respectability. If only he could join this elite! This was a band of people who had aspirations to be influential in politics, education, law and the media. This was a different universe to the Gorbals with its drunks and thieves and people who spoke with accents so broad that even people from other parts of Glasgow struggled to understand.

The inhabitants of the West End did not live in rat-infested slums, they resided in fine upstanding Victorian tenements which were kept meticulously clean. But they were at times derided by fellow Glaswegians, mostly of the lower order, as "aw fur coat and nae knickers."

He was looking good that day, the spring weather had given him a glow that exuded sex appeal. He noticed as he walked along Byres Road that many of the bourgeois girls gave him a second glance. And even a third glance but were slightly put off by his proletarian gang boy attire. This suggested that he was a common man from a common place full of common people. Johnny's accent was also a problem, he spoke in tough guttural tones and on hearing this the respectable posh girls would never go near him. Not for a relationship anyway. But some girls liked "a bit of rough" and there was no doubt that he fell into this category.

He had shagged posh birds before. They had taken him to their bedsits, adorned with Picasso prints, played him classical music and poured him large glasses of red wine. But after the shag, Johnny was quickly dumped. As a Gorbals gangster, he was certainly not in the same class division as a teacher or lawyer. Johnny knew full well about this class division but as he said, he "did not give a fuck."

He walked into an antiques shop down a lane just of Byres Road. A little Jewish looking man stood behind the counter. The place was adorned with paintings, jewellery, crockery, antique swords and even a few deer heads.

"Hello sir, can I help you with anything?" the man asked. Johnny modified his accent to give it a more middle class tone. "Yeah, I like the look of that antique sword in the glass case." The little man toddled off to get it, Johnny noticed that he had small legs like Dopey from Snow White and the Seven Dwarves.

Dopey brought back the sword, placed it on the counter and said in an upper class accent, "This, sir, is a fine piece of Victorian craftsmanship. It is a beautiful souvenir and would hang proudly on any living room wall."

Johnny chuckled and thought about all the damp living rooms in the Gorbals. "Yeah, looks like a nice piece. How much is it by the way?" He had made a significant mistake by adding "by the way" to the end of the sentence. It was part of the Gorbals low life lingo, "Where are ye gaun? By the way." Or, "Ah'm aff tae the dancin', by the way."

The little man gave a truly dopey grin, fingered the handle of the sword, and said, "To you, sir, ten pounds cash." Johnny picked up the sword and waved it about. Dopey began to look nervous. It was a fine sword, the sort he had seen in the movies when medieval barons fought each other.

Johnny then discarded the pretence of having a posh accent. "Are ye trying tae take me for a mug, wee man?"

Dopey looked frightened, "Oh no sir, I would never do that. What do you suggest then?"

Johnny was still holding the sword in his hand, "Ah'll gi' ye a sky diver, wee man."

Dopey was confused, "A sky diver?"

"A fiver, five pounds." Johnny explained.

Dopey hesitated for a minute but looked at Johnny with the sword in his hand, "Well sir, I think on reflection five pounds will do nicely."

He told Dopey to wrap the sword up in paper and he did so with trembling hands. Johnny reached into his trouser pocket and pulled out a wad of pound notes. He began to count them on the counter, "Wan, two, three, four, five – there ye go, wee man."

Johnny left the shop with a confident stride. Dopey said, "Thank you sir. Hope to do business with you again." Johnny nodded and chuckled inside, he had given him five forged notes. "Five duds for the wee man. Dopey bastard!"

He made his way to the subway as fast as he could. After a short journey he found himself in Partick, a working-class area of Glasgow full of tenements, not half as bad as the Gorbals. He felt at home there, sure it is where his father Jo Jo had been born and brought up. The Partick people were not really known as fighters but more as patter merchants who were always good for a tale or two,

He walked into the Dolphin Bar, known locally as a "Celtic shop" and sitting in the corner was Wullie McKay. They had both been at primary school together. From an early age, Wullie had shown a knack for writing. His essays were so good they were often read out to the whole class. One essay was of such "outstanding merit" that Wullie was sent to the headmaster's study to read it to him.

While Johnny went on to St Bonaventures – a tough junior secondary for dunces and hardmen – Wullie proceeded to Holyrood for the brainy boys and girls. He was now studying English literature at Glasgow University.

Wullie, a red-haired bespectacled fellow with a friendly demeanour, was reading Crime and Punishment by Dostoevsky. Johnny sat down at his table with his lager, "That looks like a good book, is it Wullie?" he asked.

Wullie put the book down, "Aye, it's about a guy who murders a pawnbroker and then is pursued by the polis."

Johnny laughed, "Sounds like the perfect book tae read in jail. So, what are ye up tae Wullie?" He said it in a tone of respect that was the complete opposite of the tone he had used on Dopey.

"Ach still at college, studying and aw that" Wullie said.

"Are ye gonnae be a teacher?" Johnny asked.

Wullie shook his head, "Nah, ah really want tae be a scriptwriter, a comedy scriptwriter, writing jokes. Ah seem tae have a talent for it, there are loads of comedians looking for a good comedy writer."

Johnny thought of the Scottish comedians he was aware of – Lex McClean, Glen Daly, Stanley Baxter, Francie and Josie, sure there was a big market out there for new material.

"Ok then, Wullie, give me a joke," Johnny said.

"Clean or filthy?"

"Up to you pal."

Wullie took a sip of his Guinness and said, "Ok then, here's a wee filthy one - what's the definition of an egg head?"

"Don't know."

"Mrs Dumpty giving her man a blow job."

"Go on then give us another, Wullie!"

Wullie nodded and replied, "What's the difference between the Gorbals Mafia and the Italian Mafia?"

"Dunno."

"The Italian Mafia make you an offer you can't refuse and the Gorbals Mafia make you an offer you can't understand."

Johnny chuckled, "And ye get paid for that. What do these comedians pay for a joke?"

"It all depends – anything from a fiver tae twenty quid for a good one."

"Ah'm in the wrong game Wullie. Have ye got a Gorbals joke for me?"

Wullie smiled, "Two guys, Joe and Billy, who are skint and out of work, are walking through Gorbals Cross and see a paypacket on the pavement. They pick it up and inside there is a twenty pound note. Joe says tae Billy, 'Let's hand it intae the polis station and maybe we'll get reward.

"But on their way there, Billy says, 'Let's have a wee bevvy oot of the money and then we'll hand it in.' They go intae a pub and one round leads tae another. By closing time, they had spent all the money.

"They go outside the pub and Joe says to his pal, 'If that lazy bastard had done some overtime, we'd have had enough tae buy a carry out.'"

Johnny left the pub and felt elated. Good patter always cheered him up.

When he sat on the Underground train on his way back to the Gorbals, he clutched the sword wrapped in paper. His mood changed suddenly. It was as if a metamorphosis had taken place

"Some bastard is going tae get this soon," he murmured in an alcohol-sodden voice as the carriage pulled into Bridge Street.

Chapter 18

NUTCASE

Johnny was perturbed about yesterday. His sudden mood change after buying the sword began to worry him a bit. One minute he was acting like a respectable business man with (what he thought) a posh accent, the next he became all gangster, guttural language to the core.

The change in behaviour got him thinking, one minute he could be as soft as shite, then next, as hard as nails. But he had been like this all his life, he blew hot and cold with people. In fact, some schoolmates, behind his back of course, had nicknamed him "the hairdryer." But it was not only his schoolmates, the teachers had noticed – his sudden mood changes would take everyone by surprise.

He thought back to when he was in primary school. He had gained a reputation for being a comedian one minute, the next he was battering the living daylights out of some poor soul. After setting about "one wee cheeky bastard" called Danny in the playground, also aged 12, the police were called as he had almost put the boy in hospital.

But because of his age, and the Gorbals mantra of not dealing with the police, the boy's parents decided not to take the matter any further. However, the headmistress did give him six of the best, with a big leather belt, and social workers were called in for an assessment. Johnny had never seen the social work report, but he knew his mother kept it in a big brown envelope in a drawer in her bedroom.

He sneaked back to the house, knowing she was "oot for the messages"– out shopping, and rifled through the drawers in the sideboard.

He found the brown envelope in the bottom drawer. It said on it "Department of Social Services, report on John McGrath." He pulled out a single piece of paper and read it. "John McGrath is a child of 12 who comes from a good family background and has hard working and caring parents. But at times they have expressed their concern at his violent outbursts and say one minute John can be 'as nice as ninepence', the next, 'a right wee monster.' After extensive discussions with his parents and teachers, we have concluded that this is perhaps adolescent behaviour which he will grow out of once he has reached a mature age.

"John was also interviewed by a psychiatrist who said he did show slight signs of paranoid schizophrenia but this was quite common in boys from the Gorbals of his age.

"It is common for boys of his age, background and behavioural patterns, to end up in approved schools, borstal and even prison in later life. As a precaution, we will be keeping this assessment on our files until the boy grows up and ceases to use such violent behaviour."

So that was it, he had always known that he was different, always known he was "a wee bit odd" but to be labelled a paranoid schizophrenic at the age of 12 had put the icing on the cake. It was official then; he was a nutcase. "A halfpenny short of a shilling, no' the full bob."

He went into the kitchen to make a cup of tea. He thought about the report and felt a bit proud he had been branded a violent fruitcake from the age of 12. But the problem was he was still a violent fruitcake, although the cake had matured with age.

To gain kudos, and enhance his reputation, he might even tell his pals about the report. They were used to his wild behaviour and violent ways from an early age:-

*Once, aged 14, he had head-butted a man through a shop window just because he had looked at him the wrong way.

*At the age of 15, and drinking underage, he had smashed up a pub when the barman refused to sell him any more drink.

*One of his first jobs after leaving school was in a factory. He got the sack after only two weeks for being continually late. He later burnt the place down and 200 people were laid off.

*At the age of 18 he had slashed three rival gang members at Glasgow Cross after bumping into them

There were other stories, too numerous to mention. But in many ways, they all had a common thread- they were committed by a young man who had let his behaviour get out of control.

He thought of these violent incidents and how he often felt aggressive and had the urge to "stick the nut" on somebody or even slash them with his razor. He then thought of Cathy and his mood changed accordingly, now he was as soft as shite. Perhaps love was the only thing that would change him. The Beatles were right when they sang, "All you need is love…da ra ra ra ra…"

He also tried to analyse his dramatic mood swings. What made him angry? Arrogant people, people with no manners, ignorant people, cardboard gangsters - guys who pretended to be hardmen.

So was easy then, it was love versus violence, and love won every time. But in the Gorbals to show love was seen as a sign of weakness. They might think he had turned into a poof if he turned on the lovey dovey patter.

So, in the meantime, violence and violent behaviour led the way, except when it came to Cathy. She was in a different division. He tried to psychoanalyse himself even more – he thought he always changed after alcohol. One minute he was as cool as a cucumber, the next, after a drink, a fucking lunatic. This bevvy business- what a palaver! It was an ingrained part of Gorbals culture. Everybody wanted a bevvy, that's why there were so many pubs and alcoholics in the area.

Feeling fed up? Have a bevvy. Feeling on top of the world? Have a bevvy. Budgie's birthday? Have a bevvy. Johnny tried to stay clear of certain beverages like whisky. Usually he would only drink them if there was a special occasion or when he wanted info from somebody. The biddy, cheap red wine, like Eldorado, Lanliq, and Four Crown, had to be avoided at all costs. Most of the guys who drank that stuff ended up in jail.

Indeed, Johnny recalled at least 90 per cent of the people he knew in Barlinnie had been on the biddy before committing offences. He thought of one night when he had bought a bottle of Eldorado wine from an off licence and promptly smashed the empty bottle over a pal's head. Sixty-six stitches. He apologised profusely to the fellow the next day – he could not explain what had come over him. His heavily bandaged pal, a lifelong school friend, replied, "Well, ah know what came over me- an Eldorado bottle!"

Suddenly there was a loud banging on the door. He opened it up – it was big Manny, one of the boys. "Hey Johnny, just had a win on the horses, fancy a bevvy?" Johnny put on his jacket and ventured out into a cold Glasgow evening. They ended up in the Turf Bar in Hospital Street. It was packed with bevvy merchants and the bevvy merchants were all doing what they did best – having a bevvy. Both Johnny and Manny got stuck into the lager.

"So, what's the score wi' the horses, Manny?" Johnny asked his pal.

Manny laughed, "You'll never believe this Johnny but until today ahv'e never had much luck wi' the gee gees. Ah was backing losers all the time, until this afternoon. Ah had ten bob –fifty pence – left in ma pocket when ah helped this old Irishwoman to get across the road. She pressed a good luck charm into ma hand, thanked me and made off." Manny pulled out a little leprechaun from his pocket. "Before she went, she said it would bring me luck. So, wi' ma ten bob I stuck it on a horse called Irish Beauty at odds of 50-1. It romped home. Aw thanks tae the wee woman and the leprechaun." The lager continued to flow and so did the stories.

Johnny had never been a betting man but he did have a flutter now and again, especially on the Scottish Grand National in Ayr. He had once won a fiver after sticking a bet on there but that was it, he had never taken a fancy to it. He was aware that gambling could destroy whole lives, leaving families to starve, all because the head of the household "liked a flutter."

But he loved the punters and their stories, they seemed to have more exotic and interesting lives - like rollercoasters –up one minute, down the next. Manny was one of them and his tales would have made the basis for a good book about gambling.

Manny went into patter mode, "Ah woke up at 3.30 in the morning and realised it was the third of March, the third of the third. Later ah walked to the bookies and there was a horse running called Triple Chance at 33-1. Ah put my life saving on it –£330 quid."

Johnny smiled, "So how much did ye win?" Manny took a sip of his lager and said, "Nothing… it came third."

As they were laughing, a big drunk navvy approached their table in his donkey jacket and mud stained wellies.

He shouted, "Have you fuckers been laughing at me?"

Johnny looked up at the red-haired navvy and retorted, "Nah pal we were laughing at a joke, no' laughing at you for fuck's sake."

The labourer seemed to get angrier and clenched his large fists, "These hands will knock ye out – you've been looking and laughing at me all night."Johnny rose quickly from the table. Manny did not feel afraid, he knew his pal could handle himself. The navvy squared up to Johnny and growled, "You've be staring at me, dae ye want ma picture?" Johnny replied, "Nah, you're too fucking ugly." He punched Johnny on the jaw. It sent him flying across the barroom floor. Johnny got up and promptly grabbed a beer bottle from one of the tables and crashed it over his head. The navvy collapsed on the floor, but no-one said anything. The bevvy merchants had seen it all before and carried on doing what they did best. Manny downed his pint of lager and said to Johnny, "Time tae get tae fuck." They walked out of the pub as the unconscious man lay on the floor.

They soon bade each other farewell. As Johnny walked the few blocks to Crown Street, he saw a couple of his pals coming towards him with a large carry out. One of them shouted, "Hey Johnny… fancy a bevvy?" There was no escaping it.

Chapter 19

BEVVY

There had to be a solution to this bevvy business. Of course, Johnny could not give up and completely sign the pledge. He thought it would contradict his cool hardman image. A gangster without a bevvy would be like Laurel without Hardy or Francie without Josie. Johnny was sufficiently worried enough about his excessive drinking that he decided to see the family doctor, Dr Mackenzie, who had a surgery in Old Rutherglen Road, not far from Florence Street. He had known the doctor all his life and after 20 odd years he was the medical practitioner who he trusted most.

Doctor Mackenzie was an old Highland guy with grey hair who had a respectable, superior manner. The receptionist said it was his lucky day as soon as he walked into the surgery. Someone had just cancelled their appointment a few minutes before. Dr Mackenzie was a very busy man and during his many years in the Gorbals he had seen it all. Alcoholism, wife and child battering, people with chronic illnesses and even more fatal ones.

But he dealt with it all in an utterly professional and detached manner. He made it a point not to get too friendly with his patients. If they saw a sign of weakness, they might take advantage. Because of his intelligent manner and accent, the Gorbals people looked up to him. Besides, he was the man who knew all the dark secrets about his patients. He knew stuff about people and their families that equalled the secrets heard by a priest in the confession box.

After waiting half an hour, while the doctor treated an old smoker with a bad cough, Johnny entered the doctor's room. Dr Mackenzie was reading from some notes at his desk and looked up through his gold rimmed glasses to see Johnny standing there. "Oh, it's you John. Nice to see you. Haven't seen you for a couple of years since you got injured in that gang fight. I hope you have been behaving yourself, young man."

Johnny sat at the desk facing the doctor, "Oh aye, doctor, ah've been a good wee boy." The doctor laughed at the impertinent pun.

"How's the family? Your mother, father and brother?" the doctor enquired.

"Good doctor, all well, otherwise they'd be in here to see you."

Johnny felt slightly nervous about what he was about to say. There was a pause for a few seconds, then he said, "Well doctor, ah think ah've been on the bevvy too much, drinking, and it's landing me in a lot of bother, like fighting. What do you recommend ah do?"

Dr Mackenzie gave a weak grin, "I get men and women in here all the time with the same story. It's the Gorbals for goodness sake. Everybody wants 'a wee drink' to cheer themselves up. But I tell them it can only lead to depression and even prison. The best thing to do is drop alcohol completely or cut right back."

Johnny nodded his head in agreement, "I think you are right doctor but if I give up the boy's might think ah've gone aw sissy, gone aw soft."

The doctor knew what he was on about, there was great pressure on people in the Gorbals to drink and "be sociable." He looked directly at Johnny and said, "Alcohol is a dangerous drug, if you become addicted. Drinking things like the cheap wine and whisky can cause so many problems both physical and mental. The problem is alcohol may cheer you up in the short term but it acts as a depressant in the long term. People are depressed enough without making it worse with alcohol addiction."

Johnny asked, "So what dae ye tell the bevvy merchant and winos who have depression?

"I give them a wee sermon. I say, you are lucky to be alive, so don't waste it with drink. For the tiniest moment in the span of eternity you have the miraculous privilege to exist. For billions of years you did not exist. Soon, you will cease to be once more. It is a short life."

Johnny was impressed. He had never known any man to impart so much knowledge in such a short period of time. His next question was mundane, "But doctor what do ah say tae ma pals as an excuse tae stay aff the bevvy?"

"Simple," Dr Mackenzie replied, "tell them you are on antibiotics and you can't take alcohol. I'll give you a prescription for antibiotic tablets, you don't have to take them of course. Show your pals the bottle and they'll be convinced."

Johnny rose from his chair and shook the doctor's hand, "Thanks for the wee sermon and advice. You are a genius!" Dr Mackenzie gave another of his weak grins and sighed, "If I was a genius, I wouldn't be working in the Gorbals. Good day to you."

Johnny walked through the packed waiting room. It was full of crying children and people sneezing and coughing. But then his heart missed a beat. He saw Cathy sitting in the corner with her mother. Her mother looked terrible, as white as a sheet with trembling hands. She had lost a lot of weight.

Cathy rose from her chair and walked over to Johnny. They went outside for a few moments.

"No' seen you for a wee while Cathy, what's the score?" he said.

She began to cry and grasped his hand, "Oh Johnny, she's had a bit of a breakdown after ma father disappeared. She's no' the same woman and looks like a skeleton. Ah'm here tae see what the doctor can do."

Johnny felt deeply emotional, as if a dagger had pierced his heart. "Tell her no' tae worry, everything will be alright, just wait and see."

Cathy wiped the tears from her eyes and said, "Oh ah hope so. Anyway, she's thinking of going down to Ayr to stay with her sister for a bit. The sea air might do her the world of good."

Johnny nodded his head in agreement, "Aye, a bit of sea air could well be just the ticket for her. Listen, when can ah see you again?"

"She's away this weekend with my sister and it means I'll be on my own. How's about meeting at the dancing on Saturday night, the Plaza in Eglinton Toll?"

"Ideal, Cathy, see you there, remember be there or be square!" She smiled, let go of his hand, and went back into the surgery. Johnny felt tormented – he knew her father was part of the concrete propping up the Kingston Bridge – but like the doctor he had to keep it a secret.

He had just crossed the road when he saw a taxi pull up outside the surgery. Two men got out. One was helping the other – a heavily bandaged man… it was McCoy and his father. They did not see him but he sure as hell saw them go into the surgery. "Those bastards will be seeking vengeance as soon as he's better," Johnny thought.

He walked into Angus, the chemists in Crown Street and left clutching a bottle of pills. A group of about 12 guys, all members of the Young Cumbie gang were standing outside John the Indian's grocer shop. Johnny went over to them, regaining his gallus walk, "What's happening, boys?" he shouted.

One of them said, "Celtic versus Rangers this Saturday. All the boys are up for it, you tae?"

"Fuck aye," Johnny replied, "We'll get aw the troops together for this." Some of the boys clapped in anticipation. One of them said, "Wi' you leading us aff we'll be a real force tae contend with."

"Hopefully," Johnny said, "I've just bought the ideal weapon for the occasion - a Victorian sword."

He went to make his way back to his house. One of the boys shouted, "Hey fancy a few pints, Johnny?"

He pulled out the bottle of pills and shook it. "Nah, nae chance. Shagged some bird a while ago and she's given me the clap. Nae bevvy wi' the antibiotics."

In the Gorbals lying was part of survival and Johnny planned to survive as long as he could.

Chapter 20

CUMBIE!

Johnny was the undisputed leader of the Young Young Cumbie gang. How he had landed this esteemed position had involved a long passage of trial and error. The Cumbie were arguably Glasgow's most feared gang, along with their rivals The Tongs from nearby Gallowgate. Both had similar structures.

At the age of 12 Johnny had joined the Tiny Cumbie which consisted of young guys aged from 12 to 15 years of age. It was in these formative years he learned, first of all, to fight with his hands and feet and then with knives, hammers and open razors.

It was a form of apprenticeship. He also learned how to win at "square goes" – using his head to give a "Glasgow kiss", and his feet to kick his opponent "in the baws." But gang warfare meant he had resorted to hitting rival gang members over the head with a hammer and on occasions using an open razor to slash a rival gang member down the jawbone.

He would rarely use a knife, not if he could help it, he saw it as a cowardly way to attack an enemy. After three years, building up a reputation as a young gangster, he eventually became the leader of the Tiny Cumbie. He then progressed to the YYC, a lot of young guys in the Gorbals, aged between 16-21, followed the same route.

These fellows were the equivalent of New York's wise guys. They talked fast, acted fast and dressed in clothes that made other young working-class guys look inferior. It was image with them, good smart suits, handmade shirt, and classy brogue shoes. The attire changed between day and night – during the day it was handmade Arthur Black shirts with personal logos, bright braces, Levi Sta-Prest trousers and Doc Marten boots.

At night, the suits and shoes went on, making them look like real gangsters. Above the YYC was another division, the Big Cumbie. They were mostly guys in their 20s, 30s and 40s who were considered to be the real deal and some even carried guns. Many of them were involved in dodgy schemes including running illicit drinking dens – "shebeens" – protection rackets, moneylending and even bank robberies. Across the Clyde, the Carlton Tongs had much the same set up, there was the Tiny Tongs, the Young Tongs and the Big Tongs.

The Tongs came into being in the 1960s after the movie The Terror of The Tongs was shown. Young guys rioted shouting "Tongs, ya Bass", which was short for "Tongs, ya bastard". As a result, the Gorbals gang began to use the same expletive, shouting "Cumbie, ya Bass." when in warfare.

Both were Catholic gangs but hated each other mainly due to their geographical differences. Over the Clyde, the Tongs ruled from the Saltmarket, Glasgow Cross and right up the Gallowgate

The Cumbie ruled the Gorbals right up to Castlemilk several miles away. There was a halfway point in the city centre, where the Cumbie and Tongs occasionally clashed - at St Enoch's Square. Johnny had been approached by a couple of the Tongs at St Enoch's Square and had promptly hit one on the head with a hammer. On another occasion he had shot several of the Tongs with a Webley air pistol. It all enhanced his reputation as gang leader.

Both the Cumbie and the Tongs could muster around 200 men and boys each – given the occasion. This was usually when Celtic met Rangers, or during the Fair Fortnight when the carnival came to the Glasgow Green in the summer. The rival gangs had massive battles there with many of them getting stabbed or slashed. During these skirmishes, Johnny led the YYC into combat like a general, shouting "Cumbie, ya bass!" as he laid into the opposing force. Indeed, he had often used a sword in such battles but it had fallen apart after much use. Thus, the reason for the new acquisition from Hillhead.

Although the Tongs and Cumbie were deadly enemies, there was another force to be reckoned with – the Bridgeton Derry. They were based a few miles away from the Gorbals in the Bridgeton area. They were all staunch Protestants and rabid Rangers supporters. All three gangs had strong historical connections when it came to rivalry and warfare.

The Tongs could date back to the 1930s when their predecessors the San Toi ruled the area (by the 1970s there was still some guys calling themselves the San Toi but they were considered merely to be an extension of the Tongs.) During the same historical period the Cumbie, named after Cumberland Street, had evolved from the Bee Hive gang which had named itself after a local haberdashery.

The Derry gang were the evolution of the Billy Boys of the 1930s who were led by a staunch Protestant called Billy Fullerton. The antics of such gangs formed the basis of the controversial book No Mean City, which focussed on a "razor king" in the Gorbals. Their names might have changed over the years but 40 years on the rivalry between the razor gangs remained exactly the same.

Johnny knew the big danger for him and the rest of his troops was when they arrived at Bridgeton Cross marching all the way to Parkhead for the game.

Folk singer Hamish Imlach had his finger on the button when he composed the song The Cumbie Boys. The Catholic Cumbie saw Celtic manager Jock Stein as a latter-day Jesus Christ and Parkhead was their new Jerusalem. The Derry Boys ran down the Pope and hated Catholics. Imlach sang when the gangs were asked about religion, they said, "Ach religion's aw right" but they were only religious when they wanted an excuse for a fight. In the song, people were advised not to wear a green scarf in Bridgeton or a blue scarf in Cumberland Street, "unless you are a heavyweight champion or hell'uva fast on your feet."

On the morning before the Old Firm match Johnny had every intention of wearing a green scarf in Bridgeton. Looking forward to a battle with the Derry. He put on his large woollen green and white Celtic scarf and then an old Crombie coat. It had thick lining, so he cut a hole in it and put the sword inside. When he put the coat on no-one would have noticed he was carrying a deadly weapon.

Johnny went out of his close and looked across the road, it was an impressive sight, 150 guys of all shapes, sizes and ages, all dressed in Celtic colours. This was the Cumbie ready for battle.

There was a group of old men in their bunnets standing outside his close. One of them said to Johnny, "Hey son, you show those dirty orange bastards who the real people are." His pals said, "Aye Johnny, fuck King Billy, up the Celts and the Fenian cause."

Johnny smiled, "Will do boys, we'll teach those Orangemen a lesson they won't forget." He and older Cumbie guys led their troops towards Bridgeton Cross. They were a formidable sight – here you had the toughest men and boys in Glasgow going off to battle.

People were hanging out of their windows as the gang walked along Ballater Street towards Bridgeton Cross. Johnny and his troops may have looked brave and gallus but they were secretly apprehensive. But so far so good. It was quiet even when they got to Bridgeton Cross. They were surprised to see none of the Derry gang there. One of the older guys from the Big Cumbie said to Johnny, "Where the fuck is this Derry mob?"

Another gangster guy, wearing a green and white Celtic shirt, said, "The Derry are probably too scared tae face the Cumbie. Sure, our mob would scare the shite out o' anyone – including those Protestant bastards." Johnny was not so sure, "Hah, those guys are no' daft, maybe they are planning an ambush after the game."

As they walked towards Parkhead they began to sing "Hail! Hail! The Celts are here what the hell do we care…" It was a good day for Celtic supporters, they beat Rangers 2-1, with no 7 Jimmy Johnstone playing a blinder.

During the course of the match, the boys passed between themselves half bottles of cheap wine, whisky and beer. But Johnny stayed sober, he was still acting out his antibiotics charade.

After the match they marched from Parkhead to Bridgeton Cross singing, "Celtic! Celtic! Ah'd walk a million miles for one of your goals, oh Celtic!" But when they got to Bridgeton Cross, the situation had changed dramatically. There were around 100 blue scarfed Derry boys amassed. On seeing the Cumbie they charged forth shouting, "F*** the Pope, up King Billy." Both sides began grappling with each other. Some of the more bevvied Cumbie guys fell to the ground and took a kicking. Two were slashed and three more were stabbed. But due to the lack of alcohol Johnny had all his wits about him.

Two guys wearing Rangers scarves charged towards him. One of them was an ugly looking guy, with a scar, in his 20s. He shouted to Johnny, "You're gonnae get it, ya Fenian bastard ye." As he approached Johnny, he was waving a knife wildly in his direction. The other guy ran towards Johnny shouting his battle cry, "Bridgeton Derry!"

Johnny pulled the sword out of his coat and lashed out. The first blow hit the dark-haired guy on the head and cut him wide open. The other fellow with the scar was about to stab Johnny and lifted his knife.

Johnny swung his sword, hitting the guy on the hand, two fingers and the knife went flying into the air. The guy hit the pavement holding his bleeding hand shouting, "Ya Bastard ye, you've cut aff ma fingers."

Johnny and the rest of his gang heard police sirens and made off quickly in the direction of the Gorbals. They split up into smaller groups and pretended they were ordinary Celtic supporters walking back from the game. They all reassembled in Crown Street, slapping each other on the back shouting, "We showed those orange Huns, naebody fucks wi' the Cumbie." Johnny shouted.

He was proud of his boys and they were equally proud of him. Cutting the guy's fingers off with an antique sword would make him a Gorbals gang legend.

They were all elated, victory had proved that the Cumbie were the most powerful gang in Glasgow. They looked bigger and more ferocious than the Tongs and made the Derry look like meagre opponents. There had been five stabbings on the Derry casualty side and two on the Cumbie side. "5-2!" Johnny shouted as if it was a football score. They all cheered.

One of the Cumbie boys, aged about 16, looked at Johnny as if he was a movie star. "Johnny, see that guy you chopped the fingers off. Dae ye think he'll ever work again?"

Johnny laughed, "Aye certainly… as a shorthand typist!"

He left his gang and headed back to the house to get changed. Sure, he had to meet Cathy at the Plaza later on.

Chapter 21

DATE

He studied himself in the mirror and looked fabulous. He had his shiny Hong Kong suit on, cream coloured Arthur Black shirt, dark tie, silk hankie in the breast pocket and highly polished dark brogues.

His mother looked at him and said, "Johnny, you look smashing, what a good looking fella you are! Have ye got a wee date on?" He began to blush slightly, the sort of blush a son gives his mother when he is being teased about his aspiring love life. His little brother entered the room with a cheeky grin. He put on a parrot's voice, "Who's a pretty boy then?" He pointed at Johnny's gear, "You look like one of those Chicago gangsters you see at the pictures." Johnny felt irritated but regained his composure to reply, "At least ah don't look like a horror movie star like you!" Joseph laughed and shouted in a mocking voice, "Johnny's got a wee bird on! Johnny's got a wee bird on!"

His mother shouted to him, "For goodness sake, leave your big brother alone. He's at the right age for courting." Johnny laughed, "Aye, there's nothing wrang wi' chasing the birds. It could be worse… ah could be chasing men."

He left the tenement and walked along Eglinton Street. He felt a bit nervous and somewhat paranoid. What if Cathy did not like the way he looked? That would be a bad scenario but what if she wasn't there? All done up and nowhere to go.

As he neared the Plaza Ballroom, he saw two young Cumbie guys coming towards him. They had big grins. Johnny paused for a few moments. Although they had not been there at what was now being called "The Battle of Bridgeton" he presumed that they had been regaled about his sword fighting exploits. He was spot on. The two youths looked extremely scruffy as they stood next to him. One of them said with deference, "We heard you were like Robert the Bruce in Bridgeton. You gave the Huns a good tanking wi' your sword."

Johnny nodded with a light grin but gave no immediate reply. He had a detached air about him. Besides, he did not like lower members of the Cumbie talking to him in such an over familiar way. The young guys had not given him the respect, as leader of the YYC, he was due. The reference to Robert Bruce irritated him. The other guy could sense that his pal had made a faux pas and attempted to paper over the cracks. "You look like a million dollars, Johnny. You heading for a lumber?" Johnny said nothing and just nodded his head briefly. With a straight face, that looked menacing, he walked off. The two young guys looked nervous, just hoping that they had not been too familiar, been too cheeky to their gang leader, who was now after all a bit of a legend.

He walked into the Star Bar at Eglinton Toll, just across from the Plaza. He was gasping for a pint to soothe his nerves before, hopefully, meeting Cathy. But he was still off the drink. "What can ah get ye son?" said the old grey-haired barman who reeked of fags and booze. "An Irn Bru pal." Johnny said in an aggressive tone.

"An Irn Bru? Surely ye want a pint before the dancing?" the old barman said.

"How dae ye know ah'm gaun tae the dancing?"

"Well you look like it the way yir done up and aw."

Johnny believed the barman was being insolent. Did he not know who he was? This was Johnny McGrath, leader of the Cumbie! "Look pal, gi' me a fucking Irn Bru and if ah get any more of your crummy patter, ah'll wreck this joint."

The barman suddenly looked frightened and moved off to get a glass of Irn Bru. When he did so, Johnny saw two men talking to him in hushed tones. The barman gave Johnny his glass of Irn Bru and said, "On the house. Sorry, ah didnae know who you were." Johnny picked up the glass, his temper had subsided. "Oh, that's ok pal, it's just that ah'm on antibiotics and ah would love a pint." He then put on a menacing tone, "In fact ah could MURDER a lager."

The old barman's beer-sodden face drained of blood. He moved off quickly to serve another customer. Johnny finished his soft drink and walked across the road into the Plaza. He paid his admission fee and the place was teeming with people. Men after women. Women after men. He thought it looked like a cattle market. He concentrated on the women and was sure many of them would sleep with him at the drop of a hat, or their knickers

There were fat birds, thin birds, tall birds, short birds, ugly birds, plain birds and a smattering of beautiful birds. He had been here several times before and thought how alcohol changed one's perception. At the start of the night the ugly birds, well, looked ugly. But after a few bevvies they became more beautiful by the minute. By the end of the night, thanks to the power of alcohol, every bird in the place looked beautiful.

On the dance floor there were hundreds of couples dancing to a live band who were playing Marmalade's Ob-La Di, Ob-La Da... "Desmond has a barrow in the marketplace..." There was a giant glitter ball above, radiating a light that gave the couples a glamorous look. Johnny scanned the dancefloor, there was no sign of Cathy among the dancers. He looked at the packed bar, still no sign of Cathy. "Stay cool," he murmured to himself, "Stay cool and look confident."

He walked around the edges of the dancefloor. There were tables full of people. Some sat in little alcoves giving each other the "lovey-dovey patter." He heard one scruffy looking numpty, with matted black hair and a moustache that reminded him of Hitler, saying, "Ye know, ah fell in love wi' you when we first met." The recipient of the compliment, a big fat lady with a crooked nose, took a drink of her vodka and coke and replied, "But Charlie, we only met an hour ago." Charlie grinned with chipped teeth and replied "Ah know,

Sadie, but time disnae matter. For me it was love at first sight."

"What a fucking patter merchant!" Johnny thought, "His patter is so bad, it's good." Charlie and Sadie kissed passionately. Johnny imagined what would happen next. They would probably stagger out of there and end up humping in some dark lane nearby. It was when he was thinking this he saw Cathy. She looked radiant and was talking to another person facing her. His heart sank, maybe she had met another bloke. Maybe she had fallen for another Charlie. He thought of his modus operandi. If another bloke was chatting her up, he would beat the shite out of him and he did not give a damn for the consequences. They could lock him up, jail him, but nobody, no man, could come in the way of their love. A love that was destined to be.

He approached the table with apprehension. But this evaporated when he saw she had been chatting with another woman, one of her old pals. Denice was an attractive looking girl, aged around 23, who worked in the same factory as Cathy. Several years before, she was at a party when Johnny walked in and she made a drunken pass at him.

Perhaps she had forgotten but Johnny had not. He prided himself that he was like the proverbial elephant who never forgot. He put on his most confident swagger and gallus accent, "Hello dolls, fancy seeing you here!" Cathy's face flushed, he knew it was the flush of love. She rose from the table, "This is Denice, a pal fae work. She said she'd keep me company until you turned up. Do you know each other?"

Johnny grinned, "Aye ah think we met at a party a long time ago."

Denice looked nervous, "Aye it was a long time ago Johnny, nice tae see you again." She shook his hand and left. Now he and Cathy were alone! The band began to play an apt song – Strangers in the Night.

During the course of the evening, he bought Cathy several glasses of lager but stayed on the Irn Bru. When they sat at a little candlelit table everything seemed just right. And when they danced together, they looked like the perfect couple, young slim and beautiful, and very much in love. A contrast to patter merchant Charlie and fat Sadie. Out of breath dancing, they went back to the table for a long chat.

"Johnny, the reason I've no' seen you is ma mother has been steadily going downhill since ma father disappeared," Cathy explained.

"Ah know Cathy, it must have come as a terrible blow."

"It was not only to her but tae me as well. Ah just hope he comes back fae Ireland soon."

Johnny felt gutted inside, he was dying to tell her the truth, but he couldn't. Lies do not mix well with true love.

"Ah think your father is lying low until the heat is off. Then he'll be back."

Cathy became tearful, "Do you really think so, Johnny?" She put her hand on his. It felt so soft and loving, so beautiful. They were connected now and no-one on Earth could break that connection. They kissed. It was a passionate lingering kiss. The power of a kiss can light up a million years!

Cathy looked him in the eye and said, "Johnny, ma mother and my sister have gone tae stay wi' my auntie in Ayr. It means ah'm all alone in the flat. Ah feel a bit frightened."

He took both her hands and squeezed them gently, "Frightened? Nae need tae be. You've got me, the leader of the Cumbie gang behind you. So, there's no' a problem."

"Oh, thanks Johnny, you have got a big head! Will you walk me home?"

"Of course, nae bother, goes without saying."

They walked out of the Plaza into the cold Glasgow air holding hands. They were now a couple officially. Good things come to those who wait.

Chapter 22

LOVE

They walked hand in hand from the Plaza. On their way back to the Gorbals epicentre drunks were streaming out of pubs, obscenities were being shouted, out of tune songs were being sung. The bevvy merchants were fighting their fellow bevvy merchants while the rats skulked about the place.

But Johnny and Cathy were oblivious to it all. As far as they were concerned, they were in their own world, a world that shut out the obscenities of life, a universe that had no time for the banality of people and their vulgar ways. Johnny gripped Cathy's hand tightly and she his, that was all that mattered. When they strolled towards Gorbals Street, a drunk man was urinating against a wall singing, "Fuck them all, fuck them all, the long and the short and the tall." A few yards away two scruffy-looking mongrels were humping each other, for an instant Johnny comically thought that these dogs may have been in love as well.

He was mystified about this love thing because he had been used to shouting the gang slogan, "Cumbie, ya bass!" for all the world to hear but now he had an overwhelming compulsion to shout, "I love Cathy!" But, of course, this was something he could never do. It would hardly fit in with his gangster image. People would have thought he had gone soft or mad, or maybe both.

As they walked through the streets to Cathy's flat in Queen Elizabeth Square, he thought that love gave him a feeling that was more intoxicating than the cheap wine or lager he had been used to. Sure, it was free as well, but the other interesting side effect was his violent tendencies seem to have subsided. Inside he felt like a big marshmallow. Soft and sticky. It was a weird yet wonderful feeling.

They passed a couple who were arguing on the corner of Florence Street and Old Rutherglen Road. The woman in her 30s was shouting to her man, "If you sat on your arse instead of talking through it, we might get somewhere." Her man, a wimpy-looking fellow, with horn rimmed glasses, looked frightened at the battle axe before him but he summoned up enough courage to retaliate, "If ah had a face like your, ah'd teach ma arse how tae speak." Infuriated, the woman punched her lover full force in the face. He went flying across the pavement before landing into a puddle nearby.

Cathy looked at Johnny, "What a carry on, some people just cannae behave themselves. Can they Johnny?"

"Nah they both deserve each other," he replied. But he had a strange thought, perhaps this couple were also in love. Perhaps they loved each other as much as he loved Cathy but showed it in a different, more violent way. His mind was racing. They came towards Cathy's high-rise flats and then saw his auntie Agnes coming towards him. He had not seen her since she had given him the confidential information from the police station.

She had a pensive look on her face. Johnny stopped with Cathy to talk for a few moments. He said to her, "Is everything ok? You look miserable, your face is tripping you."

Agnes sighed, "It was ok until two weeks ago, hassle that's when two daft guys, alkies, moved intae the flat just across the lobby fae me."

Johnny looked concerned, "Why, what's the matter, are these guys giving you any hassle?"

She looked apprehensive, "Well, aye, they're drinking all the time, ah don't know where they are getting the money fae. But somebody told me they were shoplifters and all their money goes on the bevvy. They invite their pals up night and day and they are always causing a racket and other trouble."

Johnny's concern accentuated. "Oh aye, what sort of trouble?"

"Well apart from the shouting and bawling at aw times o' night they are pishing up the close and causing a stink, a terrible stench."

"Did you no' tell them aff?" Johnny enquired.

"Oh, aye, but they threatened me and one of them said he'd throttle me wi' his belt. He even took it off and said he'd whack me before he throttled me. Ah was terrified. The other guy was pishing up the close the other night and ah told him tae stop and put his dick away. You know what he did then?"

"What?"

He flashed his dick and shouted, 'Maybe you need a bit of this!' He was disgusting."

Johnny gave Cathy a look of concern and said to his auntie, "What do these two bampots look like?"

"One is a fat guy, brown hair wi' a scar doon his right cheek, the other is daft looking eejit, wi' grey hair and a squashed nose. It looks like he was a boxer."

"Looks like he's gonnae get it squashed again." Johnny said before moving off with Cathy. As they stood outside the Queen Elizabeth flats, they kissed passionately again. Cathy said, "Dae ye want to come up for a cup o' tea?"

Johnny could feel his pulse racing. It was pulsating at the same rate as when he was at full throttle during gang fights. He felt his penis getting harder.

They took the lift up, walked along the corridor and entered Cathy's flat. There were photos of her father and mother in the living room. He sat on the couch "How many sugars?" Cathy asked. He rose and took her in his arms. They both fell onto the couch kissing wildly. Their clothes fell to the floor and Cathy gasped and moaned as Johnny penetrated her. It was a first for them. Cathy had never made love before and Johnny had never made love while being in love. Later they went into Cathy's small bedroom and made love all night.

In the morning Johnny awoke with Cathy in his arms. He looked at her face as she slept. He had never seen her look so content and did not want to wake her. He put his clothes on and slipped quietly away. It was about 8am and the sunlight was being kind to all those who walked beneath it. He went into a shop and bought a bottle of milk. He headed up to his auntie's tenement and knocked on the door opposite her flat. No-one answered. He knocked again. A fat man appeared at the door, "What dae ye want?" The next minute, a grey-haired man with a squashed nose stood behind him slugging from a wine bottle.

Johnny was straight to the point, "Ah've come tae tell ye to start behaving yourselves and cut the noise doon, ok?" The fat guy snarled, "No, it's no' ok, ye cannae tell us what tae dae, that's oor business." Squashed nose shouted in agreement, "Beat it, ya bampot!" Johnny smashed the bottle of milk over the fat guy's head. He collapsed outside the door. He grabbed squashed nose and head butted him, squashing his nose even more. Johnny made off quickly regretting he had wasted so much milk on the fat man, but then again there was no use crying over spilt milk.

It had been a strange 24 hours. It was like he was two different people. One minute the lover, the next a warrior gangster. He thought of all those losers who had love and hate tattooed on their knuckles. But surely this was what life was all about. Love one minute, hate the next. It was a strange combination but a combination that the Gorbals seemed to thrive on.

If he had to choose between love and hate, he certainly knew what he'd go for every time – love.

Back in the house he turned on Radio Clyde and The Beatles were singing All You Need is Love. He thought of it as an omen. Love is what everyone needed but few people actually got it.

Chapter 23

DOLE

It was 8.45 am the next day. There was someone knocking at the door. Johnny was having a shave in the sink and looking out of the window it was a fine day in the Gorbals. Children were scurrying to school, while people went about their daily duties. Cars and vans were going along Crown Street at a steady rate, business as usual! He opened the door and was greeted by Chris, covered in bruises. Two black eyes and a scratch mark on his nose.

Johnny also noticed a lump had been ripped out of his fine Irish red hair. "Can ah come in?" Chis asked. "Aye, certainly big man. "What the hell has happened tae you?" Johnny said in a humorous voice. "Ach, had an argument wi' two tubes in the pub, it ended up as a bit of a rammy."

"What, did ye get a kicking?"

"Ah think ah gave as good as ah got, they must be in a state as well."

Johnny made his pal a cup of tea, they had known each other all of their lives and had no secrets to hide. In a way he looked up to Chris. When he was younger and weaker at primary school, it was Chris who had stood up for him against the school bullies. Chris had even taken "a doin" for his pal a couple of times. When one bully battered into Johnny, Chris promptly intervened and kicked the shit out of him.

The incident did not go unnoticed by the head teacher and Chris was promptly given the maximum punishment, six of the belt with a big leather tawse. But he took his punishment like a man, or rather an Irishman. After getting six of the belt, he smirked to Johnny and his classmates, indicating that the punishment had not been that painful but merely an irritation.

Johnny had been impressed. Chris seemed fearless. The only thing he was afraid of was fear itself. On another occasion, when they were both aged around 11, two scruffy bullies turned up in the backcourts, while they were playing football, and tried to join in. Chris told them to "get tae fuck" which resulted in him getting a beating. But he was used to beatings. His father, a big burly Irish labourer from Donegal, often beat Chris up for one of his many misdemeanours. He got one such bashing after secretly taking money from his mother's purse – a ten bob note which he and Johnny spent on big bottles of Irn Bru and apple pies. This had happened many times. But on one fateful day, Chris' father found out and he was given an old fashioned Irish beating.

Chris' father took his belt off and whacked the boy hard. Ironically Johnny was usually there to witness such beatings. Before another beating, Chris jumped under a big double bed thinking he could avoid any punishment. But his father resorted to using a sweeping bush and pummelled his son that way. To Johnny it did not look like a serious punishment but more of a comedy farce with the big Irishman shouting, "Ah'll teach ye no' tae steal money fae your mother's purse."

Johnny thought himself lucky. His father and mother had never laid a hand on him. There was one occasion though when Johnny, aged 12, had been too big for his boots and he had sworn at his mother. She threw a loaded purse at him, bursting his nose. But this solitary act of violence made her remorseful. She ended up crying and apologised. But Johnny felt deep remorse as well. He had sworn at his mother, which really was unforgiveable.

His father had once slapped him for being too cheeky and not going to bed when told to, but it was a flimsy slap, "a poofy slap" as some would say. Chris was of a different stock, a different race, a different breed, no poofy slaps at home. Just plain old Irish family violence.

Johnny recalled Chris's father confiding in him, when he was aged 12, saying, "What am ah gonnae dae wi' that boy?" But to Johnny, Chris had no faults. If he was a diamond, he would be 21 carat, or as the Cockney's say, "a diamond geezer." He took a sip of his tea and said, "So what's the score man?" Chris put his hand on his head where the clump had been torn out. "Ah've got a wee problem. Ah've got tae sign on the dole at 11 this morning and wan o' those guys, ah had a fight wi', signs on at the same time, so ah need back up."

"If you are looking for back up, look no more," Johnny said in his most aggressive voice. The phrase made Chris feel more confident, more at peace with the world. No-one knows where confidence comes from, and no-one knows where it goes. Chris was in a confident, yet naughty mood. Although he had the clump missing from his head, Johnny's patter had rejuvenated him. The battery might have been running low, but now it was fully charged.

They headed for the dole, in many ways Chris and Johnny felt elated. They always thrived on a bit of drama and a giro at the end of the week was the icing on the cake, man!

When they arrived at the employment exchange in Eglinton Toll there was a long queue of men, some shabby, some well-dressed. Johnny thought of the joke, "What's green a gets you drunk? A giro." In the dole queue, a shabby-looking fellow looked over to Chris and shouted in a nervous tone, "Awright, big man?" Johnny noticed that he had several clumps of hair missing from his scalp. He presumed this was one of the fellows Chris had the drunken argument with.

After both had signed on, the guy approached Chris and said in an apologetic fashion, "Sorry about last night, big man, ah was right o' order."

Chris smiled and shrugged his shoulders, "So was ah, ah'm sorry as well. It was aw the bevvy, it sent me bananas." They both shook hands and joked about the brawl. The guy said, "Ah was drinking vodka and coke aw day. By the time we had the fight ah was speaking fluent Russian!" Once again, drink had a lot to answer for. As Johnny and Chris walked towards the Gorbals a pretty woman in her 20s shouted, "Hello, Johnny boy!"

It was Margaret, an old girlfriend. He had shagged her on several occasions, a few years back, but she had met a bingo caller Barney and had got married with two kids. She was now a divorcee. "Awright Margaret?" Johnny said, "No' seen you since the Pope was an altar boy." She blushed and it made her look even more attractive accentuating her shiny blonde hair, pert breasts and a smashing 5'2" figure. "Up here tae sign on Johnny, must hurry" she said in a sexy voice that gave him a hard on. "Aye, same here," Johnny said, "Me and big Chris." She giggled and made off, her boobs bouncing in an erotic way.

Chris looked on, "Ah'd shag that, eat chips oot her knickers!" Johnny laughed, "Been there, done it, got the t-shirt man!" Chris gave a comical look, "Ah widnae mind that t-shirt."

As they walked along Eglinton Street, a dishevelled looking beggar approached them, "Hey boys, ye couldnae gi' me your spare change by any chance?" Johnny always felt sorry for beggars, there but for the grace of God…. He fumbled in his trouser pocket and gave the beggar "two bob", a shiny ten pence piece. The beggar thanked him profusely, "Cheers young man, you are a saint, or you will be when ah have a wee word wi' the Pope!"

Chris laughed, "By the way, what are ye gonnae dae wi' the money?"

The beggar looked at the coin in his hand, "Look, what ah dae wi' ma money is ma business, so fuck off." They all laughed at the audacity of the comment. Many people in the Gorbals were short of money but rich with laughter. Johnny thought that if you could bottle such laughter and sell it, you would make a fortune.

Cry and you cry alone. Laugh and the rest of the Gorbals laughs with you. The absurdity of poverty turned many people into comedians.

Chapter 24

GUITAR

It was a cold, brisk Saturday morning. The boys, Alex and Chris, had arrived at Johnny's door, as was usual on most weekends. They were up for a laugh and a bit of banter, wherever their feet took them. By contrast, Johnny was a bit subdued. He had not slept well during the night. The nightmare of having a giant machine chasing him had returned. On waking up in a sweat, Johnny pondered what the dark dream actually meant. Surely it was simple enough, the machine represented danger and perhaps signified there were enemies out there plotting against him.

"Hey Johnny boy, fancy a wee donner up the toon?" Alex said in a cheerful voice which led to images of the bad dream fading quickly. "Aye" said Chris, "Let's have a wander and we'll turn the patter on." Johnny smiled, maybe that's just what he needed, a good laugh at the ridiculousness of life. The three of them headed over the Albert Bridge to the Saltmarket and then into Paddy's Market. As usual there were hundreds of stalls there with people standing in a dirty lane selling what Chris aptly described as "clatty gear for clatty people."

Johnny and his pals got a kick out of walking through Paddy's Market, for this was Glasgow of old. As described earlier, it was an old-fashioned Glasgow that had more of a connection to Victorian times rather than the 1970s. The place was a real living theatre with hundreds of dramas being played out there, especially on a Saturday morning. Chris said, "Look at that poor bampot there!" He pointed to a shabbily dressed man in his 50s who was trying to sell an old battered guitar for the price of a couple of pints. The ironic thing was the guitar, which had definitely seen better days, had only one string. But this did not deter the shabby alcoholic who began to sing "I Belong to Glasgow." His voice was as out of tune as his single string. "Ah belang tae Glesga, dear auld Glesga toon, there's somethin' the matter wi' Glesga for it's goin' roon and roon."

Johnny and the boys laughed at this comical sight. "Come on, boys," the man shouted to them, "A rare wee guitar for two quid. It used tae belang tae Eric Clapton." "Two pounds for Eric Clapton's old guitar, now that was a bargain! Chris said to the man, "Ok, gi's a wee shot then!" The alcoholic handed him the guitar. Chris strummed it hard, too hard, the remaining string broke. The scruffy man looked crestfallen, his means to a couple of pints had just been destroyed within a few seconds. "Ya clumsy bastard ye." He snarled at Chris, "You've wrecked ma guitar." Chris replied, "Aw, sorry about that mister." He pulled a pound note out of his pocket and handed it to the fellow. The man's face lit up with joy, now he would be able to afford a bevvy.

He offered Chris the guitar but he replied, "Nah, ye can keep it pal, but can ye do me a favour?"

"What's that?

"Next time ye see Eric Clapton, tell him ah was asking for him."

The man laughed and wiped his snotty nose with a large dirty hankie before replying, "Will do, son. Thanks for the wullie hound (pound), much appreciated." He then made off, guitar in hand, to the nearest boozer. This was human theatre with situations that few scriptwriters could envisage. They went inside one of the dingy tunnels that housed hundreds of stalls. They were selling everything. You name it, if it was knocked off and dodgy, they had it.

One desperate-looking woman was standing next to what looked like a pile of worthless rags shouting, "Babywear" Babywear! A shilling a go!" Johnny noticed another stall that was punting "Old Firm babywear"

There were little vests and pants, green and blue, for babies that presumably would grow up being Celtic and Rangers supporters. He announced to his pals, "Ah'm starving, let's have a bite before we have a pint." It was Saturday after all and he felt that he could drop his Irn Bru, antibiotics, charade for at least a day. At the back of the market there was a ham rib cafe. It sold steaming hot ham ribs with mashed potatoes, straight from the pot. The cafe was cheap, around "two bob" (10p) for a giant dinner. It also sold huge plates of "mince and tatties" It was reckoned to be the best value meals, for the poorer working classes, in the whole of Glasgow.

Johnny and Chris ordered the ham ribs and Alex went for his favourite, mince and tatties. The food was delicious. Alex said, "If only ma auld maw could cook like this, ah'd never leave home. She cannae cook, the last time she tried tae boil an egg, she burnt it."

Chris agreed about the food, "If ye went tae a fancy restaurant like the Rogano up the toon, they'd charge ye a tenner for a plate as good as this."

Johnny chimed in, "Aye, too right but those snobs who eat at the Rogano, don't know what they are missing. Give me the nosh in Paddy's Market any day."

The three of them headed to The Old Ship Bank pub nearby. The place was jam-packed with singing and dancing old age pensioners. This was definitely old Glasgow, full of colourful characters. It was a cornucopia of amateur singers and street comedians who had patter that would put the professional comedians to shame. As Johnny and the boys downed their lagers, they felt elated. The place was buzzing with singing, laughter and, of course, patter.

On the stage one fellow in his 60s, smartly dressed in a three-piece suit, remarked to the two fat sisters sitting at a table near the stage, "Hey you two, where's Cinderella?" Before singing My Way, he launched into a joke, "In the Wild West there were two soldiers guarding a fort. One of them says tae the other, 'Hold the fort for me, ah'm slipping away for an hour. Ah'm going tae the I.R. find an I.S. and take her tae the I.W.'

"The other guard says, 'What the fuck does I.R. I.S. and I.W. stand for?' His pal replied, 'Indian Reservation, Indian Squaw and Indian Wigwam.' So, the next day he tells his pal tae take time aff and dae the same. But a couple of hours later his pal comes back wi' a broken nose, two black eyes and all his uniform ripped.

'What happened tae you?' he asked his pal.

'Well ah did what you said. Ah went tae the I.R. met an I.S. and headed tae the I.W. but then the F.B.I. turned up.'

'What, the Federal Bureau of Investigation?'

'No, a fucking big Indian.'"

The audience, well tanked up, clapped and cheered enthusiastically. Las Vegas it was not, but to many the entertainment, good old- fashioned stuff, was brilliant.

A few minutes later, an old grey-haired woman got up on stage to sing It's a Sin to Tell a Lie. The atmosphere changed yet again. Couples who had been laughing a few minutes before now had tears in their eyes.

For a few brief moments, Johnny himself felt a bit sentimental, a trifle melancholy, especially when he thought of Cathy and her missing father. Chris went to the bar and bought back three pints of lager and three double vodka and cokes.

They downed the drinks quickly as a man with a blackened face got on stage to do an Al Jolson impersonation, "Mammy, mammy, ah'd walk a million miles for one of your smiles…" The Jolson fanatic was good, perhaps too good for a pub like this.

Chris said, "That guy should be on the stage… it leaves at 12 o'clock."

Johnny felt a tap on his shoulder and when he looked round it was Margaret who he had met coming out of the dole. She looked as sexy as ever as she clutched a large vodka and coke and said, "Fancy seeing you here. Ah don't see you for donkey's years and now twice in one week. It must be fate Johnny!"

He smiled, "Aye, fate right enough. Ah suppose people are like buses, ye don't see wan for a while and then three turn up at the same time." He quite fancied Margaret but he was aware she was a woman in her 20s with a dubious past. A few years back, they had 'a wee fling' before she met and married the bingo caller. But Johnny had been told by a reliable source that she had once been 'a line up merchant.' But even now he surmised that she was a nymphomaniac, a sex addict, who felt it hard to give up her old ways.

Margaret looked at Johnny in a salacious way and replied, "You say people are like buses. Does that mean ye want tae take me for a ride Johnny boy?"

There was an obese woman on stage singing in a loud voice Bonny Mary of Argyle. Margaret whispered into

Johnny's ear, "Dae ye fancy joining me outside for a few minutes while ah have a fag?"

He smiled and nodded his head in agreement and they headed outside. They stood in the doorway and she offered Johnny one of her Embassy Regal cigarettes. He refused politely. He hated smoking and used the old Glaswegian cliché, "The only time ah'll smoke… is if somebody sets me on fire!"

She laughed in a flirty sort of way. The rain began to come down. She pushed her breasts against him and said suggestively, "Let's stand in that close tae keep oot then rain." They went into the dark close nearby, in the Saltmarket.

She pushed her hand down Johnny's Levis and soon they were making love standing up. "Johnny ah've always fancied you," she was moaning. By this time Johnny's trousers were around his ankles and her underwear the same. But, suddenly, a little old man with an Alsatian dog came into the close. He was one of the residents. Alarmed at what was going on, he shouted, "Get the fuck oot ma close ya dirty bastards ye!" It was no time to argue. Johnny and Margaret quickly got dressed and went back into the pub. Chris and Alex were both the worse for wear. Chris said to the fat lady who had sung Bonny Mary of Argyle, "If singing was a crime, you'd be found not guilty." But the woman was not short of repartee, "Aye, well, if ah had a face like yours ah'd top myself."

She slapped Chris on the face and he stumbled, falling onto a table full of glasses. A drunk man, presumably her husband, tried to intervene but Alex headbutted him, sending him flying over another table. Meanwhile, there was a guy on stage in his 50s singing Elvis' It's Now or Never. Johnny shouted to the boys, "Aye, it's now or never, let's blow before the polis come."

They left the pub quickly and a few minutes later found themselves outside of the High Court which was closed. There was a group of well-dressed men and women outside, all with middle-class English accents, presumably on a tour of Glasgow. Johnny assumed they were all lawyers from places like London on some kind of legal, academic tour.

One of the party, a man in pin-striped suit, with smart Bryl-creamed hair, was giving an impromptu lecture, "And this is Glasgow's famous, or should I say infamous, High Court. As you are aware, there have been numerous, some would argue legendary, murder cases held here. Of course, in this city there is no shortage of criminal clientele. Just across the bridge, we have the Gorbals, which is a breeding ground for rogues and rascals, enough to fill any High Court and keep our legal counterparts in Scotland extremely busy."

The party of men and women all laughed and nodded in agreement. It was clear they were the rich, moneyed legal classes who thought that people like Johnny and his contemporaries were only slightly better than the Gorbals rats they were surrounded by.

Alex suddenly broke away and walked up to the party, addressing the posh fellow who had given the humorous speech, "Excuse me, dae ye speak English?" Alex asked. The man put on a pompous tone, "Of course we do, we are all used to speaking a high standard of the Queen's English when we are representing our clients in courts like this."

Alex replied, "That's good. Do you know anywhere about here that I can have a good... shite?"

The man and his party looked aghast. Some tut-tutted and moved off quickly. "Gorbals scum," said one of the party. The boys, half-cut and giggling, walked over the Albert Bridge to the Gorbals. When they got to Crown Street, they saw a group of drunken men outside the Wheatsheaf pub.

As they walked past, one of the men shouted to Johnny, "Hey you, ya bastard, you set about ma boy, you're gonnae get it!" He moved towards Johnny. It was McCoy's father, who had obviously been on the cheap wine. Two of McCoy snr's cronies held him back. Johnny reached into his pocket and pulled out an open razor. He waved it towards the drunken McCoy snr. "Oh aye, do ye fucking want it as well?"

The other men looked frightened. They were well aware of Johnny's reputation and had no doubts he would have slashed McCoy snr, and even them, on the spur of the moment.

They led McCoy snr away as he was shouting, "You've no' heard the last of this. Vengeance is mine!" Johnny, in his half-drunken state, was unperturbed. He bade the boys farewell but was aware that even in his inebriated condition, vengeance was heading in his direction.

Chapter 25

CARNIVAL

The Cumbie gang had amassed, a bigger force than the last outing to the Celtic v Rangers match. Johnny was like a general giving orders to those lower in command. He looked at the gangster throng, around 150 guys, all ages, all sizes. Guys in their 30s, guys in their 20s and teenagers. The thing about the Cumbie that was noticeable was that they were all well-dressed. As usual many of them looked like they had stepped out of the fashion pages – neat crew-cut haircuts, handmade tailored shirts, Levi trousers and Doc Marten boots, ready to give any fucker a kicking if they fancied their chances. This attire had become like a uniform for the Cumbie gang.

They might have lived in the worst crime-ridden area in Britain, with its crumbling buildings and rats, but they took pride in their appearance, and looked nothing like what they were in reality – slum dwellers. The Tongs from the Gallowgate were the same. Also well dressed, fashionable to the core. Members of the less fashionable, less prestigious gangs like the Hutchie from nearby Oatlands, or the Govan Team, were dressed likes tramps in comparison. They wore jeans and t-shirts or scruffy-looking shirts, nowhere near the league of the Arthur Black's the Cumbie and the Tongs wore.

On this particular day, Johnny and his 150 strong comrades all looked immaculate, as they usually did, going into battle with the Tongs at "the shows" in the Glasgow Green. The event was held every year, a carnival for the Glasgow workers who had two weeks off from the factories during "fair fortnight." The carnival was quite a big affair, and included dodgems, waltzers, coconut shies and all the palaver that made up a carnival.

Like the rest of his troops, Johnny was well armed – he had two open razors in his trouser pockets, and a hammer tucked into his waistline. Before they walked through the Glasgow Green to the shows he made a short speech to his fellow gang members, with some of the less experienced guys listening in awe, "Right troops we're aw heading tae the shows and if the Tongs turn up we'll gi' them a battle they'll never forget. Last year we got a wee bit of a tankin', twelve of us either got stabbed or slashed, but we set aboot them as well. This year we're stronger and better. So, try no' tae get chibbed or arrested… Cumbie, ya Bass!"

The boys replied in chorus, "Cumbie, ya bass!" The gang all headed through the Glasgow Green. Johnny had considered taking his sword with him but left it at home at the last minute. He could throw away the razors and hammers during any pursuit but the disposal of a sword would have been more hassle and certainly more detectable. Besides, he had read in the papers that sword-carrying gang members were being given heavy sentences with headlines like – **GANG MEMBER GIVEN TEN YEARS FOR SWORD ATTACK.**

At the Glasgow Green he surmised there might be undercover police there spectating secretly on any gang fights. During last year's battle with the Tongs, 27 of the Cumbie got arrested for mobbing and rioting, much the same as the Tongs side. 24 gang members from both sides were sent to jail for 12-15 months. Johnny was not a great lover of porridge and to him jail was for the "lower bampots". Indeed, his motto was, "You can do anything you want, but don't get caught."

To be less easily detected, the Cumbie gang split into small groups of two and three before they arrived at the shows. Johnny's partner in crime and second in command, was big Malky, a labourer in his mid 30s. He was reckoned to be "as game as fuck" and a powerhouse in any battle, especially against the Tongs. Like many of the major forces, the Tongs regularly had changes of leadership, many of them having been sent to jail. Their leaders had been arrested because at the end of the day they were not as lucky as the Cumbie when it came to being apprehended. Johnny put it down to the fact that at that time, the headquarters of the Glasgow Police was based bang in the centre of Tong territory near Glasgow Cross. The magistrates' courts were also there.

A short walk away was the Sheriff Court and High Court, so when it came to being hung drawn and quartered, the Tongs had a geographical disadvantage. They were the on the wrong side of the river and too near the authorities.

As they began to walk through the shows, the carnival was buzzing with loud rock and pop music. Malky said to Johnny, "Hey, some buzz man. It always gets ma adrenalin going. Chibbed three o' those Tong bastards last year. Maybe ah can make it four this year!" He then gave out the laugh of a maniac, a maniac ready for violence. A madman who thrived on the aggression of gang warfare. "Aye ye might well do Malky," Johnny laughed, "But don't let the polis see you do it. Five years is a long time in jail." Malky grimaced, "Five minutes is a long time in jail, Johnny boy."

Johnny had been lucky. He had never been in jail, but had probably been in more violent skirmishes than Malky. But the difference was he never got caught, Malky did. He had spent time in approved school, a young offenders' institution and then Borstal. He seemed quite proud of the fact. Jail was just a minor irritation to him, part of his lifestyle and he made numerous friends during his various spells inside. Over the years, he had enthralled Johnny and his pals with his exploits while inside, which he often described as "the university of crime." He was not wrong in his surmise. While serving time, he took lessons from a safe blower, a pickpocket a professional shoplifter, and even an old razor king.

They all showed him how easy it was and in some cases, how lucrative it could be to live on the other side of the tracks. In jail, he had met all sorts of colourful characters, including the sort of people Johnny would never have mixed with, bum boys, grasses and even "stoat the baws" – paedophiles. While most men would have cracked under the pressure, Malky never did. He put it down to his tremendous sense of humour.

While some may have been crying in their cells, Malky was a laugh a minute kind of guy who joked his way through the sentences. But he was no mug. Like Johnny, one minute he could be laughing with you, the next, head-butting you. He could change like the weather.

A few years before, Johnny had witnessed Malky hitting his Borstal day's pal over the head with a half brick. They had been joking one minute, all laughs and back slapping, the next, nasty and violent, like a scene from a Hammer horror movie. Afterwards, Johnny had asked Malky why he had hit his pal over the head with the brick and Malky replied, "Ah just had tae knock some sense intae him. Since that day he has been a far better man. He's kept oot o' jail, got a decent job and has a wee wifey and kids. A brick on the nut can work wonders for some people." Johnny thought about the remark carefully. Sure, he knew quite a few people in the Gorbals who needed a brick over the nut. It might have led them on the road to respectability.

They went deep into the carnival and ended up standing at the waltzers. "Hey, this looks fun Johnny," Malky said, "Fancy a go?"

They jumped on a waltzer and a man spun them round and round giving them a feeling of exhilaration. Malky began to shout, "Cumbie, ya bass!" as they were being spun around. Johnny laughed, but was aware that there could be an undercover policeman listening in. He told Malky, "For fuck's sake, keep the Cumbie shouts doon, we don't want tae get lifted, we've just got here."

They got off the waltzer and Malky looked a little subdued. There was one thing he did not like and that was being told off. But he responded to the fact that Johnny was the leader and further reflected that his pal had never been arrested and done time. As they stood pondering what part of the carnival they should go to next, a boy of about 17 ran over and stabbed another teenager in the side and made off. The bloodied victim staggered and fell as the waltzers spun around.

"What the fuck was that?" Malky asked his pal. Johnny replied, "Oh some loser taking a liberty. The scruffy-looking bastard is certainly no one of oor gang. He must be a member of the clatty Hutchie mob and ah think the chibbed guy must be a member of the Fleet gang." Johnny said in in such a way to imply that those gang members were the scum of the earth, low life, badly dressed fellows who were nowhere in the same league as the Cumbie and Tongs.

They passed the ghost train and Malky's mood changed again into a more humorous one, "People pay tae be frightened by shite like that. They should try walking through the Gorbals on a Friday night when the pubs are coming oot!"

They giggled like schoolboys and walked on to meet up with other members of the Cumbie. "Anything tae report?" Johnny said to a group of them standing near the dodgems. "Nah, Johnny," one of them said, "Nae sign o' any Tongs. They must be too frightened tae go intae battle wi' us." Johnny pulled out an open razor, "Well, boys, if those bastards want tae fight, they'll end up getting this." The teenage guys all laughed nervously and nodded in agreement. Johnny put the razor back in his pocket and repeated his well worn mantra, "Remember, boys, ye can dae what ye want, but for fuck's sake don't get caught." They dispersed, walking off again in twos and threes.

When they walked towards a coconut shy, a strange feeling came over Johnny, it was like a mini thunderbolt. Nearby, he spotted Cathy and her mother. Cathy looked as beautiful as ever, her mother certainly looked better than when he had last seen her. A spell in the Ayrshire air must have done her some good. Johnny walked over to them and said, "What are the two most beautiful women fae the Gorbals doing at the shows?" Cathy blushed heavily and her mother gave a weak smile. Cathy said, "You are a charmer, Johnny. Me and ma maw are oot for a wee walk. Ah thought it would cheer her up a bit. Her face had been tripping her for weeks."

Johnny looked at her mother and said, "And how are ye bearing up missus, how are ye coping?" She shrugged, "Ah've been worse Johnny. Ah'm feeling a bit better after ma wee holiday in Ayr. But ah'm still missing ma man. Ah think he's still hiding in Ireland. Just hope he comes back soon."

Johnny nodded, "Don't worry, he'll be back soon, nae doubt about that." The confident remark certainly cheered both mother and daughter up. But Johnny felt terrible inside. How long could he keep on with this charade? How long could he keep the pretence up, knowing that the man they were talking about was now part of the concrete foundations of the Kingston Bridge?

"Right, see you back in the Gorbals, we're off tae meet a couple of pals." Johnny said before making off with his comrade.

Malky said, "Was that your bird and her maw?"

Johnny nodded his head.

Malky said, "Did her father no' go missing?"

"Aye, he's supposed to be hiding out in Ireland, the polis and the taxman are after him," Johnny explained.

Malky gave out one his mad laughs, "Ireland? That's as good a place as any tae hide oot. Naebody gives a fuck in Ireland." Johnny could feel his stomach churn, the big lie was getting to him.

They met up with other gang members who were dotted strategically all over the shows. There had been no sightings of the Tongs, which Johnny felt was suspicious. Were they playing the same game as the Derry had played in Bridgeton? He told some of the younger gang members, "It looks like the Tongs hivnae turned up for battle, but they're fly, cunning bastards and as the auld saying goes, don't count your chickens before they're hatched."

All the Cumbie guys reassembled on the edge of the shows and the 150 strong outfit began to walk back through the Glasgow Green, towards the Gorbals. When they were halfway through the park they heard the shout, "Tongs, ya bass!" and hundreds of guys ran towards them, brandishing razors, knives and hammers. Malky was hit over the head with a hammer and plummeted to the ground. It was a well thought out ambush.

There was hand to hand fighting with people being stabbed and slashed on both sides. A guy, in his 20s, lunged towards Johnny with a Ghurkha knife shouting "Tongs rule!" Johnny quickly pulled out his razor and slashed his right jaw with a single swipe. It was the biggest brawl Johnny had ever been involved in. Then they heard the police sirens, the gang members on both sides dispersed. As Johnny ran towards the park gates heading to the Gorbals, he glanced around briefly and saw a fair-haired youth throw something towards him. Thud! It hit him in the back and blood began to ooze.

One of the Cumbie shouted, "Johnny, you've got a potato stuck in your back!" Johnny felt weak and staggered shouting, "Pull the fucking thing out!" One of the boys did and it was extremely painful. He showed Johnny the bloodied potato with a razor blade sticking out of it. This had been used as a weapon by the Glasgow razor gangs dating back to the 1930s. Johnny was getting even weaker as the blood gushed from him. He was helped into a close and they tried to stop the blood flowing, but it seemed fruitless. Johnny conked out. He was sure his time had come to die.

The next day he awoke in a bed in the Royal Infirmary with his mother sitting beside it, "Oh Johnny you're awake! Ah thought you were gonnae die." He had a huge bandage on his back. "The doctor says ye were hit wi' a tottie wi' a razor in it. You're lucky tae be alive." A few yards away Malky was in another bed with a large bandage on his head. He gave Johnny a painful wave. Malky beamed, "Hey Johnny we got out alive. We live tae fight another day!"

Johnny gave a weak smile, "Aye, Malky, he who fights and runs away lives to fight another day!"

Chapter 26

RECOVERY

The boys were out of hospital after a week. Both Malky and Johnny recovered rather quickly, but in some ways the incident, being ambushed in the Glasgow Green, had left them with mental scars. It had drawn home to them the futility of gang warfare. Malky, still with a large bandage on his head, turned up at Johnny's house to visit his injured pal. He was still feeling the pain after having the razor blade stuck in his back and in many ways, he had been lucky not to have been murdered. "What a way to go," he thought- "Murdered by a tottie!"

He had been used to face-to-face combat with real men, not those cowards who threw a potato at you, loaded with a sharp razor blade, and then ran off. Bastards! Complete and utter cowardly bastards, who would shite themselves in a real square go. Mammy's boys to the core. Johnny was in a lot of pain and let Malky make him a cup of tea to cheer him up. A wee cup of cheer! In The Gorbals, tea was always the great soother in times of trouble. Facing problems? Put the kettle on. Someone coming to visit? Put the kettle on. A cup of tea was the great prophylactic to life's problems.

Being hurt gave Johnny the time to think about his life as a gangster and the futility of it all. Drama and violence had certainly given his life some sort of meaning. Sure, it provided him with several roles,

Johnny the hardman, Johnny the gang leader, Johnny the part time seducer. He took a sip of his tea and said to Malky, "What's it all about, man."

Malky replied, "What's what all about?"

Johnny looked him straight in the eye, "This life business, what's it all about?"

Malky shrugged his shoulders and gulped a mouthful of tea, "Who knows what it's all about. We just go out and do it, like actors on a stage. We're the main performers on the Gorbals stage"

Johnny smiled, "What, like those actor guys in the Citizen's Theatre?

Malky nodded, "Aye, we're just like them, the only difference is their world is made up, a fantasy, ours is real."

Johnny thought that Malky had hit the nail on the head. So that's what it was all about- playing parts according to your audience. To his family, Johnny was the loving son. To his fellow gang members, a leader and violent psychopath. To the rest of the Gorbals, he was a friendly, strutting hardman, a game guy who never backed down from a confrontation. He played many roles.

The sweet tea had given him a warm, almost contented feeling.

"Awright," he said to Malky, "If we were both actors in a true life situation, who do you think could play us in a movie?"

Malky laughed. It was an absurd question but he enjoyed the banter with his pal.

"Ah think James Cagney would be good as you," he said to Johnny.

Johnny smirked, "Yeah, but he'd have to have a Scottish accent, maybe change his name to Johnny McCagney. And who do ye think could play you?"

Malky replied instantly, "Humphrey Bogart, he's the man, nae bother at aw." They started to laugh loudly. Johnny said, "Malky McBogart and Johnny McCagney, sounds good to me."

Johnny's brother Joseph entered the room wearing his school blazer, which instantly suggested that he was a cut above, more intelligent, than most of the other boys in the area.

"Hey bampot wi' your posh blazer, who dae ye think could play us in a Hollywood movie?" Johnny shouted to his brother.

"Easy peasy," he replied with a massive grin, "Laurel and Hardy, a right pair of idiots who've got ideas well above their station." A pair of bumbling buffoons like Laurel and Hardy? Johnny could see that Malky had been slightly wounded by the humorous remark and if it had been said by anyone other than his younger brother, he would have got a beating. Malky finished his tea and said, "Got to go boys, got to see a man about a dog."

After Malky and Joseph left, Johnny thought about the cheeky remark. Maybe his brother had been right, perhaps they were just a couple of idiotic buffoons. A pair of numpties who had delusions of grandeur. The thought began to make him feel slightly dizzy, also the dull pain in his back did nothing to help things. He decided to get out and breathe in the fresh air of the Gorbals stage.

He walked down the stairs of the tenement and went into the back court. There was a shabby-looking man there singing, "It's a long way to Tipperary." He was a back court singer who sang until people threw money from their tenement windows, usually a few coppers at a time. He actually had a fine voice. Johnny put his hand into his pocket and threw the man a few pennies. He knew the singer would be grateful as it would provide enough money to buy a couple of pints at the end of a hard day in concert. "Thanks pal." The singer said, "Any requests?" "Aye," Johnny replied, "Get tae fuck." The singer gave a weak smile and made off to the next back court.

The fresh air and the singing had boosted Johnny's mood considerably. The throbbing on his back seemed to subside. Suddenly he felt very hungry, enough, as he would say "Tae eat a scabby donkey between two bread vans."

He entered a dingy cafe in one of the back streets, which laughingly called itself a "restaurant." He was unsure about the hygiene of the place as a manky-looking woman with a fag in her mouth, took his order, "Big plate of mince and tatties, two slices of bread and a mug of tea."

The woman was back a few minutes later with his order. When she put the plates on the tables some of the fag ash fell from her cigarette onto the bread, giving it a streak of grey. He also noticed that the woman's fingernails were dirty, with black ingrained dirt underneath them.

"Anything else ah can get ye son?" she said in an irritating voice. But Johnny decided to be diplomatic, he had an urge to tell her to "go and get a good wash" but he stayed silent and tucked into the mince and potatoes. It was delicious, just what the doctor ordered. While eating he thought about the dubious hygiene of the place. The waitress was manky but what about the cook? What the hell did she look like? It was a matter he did not wish to concentrate on. The cook was probably a filthy-looking bastard as well, but certainly knocked up a good plate of mince. When he finished the meal, Johnny was taken by surprise. The manky waitress, who was in her 60s, sat opposite him, "Nae charge for the mince son, it's on the house, 'cause we know who you are."

"Oh, aye missus, "Johnny replied, "Who am I then?"

She smiled through broken teeth, "You're that boy fae Crown Street, the leader of the Cumbie gang. Am ah right or am ah wrong?"

Johnny smiled with some mince stick in his teeth, "You're right, missus."

"Oh, that's good son. Ah wonder if ye could do me a wee favour?"

So, this was the reason she had not charged him for the dinner. He put his knife and fork tidily on the plate before saying, "And what is this wee favour?" The waitress changed her expression from mock friendly to deadly serious.

"Well, ma granddaughter is often playing across the road but she and the other weans are complaining that an auld stoat-the-baw is turning up offering them sweeties."

If one thing got on Johnny's wick it was a stoat-the-baw. He had encountered a few growing up and experience had taught him they had to be subjected to instant, merciless punishment. When one paedophile approached Johnny and his pals when he was aged about 10, a gang of the older guys had almost kicked him to death. The waitress walked over to the window and pointed out, "Look there he is now talking tae the kids." Johnny rose from the table and looked, out of the window. There was a grey-haired man in his early 70s talking to the children and handing them sweets. He looked like a retired accountant type, they usually did. In Johnny's experience there seemed to be a plethora of elderly middle-class men from the suburbs like Hillhead or Giffnock turning up in the Gorbals with dubious intentions towards children.

Despite the throbbing in his back, Johnny could feel his energy return. He walked towards the elderly man. On seeing this, the man's face drained of blood and he moved off a few hundred yards away near a pile of rubble. "Hey you!" Johnny shouted, "What are ye doing hanging aboot and giving weans sweeties? Ya dirty auld bastard ye."

The man froze with fear, like a rabbit stuck in the headlights of a car. He looked at Johnny and tried to cover his tracks. "Oh, I was only being friendly," he said in an accent that gave away his lower middle class roots. "Friendly? Ah'll gi' ye friendly, ya pervert," Johnny shouted and pulled a fork out that he had been eating with in the restaurant.

He stuck it underneath the man's jaw. It stayed there firmly until the elderly man collapsed onto the ground with blood gushing everywhere. Johnny left him in a pool of blood and quickly made off. There were no spectators, more importantly no witnesses. The fork from the restaurant might be a giveaway but the waitress would not be providing any information to the police.

He stood at the corner of Crown Street and Old Rutherglen road, watching the traffic come and go. After about ten minutes he heard the sirens of an ambulance and a police car heading in his direction.

They turned into where the man had been stabbed with the fork. Johnny could see from a safe distance, the stoat-the-baw being placed onto a stretcher with the fork still stuck underneath his jaw. The ambulance rushed off to the hospital with sirens blaring.

The excitement of the attack had made the throbbing in his back almost disappear. But when Johnny got back to his house, he had another throbbing, in his belly.

He sat on the toilet and felt sick as the poisonous mince gushed out of his system. It was the worst case of food poisoning he had ever experienced.

"A good deed never goes unpunished," he muttered to himself as the flow of diarrhoea continued like a waterfall.

Chapter 27

ABERDEEN

Once the throbbing in his back (and belly) had dissipated, after a week or so, Johnny felt well enough to once again submerge himself in the Glaswegian subculture. A trip had been arranged from an Irish dominated pub, Derry Treanors, to a Celtic cup match against Aberdeen FC in the Granite City. Three buses were leaving with mostly Irish labourers and a smattering of Johnny's cronies. Malky, Alex and Chris were on a bus to greet Johnny as he boarded. They were all clad in Celtic gear, big green and white scarves and some wearing Celtic jerseys.

In the past, Johnny had been a diehard Celtic fan. He grew up watching outside right Jimmy Johnstone, and the swerving skills of this player almost took his breath away. Indeed, when Celtic were the European Cup winners in 1967 it made most of the local Catholic inhabitants of the Gorbals feel as if they could go out and conquer the world. The players who had won the cup in Lisbon, summed up what every Glaswegian should be – gallus and fearless.

From an early age that's what Johnny aspired to be, gallus and fearless to a point where people looked up to him. He loved the word gallus, meaning having a superior style with attitude. The word gallus seemed gallus in itself. The boys were certainly acting in a gallus fashion. They had chipped in for a large carry out – several bottles of cheap and strong South African wines – Eldorado, Lanliq and Four Crown. Malky and Chris passed around the bottles and cans of Tennent's lager which they all slugged from. Johnny usually avoided the cheap wine, but made an exception for football matches.

The other passengers on the bus, all Celtic FC Irishmen to the core, were operating the same drinking system. In fact, most of them seemed half-cut before they got on the bus. As the cheap wine soared through his veins, a soothing, contemplative emotion came over him. At times cheap wine could be your best pal and at other times your worst enemy, landing you in jail.

But it was almost a perfect day, Johnny was with his pals and fellow Celtic supporters who were all psychologically bonded together. One of the Irishmen began to sing Off to Dublin in the Green, "Oh I am a merry ploughboy…" Johnny joined in enthusiastically and the wine had given him the strange inclination that perhaps he should join the IRA and be a soldier that would fight for the cause.

There were shouts of "Up the IRA...our day will come," and "Fuck King Billy." It was real tribal stuff, Fenian banter which made Johnny feel at home among his own. Apart from the songs, the bus was full of jokey banter. Chris said, slugging from a large bottle of Eldorado, "Ah hear Rangers have bought a submarine, there are twenty thousand leagues under the sea and they've got a chance of winning one of them!" He had heard a lot of these crude jokes before but in his semi wine-sodden state he laughed at them as if he had heard them for the first time

In his mind, this was solidarity. This is what gave most of them, with meaningless lives, a meaning. A good song, a good bevvy and a joke with his Fenian pals was all that he needed to feel contented. The love for Cathy made him feel contented in a different way. His mother's love, at times, also made him content. But with the boys, it was a different kind of contentment, a gallus contentment, if you like.

As the bus trundled along the highway, Johnny looked out of the window and scanned the countryside. It looked beautiful, a different world from the Gorbals. A world of farmers, sheep, horses and cows, far away from the grim reality of the dingy and filthy streets of Glasgow. Johnny looked over to Malky. The cheap wine made his pal resemble a madman. His eyes had taken on the look of a lunatic, which he probably was anyway. Johnny also noticed that Malky's nose began to get redder and redder by the minute. He knew from past experience that the cheap wine made Malky's nose glow in the dark.

The wine affected the boys differently. While Johnny (this time) felt content, Malky was aggressive and was looking for a punch up with any fool that got in his way. Chris became a bit solemn and subdued when too much vino took over. Alex would go through a metamorphosis. He came up with such erratic and wild behaviour that often surprised and even shocked Johnny. One time they had been in a pub, near the

High Court, when a couple of middle aged gangsters walked in, all suited and booted, after being cleared of attempted murder. Johnny had seen a photo of one of the gangsters in the Daily Record.

He was definitely not a guy to be messed with. But after being on the cheap wine all day, Johnny was mortified when Alex walked up to the gangster as he sat at a table in the pub, slapped him on the back and shouted, "You're just a cardboard gangster. Ah could bend you no bother!" It resulted in Alex being thrown through the air like a rag doll and being given a kicking in the bar with tables and glasses flying everywhere.

But Johnny had not intervened. Not because he was scared but because he realised on such occasions Alex had to be punished for his eccentric behaviour. He was mad but certainly not bad.

Suddenly Alex shouted on the bus, "Long live the Pope!" This was a surprise because Alex had been brought up as a Protestant and Johnny was sure he did not even know who the Pope was. He was just being controversial, it was part of his nature. Even his mother admitted, "Alex is never satisfied until he's causing trouble." They were almost on the outskirts of Aberdeen, and sitting at the back of the bus, when a large fellow came from the front to join them. It was John the Irishman from the Portland Dancehall.

The Irishman sat next to Johnny and talked quietly, "Have you had a think about ma offer?" Johnny at first pretended not to understand, "What offer was that?"

"To join the cause."

"Aye, ah've been thinking about it, in fact it crossed ma mind a few minutes ago."

The Irishman smiled saying, "Well, we need guys in the IRA who don't just think but act."

Johnny understood immediately, "Ah know what you mean, but what exactly dae ye want me tae dae?"

The Irishman laughed, "That's for me to know and for you to find out."

Johnny grinned and took another sip of the red wine, "Awright, so when can ah find out then?"

John replied, "After the match when we get back tae the Gorbals. Meet me at the dancehall and I'll show ye. Take a couple of your boys with you." Johnny nodded in agreement and asked the Irishman what he thought the score would be. The Irishman thought for a few moments and said, "Two nil tae Celtic, nae bother, us Fenians always win!"

He rose and shook hand with Johnny and the rest of the boys. They all showed respect for the Irishman except Alex who laughed and sneered as he walked away. "Ah think you're heading for a knee capping, Alex," said Malky.

Chris agreed, "Don't fuck wi' that fella, he could make you disappear faster than Harry Houdini. For fuck's sake Alex, only you could insult the head of the IRA and get away wi' it."

Alex took another slug of what was left of his Eldorado wine bottle, "The IRA are too scared of me, they know ah'm fucking insane." The boys laughed at the remark but could sense there was some truth in it.

They were not far from Aberdeen city centre when suddenly a drunken navvy stumbled past them in a state shouting, "Ah need a pish now." He began to urinate heavily at the back of the bus.

The urine began to flow down the aisle, splashing on Alex's shoes.

Alex rose and smashed his wine bottle over the navvy's head. He collapsed onto the floor in a puddle of pish.

The boys left the bus and strolled towards Aberdeen's ground. Johnny liked the feel of Aberdeen. He had never really been before, just once as a kid, and had hazy memories of it. As they walked through the streets, albeit in a wine-sodden state, Johnny liked the fresh air which was far fresher than the Gorbals. He was also impressed with the pretty buildings and the pretty young ladies. He noticed they were different from the wee herries he had grown up with. As the girls passed him, they did not avoid eye gaze but gave a brief smile in his direction. He felt aroused by them, and the general ambience of the Granite City. Ironically, there was a bar in the Gorbals with the same name. But it certainly differed from the atmosphere of the real place. It was full of drunks and ugly women who would have put Aberdeen to shame.

The Aberdonians had a different reputation to the people of Glasgow. Glaswegians had a reputation for being rough and uncouth whereas people from Aberdeen were said to be more timid and very careful with their money. The standing joke was, "What's the emptiest place in the world? Aberdeen on flag day." In the event Celtic played well that day with Jimmy Johnstone showing with his swerves and dribbling why he was such a legend. The Irishman had been right, Celtic beat Aberdeen 2-0 heading for the final of the Scottish Cup at Hampden Park in Glasgow, which is not far from where they all lived. The boys all got back to the bus feeling exhausted but elated. The drunken navvy was still unconscious in the puddle of pish, but he was certainly still alive as he snored heavily.

Johnny and his pals all had a kip until they arrived back in Glasgow. Still exhausted, Johnny bade his pals farewell and headed to his tenement. What a day! What a bevvy! What a victory for Celtic! The IRA could wait for the moment. He was going to bed for a well-earned rest. A sleep that would take him away from the absurdity of his life in the Gorbals.

Chapter 28

I.R.A

A message got to Johnny that he was to meet the Irishman not at the Portland dance hall but at a tenement in Thistle Street which was only a few minutes way from where he lived in Crown Street. As he walked towards the tenement, he noticed there was a large car parked outside. It was an incongruous sight as most of the people who lived in Thistle Street never earned enough money to buy a car. Well, a Dinky perhaps.

As Johnny approached the close, he had a quick glance at three men who were in the vehicle. All had ruddy faces and thick hair, this was usually a sign that they were all Irish guys. The Gorbals guys tended to look thinner and paler, the Irish had that certain look about them.

As he passed the car, the ruddy-faced man at the wheel gave him a smile and a nod as if to say, "We know who you are, we know where you are going." Johnny climbed the tenement stairs and three rats scurried past him. In a strange way he thought it somewhat of an omen, he always thought that the number three had been lucky for him, just like the betting joke he had heard from his pal, Manny.

At one time he had three birds on the go, he had scored three goals in his first schoolboy football match and had a minor pools win by using combinations of the number three. So, in his mind, three rats were good. He knocked loudly on an old battered Victorian door. It had a nameplate on it saying "McCafferty". He heard slow footsteps and the door opened. It was an old Irish woman with white hair wearing a pinny. She gave Johnny a suspicious look before saying, "Can ah help ye son?" "Aye," Johnny replied, "Ah'm here tae see the big fella." She smiled and welcomed him in saying, "We've been expecting you."

Johnny entered the flat and there was an overwhelming smell of cabbage. It did not irritate him as he loved the smell of boiled cabbage. It reminded him of when as a child, he went to visit his grandmother. Cabbage, or rather the smell of it, evoked happy memories. "Come away in," the old lady said and pointed to a door leading to another room. He twisted the handle and inside, seated at a table were three men – John, and two other fellows he had never seen before.

"It's yourself Johnny boy," the Irishman said as he rose from the table to shake his hand. Johnny noticed his handshake was soft, almost like that of a woman. John introduced the other two fellows, "This is Liam," he said. Liam, a fat looking fellow in a donkey jacket grunted and shook his hand. His handshake was firm. Johnny thought briefly, semi violent, the hand of an Irish labourer who had IRA connections. Liam looked at Johnny suspiciously before sitting down. "And this is Danny," John proclaimed. Danny, a grey-haired man in his 50s was wearing a smart three-piece suit and looked very inch a prosperous businessman.

"Pleased to meet you, Johnny," Danny said before shaking his hand. Like Liam, Danny's handshake was firm and strong, so strong in fact it made Johnny's knuckles go white. "This is the handshake of a leader", Johnny thought, perhaps an IRA leader.

He sat down at the table with the men. The old lady made them a large pot of tea. There was also baked Irish soda bread, scones and sandwiches on the table. Johnny spoke first in the most confident and gallus Glaswegian accent he could muster, "Right boys how can ah help you?" Liam looked slightly annoyed, scowled and grunted but said nothing. It was left to Danny to do the talking, "It's not about you helping us, but how you can help the cause." Johnny feigned confusion before replying, "The cause?" Danny gave a sly smile, "You're no' that daft Johnny, the cause to make Ireland one nation again. You can do your part."

There was a pause as Johnny sipped his sweet tea, "Oh aye and what's that?" Danny was straight to the point, "A lot of our best men are in jail or been interned. We need fresh blood. A young fella like you who is not on the army radar and can slip through the net."

Johnny was grateful for the compliment, "So, tell me, what does it involve?" John was first to reply, "Danny is the leader of the Provisional IRA in Belfast and Liam is his right hand man. They have secured a load of rifles that need to be smuggled back to Ireland." Johnny was interested, very interested, it sounded like a plot from a Hollywood movie. Danny clarified the situation, "Look we've just had a shipment from the Middle East. Guns and dynamite. We need you and your gang pals to shift them for us."

Big John joined in, "They're hidden in the dancehall. I had arranged for a couple of our fellas from Belfast tae pick them up but they've been incarcerated. Interned by the fucking British who should not be in Northern Ireland anyway." Liam agreed saying, "We will not be mastered by some English bastards."

"Ok boys, I agree," Johnny said. "So what's the score then?"

Danny replied, "The score is you and some of your boys pick up the gear from outside the dancehall and load it into a van, which we will provide, then drive it to Portpatrick. There, you will be met by a fishing boat which will take the cargo back to Ireland. Job done!"

"Sounds a doddle," Johnny said, "Is there any money in it for me and the boys?" All three Irishmen looked annoyed with Liam giving him a violent stare. Danny sighed, "Johnny this is for the fucking cause – no money involved but we can give you the greatest gift of all." Johnny looked confused, "Oh aye and what's that?"

Danny replied, "The backing of the IRA. You get into trouble with anybody and we, the IRA, will be behind you. And I'll tell you what, when we are behind you nobody will fuck with you again."

Johnny nodded his head in agreement. Any future backing of the IRA would be worth far more than a couple of hundred quid in the bank.

John clarified the matter even further, "Look, we work on the principle that if you do us a favour, we owe you a favour. And when the time comes for you to collect that favour we will be there to back you up all the way. A favour from us is worth more than any money."

It was then the plan unfolded. There would be a van waiting for Johnny and his crew at midnight on Saturday. All Johnny had to do was drive the van to Portpatrick, hand over the gear and then fuck off. The only problem was Johnny could not drive. Well, he could technically, as he had a provisional licence and had taken a few lessons from his father a couple of years back. But he was hardly confident enough to drive a van full of guns and explosives all the way to Portpatrick. It was a minor problem to him. He knew one guy who was a proficient driver, his old pal Malky. Johnny bade the three IRA men farewell and as he did so, they all shouted in unison, "Our day will come. Up the IRA!"

As he walked down the tenement stairs towards Thistle Street, he felt once again elated. Sure, he was now an IRA gun runner with the backing of no less than the leader of the Belfast IRA. But it was frustrating in a way, he could not exactly boast about it. He could not go into a pub and announce, "Ah've got a new job, an IRA gun runner!"

The thought amused him until he got onto the street. The three Irishmen were still in the car. The driver smiled once again and gave Johnny the thumbs up. Johnny gave the thumbs up back and winked.

The wink summed it up, he was going places, even if it was only Portpatrick.

Chapter 29

ADVENTURE

Malky agreed to the plan straight away. Not only was he a car fanatic but an adrenaline junkie – he thrived on adventure, the more dangerous the adventure, the more his adrenaline flowed. He liked the odd pint but to him nothing could replace the feeling of all that adrenaline pumping through his body. He was a proficient driver and an experienced car thief. His uncle Roger had taught him from an early age how to hotwire cars. If you fancied a stolen car with equally stolen number plates, Roger was the man to see. He could get you any car on the black market if the price was right.

He was always cruising round Glasgow in various cars which he had hot-wired. Malky had been his apprentice in crime, learning the tricks of the trade. Roger taught him to acquire and sell stolen licences and where to obtain dodgy plates.

But it all went wrong for Roger when he spotted a cracking looking red Jaguar just off Sauchiehall Street. Malky, then aged 12, was with his uncle at the time. They nicked the car and made off laughing all the way to a secret garage in Maryhill where they hid the vehicle. He said he had a "Paki business guy" who owned a string of shops who was quite willing to buy the stolen Jag for several thousand pounds. His plan was to ship it back to Pakistan.

All was going well until reports in the Glasgow newspapers proclaimed, **CHIEF CONSTABLE'S CAR STOLEN.** Of course from then on every bobby on the beat, every CID guy, every PC plod was on the look-out for the red Jag. The word got out amongst the cops- find the chief constable's Jag and get a promotion.

Another thief, who was in custody for numerous vehicle thefts, gave police the information they were looking for. He grassed Roger up to escape an 18 month sentence. Both Roger and Malky got caught red-handed cruising in the Jaguar through Maryhill towards the Pakistani man's shop. Roger ended up doing two years. Malky got off because of his young age and the two police officers who arrested them got promotions. The message was – don't fuck with the chief constable, and don't ever fuck with his red Jaguar.

Meanwhile, back in the present, Johnny met up with Malky and Chris in the Dixon Blazes bar in Caledonia Road. The place was empty. It was clear Malky was excited to be a part time recruit of the IRA. Chris, who was from an Irish background, was more sceptical. But after a few pints went down his throat, he seemed to go through a metamorphosis.

They all shook hands on the matter and just when they thought it was all sealed without any hassle, wee Alex turned up. He was told briefly about the plan and began to shout, "Ah want tae come, ah wan tae come, ah'm in." But they made it clear he was not needed.

Besides, the last thing they required was a complete and utter nutcase sitting on a pile of guns. They would have all ended up in jail or in an asylum. "Nah," Johnny said, "Ah've got enough handers at the moment Alex. Besides, there is only room for two passengers in the van, so maybe next time,"

Alex looked disappointed, "OK then, but if ye change your mind, let me know and I'll be there in a jiffy."

"Sure you will, Alex, sure you will," Johnny said while patting Alex on the back. He looked like a social worker patting a spastic on the back before putting him on a bus for children with special needs. Saturday night came and the boys stood in South Portland Street waiting for the van to arrive. It was freezing cold and they waited and waited until their teeth chattered.

"Ach, ah don't think those IRA tubes are gonnae turn up. Let's fuck off, it's freezing," Chris said clapping his hands together to keep warm.

Malky agreed, "Johnny, they'll no' be turning up now, something must have gone wrong. It's well past midnight." Just as he said this, a large white van appeared and drew up beside them. John was at the wheel. He got out of the van and handed Johnny the keys who promptly handed them to Malky.

The Irishman took them to the back of the van, opened the doors and it was loaded with crates. They had stickers on them saying: ELECTRICAL PARTS. DO NOT OPEN AS COLD AIR WILL DAMAGE CIRCUITS.

John told the boys that as a decoy the first two large crates did indeed have electrical parts but the crates stored behind had guns, rifles and some hand grenades.

"Right boys" said the Irishman, "Keep to the story. If you are stopped by the police, tell them you are delivering electrical components to a factory near Portpatrick." He handed Johnny a small loaded revolver, "And if any polis fucker tries to arrest you, shoot the bastard and make a quick getaway."

Johnny was nervous and put the revolver is his coat pocket, as the Irishman walked away through the darkness, leaving them to their own devices. "Good luck boys," he shouted in his thick Irish brogue.

Johnny, Chris and Malky went into the van. Johnny looked at the gun,"For fuck's sake, ah've carried razors, knives and even a sword but never a gun."

Malky laughed, "Shut up, ya big girls' blouse, you're in the IRA now. When in Rome, do as the Roman's do." Chris quipped, "More like when in Scotland do as the IRA do."

They all burst into uproarious laugher as they drove through the night towards Portpatrick. It was a beautiful evening and the stars glistened like diamonds in the sky. Johnny felt less nervous when he hid the revolver under the passenger seat. Malky decided to drive the van fairly slowly through the back roads, so the journey of 100 miles would take about three hours. This way they would not attract the attention of the police.

Through the night everything went well until they were about 20 miles from their destination when they saw a blue flashing light behind them.

"Fuck's sake, it's a panda car, we're all done for now, "Chris said in a nervous voice. Johnny was calmer but had beads of sweat on his forehead, "Shut up Chris, keep the head. Right Malky, you give the polis the patter, you're the fucking motoring expert."

They stopped the van and the panda car stopped behind them. A big policeman looked through the van's open window at Malky and his passengers, he said, "Evening sir." Malky was quick to reply, "Evening constable. Can we help you by any chance?"

The constable shone his torch into Malky's face, "Can you tell me what you have in your van?" "Certainly constable," Malky replied in what sounded like a posh Glaswegian voice, "We are delivering electrical components to a factory near Portpatrick."

The constable replied, "Oh aye, do ye mind if you show me your load?" "Certainly officer," Malky replied as he got out of the van. He opened up the back door and the policeman shone his torch inside. Johnny fingered the gun which he now had in his coat pocket. He would shoot the polis bastard if needs be. No way was he doing 20 years for this, even if it was for the IRA.

After looking at the crates with his torch, the policeman said, "That looks fine to me. Can I now look at your driving licence, sir?"

Malky replied with a smile, "Certainly officer, no problem." He produced a driving licence from his pocket that said, 'George McKinley.' The officer studied it for a few seconds. Johnny fingered the gun. The policeman said, "That looks fine to me Mr McKinley. Sorry to have bothered you, but recently, there have been a lot of break-ins to farmhouses near here. I hope you understand that there are thieves and rogues everywhere at this time of night."

Malky nodded in agreement, "I know what you mean, officer, you can never be too careful. There are lots of dodgy characters about. Thank goodness for policemen like you." The policeman enjoyed the compliment and got into his panda car then made off through the night.

Johnny said, "Fucking hell, Malky, that was a close one. Good job you had the patter and the stolen licence"

"Aye, otherwise we would have been well done for, "Chris said with a sigh of relief. Johnny agreed and waved the revolver, "Ah was ready tae shoot the bastard... he's a lucky man!"

The journey continued with Malky looking nonchalant at the wheel, "The trouble wi' you guys is you're too nervous. Take it easy."

When they arrived at Portpatrick harbourside there was not a soul around and then, suddenly, two men approached the van. Johnny recognised them immediately, they were the Irish fellows he had spotted in the large car a few days before in Thistle Street. He handed one of them the revolver and instantly felt relieved. The two IRA guys carried the crates of guns to another vehicle before driving slowly away. Not much was said but the ruddy-faced driver gave Johnny the thumbs up sign which he had done in the Gorbals. Johnny did the same and added the familiar wink.

As they were heading back to Glasgow, Chris said, "Ah'll tell you what, that was better than being at the pictures. Fucking unbelievable."

"Too right Chris," Malky said, "When you work for the IRA it's just like being in a movie and we're the stars!"

Johnny was pensive for a few moments, then replied, "Aye, like stars, in a fucking gangster movie!"

Chapter 30

TONY CURTIS

Johnny, once again, had terrible dreams. The big machines were chasing him and the faster they ran the slower his progress seemed to be. They caught him, almost crushed him. But he woke up in the nick of time, drenched in sweat. It was around 4am, the Gorbals was quiet but there were some sounds of rats fighting and a dog barking continuously. He hated the fucking barking! He had a good mind to get dressed find out who the owner was, and kick the fuck out of him. He smirked briefly thinking that the Gorbals was full of mad people with mad dogs. He then fell soundly back to sleep and this time the machines had gone, only to be replaced by Cathy with flowers in her hair standing in the Glasgow Green saying, "I love you" over and over again.

When Johnny did get up just after eight, he went as usual for a wash and a shave in the kitchen sink and looked at the world coming and going in Crown Street. Much to his surprise, something very interesting caught his eye. Passing by Thomson's furniture shop, across the road he spied McCoy, fully recovered, with his father, accompanied by two men. One was short, fat and bald with a slight moustache, perhaps in his late 30s. The other was a tall, athletic-looking fellow, in his 40s, who could have passed for an ex-boxer.

The important thing was, as Johnny shaved, he saw them but they did not see him. Forewarned is forearmed. What the fuck was McCoy and his dad up to? Who were these two guys they were with? He had no doubt they were all part of a team planning to exact revenge on him.

He felt a shiver go down his spine, but it was not a shiver of fear. It was a shiver of apprehension. He was confident he could set about these four guys on his tod but if he needed reinforcements, they were on hand. He got dressed quickly and put on his new dark blue Arthur Black shirt. He looked in the mirror and combed his thick black hair, murmuring to himself, "Looking good Johnny boy, but you need a haircut." He went into a chest of drawers and pulled out a hammer which he tucked into his waistband. "Just in case," he thought. If they were going to attack him now, they were going to get beaten into a pulp.

He came out of the close into Crown Street but there was nothing to be afraid of, just the usual mob of faces, old men standing at the bank corner, families out for their messages. He went into Felix the barbers in Rutherglen Road and the place was empty. Felix looked pleased to see him, "How ya doin', young fella. Same as usual?"

"Aye" Johnny replied, "Same as usual – a Tony Curtis." Over the years, the haircut had become popular with gang leaders. The haircut gave Johnny a style that separated him from the other Cumbie gang members. "So, Johnny what have you been up tae?" Felix said while cutting his hair. "Ach a bit of this and a bit of that, ye know. If ah told ye, ah'd have to kill you!" Johnny replied in a humorous tone.

Felix laughed, "Ye cannae kill me ah'm the best barber in the Gorbals!" Johnny laughed, "Too true, Felix, you're safe for the time being, until a better barber appears on the scene. But gi' me any more of your cheeky patter and I'll have tae give you a short back and insides!"

The banter continued until the Tony Curtis haircut was complete. Johnny looked in the mirror, "Good job as always, Felix." The barber blushed with pride, the leader of Glasgow's toughest gang was wearing one of his haircuts. Now that was an accolade!

Johnny felt more gallus than usual, the haircut had given him some kind of power. Some kind of charisma that he had been lacking in recent weeks. But he was careful- he scanned Crown Street for any hint of the McCoy mob, but no sign. But he did see 'Mick the mixer' standing outside a shop in Rutherglen road. He had known Mick from the age of five but even after all these years he still did not trust him. Nice enough guy to your face but he was two faced. He was always stirring things up between the boys at school. He would go up to one boy and say, "So and so has been saying something about you." He would then go up to another boy and say the same thing. Result? A square go between the boys resulting in much bloodshed.

But he did go too far on one occasion – one boy was stabbed after Mick told the assailant that another boy had called his mother "an auld cow," in other words a prostitute. There was an investigation at the school and Mick the mixer was promptly expelled. But even after that, his mixing ways continued, causing fights between men (and even women) in bars and dancehalls. But Johnny knew the score, Mick might have been an excellent mixer but he was also an excellent source of information about what was happening on the street. Mick was a short fellow, 5'2", with thick, sandy hair and a slight stammer.

As Johnny approached him, Mick looked slightly edgy. "How, how…how's it gaun Johnny?" Johnny could tell that Mick was slightly afraid of him, probably because he had once beaten him up after he had tried to mix it up in the playground. From that day on, Mick had behaved himself with Johnny. No more stirring it up in his direction.

"No' bad, Mick, what's the Hampden roar, man?"

Mick looked even more edgy. He was aware that Johnny would have no hesitation in punching or even slashing him, if he stirred things up. "Eh well a wee bird tells me you should watch out for yourself."

"Oh aye," Johnny replied, "Just what else did the wee bird tell you?"

Mick's face reddened, "Ah would watch out for McCoy and his cronies. Ah...ah...hear they're out tae get you, four of them."

Having seen the four guys, Johnny instinctively knew that Mick, this time, was not mixing it up but telling the truth.

"So, what else did ye hear Mick?" Johnny said in a tone that was slightly menacing.

"Well, turns oot that McCoy's cousin, a wee guy called Jimmy, is just oot o' jail and he's a bit of a chib merchant. He's telling everybody he's gonnae get you." Mick described Jimmy in detail so he would know him when he saw him. The description matched the guy he had seen from his kitchen sink window.

"Anything else?" Johnny said. Mick thought for a moment, tried not to stammer too much and replied, "The McCoy mob have been mouthing off that they're gonnae throw acid in your face or even burn your house down."

Johnny smirked, "Aye, fucking acid drops, sweeties. It's a joke, Mick, in fact those cardboard gangsters are a joke. You tell them fae me, ah'm ready willing and able tae go ahead!"

"Will…will do John…Johnny," Mick replied shaking his hand.

Johnny walked away feeling angry but glad that Mick had spilled the beans. He felt the hammer in his waistband, he was so angry he was willing to launch an attack on these guys straight away.

He walked to Gorbals Cross, along Gorbals Street and then turned into Cleland Street. His luck was in.

Standing outside the Asian corner shop was Jimmy from the McCoy gang. He looked unperturbed at the sight of Johnny. For although he had heard a lot about Johnny, Jimmy had never seen him in person.

Johnny walked straight up to him, "Are you Jimmy?"

Jimmy gave a quizzical look, "Aye, who's asking?"

"Ah'm fucking asking, Johnny McGrath."

Jimmy showed no fear, took a draw of his cigarette and replied, "Don't know what you're talking about pal. Ah don't know ye, never heard of ye, so get tae fuck"

Johnny pulled the hammer out of his trousers and hit him full force on the head. The blow made Jimmy turn in a circular motion before he fell to the pavement. There was blood gushing from his head.

Johnny walked into the shop and said to the Asian man behind the counter, "Better call an ambulance some poor fella has just been attacked outside."

He walked off towards Crown Street as a crowd gathered round a stricken and bloodied Jimmy.

When he got back to the house, he admired his haircut in the mirror. Felix had done a wonderful job. "One down, three to go," he mumbled to himself, trying to mimic Tony Curtis in The Boston Strangler.

Chapter 31

RATS

Things were quiet for a few days. Johnny expected some kind of comeback from the McCoy mob, but nothing. A small story did appear in the Evening Times though:

"A 37-year-old man was hit on the head with hammer in the Gorbals area of Glasgow, while trying to fend off two muggers."

Johnny was amused. Where the fuck did the two muggers bit come from? He had battered Jimmy on the nut, maybe it had knocked the sense out of him. Or maybe, as he suspected, Jimmy had told the police, while lying in his hospital bed, he had been mugged to cover his tracks. It was the old Gorbals adage, tell the polis nothing and if you did, tell them lies.

Johnny had made his mind up, he must attack the other three guys as soon as possible. Attack after all, is the best form of defence. He had a meeting with Malky, Alex and Chris in the Turf bar. But the consensus was that after the attack McCoy and his cohorts were nowhere to be seen. It was as if they had disappeared into thin air. Malky summed it up, "Those bastards are fly. They'll hide until they decide to make their move. You mark my words, so keep your wits about you Johnny," Chris more or less uttered the same message, "From now on you'll have to have eyes in the back of your head to deal wi' that bunch of sneaky bastards."

Alex agreed, "You'll have to have the eyes of a shitehouse rat when dealing wi' those no users. But no' to worry, you've got us behind you all the way."

The conversation cheered Johnny up but he had an inkling in his mind that it was too quiet, with no immediate comebacks. The McCoy mob must be planning a big revenge mission against him and waiting for the right time to strike. The atmosphere was similar to the ambushes he had experienced in the gang attacks.

He did not know where McCoy and his father lived but he heard from one source that they were now staying with relatives, in the Calton area. This was real Tong gang country, there is no way they could go on a search there, they would be outnumbered and mollicated by the Tongs. It would be a bit like a cowboy going into Indian country. The best thing to do was to wait and see what happened. Malky agreed, "Do nothing. Let them make the first move. They're bound to slip up and when they do, we'll give them a lesson they'll never forget."

Johnny nodded in agreement, "You're right Malky, it is a waiting game but how long have we got to wait?" Alex was quick off the mark, "Those guys are cowards. I'll tell you what, you'll wait so long you'll have forgotten what you were waiting for."

They parted in high spirits but when Johnny walked towards Crown Street he felt apprehensive that he could be attacked at any moment. He touched the hammer in his trouser waistband and for a few moments it gave him a modicum of comfort. Suddenly he saw around a dozen young guys coming towards him, they were all members of the gang's junior division, the Tiny Cumbie. Their leader, Goo Goo, shouted, "Ok, Johnny? We hear you having trouble wi' a few cardboard gangsters. If ye need any help we're here for you."

Like Johnny, Goo, a boy of around 15, was well dressed and had handsome features. He was undoubtedly a rising star in the gang structure and had been tipped to take over the leadership of the YYC when the time was right, after Johnny moved on to fresher pastures. Perhaps when he got a proper job, got married, had kids and settled down. Goo was the future… but not yet.

For the foreseeable future Johnny was the undisputed leader, the guy they all looked up to.

"Thanks, boys," Johnny said, "Nice to know ah've got friends in high places. Or should I say low places?" They all laughed as Johnny moved off. When he entered the close he looked back and was sure he saw one of the McCoy's appear across the road, but it was all in the blink of an eye. He turned back and looked up Crown Street, just drunks staggering by, no sign of the McCoy mob. He was aware that the McCoy gang were basically cowards but even experienced cowards can do you more harm than brave bastards. As an example, he thought of the razor potato in his back.

He also thought cowards were like backcourt rats. Skulking about the place in darkness, waiting to pounce on their prey. Sure, a coward had almost killed him with a razor potato and then ran off, just like a rat. That's what cowards did. They would not face you man to man. They were people who hid behind lies and deceit. Rats to the core!

When he got back to the house he was surprised to see his father there. He had a glass of red wine in his hand with a bottle of Eldorado wine and cans of Tennent's lager on the kitchen table. His mother and brother were also there sitting opposite the coal fire.

"Come away in Johnny and have a drink," his father shouted. Johnny replied, "No problem da, but what are you doing home? Ah thought you were away on a long cruise." His father poured Johnny a large glass of Eldorado and handed him a can of lager.

Johnny's brother had a small glass of Irn Bru and his mother a small glass of wine, they did not look happy. Johnny could tell something was up. The atmosphere was very subdued.

"Engine trouble, Johnny, bloody engine trouble. The ship has to have a new engine fitted and we've all been laid off until the problem is sorted out," his father said. But he could read his father like a book and could tell when he was being economical with the truth. The look on his mother's face said it all, she barely smiled during the homecoming celebration.

"So how long are ye here for, da?" Johnny asked sipping his Eldorado.

"As long as it bloody well takes. Ah'm fed up wi' the boats anyway. Being away fae ma family for so long has been doing ma nut in. So how you been doing? Ah heard you had a wee injury recently, your maw was telling me." Johnny shrugged his shoulders, "Ach, it was nothing, ah'm fighting fit now."

His father laughed, "Aye, fit for fuck all!"

More drink was poured and the atmosphere seemed to improve considerably. Johnny's father looked at Joseph, "So how's it going at your posh school, wee man?" Joseph took a sip of his Irn Bru, "No' bad, da, ah'm learning a lot, subjects like History, English, Maths and even Latin."

His father spat out some wine with laughter, "Latin? What good is that? Are ye gonnae get a job as a Roman centurion when you leave school?"

The boy did not look amused. He gave his father the sort of stern look a teacher gives a naughty pupil. "Nah, Latin is great. It helps you understand the English language better."

"Like what?"

"Well, take, for example, on the side of every Glasgow polis car it says, semper vigilo. You know what that means?"

"No"

"It means "always watching". And that's what they are doing, always watching people like Johnny and his gang pals!"

For a few moments his father looked impressed, "It sounds better than the crap schools me and your brother went to." Johnny and his mother gave weak smiles because they knew he was speaking the truth. Many a true word is spoken in jest.

"Ma da's right," Johnny said, "The only thing we learnt at school was to fight and duck and dive. They call that an education, some people would call it torture!"

Suddenly there was loud banging on the door. 12 o'clock at night and someone was knocking on the fucking door. Johnny leapt from his chair, "Who the hell can that be at this time of night?" He had a hammer in his hand. It must be McCoy and his gang. Now was the time of reckoning. "Who is it?" Johnny shouted. No answer. He raised his voice higher, "Who the fuck is it?"

Suddenly he heard a woman's weak voice say, "Lorraine. It's Lorraine, Johnny."

Still clutching the hammer in his hand firmly, in case it was an ambush, he opened the door. Lorraine was standing there, unsteady on her feet. She looked as though she had been crying and her breath smelt heavily of alcohol.

Johnny shouted back into the house, "It's awright, it's for me." He closed the front door behind him and said to Lorraine, "What the fuck are you doing knocking at my door at this time of night?"

She shivered and muttered, "Johnny ah don't care about the time, ah had tae talk tae ye."

"About what?"

"Remember that night at the Railway Club?"

"Aye"

"Well....."

"Well what?"

"Well, ah'm pregnant.

This was more painful than having a razor blade stuck in his back.

"How da ye know it's mine"

"You're the only man ah've been wi'."

It was a difficult situation. He decided to walk Lorraine back to her house a few blocks away in Florence Street. As they walked through the cold Gorbals streets he looked at her, she was young and beautiful. Any man would give his right arm to have her as a wife.

She looked at Johnny pensively, "So, what are we gonnae do Johnny?"

"Do about what?"

"About the baby."

He felt confused, it was a big question for a big situation, "Listen, doll, this has come as a shock. Right out of the blue. I'll have to think up a battle plan."

"Battle plan, what dae ye mean? You have to marry me Johnny McGrath, then we'll aw live happy ever after. You, me and the baby. Ah'll be a good wife and mother, ah promise." Johnny led her to her close and kissed her on the cheek, "Look, Lorraine, you've just sprouted this on me. Let me think about it and ah'll get back to you." She pleaded with him, "Soon Johnny, sooner rather than later, for the baby's sake." He walked through the darkness just thinking that a future with Lorraine would be far darker.

Chapter 32

PISH

Johnny mulled over his problems for a couple of days. What the hell was he going to do about the Lorraine and baby situation? How was he going to deal with the McCoy vengeance squad? Also, his father had turned up, out of the blue, with some cock-and-bull story about his cruise ship having engine trouble.

He realised he was surrounded by lies and deceit. It was just past 8pm and he was walking down his tenement stairs, armed as usual with his hammer tucked into the waist of his trousers. How he loved his hammer! At times it had been a life saver getting him out of scrapes that could have left him a defeated man if he had not resorted to using it quickly and effectively. As he neared the ground floor he could hear the sound of men's voices and the sound of heavy urination.

Sure enough, two drunk men were pishing up his close. Johnny shouted to them, "Hey boys don't pish up ma close, use the back court. Some poor wee woman has got tae clean aw your pish up."

One of them, a fat scruffy looking man in his 50s, zipped his fly up and said, "Sorry about that pal, we were bursting and when you've got tae go, you've got tae go!" Johnny replied instantly, "Ah know but dae me a favour, pish somewhere else in the future." The other man, in his 40s, wearing a pair of thick-rimmed glasses, was far more intoxicated than his friend. He sort of staggered towards Johnny shouting, "We'll pish where we want, ok?" Johnny pulled out his hammer, "Well if ah see ye here again, you're gonnae get this." The fat guy was taken aback. There was no way having a pish was worth having a hammer over the head. He pulled his partner in crime away shouting, "Come on, Bobby, let's get to fuck oot o' here." But Bobby was far gamer, far drunker than his friend.

"Ah'll go when ah'm ready, no' when ah'm told tae. That hammer disnae frighten me a bit, ah used tae be in the army you know."

"Aye, the fucking Salvation Army," Johnny retorted. At first he had thought of giving the two men a quick doing but there was something in their brave demeanour he liked. Two middle age men still as game as fuck! He always admired old guys who were still game. He just wished that he would be like that when he eventually submerged into middle age. Nevertheless he raised his hammer and said, "Ok boys, are you going or what? Or dae ye want me tae knock the fucking daylights out of you?"

The fat guy sobered up, saying to his pal, "For fuck's sake, Bobby, ah don't think he's bluffing." They made off into the street with Bobby shouting, "He disnae scare me, ah fought tougher men when ah was in the Highlanders." It was a brief interaction, but Johnny believed they had got the message, they would not be pishing up his close again. To use a pun, he was glad they had pissed off.

Out in Crown Street, he glanced up and down. There was the odd drunk staggering about and a few of the Cumbie gang members were having a bit of banter just up the street. Two dogs were humping outside the George Cinema. A woman from a nearby tenement came out with a bowl of cold water and threw it over the mongrels shouting, "Get away tae fuck ya dirty beasts." Johnny laughed to himself, just thinking if the same wee woman had thrown a bucket of water over him and Lorraine at the back of the Railway club, he would not be in the bother he was facing.

Suddenly he saw his father approaching, perfectly sober and perfectly dressed as usual, "Hey, come on son, let's a have a quick pint," he shouted. They headed into the nearby Wheatsheaf pub.

They sat down in the corner with their pints, "Johnny boy, ah've got a wee confession tae make," his father said, "Ye might have guessed ah hivnae really told you the real story why ah'm not working on the boats."

Johnny replied, "Ah could tell straight away you were telling porky pies. So, what's the score man? The real story?" His father looked nervous as he sipped his pint, "Well, to tell ye the truth, ah got the tin-tac, the sack."

"What for?"

"For fiddling"

"But you always had a wee fiddle on the go, what happened this time?"

"Ah got careless. Ah was supposed to put ma tips into a box like everyone else so that they could be shared out at the end of the cruise, but ah was just pocketing ma own tips."

"But you've been doing that for years."

"Too true, but a new restaurant manager took over, a right bastard, an Italian. It was him that fired me when he found out about ma tip scam."

"So, what's your next move?"

"Ah've been up tae the Bromielaw, trying tae find a new boat. Ah went tae the seaman's union office and the union guy there says he's gonnae try tae get me reinstated, saying the tip fiasco was a misunderstanding."

"So, what next?"

"It's a waiting game. The union guy says around two months and then it might be sorted. Meanwhile, ah'll try for part time waiting work in a restaurant up the toon. What about you? Still got money fae your wee pools win?"

"Aye, but it's running down now, ah had a couple o' scams on the go and it built up ma nest egg but it'll no' last forever. Maybe like you, ah'll give it a couple of months and start looking for work."

"It's hard work, looking for hard work!" his father joked.

"Ah've got a confession as well," Johnny said.

"Oh aye, what's that?"

"Got a wee bird pregnant after a drunken shag."

"So, what are ye gonnae dae about it?"

"Nothing at the moment, nothing at all but, like you, ah'll make a decision when the time is right"

"Bloody hell Johnny, it's all happening. Ah came in intae this pub as a father and ah'm leaving it as grandfather. They say a week is a long time in politics, well an hour is a long time in the Gorbals!"

They both left the pub in better spirits than when they entered. His father headed home and he went for a saunter towards Gorbals Cross. He was obviously on the look-out for McCoy and any of his vengeance squad. But it was comparatively quiet. Crowds of old ladies were coming out of the Palace bingo hall. Some of them looked elated and were shouting, "Wee Maggie's won the snowball, 550 quid!" Winner Maggie appeared clutching a fistful of fivers and she and her pals jumped into a taxi, presumably to party all night and toast the magic of bingo.

This bingo business! Many middle-aged women lived for it. They travelled from all over Glasgow for a night out at the Palace bingo hall. Ironically, a few yards away was the Citizen's Theatre where middle class women, and their partners, went to see high-brow productions.

Johnny often watched the crowds at night with the posh avant-garde women on their way to the theatre mingling with the working class women, some in curlers, on their way to the bingo. It was debateable who had the best night out, the snooty teachers who went to see productions such as A Lily in Little India, or the working class cleaners who enjoyed responding to shouts like, "Two fat ladies, 88" or "Clickety click, 66." He thought that they should all swap places for one night only. Would the posh ladies enjoy themselves at the bingo? Would the working class women not equally enjoy themselves going to see a play? The jury was out on that one.

As he looked at the crowd of women coming out of the bingo he heard one of them shout, "Johnny! Johnny!" It was Cathy's mother. She certainly looked better than when he last saw her. She said, "Cathy's been looking for you. She's been around your usual haunts but no sign of you. Where have you been?"

He smiled, "Ah got injured in a fight. But everything is hunky dory now. Tell her to meet me in Lombardi's' café about two tomorrow, and we'll have a laugh, and an ice cream."

Cathy's mother nodded and looked pleased. It was clear the news meant more to her than any bingo win. "Ok son. She's got a lot to tell ye."

"Well ah hope it's aw good news!"

She smiled weakly and said mysteriously, "Ah'm sure it is son, for both of you." She made off through the crowds. It was then he saw three men. But because of the bingo and theatre crowds they did not see him – it was McCoy, his father and another fellow. He felt the hammer in his waistband and moved through the hordes.

He was ready to launch a major attack on the three men. But two beat Bobbies appeared outside the Citizen's Theatre. Then another two appeared. He surmised that there was increased police presence because there had been a number of break- ins of cars belonging to the posh theatregoers. This had been the perfect time to strike and end the matter once and for all. He was confident that he could take the McCoy gang easily. But now, he was scuppered by the polis. The police were like buses, you didn't see one for a while then loads of them turned up at one time. The McCoy gang made off when they saw the police. Johnny was frustrated, he had to let them go. Bastards! Inadvertently the constabulary had saved their skins.

Later, he lay in bed reflecting on the day. He had enjoyed meeting his father, enjoyed seeing the wee woman after her bingo win, and enjoyed meeting Cathy's mother. On further reflection, he had enjoyed not having to set about the McCoy gang. But the last thought slightly disturbed him. Was he getting soft? There was no room for softness in the Gorbals, unless you were a couch.

Chapter 33

ICE CREAM

Johnny sat in Lombardi's café at 2pm. He liked being punctual and he remembered what a teacher had told him at school – punctuality is the prerogative of kings. So King Johnny sat there and waited for Cathy. He drank his tea slowly and observed the Italian men behind the counter. He admired their work ethic. They opened the cafe in the early morning and closed late at night. They also had the best ice cream he had ever tasted. He found their accents comical, a mixture of Italian and Glaswegian which made them sound like Stanley Baxter in the TV comedy programme Parliamo Glasgow.

When he entered the café one of the Italians announced, "Mama mia! It's the Johnny boy fella, bene'." Cathy was late, half an hour had gone and still no sign of her. He was about to give up when suddenly she rushed through the door. My god, she looked more beautiful than ever. Flaming red hair and glossy red lips. She was also wearing a dark dress that accentuated her voluptuous figure. She sat down opposite Johnny, kissed him on the cheek and said, "Where the fuck have you been? Ah've been all over the place looking for you. Ah was gonnae call to your house but ah decided to wait until ah bumped intae you."

He was taken aback by her beauty and her foul mouth only made her more attractive. Sure, she was a gangster's daughter, a cut-above Lorraine whose father was a porter at Glasgow's fish market, "You look like a star," Johnny said. "Aye," she replied, "I am a big star it's just that the picture got smaller. So, where have you been hiding Johnny?"

"I got injured in a gang fight, blade in the back. But ah'm all right now."

She looked furious, "Gang fight? Blade in the back? It's time you grew up. You're in your 20s, not fucking 12. It's time you started acting like a man, a real man."

No-one had ever talked to him like that, not even his mother and father. In a way it turned him on, he felt like a scolded schoolboy as she continued her tirade, "I'll get straight tae the point… no messing… ah'm pregnant with your baby."

For a few moments he was lost for words. "That night we spent together was different, Johnny. We did not shag, we made love. If you don't want the baby ah'll go tae Manchester or London and have an abortion. Ah'll get rid of it, no bother."

He was lost for words but suddenly said, "Let's have some ice cream and we'll talk about it." He ordered two ice cream snowballs and when the plates were placed on the table, Cathy mellowed a bit but she was still as hard as nails.

"Mmm, nice" she said putting the ice cream into her mouth. "Plenty of men are after me, so really ah don't have tae bother wi' a no hoper like you." When she got angry he noticed that her cheeks got redder and redder and her blue eyes flowed with intensity, making her look even more beautiful.

He had never seen a woman look so fiery and beautiful at the same time. Lorraine, by contrast, was a pale imitation of the real thing. Cathy continued, "Forget about this love shite, stand up and do your duty like a man. Instead of running about like a numpty with all those other idiots."

He was not offended because he realised that she was talking to him like a wife. "So, Cathy what do you want me to do?" he said in a voice that sounded rather timid for him.

"Either you marry me or you can get tae fuck. If you don't ah'll get rid of it and find another bloke. Someone who acts like a man. No' a stupid wee boy who runs about the streets beating people up."

For the first time in his life he felt afraid. Was this the time he at last grew up? Became a grown man at last?

"So, what's the next move?" he said meekly.

She thought for a moment, put the last spoonful of ice cream in her mouth and replied, "We're gonnae get married and have a big reception paid for by you. If no', get tae fuck."

She then continued with her ultimatum, "You've got 24 hours to make your mind up. I want a ring, no' a wee cheap crappy one, but big and sparkling wi' diamonds. So get your cash out."

He was flabbergasted but realised it was a key moment in his life, a moment he would never forget until his dying day.

Cathy knew she had got the better of Johnny. She knew how to deal with the so called Gorbals hardmen. Her father was one, and she had learned how to play her dad like a violin from an early age.

"Ma mother knows ah'm up the stick. Ah told her last week. She thinks you're a nice boy, if only she knew the truth. A nice boy who goes about chibbing people! If she knew the real truth about you, she'd tell me tae drop you like a hot potato."

He tried to diffuse the situation, "So, how is your mother? She looked a lot better when ah saw her outside the bingo last night."

"She's a lot better now that she knows ma father is coming back after hiding in Ireland."

Johnny gulped, "What, your father is coming back fae Ireland? When?"

"In the next couple of weeks"

"How do ye know?"

She fetched a piece of paper from her handbag and put it on the table in front of him. It was a telegram – "Everything is fine. Will be back soon. Dad." She smiled," So that's good news is it no' Johnny? When he gets back we'll tell him about the pregnancy and getting married. He's been through a rough time recently and the news will put him on top of the world - if you grow up and play the game."

She got up, kissed him on the cheek, and left as quickly as she had come. Before she left, she said, "Remember, you've got 24 hours to man up. If no', you are toast." He felt a shiver go down his spine. The Irish fellow who had sent the first telegram must have sent another to cheer the family up and given them even more false hope. What a dilemma! What a pickle he had found himself in.

He rose from the table slightly shaking and the Italian guy behind the counter said to him. "Wow, what a bird. Bellisimo!"

"Too right, Giovanni," Johnny replied, "But she's got a fiery temper, a bit hard going at times."

Giovanni laughed, "Johnny boy, that woman is so good looking any fella in his right mind would put up with her fiery temper."

"I know that," Johnny replied, nodding his head in agreement, "She even puts the wind up me and ah'm supposed tae be scared of nobody."

The Italian agreed and gave him some advice, "Listen, young fella, beauty has a price. All beautiful women are like that, they are works of art. They're no like all those old dogs who put up wi' any shite."

Johnny laughed, "Ah suppose you're right, Giovanni, there's a price to be paid for everything, even a beautiful work of art like Cathy."

Giovanni smiled and decided to take the mickey, "She needs to go to the opticians. Because ah don't know what she sees in an ugly looking bastard like you!"

Johnny took the ribbing well and shook his hand before leaving. But Giovanni had hit the proverbial nail on the head –what the hell was a beautiful woman like Cathy doing with a hooligan like him? Maybe she was right, it was time to man up, grow up and throw all this insane violent behaviour away for good.

But his mind changed within seconds. Meanwhile, as a last hurrah, he had a few scores to settle with the McCoy gang. But the new telegram news seemed to haunt him. He walked up to the Irish club in Govanhill and looked for the fellow who had sent the first telegram.

The barman said the guy had been in Ireland but expected him in that night. Johnny sat in a corner with his pint and sure enough half an hour later he walked in.

"Welcome back fae Ireland! Let me buy you a pint of Guinness," Johnny sad to him. "So how was the Emerald Isle, is your auntie getting better?

"Aye, she's coming along fine. It means ah'll no' have tae go over so often."

Johnny smiled and nodded his head, "Anyway, ah'd just like to say thanks for sending Cathy and her family that second telegram. Good thinking man."

The Irish fellow looked confused, "What the fuck are ye talking about? What second telegram?"

"The one you sent saying Cathy's father was coming back soon."

"Are you pished? Ah never sent a second telegram."

Johnny was shocked, he spat out some beer from his mouth, "Well who the fuck did then?"

"Hivnae a clue, maybe he's still alive and is hiding in Ireland after all."

Johnny left the club feeling slightly disorientated, but it was not because of the beer. He had two pregnant women to deal with, the imminent return of a missing man who he had presumed dead and the matter of the McCoy vengeance squad. It never rains but it pours.

Life was complicated, far more complicated than he could have ever imagined.

Chapter 34

FLAMES

"Johnny, wake up! Wake up! There's a fire" Joseph was shouting to him as he lay in bed. It was around 5am. He jumped out of bed in his underpants and ran into the lobby. His mother and father were there throwing water over the flames that had set the front door alight.

Also, the fire had spread its way along the lobby but luckily his father had managed to stamp it out. Johnny rushed to the kitchen sink and filled up a bucket of water. He ran back and threw it over the flames. His father and mother were also throwing water over the flames which were still progressing along the lobby. His wee brother Joseph was also stamping out the flames in his school shoes. After about ten minutes the flames were under control and eventually put out.

The front door was dark and charred as was a major section of the lobby. His mother began to cry, "Somebody has tried to burn us to death, look at that." She pointed to a charred burnt rag in the floor. His father picked it up and smelled it, "Fucking petrol, somebody, a headcase, has put this lighted rag through the door."

Johnny full well knew what sort of headcase, an arsonist from the McCoy gang. "Bastards!" he shouted. "Wait till ah get ma hands on them." His mother gave a quizzical look, "Do ye know who did this Johnny?"

He decided to spare her the details, "Nah, ma but ah can find out soon enough, nae bother." His father said, "It's a good job ah'm no' on the boats. Ye would have all been burnt to death. It was me that smelt it first."

Johnny was suffering from some kind of shock. Not in his wildest dreams had he imagined this would happen. It was the same old story, cowards who could not fight a man face to face. The modus operandi, once again, was attack like cowards, run away like rats.

Two beat Bobbies and a couple of CID guys turned up. Of course, the beat Bobbies knew Johnny well or rather his reputation well. One of the constables took Johnny aside and said in a soft voice, "Johnny boy, it looks like your past is catching up with you. Give us a clue who it was and we'll nick them. Simple as that." He was glad of the offer but the unwritten Gorbals rule was never talk to the polis. He would sort out this mess his own way. "Look, officer," he said in an equally soft voice, "They'll regret the day they were ever born"

The policeman grimaced and shrugged his shoulders, "I don't think that's a wise move son. Whoever did this could end up doing at least 10 years in jail. That would be worse than any hammering you might give them."

He nodded his head in agreement but he must have been still in shock because he never agreed with the police, "You might be right officer but let me do things my way."

"Up to you son, but you'll end up doing time, not them."

"Thanks for the advice officer but ah'll take ma chances," Johnny said moving away from the constable. He thought the policeman was only doing his job, an agreeable, caring sort of fellow who he secretly liked. But him being a policeman barred him from any future friendship.

The two CID guys looked at the charred door and floor. One of them examined the petrol smelling burnt rag. He said to the McGrath family, "This is a very serious crime, attempted murder, in fact three attempted murders. A bid to wipe out a whole family. It is often used in Northern Ireland between the Catholics and Protestants. Have you any idea who did this?"

They all shook their heads. Johnny's father replied, "No' got a clue, ah'm away most of the time and I have certainly no' got any enemies who would dae a thing like this?"

Some forensic men arrived and took fingerprints from the parts of the charred door and a lighter that they had found outside on the tenement stairs. The family were advised to seal up the letter box until further notice.

After the police left, Johnny's mother sat in the kitchen crying her eyes out, "Who would want tae burn us tae death? It disnae seem right. I hivnae harmed a soul, ah've got nae enemies."

Johnny's father shouted, "This is a nutcase who did this, a dangerous fucking nutcase. Johnny, you're always getting intae bother wi' the bampots. Who dae you think did this?"

Johnny kept up his pretence of feigning ignorance, "Could have been anybody da, probably somebody that's escaped fae an asylum. There's a lot of nutters roaming the streets of the Gorbals. In fact, there's mare out than there's in."

Wee brother Joseph, who was now dressed in his school blazer looked less worried, "Wait till ah get to school and tell ma pals, they'll never believe ah was almost burnt to death, ah thought ah'd be at least eighty before ah got cremated." He left for school in what appeared to be a happy and excited mood. His mother was still crying, "What are we gonnae dae? We can't keep living like this, we're no' safe."

Her husband consoled her, "Don't worry, everything will be all right. Just make sure that letter box is sealed at all times, especially when we are asleep."

Johnny said nothing, he was still in shock. The McCoy bastards had tried to murder his family. They had to pay.

He had a walk round the Gorbals and rounded up his pals, Malky, Chris and Alex. They sat in a café pontificating on the situation. "Well it looks like those guys don't fuck about, they mean business Johnny," said Malky.

Chris agreed, "McCoy and his gang have made a mistake, a big fucking mistake. It's comeback time."

Alex, as usual, was more extreme, "Ma uncle has a few cans of petrol in his garage. We'll track the McCoy mob doon, pour the petrol over them and set them alight. Human fireballs. That would be a laugh… whoosh!"

Johnny knew Alex's suggestion was honourable but highly impracticable. He emphasised the fact that they had to find out where the McCoy gang were hiding and then strike. Malky said he knew they were still hiding out in the Gallowgate but it would be too dangerous to go there. They came up with a solution. They had to find Mick the mixer again and see if he had any new info on where to find the McCoy mob. Mick was known to go into the Mally Arms around eight every night.

Meanwhile, Johnny and his trusted hammer patrolled the streets of the Gorbals on the look-out for his enemies, but after a few hours, there was no sign.

Just after eight they were sitting at a table in the pub when sure enough Mick the mixer walked in. Johnny bought him a pint and Mick sat down with them. Johnny got straight to the point, "So, what's the score wi' that McCoy wanker? He and his mob tried to set fire tae ma house."

Mick looked unsurprised, "Ah know all about it. That's what they dae, they wait until you think everything has gone quiet, then they strike."

Malky became aggressive, "Tell us something we don't know Mick. How can we find those cowardly bastards?

"It's no', no', no' that simple boys," Mick stuttered, "Ah've heard they are hiding out in a tenement near the Barras. Now that's real Tong country, so ah widnae go near there."

"Anything else?" Johnny said.

"McCoy and his father have brought in a couple of their relatives from Northern Ireland as reinforcements. They were in the UVF, right Orangemen who hate Catholics."

Malky replied, "The UVF, that mob of mad protestant fuckers? I've read about them in the papers."

"Aye, the UVF is like the IRA only for Protestants. All's ah know is one of the guys has a King Billy tattoo on his right hand. But watch out Johnny they are dangerous bastards. Be on your guard from now on."

Johnny was not afraid as he fingered his hidden hammer. "Ah'm no' scared o' those Huns, they'll get sorted out soon enough."

Mick the mixer's information had given them a buck up and he said he would have another word with "the wee bird" to obtain more information.

The boys were in a mercurial mood and as a result, the beer flowed. When the pub closed its door at 10pm they left each other in high spirits, staggering their separate ways.

When Johnny got to his close it was in complete darkness. Suddenly two men ran towards him with large baseball bats and battered into him. Johnny was thrown to the ground as the two guys rained down blows.

For a brief moment, he saw McCoy and his father standing behind them as they continued to batter into him. One of them had a tattoo of King Billy on his hand.

As they battered him even more, Johnny's blood ran all over the tenement stairs and walls. Johnny lost consciousness but as he did so an elderly man came into the close and shouted, "What the fuck is going on here?"

It was one of Johnny's neighbours, 72-year-old Duncan Mackintosh. The men, covered in blood rushed past him out of the tenement into Crown Street. Duncan Mackintosh looked at the bloodied heap that was Johnny. He put his ear to his mouth to see if still breathing.

He was breathing - only just.

Chapter 35

TUNNEL

Johnny was once again dreaming but it seemed he had been dreaming for a long time. He was in a long dark tunnel with no sign of light at the end of it. He marched on through the darkness but the further he marched the darker it seemed to get. How the hell had he landed in this tunnel? A tunnel that seemed to go on forever. After what appeared to be an eternity there was salvation. A little glimmer of light approached him but it was approaching slowly.

At first it was a dull light but as time went on it got brighter and brighter. Was this danger in disguise? Was it a train heading towards him intending to knock him down? The light began to close in on him, getting closer by the minute. Suddenly he heard a soft quiet voice saying, "Johnny, wake up son. Wake up." His eyes opened, the dream had come to an end. No longer was he in a dark tunnel but in a hospital ward. Sitting beside his bed was his mother, father and Cathy. His mother gave a gasp of relief, "Thank god, he's awake." She said, perhaps she had been the light at the end of the tunnel. He heard his father say, "About bloody time as well. Ten days in a coma but now he is back in the land of the living."

Cathy's soft voice joined in, "He's a fighter sure enough. Ah've told him tae forget about aw this gang warfare garbage. But he widnae listen and look what's happened to him." He began to speak slowly, the long dream had affected his senses, "How long have ah been asleep?" His father replied, "Ten bloody day's son, ten days when we did not know whether you were going to live or die."

"It was touch and go son," his mother said. Cathy nodded her head, "You've put us through ten days of torture. It's been the longest ten days of our lives." He felt pain all over his body. He could barely move his right arm and his left leg was as stiff as cardboard. Also when he breathed a searing sensation seemed to overwhelm his ribs.

He did not feel like speaking but did so in the voice of a defeated man. "So ah've been sleeping for ten days? That was some doin' ah had" His father was quick to reply, "Ten days out the game, you're lucky to be alive. If it wisnae for auld Duncan Mackintosh, you'd be propping up the daisies." Johnny was confused. He said in a weak voice, "Auld Duncan Mackintosh! What's he got tae dae wi' it?"

"He saved your life son. Luckily he was in the Army medical core years ago," his mother said. His father smiled and nodded his head, "After those bastards beat you to a pulp it was Duncan who gave you the kiss of life. It was him that saved you from an early grave." Cathy chimed in, "He saved your bacon, got you breathing again before the ambulance arrived."

The pain seared through his body. It was all a bit much to take in. Sure, he was a Gorbals' hardman, a gang leader, and had been saved by the lips of an old age pensioner! A doctor appeared at the bedside. He was a young cheery looking guy in his late 20s, "Good to see you have survived such a savage beating. At one point we thought we had lost you."

Johnny gave a weak smile, "So, doctor, what's the verdict? How badly am I injured?" The doctor looked at a medical chart he was holding, "Broken right arm, broken left leg, severely broken ribs. Whoever did this certainly intended to kill you."

He thought the doctor was stating the obvious and asked him, "How long will it take me to recover?" The doctor sounded optimistic, "At least three months but you must rest as much as you can. The beating has given you serious injuries. But now you are out of a coma they aren't life threatening." The message got through and the atmosphere around the bed seemed more upbeat than before. After the doctor left a nurse told those beside his bed to leave as Johnny needed to rest.

The next day he felt somewhat better when the nurse said, "There's an auld guy called Mackintosh outside asking if it all right to come in and see you?"

He replied through the pain, "Aye, he's all right, send him in."

The young nurse sighed, "Ok, Johnny but only for a few minutes. You have got to have time to regain your strength and recuperate." Duncan Mackintosh approached his bed, "Hey, Johnny boy, glad to see you've survived. At least you've shown those bastards that tried tae kill you that you're a real fighter!" He was clutching a bottle of Lucozade and a bunch of grapes. Duncan sat down beside the bed and they talked quietly so the nurses and other patients could not hear.

"So, what happened then Duncan?" Johnny said. Mackintosh was quick to put him in the picture. "Well ah went oot for a walk around the Gorbals and when ah walked into our close there were four guys beating the hell out of you wi' big clubs. When they saw me shouting they ran off leaving you in a pool of blood. I put ma ear to your mouth and there was barely any breath and you had a faint pulse. Ah gave you the kiss of life and your breathing got better. Man, you had a lucky escape ah can tell ye!"

Johnny shook his hand, "Thanks for saving ma life, man. Did you recognise any of the guys?" Duncan replied, "There was a middle aged guy and a younger fella who I've seen before about the Gorbals, but no' the other two guys."

Johnny presumed he was talking about McCoy and his father, "The other two guys, did anything stand out?" Duncan thought for a moment, "Come tae think aboot it, aye. As the two of them were shouting, they had Irish accents. But ah think they were Northern Ireland accents. Also, ah noticed one of them had a King Billy tattoo on his hand."

The nurse came over and told Duncan his time was up. He rose to leave saying, "Don't worry son, you'll be on the mend soon and be fighting fit before you know it. Fit enough tae sort out those Orange bastards."

Over the next few days his parents and Cathy said the attack had been a warning that he should give up his gangster days. His mother said, "The game's a bogey, no more gang fighting for you. Settle doon and get a job, otherwise you'll end up dead." Johnny's father agreed, "Once you've recovered you'd be better getting the hell oot o' the Gorbals. When ah get ma job back, ah'll try tae get ye on the boats wi' me." Johnny noticed that Cathy said little when his parents were there. His parents presumed she was another of his many girlfriends. They did not know that Cathy was pregnant with his child. And when he recovered, a marriage would be imminent.

After a few more days Cathy visited him alone and had him all to herself. He might have looked a wreck, but the pregnancy had given her a bloom.

"Look ya stupid eejit," she said, "This is a message to you saying your daft gang days are over. Besides, we've got a new baby on the way. It needs a father and mother, no' a widow and a corpse."

He agreed and nodded his head meekly, "You're right Cathy, it is time ah grew up, all this palaver has been a lesson to me." But when the words came out of his mouth, inside he was not entirely convinced that he was ready to give up his hardman ways. He had to tell the mother of his child what she wanted to hear. Afterwards Cathy kissed him on the cheek and left in a consoled mood. But there was only one thing on his mind… retribution.

During his weeks in hospital he had an assortment of visitors. Two CID guys turned up and as he had expected, played the Mr Nice guy, Mr Nasty guy game. They sat beside his bed with Mr Nice guy starting off the conversation, "Look pal, if you tell us who it was that nearly beat you to death, problem over. We'll do them for attempted murder, 10-15 years, and that's the end of them"

Johnny politely refused to co-operate saying the savage beating had given him amnesia. Mr Nasty guy took over with his psychology, "Ya daft bastard, why are you trying to protect those no users? Maybe you've got vengeance on your mind. But if you do, it's you that'll end up doing 15 years, not them. So, it's time to stop being a silly idiot and give us some names, otherwise it's you who'll be in big trouble. That is if you don't get murdered first."

Johnny kept up his pretence saying the amnesia meant he could not recall any of the events leading up to the attack or any of the assailants. They left empty handed, he hoped he would not see them again.

The visitors he was glad to see were the boys. Malky, Chris and Alex all turned up with Lucozade and grapes. Malky put Johnny in the picture, "The word on the street is McCoy, his father and the two Northern Irish bampots are going about boasting how they almost battered you to death and put you in hospital."

294

Chris agreed, "They're supposed to be gloating about it. But we'll sort them out when you are fighting fit and back on the streets."

"Too right," Alex said, "Naebody messes wi' us and gets away wi' it. We'll fucking mollicate them! I've just bought an air pistol- I'm gonnae shoot them!"

After a couple of weeks he could feel that he was on the road to recovery and was now able to walk through the ward, a few steps at a time ona crutches and an arm sling.

The doctor was pleased with his progress, "You're coming along fine, Johnny. Your ribs, arms and leg are coming along well. It's probably because you were in a fit physical condition and your age means you recover faster than most people." After these consoling words he certainly felt ten times better but he got a bit fed up eating all those grapes and drinking all that Lucozade. What he yearned for, once he was discharged, was a big greasy fish supper and a pint of Guinness.

But vengeance was still very much on his mind. It was destined that the McCoys and the two Northern Irish bastards would feel the full force of his wrath.

It was just as he was thinking this the young nurse approached the bed, "There's two men here to see you."

"Who are they?"

She replied, "They did not give their names but they say they're your pals. They sound Irish to me."

He thought the two Northern Irishmen had turned up at the hospital to finish him off. He picked up his crutches and hobbled a few yards from his bed. He glanced down the corridor and what he saw took him aback, it was John, the Irishman from the Portland dancehall and his leader Danny.

The IRA had come to visit him. That was the best get well message he could ever have.

Chapter 36

LUCOZADE

The two Irishmen entered the ward and looked genuinely pleased to see him. He was on the road to recovery but still did not look like the robust virile Johnny of old. The beating seemed to have knocked something out of him but the Irishmen concealed their concerns about him with fast friendly banter. Johnny smiled weakly as they placed a bottle of Lucozade and a bunch of grapes on his bedside cabinet. He felt slightly nauseous looking at the Lucozade and grapes, psychologically to him they had become symbols of failure and ill health.

If he never saw Lucozade or grapes again, it would not perturb him. The big Irishman from the dancehall was first off with the breezy patter, "We hear a few cowardly orange men tried tae dae you in."

"Aye, they attacked me in the close when ah was steaming drunk."

The big Irishman raised his eyebrow, "In a way it serves you right. You should have had your wits about you at all times." Danny joined in, "We often say that things can sometimes get a wee bit dangerous, so dangerous you've got tae sleep wi' your eyes open."

Danny leaned over to speak in Johnny's ear, "We know who did you, Pinky and Perky and the idiot father and son the McCoys."

The big Irishman laughed, "Aye, Pinky and fucking Perky. We've been after those bastards for a while"

"Who the fuck is Pinky and Perky?" Johnny asked.

Danny replied, "They're two no-users from Belfast. They used to be in the UVF but they're on the run here in Glasgow." Johnny was aware of Pinky and Perky from watching TV, two ugly pigs who sang in high pitched voices. In fact, when he was kid he had grown up laughing at their childish antics.

"Why do you call those guys Pinky and Perky?" he asked.

Danny smiled, "Because they look like a couple of ugly swines with squeaky voices. The big fella with the King Billy tattoo, we call Pinky. He's wanted in Northern Ireland for shooting a couple of our guys and blowing up a few others. His mate Perky, a short fat fella, tried tae shoot me while back in Belfast but ah was quick enough tae dodge the bullets."

"Missed you by a couple of inches," the big Irishman nodded.

Danny replied, "We've got an idea where those bastards are hiding out and we have plans in place tae kidnap them."

"And then what?"

Danny replied with a grin, "Then they disappear. Pinky and Perky become the invisible men, or should I say… invisible pigs?"

"What about the McCoys?" Johnny asked.

Danny smiled again, "They beat the living daylight out of you but to be fair they did not shoot or bomb you. So perhaps we might just show them a wee bit of mercy. But it's up to you Johnny. If you want them to disappear with Pinky and Perky, then that can be arranged as well. Your decision."

Johnny contemplated the situation. Sure, he hated the McCoy's but could he really give the go-ahead for a death sentence? Pinky and Perky were a different matter, two members of the UVF, who had murdered IRA men, they had it coming to them. They had also set fire to his house.

"Let me think about it," he said.

The big Irishman and Danny nodded. "No hurry," Danny said, "Wait till we work out a battle plan then we'll be in contact." They got up and began to leave. Danny shouted, "Enjoy the grapes!"

Johnny replied, "Grapes? Ah've had so many ah think ah might be turning intae a grape!"

"Those bastards who we were talking about will be getting grapes as well – the grapes of wrath!" the big Irishman said.

After they left he felt consoled. Consoled not only because the might of the IRA was behind him but because of the fact the act of vengeance was now out of his hands. The two ugly pigs, Pinky and Perky, were consigned to end up in the IRA abattoir. But the

McCoys were a different matter. Would he, like a Roman emperor, give the thumbs up for them to be spared, or the thumbs down to be killed? He had mixed emotions about the matter. He reflected that maybe he had deserved a doing after putting the young McCoy in hospital. Maybe he had gone too far by ridiculing his father. They might just get a thumbs up to show some mercy but they certainly needed to be punished in some way.

As for Pinky and Perky, the IRA had already decided they were thumbs down material. Emperor Nero, a la Danny, had decided they were to be thrown to the Fenian lions.

A wave of tiredness overcame him. He had taken an assortment of pills, all different colours that reminded him of Smarties. He drifted off to sleep for several hours. But then he was awakened by a soft voice, "Johnny it's me. Wake up" He thought it was the voice of Cathy but when he opened his eyes it was Lorraine.

She looked as pretty as ever, and like Cathy, the pregnancy had given her a glow. In fact, it was more than a glow, it was an aura, an aura of love. She was clutching a bunch of grapes and a bottle of Lucozade, par for the course.

She sat beside his bed and held his hand, "Oh Johnny, those bastards could have murdered you. At least you're alive and on the road tae recovery and our wee baby still has a father!"

He was lost for words, there was no way he wanted to be a father to her baby. Cathy was a different matter. He felt that in such situations it was better not to do or say anything that might in anyway cement their relationship, or rather the lack of it. A drunken shag behind the Railway Club had led to this! To placate Lorraine, and appear to seem normal, he put a handful of the hated grapes in his mouth and took a sip of the equally hated Lucozade. "Nice, nice," he pretended.

"So, when dae ye think you'll be getting out of hospital Johnny?" she said with pleading eyes.

"Depends what the doctor says. Those bastards in the close gave me a good doing over, so it's aw taking a bit of time tae heal."

Lorraine grasped his hand tightly. He could clearly see she was madly in love with him. Indeed, they had a love-hate relationship, she loved him but he hated her. She said, "Ah cannae wait for ye tae get better because we've got a lot of planning to do for our baby." The way she stressed "our" sent a shiver down his spine. "So, what sort of planning have ye got in mind, Lorraine?" he said. She clarified the matter, "We've got to get baby clothes, a cot and a pram. And we'll have tae work out where we're gonnae live when we get married." Johnny kept up his pretence of enthusiasm, "You've got it all worked out Lorraine, you're smarter than you look."

"Aye and you're dafter than you look." She laughed like a schoolgirl, thinking she was going to get married. Also she did not know about the Cathy situation and the fact that she was also pregnant with his baby.

He sighed, he had been involved in gang fights, involving dozens of guys that had been far less complicated than being involved with two pregnant women. How was he going to get out of this dreadful mess? Only time and a degree of cunning would tell. It would also involve telling a lot of lies which, in reality, was not a problem.

Lorraine rose to leave. She looked at him and said, "You know ah love you to bits. But do you love me?" At times like this he could be a good actor, "Of course ah do." She kissed him on the cheek and left. Oscar winning performance from the main man. As he was thinking this, Malky appeared by his bedside. He had obviously been drinking. His breath smelt heavily of cheap wine, "Just saw that bird Lorraine leave, a smashing looking bit of stuff. Ah've fancied her for ages. She been in here tae see you?"

It was obvious Malky did not know about his connection with Lorraine and the pregnancy, "Yeah she's nice but no' ma type Malky. Ah think she's more your type. In fact, she told me she quite fancies you. So you're in there man!"

Malky sort of blushed, perhaps it was the wine, "Fancies me? A great looking bird like that. Ah should be so lucky."

"Malky, no' kidding, she's mad about you." Malky rubbed his hands in glee, "Well, we'll have to dae something about that soon, probably when you're back oot and fighting fit." Johnny was secretly pleased his pal had swallowed the bait.

Malky left the ward laughing and felt invigorated that Lorraine rather fancied him. Perhaps they might even get married! Johnny grinned to himself. Sure, he must be getting better, his street cunning had come back. This was after all the human jungle. To survive in the Gorbals he had to be as sly as a fox and as cunning as a wolf.

Chapter 37

CHANGES

When Johnny eventually left hospital he was definitely on the mend. He thought rather jokingly that perhaps the overdose of Lucozade and grapes had worked wonders after all. His injuries had been quick to heal and after no time at all he dispensed with the crutches then progressed onto a walking stick, the kind he used to see pensioners walking about with, in the Gorbals. To some, his injuries only enhanced his reputation. But to others, who were more cynical, his beating had diminished his reputation, with some saying he was not the man he used to be. Some of his up-and-coming rivals could smell weakness but now was not time for a gang leadership takeover.

Johnny was still leader of the Cumbie gang and still highly respected by the majority of its members. But there were up and coming guys like Goo Goo who instinctively knew that when the time was right they would take over. When Johnny came out of hospital, with its grapes and Lucozade hell, he did feel like a changed man. Perhaps he was just getting older. Perhaps the beating had knocked some sense into him. Perhaps becoming a father to two babies had given him some kind of maturity. Perhaps! Perhaps! Perhaps! As he walked through the streets of the Gorbals, he did notice one thing. The streets and their tenements were being knocked down in a dramatic and speedy fashion.

The authorities had decided to kill the Gorbals off once and for all. The publication of No Mean City in 1935 had done the area no favours, bolstering its image as one of the roughest places in Britain. The novel reinforced the images of violence, poverty and drunkenness as an accepted way of life.

The local MP had stood in the House of Commons and lambasted the place, basically saying it would be better to knock the Gorbals down and redevelop the area. But with these plans there was barely any consideration for the destruction of a once great community. The Gorbals in the 1970s was not what it used to be, it was going through a metamorphosis and Johnny felt the same. He had to change with the times. The destruction of hundreds of tenements meant that many of the guys Johnny knew, and had been brought up with, were now making money from numerous scams, including robbing gas meters full of coins in deserted tenement flats, stealing lead from roofs, and even searching down the back of discarded sofas for any notes and coins that may have fallen there.

As he walked through Gorbals Cross he bumped into Goo Goo and other young members of the Cumbie gang. They had been breaking into gas meters in all the empty tenements and were loaded, well loaded with coins. Johnny was invited to join them in Derry Treanor's bar in Gorbals Street. He took up the offer gladly. A pint of Guinness would be a nice change from his Lucozade days. Johnny sat down with Goo Goo and half a dozen of his young comrades. Some of them looked at him in awe, it was like having a star in their presence. He was a man with a fearless reputation, a man who had fought his way over the years to become leader of the gang. It was an incredible story. But an astute young guy like Goo Goo could see the beating had left Johnny a diminished figure. It had made him look older.

Johnny felt a twinge of pain going through his body and felt weak, but he kept up the pretence of being the fearless gang leader, "So what's been happening boys while ah was in hospital?" Goo Goo took a swig of his pint and said, "Ach, the same auld shite, Johnny. We've had a few run-ins wi' the Tongs, the San Toi and the Derry but we've never been beaten.

"Good!" Johnny said lifting his glass, "The Cumbie will never be beaten. Cumbie ya bass!" The other guys raised their pints and shouted in unison, "Cumbie, ya bass!" He looked at the young guys, how virile, how gallus they looked. He had been like this once, as gallus as fuck. These young guys were following in his footsteps and had the same gear on, Arthur Black shirts and Levis. This was the new generation of the gang which Goo Goo would eventually lead.

He looked at Johnny, "Is there anything we can dae for you about those cowards who put you in hospital?" Johnny waved his hand in a dismissive manner, "Nah, its awright ah've got ma own men on it. It's all sorted or should be soon." Goo Goo was impressed, up until then he thought Johnny was a finished man.

Johnny left the young guys in good spirits. It was interesting that Goo Goo had made him such an offer. This would not have happened in the past. Was it because Goo Goo had sensed that he was weaker than before? Or was it just a fact that Goo Goo and the boys were now growing up so fast it was time for older guys like him to move on? Move on to marriage! Move on to having children! Move on to a 9-5 job! He contemplated this as he walked towards the Mally Arms. The future awaited him. They would eventually take over, but not yet. He was still the undisputed leader of the Cumbie gang and no-one would dare argue with that.

He went into the Mally lounge and stuck a few coins into the juke box. He laughed when he saw listed Pinky and Perky singing "When The Saints Go Marching In" of course it was a speeded up version with squeaky voices.

He wondered whether the IRA had caught up with the Belfast Pinky and Perky and whether they were being tortured at this very moment. He sat down with his pint and pondered his next move. His leg was strengthening and in a few days would throw away the stick. It was making him look too weak. He had a few weeks to play with and during that time Pinky and Perky, the McCoys, and the Lorraine problem would all be sorted, or so he thought. He thought of them as hurdles that he needed to overcome. Like a horse at the Grand National jumping over hurdles at Aintree. As he was thinking this, a man in his late 50s approached his table and plonked his pint down. He was scruffy and unshaven with thick, greasy black hair. Johnny was unsure who he was but had seen his face about the place.

The man looked at him and said, "Awright son?" It was said in a friendly way as if they might have some connection. "Aye," Johnny replied, "Just came in for a pint and tae listen tae a few records."

"What? Fucking Pinky and Perky? Can you no' stick on somebody like Tom Jones?"

"It's not unusual!" Johnny joked back. As he did so he noticed an overwhelming smell of fish coming from the man. "Phew, there's some smell of fish in here," he said.

The scruffy man had an apologetic look on his face, "Sorry about that son, it's me, ah work as a porter at the Glesga fish market." This jogged Johnny's memory. Stinking of fish and working as a porter? How did he know this man?

The fish porter knocked back a large Bell's whisky and then said, "Johnny McGrath? Am ah right?"

"You sure are."

"Well, ah hope you are going to dae the right thing by ma daughter."

"Daughter?"

"Lorraine ya stupid bastard. You've put her up the stick, now it's time for you stand up and show you are a man by marrying her."

Johnny gulped, this could be his future father-in-law. A dirty looking man with a foul mouth who smelt of fish!

"Aye, me and Lorraine have tae have a good talk about it and to decide what we are gonnae dae."

The fish porter did not looked pleased, "You'd better start making arrangements soon. Ah cannae wait tae walk ma daughter doon the aisle"

Johnny was taken aback thinking that this man expected to attend a wedding reeking of fish. In reality, as the say in the Gorbals parlance, the fish porter had two hopes, Bob Hope and no hope.

Johnny was once again very economical with the truth, "Lorraine is a fine looking lassie. She'll make a fine mother."

The fish porter looked Johnny straight in the eye, "And she'll make a fine wife for you and I'll be your perfect father in law."

"I'll drink to that," Johnny said putting on a massive false grin. He went to the bar and brought back two double whiskies, "To Lorraine and the baby," he toasted. The fish porter looked pleased, "Aye to Lorraine, you and the baby. Good times are just around the corner!"

After a few more rounds of double whiskies he bade the fish porter farewell. The drunk porter rose from the table and gave him a sloppy wet kiss on the cheek, "You're the best son in law a man could wish for," he said. Johnny left the pub thinking that the slobbery drunken kiss had left a strong smell of fish on his cheek. But he consoled himself thinking that his "future father in law" had not suspected a thing. It was all Lies! Lies! Lies! Lorraine and her father had dreams that were castles in the sand which would be eventually washed away by the sands of time.

Chapter 38

NO SURRENDER

A few days later he was walking along Rutherglen Road when a car pulled up beside him. The window was down on the driver's side, a man with a thick Irish brogue shouted, "Hey Johnny, Danny the main man wants to see you." Johnny looked at the driver it was the same Irish fellow he had encountered before at the first meeting in the Gorbals and then when he exchanged the guns in Portpatrick. He jumped in and was taken to a tenement in Florence Street. He was led to a top floor flat, knocked on the door, and it was opened by Danny. The flat was filthy, even by Gorbals standards. It had a vacant dirty look about it, odd pieces of furniture and there was an overwhelming smell of damp.

In the corner there was a manky looking bed with what appeared to be a large dead rat lying on it. He thought the rat looked peaceful as if it had died with a smile on its face. Danny pointed to it, "Would you look at that big bastard lying there. One of the boys woke up and caught it trying to eat his face, so he kicked it to death."

Johnny smiled, the whole scenario seemed ludicrous. Only in the Gorbals would you find the IRA having to assassinate a rat. "So, what's new Danny?" he said.

Danny grimaced, "The news is we've got Pinky and Perky and the other two eejits you were after." Johnny replied, "You haven't killed them, have you?"

Danny laughed, "Nah, the only thing we've killed today is that rat. The other rats you were looking for are still alive, just."

He led him into a back room. John the Irishman from the dancehall was there and had a large baseball bat in his hand, smeared in blood. There were four bloodied and bruised men tied to chairs. Because their faces were so bloodied and bruised he failed to recognise them at first.

But after a few minutes he recognised who the men were, Pinky and Perky, McCoy and his father. Both the McCoys were simpering with pain. But Pinky and Perky were quiet, two obstinate UVF men who were used to living by the King Billy motto, "No Surrender."

He looked at McCoy senior and his son, "Why did you set fire to ma house? Ya pair of cowardly bastards." McCoy senior spat out a mouthful of blood and sounded diplomatic, almost apologetic. "We didnae set fire to you house it was those two there," he nodded towards Pinky and Perky, "We would have been happy to have given you a doing but they wanted tae go further when they heard you were a Catholic."

McCoy junior nodded his bloodied head in agreement. Johnny thought both of them looked pathetic. They had been well battered and tortured. It had robbed them of their dignity. Johnny was taken aback by what happened next. McCoy junior began sobbing like a baby, "We would never have considered setting fire to your house. But they made up their own minds tae dae it. We tried tae stop them but they went ahead anyway." McCoy senior agreed, "We should not have got involved with those two Orange bastards, they told us they were used to burning down people's houses in Belfast."

Johnny said to the young McCoy, "Awright then, why did you attack me in the close?" McCoy junior's nose began to flow with blood, "It was revenge, remember you put me in hospital first. So, it was an eye for an eye." He understood the pathetic plea of mitigation. McCoy junior was perfectly right, he had put him in hospital first and the laws of the Gorbals human jungle meant there had to be a comeback. He stood before Pink and Perky, "Why did ye try to set fire to ma house, trying to murder me and ma family?"

Pinky looked up from his chair. The beating had left one of his eyes closed. He had a different attitude to the McCoys, "Because you are a dirty Fenian bastard. And all of you should be set on fire." He then spat on the floor. Johnny knew the Irish to be an obstinate race but he thought Pinky and Perky had taken it a bit too far.

"And what have you got to say for yourself?" he said to Perky. The UVF man looked at him with a face of hate, "You think you are a big man with your IRA pals but you're fuck all tae me. No surrender!" he shouted.

Johnny was confused as what to do, Pinky and Perky were so badly beaten it would have been pointless to hit them anymore. He would let the IRA deal with them.

As for the McCoys, he weighed up the situation. They had admitted they did not set fire to his house but had taken a hand in his beating. That was about par for the course. It was his own stupid fault that he had got drunk and let his guard down. But the McCoys did not deserve to die for that. Danny took him back into the room with the dead rat on the bed. He said, "Right Johnny, Pinky and Perky are a couple of rats and are going to die like that dirty vermin on the bed. But what do you want us to do with the McCoy idiots?"

Johnny thought for a moment and then said, "Ah don't care what you dae wi' Pinky and Perky, but you can let those McCoy bampots go, ah think they've learnt their lesson"

Danny nodded his head in agreement, "Awright, good decision but if those McCoy bastards mention any of this to the police, they are dead men walking. Ok?"

"Aye OK, now ah've got tae get tae fuck oot o here." Johnny said making a swift exit. The behaviour of Pinky and Perky had disturbed him. They were bigots, obstinate bigots who were used to burning Fenians to death. But they had met their match with the IRA. Danny would be their judge and jury and no doubt sentence them to oblivion. The McCoys were a different matter. A father who had stood up for his son. There was nothing wrong with that, at least he had shown he was still game. Still gallus enough to attack him in the close. He suddenly felt respect for the man and his son. But when he thought of Pinky and Perky, insane, murderous bastards, they deserved all they got.

The McCoys no longer posed a threat, they would keep well clear of him and the Gorbals from now on. A few hurdles gone, a few to go! He walked down the tenement stairs and there was a strong smell of shite and piss. On the first floor landing he saw a drunk man lying there covered in vomit clutching an empty bottle of Four Crown wine. He shouted, "Hey pal wake up, ye cannae lie about here in that state. You're pished out your brain."

The drunk opened his eyes, "What the fuck has it got tae dae wi' you. Dae ye want trouble pal?" Johnny did not feel afraid but said meekly, "Nah mister ah've had enough trouble for one day." The drunk man went back to sleep snoring loudly.

When he got to the bottom of the close he bumped into an old lady who he recognised as one of his mother's long standing bingo pals. She said to him, "Is it you Johnny? You've certainly grown up. Ah remember you when you were just a wee boy at primary school. A right wee bugger you were."

"It's me right enough Mrs Dalglish. Everything awright?

She shrugged her shoulders, "Ach could be better, ah'm no so good on ma feet nowadays. Ah wonder if ye could dae me a favour?"

"What's that?"

"Could you go to the wee dairy across the street and get me half a dozen eggs and half a pound of bacon son?"

She pulled out a handful of coins from her purse but he replied, "Put your money away Mrs Dalglish, ah'll get it." He walked into the small dairy across the road and said to the woman behind the counter "Six eggs and half a pound of bacon missus"

"Ayrshire or Irish bacon" she asked.

"Better make it Irish 'cause they saved ma bacon today," he chuckled as he handed over the money to the bemused woman.

Chapter 39

Goo Goo

He was aware that young Goo Goo was increasing his power base. Goo Goo was now the undisputed leader of the 100 strong Tiny Cumbie, all young guys varying in ages from as young as 12 to 18. When they got older they would graduate to Johnny's mob, the YYC. Goo Goo was walking along Crown Street in the direction of the city centre accompanied by around twenty of his gang when they bumped into Johnny, "Where are you guys off tae?" he said to the young mob. The first thing the noticed was how handsome Goo Goo looked, smart Tony Curtis haircut, tailored shirt and trousers with a sharp crease in them. Goo Goo also accentuated his gallusness by wearing a pair of tartan braces, "We're off to the city centre to see if any other gangs want to go ahead."

Johnny gave the young team some advice, "Be careful what you do. A number of different gangs are hanging about the toon, including the Govan Team, The Crew, The Fleet and The Hutchie. They are all cunning bastards, never underestimate them. The city centre is different from the Gorbals. With so many gangs roaming about the toon it can make the Wild West look mild by comparison."

Goo Goo and his team laughed, "The Wild West will be wilder when we arrive!"

They made off towards St Enoch Square and were a formidable sight. The tartan braces had impressed

Johnny, he might even consider wearing them in the future.

He was unsure Goo Goo's junior division had planned properly, had thought the battle through carefully enough. He did not think Goo Goo had taken enough troops. Twenty odd was a fair enough number but if they were going into a territory that had numerous gangs there, double that figure should have been the minimum.

But Goo Goo was a young commander who was entitled to make his own mistakes. Sure, he would learn by these mistakes, but mistakes in gang warfare could be fatal

Johnny went into the Hampden bar in Ballater Street and it was quite empty apart from a few old guys playing dominoes. He was asked to join them "for a game of doms." He liked the odd game of dominoes, sitting with the old guys exchanging patter. The older generation took the game very seriously. It wasn't an intellectual game like chess, but it needed a degree of cunning and skill.

He had often seen fights break out between old men who had argued about a shilling's winnings. He enjoyed the older raconteurs as they launched into their stories. Many of them, in their younger, days, had been gang leaders who had gone into battle to defend the notorious reputation of the Gorbals. One of the old men said to him, "Saw the young team heading up the toon. Are they off tae battle?"

"Aye," Johnny replied, "That young Goo Goo is leading them aff. Ah told him tae be careful." The old fellow, wearing a soiled looking bunnet, smiled, showing his rotten black teeth, "He'll have it coming tae him, if his battle plan isnae right. The city centre can be a dangerous place. Too many young gang bampots up for a fight." He nodded in agreement as he respected the old man's advice. The aged domino player had been the leader of the Bee Hive gang in the 1930s, and during one battle in Argyle Street he had been slashed and the scar on his left cheek was still visible after all these years.

He pointed to the scar and said to Johnny, "Ah got this 40 years ago and ah'm still looking for the bastard who did it. Somebody told me he emigrated tae Australia. If ah found oot where he was, ah would raise the money somehow, go over there and chib the bastard!" He was impressed, 40 years on and the old guy was still up for a battle.

After losing several games of dominoes and hearing more 1930s gang warfare stories, he decided to venture elsewhere. When he got outside, police cars with sirens blazing were heading in the direction of St Enoch Square. There must have been a big battle. Johnny speculated on how Goo Goo and his team had got on. Later on in the day the question was answered for him. The Glasgow Evening Times had the headline: **THIRTY INJURED IN CITY CENTRE GANGFIGHT.** The report said,"Police and ambulances rushed to the city centre of Glasgow earlier today after reports of a massive gang fight. Police sources say the skirmish took place between teenage members of several gangs. During the battle, nine gang members were either stabbed or slashed. They were rushed to Glasgow Royal Infirmary for emergency treatment.

"A police spokesman said, 'It appears the young division of various Glasgow gangs clashed in St Enoch Square. There were nine casualties and 20 arrests.'"

The report continued, "Glasgow police have been clamping down on such incidents over the years and were quick to quell the latest outbreak of mindless violence. The arrested alleged gang members will appear at Glasgow Sheriff Court in the morning."

Johnny later heard through the grapevine that Goo Goo himself had been slashed with an open razor requiring 22 stitches. He went to the Sheriff Court the next day. In the dock there were 20 young guys some from the Cumbie and the rest from other gangs.

One by one all of them pleaded not guilty to mobbing and rioting. All were released on bail. There was no sign of Goo Goo, presumably he was recovering in hospital after having stitches. That day, he had been stitched up in more ways than one.

Johnny met some of the young Cumbie mob outside the courtroom and asked what happened. One of them said, "You were right Johnny, there were too many different gang guys wanting tae battle. We took a real beating and got lifted as well. It just wisnae oor day."

Johnny nodded, "What happened with Goo Goo?"

The teenager replied, "He's still in hospital being patched up. But the good thing is the polis didnae charge him wi' anything. He told them he was an innocent bystander who had just been passing through the city centre to meet up wi his auntie."

"The stupid bastard should have listened tae me," Johnny said. "If he had taken ma advice his face widnae have been turned intae a jigsaw puzzle."

They both agreed that Goo Goo was the kind of obstinate guy who would not listen to advice and Johnny said if the lad was in hospital longer than a week he would go up and visit him with the customary grapes and bottle of Lucozade. The next day he bumped into Goo Goo's father, an Irish labourer, at Gorbals Cross. "How's your boy, Goo Goo doing?" he asked him

He replied in an aggressive tone. "For fuck's sake call him by his real name, George. I hate that Goo Goo nickname. He's discharged himself fae hospital and he's in the house now. But he's got a massive Mars Bar (scar) on his right cheek, He used tae be a good looking boy as well. Before aw this palaver."

Johnny headed for Goo Goo's tenement building in Thistle Street and knocked on the door. It was answered by the boy's mother, "Aye, what is it?" she said glumly. She looked as if she had been crying. "Is Goo…I mean George in?" "Who will ah say wants him?" "Johnny." She shouted, "George, there's a fella at the door called Johnny, he says he want to see you."

Goo Goo came to the door. Johnny was shocked at his appearance. He had a massive scar which stretched all the way from the top of his right cheek right down to his jawbone. Goo Goo, or George, looked fucked. "What happened, man?" Johnny asked him. "Just as you predicted, we got ambushed in St Enoch Square. Some bastard came from behind me and ah got slashed," he said pointing to the unsightly scar. Johnny thought the scar was horrendous and felt sick inside. He told a lie, "It's no' that bad, it'll heal up soon enough and aw the birds will be after you." The young man was unconvinced, "Johnny ah'm daft but no' that daft, dae ye really think any bird would go oot wi' me looking like this?"

"Of course they will," Johnny replied in the most confident voice he could muster, "The scar shows you are a real hardman and it turns some women on."

The boy suddenly cheered up and shook Johnny's hand. "Thanks for coming tae see me, much appreciated man. Ah should have listened tae ye and kept well clear of the toon." Johnny made his way back down the tenement stairs and thought about the reality of the young man's future.

Goo Goo would never get a job with that massive scar. He would find himself a woman though. But she would be low class who thought that going out with a scarred man was some kind of social prestige in the Gorbals. It was undoubtedly clear that Goo Goo was destined to be the leader of the Cumbie gang. Unable to get a job, he would have a life of crime and violence and perhaps extreme drunkenness.

Maybe, just maybe, he would live long enough to sit with other old scarred guys, have a game of dominoes and tell tales of his lurid past.

Chapter 40

SURPRISE

Johnny and Malky were sitting in Cha Pa Pa's fish and chip shop having a bit of banter and putting the world to rights. It was late afternoon and the place was quite busy. Because the Gorbals had a high Catholic population there was a great demand for fish on a Friday.

It was the one day of the week when Catholics, as a penance, would not eat meat. Indeed, it was quite easy to spot the Protestant contingent because they were the ones with steak pie suppers while the Catholics had fish suppers. Johnny and Malky both ordered two fish teas - fish chips, bread and butter, and a cup of tea. Malky was rabbiting on about Lorraine. He certainly did not know that she was pregnant and had no idea that Johnny had impregnated her behind the Railway Club.

Johnny had to play this game like a poker player keeping his cards close to his chest. In many ways he adored Malky but thought he would come in useful if he got involved with Lorraine. "So, do you think ah've got a chance wi' that Lorraine bird?" he asked Johnny.

Johnny was quick to reply, "Of course ye have but it's got tae be a case of slowly, slowly catch the monkey." Malky looked extremely cheerful hearing this advice, "So how dae ye think ah should play it? I mean do you think a lovely looking bird like Lorraine would fancy an ugly looking bastard like me?" Malky had low self-esteem with the opposite sex but he had certain qualities that many women looked for. He was smartly dressed, intelligent with a fast line in patter. Although he was not as good looking as Johnny, he had attractive qualities that set him aside from ordinary blokes. He was sincere and had what many guys in the Gorbals lacked – a certain amount of emotional intelligence.

Johnny was secretly playing a pass the hot potato game with his pal. If he got them together it would be one less hurdle he would have to face. It would clear the way for him to be with Cathy, undoubtedly the love of his life. He instinctively felt that Malky would marry Lorraine even if she was pregnant with another man's baby. He was that sort of guy, although he was tough and gallus, he had a naivety about him. If Malky did get together with the pregnant Lorraine, he would have to ensure that Malky would never know that he was the father.

He decided to play his best pal along, "She fancies you but she's disappointed you hivnae made a move tae chat her up. Fortune favours the bold man!" Malky contemplated the false words of wisdom, "Too right, what do they say? Faint heart never won fair maiden." Johnny nodded his head in agreement, "Ah'll have a wee word wi' her, give her the patter saying you fancy her like mad, that should dae the trick."

Malky looked impressed as he tucked into his fish supper. He felt a great deal of warmth towards his pal, who he treated as a brother. Indeed, in certain situations he would have died for him, "You're a great pal Johnny, would you really dae that for me, fix me up wi' the beautiful Lorraine?" Johnny felt ashamed that he was conning his best pal into a relationship but kept up his façade, "As good as done pal, just leave it tae me." They shook hands on the dubious romantic deal.

A few minutes later they were joined by wee Alex who looked as manic as usual and was sporting a large black eye. He shouted to the fish fryer Cha Pa Pa, "Steak pie and chips and throw in a big fucking sausage." There was no doubting he was a Protestant.

Alex sat down with his pals. "How the fuck did ye get that black eye Alex?" Malky said. Johnny was also curious, "You been fighting again wee man?" Alex smiled, "Aye it's a cracker of a black eye but ah didnae get it fighting. It's a bit embarrassing. Ma mother found me taking money fae her purse and beat me up."

Johnny and Malky laughed. Johnny said, "Only you could get beat up by your old maw. She's given you a cracker of a keeker." Alex chuckled, "She went a bit mental when she found oot ah wis stealing her bingo winnings. Battered me wi' a big rolling pin. But ah still got away wi' enough dough tae buy ma dinner here." There was no doubt that Alex was crazy, but it was a craziness mixed with humour. The boys were about to finish eating when Johnny heard a voice saying, "How do you do, little boy blue?"

He looked around and his face drained of blood, as if he had seen a ghost. Well in a way he had, it was

Cathy's father Bobby standing there as smart as usual in a three piece suit. He was certainly very much alive and kicking. Johnny gasped, "What the fuck, I thought you were dead."

Bobby smiled and shrugged his shoulders, "That's what a lot of people thought when ah disappeared. But ah've been hiding out in Dublin." He sat down to join them. Both Alex and Malky looked gobsmacked. They had also heard he had been "done in" by Glasgow's Godfather Big Arthur after a dispute over money. Johnny asked him,"We heard you were in a concrete overcoat. Bloody hell what a comeback! So, what happened tae you? Why did ye disappear?"

Bobby ordered his Catholic fish and chips and explained, "I did have a dispute wi' Arthur over money but it was only a few hundred quid. He widnae have done me in over that. The polis were trying tae pin some money lending charges against me, could have led tae five years in the nick. So, ah decided tae vamoose and live for a while in Ireland. At one point even the polis thought ah wis dead." Johnny was still shaken at seeing him in the flesh, it really was a bolt out of the blue, "So, what's the score now?" he asked. Bobby gave a grin, "Well it's all squared up. While ah was on ma wee holiday in Ireland ah had a team of lawyers on it. The polis have dropped all charges and the taxman has been given a few bob. Once ah heard the coast was clear, ah knew it was time tae fuck off fae Ireland and get back tae the Gorbals."

"So did ye square it up wi' Arthur as well?" Johnny asked, still barely believing he was very much alive. Bobby replied, "Yeah, it's aw squared up. It was a wee misunderstanding. In fact, he's put me in charge of a new project which could be very lucrative." The boys did not ask him what the lucrative project was but they had an idea. It would not have been polite to have pursued the matter. They were silent for a few minutes then suddenly Alex said, "Can ah ask ye something about Ireland?" Bobby looked bemused, "Aye, certainly, fire away." Suddenly Alex looked deadly serious, "Did ye see any leprechauns when you were there?"

Bobby smiled, "Hundreds of them. In fact, ah ended up drinking Guinness wi' them. They've got great patter." He understood that Alex was not exactly the sharpest tool in the box and treated him like a child. Suddenly, Bobby's mood changed. His eyes became more psychotic. "Right boys, if ye don't mind ah'd like tae have a wee word wi' Johnny in private." Alex and Malky left, leaving Johnny and Bobby alone. "So, what's your plans for you and ma daughter?" Bobby said.

Johnny felt nervous. Not only was he dealing with perhaps his future father in law but a gangster and murderer to boot. "Ah love Cathy and we'll get married as soon as possible. We'll have tae find a flat in the Gorbals and settle down."

Bobby nodded in agreement, "That's just what ah wanted tae hear son. Between us we'll fix a date for the wedding and I'll pull some strings wi the Corporation tae get the two of you a flat, easy peasy." They shook hands on the deal. Johnny said, "Now that ah'm gonnae be a married man, ah'd better find a full time job tae support them." Bobby shrugged, "Ah widnae bother about that, you can always come and work for me. Good money and it can be a wee bit dangerous now and again. But you're a big boy and you'll be able tae handle it. Besides, you are family now."

Johnny knew that Cathy's father was more or less inviting him to join his money lending business and other rackets. But he would have to think very carefully about the offer. It could either make him, or break him.

Chapter 41

PROBLEMS

Although there were certain problems disappearing there were some that remained and were perfectly tangible. There was no doubt that Johnny and Cathy were destined to be together, but what about Lorraine? It was a massive problem that would have to be handled with care and a degree of diplomacy, albeit Gorbals diplomacy. He headed to the bank up the town and checked his balance. It was comparatively healthy, £1,500 and a few odd pence. He walked up to the counter and said, "I'd like to take out 500 quid please." The pin-striped man behind the counter grimaced the way that bankers do when someone is extracting money from them.

"That's a rather large sum of money sir. Are you sure you want to take that amount out in ready cash?" Johnny put on a mild mannered voice, "Aye, its tae cover a wee financial emergency." "Oh," the bank teller grimaced, "Nothing serious I hope." "Nah, just a wee matter that's a bit personal, if you know what I mean." He winked at the bank teller, it was a dodgy wink, the kind of wink men use when they are sharing a secret that can't really be discussed. "Oh, I see," said the teller but of course he did not wink back. It was strictly against bank protocol to be too familiar with clients, especially one as low class as Johnny.

"How would you like the money, sir?" the teller said with a slight air of contempt. Johnny detected this immediately but remained calm, "Make it up in fivers and tenners," he said coolly. The teller showed more disdain, "Fivers and tenners, sir? Are you sure?" The guy was pushing his luck. "Look fatty, shut the fuck up and gi' me ma money and make it up pronto. Otherwise ah'll be waiting outside for you when you finish work." Suddenly the teller looked frightened, the last thing he wanted was a Gorbals gangster waiting for him after his shift.

All the money in the bank was not worth that. He coughed nervously, "I understand sir, I can put it in a bag for you." "Aye, dae that and hurry up. I've seen snails move faster than you," Johnny said with a growl. The teller understood he was dealing with a volatile hardcase and decided to limit the conversation from then on. He placed the notes in the bag while coughing nervously. Johnny took the bag and walked off before saying, "Sorry for being a bit touchy but ah've got a problem and this cash might just solve it." "I understand sir," the teller replied and gave a sigh of relief as Johnny left the bank.

Images of him leaving work flashed into his mind with a disturbing scene of this young man attacking him with an open razor. His imagination was not all that far from the truth. If he had given Johnny any more insolence he would have been attacked rather viciously by the leader of the Gorbals Cumbie. It was a thought he could not bear to linger on and nervous beads of sweat fell from his head and bounced onto the counter.

Johnny held onto the bagful of notes and headed towards Lorraine's tenement in Thistle Street. He had almost got to the close when he noticed from distance her father heading to the pub. It was early evening by his time and he presumed her mother had also headed out for a bingo session. This was an ideal time to strike. Lorraine would be home alone. He walked up the tenement stairs and knocked on the front door. Lorraine opened it up almost immediately. He was taken aback by how beautiful she looked. The pregnancy had put her in full bloom.

"Johnny it's you!" she said looking excited, "I was wondering when you were gonnae turn up. Come away in." The house was clean yet comparatively shabby compared to Johnny's own abode. As far as he knew her father had never been out of work over the years. He did not have a spectacular wage as a fish porter but it should have given him a far more comfortable habitat than this shabby hovel. The problem was Lorraine's father was used to "pishing his wages up the wa'" which left his family in abject poverty.

"Dae ye fancy a cup of tea?" Lorraine said in a soft voice. "Aye doll, strong, dash of milk, two sugars." She made the tea and handed it to him. They sat down at the kitchen table facing each other. "We've got a lot tae talk about," she said. "Oh aye, like what? Johnny replied as he sipped his tea. "Well things like what we are gonnae call our baby, when we're gonnae get married and where we're gonnae live Ma da says we could live here for a while until we get settled." The conglomeration of ideas repulsed him. Living in this hovel with a wife and baby he did not want! She had to be fucking joking. There was as much chance of that happening as seeing the Pope and King Billy at a Celtic and Rangers match.

"Lorraine, doll, there's something ah've got tae tell ye" he said. She could detect nervousness and insincerity in his voice. "Oh aye, and what's that then?" Johnny had never stuttered in his life but now he felt like a jabbering idiot, "Well…well it's just ah …ah'm promised tae another woman. We're engaged and ah cannae get oot of it." Lorraine's face drained of blood. She had a beautiful face but the mouth of a sewer, "What the fuck dae ye mean your engaged Johnny? We've got a baby on the way and you've got tae get married tae me. No' some whore you met at the dancing." She was no longer in a beautiful bloom and suddenly looked like a pale skeleton.

"Who is this whore?" she shouted. He felt rattled, "Naebody you know but we were seeing each other when you and me had a wee dalliance behind the Railway Club. "Well Johnny," she shouted as tears fell down her cheeks, "You'd better tell her tae get tae fuck, you're ma man and ah'm pregnant wi' your fucking baby." Johnny felt like a baby himself, he was helpless in this situation. Gang fights he could handle but not the wrath of a jilted woman. Hell hath no fury like a woman scorned.

"Look Lorraine, ah'm sorry but she's pregnant as well and ah've promised tae marry her." She began shrieking, "Promised tae marry her! Promised tae marry her! Ya dirty bastard ye. Ma da says you are a two-faced no user and he was right." Suddenly she picked up a breadknife and lunged towards him shouting, "If ah cannae have ye nae one will!" He realised his life was in danger but his quick reflexes and gangland experience meant he was able knock the breadknife to the floor. Lorraine began to wail, "Ah'll' kill ye, ya bastard ye. You've stabbed me in the back for a whore!" He tried to reason with her, "Nah it's no' like that Lorraine." The next line that came out of his mouth was a blatant lie. "Look ah love you and our baby when it comes. Maybe one day we can get together but not now."

He placed the bank bag on the kitchen table, "There's 500 quid in there and that should see you and the baby right for a while." She grabbed the bag and threw it across the kitchen. It sort of exploded and hundreds of notes cascaded across the room. "Ah don't want your filthy dirty rotten money," she cried, "Ah want is you Johnny. Ah want us tae be together. Money means fuck all compared tae that." She looked a pathetic sight, as if she was clutching at straws.

Johnny was dumbfounded. He had never seen a woman looking so hurt. In many ways it horrified him and a strange thought came into his head. How could a Catholic man treat a woman like this? The thought began to torture him, "Ah'll always be around tae see you and the baby. But for now, there's nothing ah can dae." She picked up a cup and threw it at him. It smashed on the wall behind his head," You are a dirty Judas bastard, you are gonnae pay for this in more ways than one. You swine!"

For the first time in his life Johnny felt defeated. He felt crushed inside. It was a worse feeling then when the giant machines chased him in his nightmares. This was a living nightmare and the very thought of him settling down with this madwoman and a baby would be a lifelong nightmare, every second, every minute, every hour of the day. He had to make excuses and leave. What came out of his mouth surprised him, "Ah'm sorry, that's the way it is. Take the money and look after the baby. You can buy it new clothes and a new pram."

She shouted back, "Fuck the clothes and the pram and fuck you!" She picked up a pile of dishes and began to throw them at him. Johnny felt cowardly. How could he lead a gang of guys into battle but shit himself when faced with a jilted woman? He rushed out of the kitchen to the front door. She picked up a pile of notes and threw them towards him, "Take your fucking money and stuff it up your fat arse." He rushed out of the door, ran down the tenement stair and down to the street. There is no greater feeling than escaping the wrath of an angry woman.

Suddenly he saw Lorraine's father coming towards him. He was half cut and looked like he had been out all day in the bevvy. "Ah Johnny boy, ma future son in law. Have ye just been up tae see Lorraine and sorted yourselves oot?" Johnny gulped nervously, "Aye we had a good blether and everything is sorted."

"Oh that's good son, can't wait until ye become a member of the family!" Johnny put on a furtive grin and said rather unconvincingly, "Neither can ah pal." The fish porter put out his hand, "Shake hands on it son. Ah'm looking forward tae becoming a grandfather." Johnny shook his hand rather weakly saying, "Yeah, you're gonnae be a great grandpaw." He left the fish porter on the best of terms. Lorraine's father had one of the biggest grins he had ever seen in a man. Sure, he was pleased as punch to be a grandfather. Perhaps it was meant to be his only great achievement in life. Johnny walked back to his tenement in Crown Street feeling shrivelled inside. But he consoled himself with the thought that the love of Cathy was waiting for him. Surely Lorraine's pain of rejection would disappear? Or would there be more trouble on the horizon? Only time would tell.

Chapter 42

PLANS

On a cold brisk winter's evening, Johnny walked towards Cathy's house in the high flats. Perhaps her mother and father would be there also so they could all sort out the future marital plans together. He took the lift up to the third floor and walked along the corridor to Cathy's flat. It impressed him how clean the corridor was and the smell of disinfectant lingered heavily in the air. It signified those who lived in such flats were very house proud and looked after their environment. It was a sort of contradiction to many of those who lived in the crumbling slums nearby with rats swarming about the place.

When he went into such tenements, the smell of pish and shite could almost be unbearable, especially on a hot summer's day. He also noticed that the high flats, like this one, were devoid of the lobby dossers who kipped in the tenements. The highly disinfected environment of the high rises and their house proud tenants probably kept them away. He knocked on Cathy's door and she opened it up almost immediately, kissing him on the cheek, "Oh, acome in we've been waiting for you tae arrive," she said in an excited tone. He went into the living room and stared briefly out of the window. Cathy's mother was there sitting at a table in the main living room.

The place was immaculate by Gorbals standards. Very well furnished and it did not have the obligatory crying lady on the wall. There were some sandwiches and a pot of tea on the table accompanied by biscuits and cakes. This signified that he had been invited to an important occasion. An occasion that would ultimately lead to his marriage to Cathy. Johnny was surprised though not to find her father present. "Oh," Cathy's mother explained, "He's had tae go out and dae a wee bit of business wi' a couple of his pals."

Johnny presumed what the business would be, dodgy business, but kept his trap shut.

They talked about inconsequential things, general chit chat, but after a while her mother tired of it all and asked him, "Right son, when are ye gonnae make an honest women out of ma daughter?" Cathy chimed in, "We've tae get it out the way before the baby arrives." He had no real plans, but unlike the Lorraine situation he knew he had to marry Cathy. It was written in the stars.

He took a bite of his ham sandwich and said, "You two decide, ah've always said that women are the best organisers." "Too right son," her mother said sipping her tea, "Ah think because of the circumstances, the pregnancy and aw that, it should be a low key affair" Cathy butted in, "But ma, ah wanted a big white wedding wi' a reception tae match. Ah know it would cost a lot of money but cost disnae matter on the big day." Her mother nodded in agreement but said, "If ye hidnae been pregnant you would have had a big white wedding. Your father isnae short o' a bob or two. But we've got tae keep it low profile, if ye know what ah mean."

"Me and your father think its best tae have a wee wedding, fifty guests or so, and a reception in the local pub." Cathy had a grimace on her face but she realised her mother and father were in a quandary. There was still, even in the 1970s, a certain amount of shame in being a pregnant bride.

She proposed they got married in St Luke's Church in Ballater Street and there would be a small reception in the Star bar in Eglinton Toll, two places Johnny knew well. The bar had a juke box in the lounge and a buffet would be laid on, sandwiches, sausage rolls, crisps and all that palaver. They would also hire a singer with a guitar.

Johnny had misgivings about such marriage plans, but outwardly he agreed, it was best to go with the flow. He agreed, "You're right, missus. Maybe it's better if we keep it a wee bit low profile." He was playing a shrewd game again. He knew that keeping it low profile might not get to jilted Lorraine and her fishy father.

Cathy sighed, "There goes ma dream of a big white wedding, it's aw gone up in smoke." Her mother gave a violent stare, "It was you who was the stupid cow that got pregnant, after aw ah told you. Men are after only one thing and once they get that they don't want tae know." Johnny said nothing, he had learnt from an early age when two Gorbals women have an argument, never intervene. Even the local police avoided such domestic disputes.

Cathy suddenly relented and agreed with her mother, "Ah suppose you're right, ah was a silly cow tae get pregnant but at least ah've got Johnny and the baby, that' s all that matters." Johnny had to be diplomatic and nodded his head in feeble agreement. He then chirped up, "How much is it gonnae cost? Ah've got a few quid hidden away in the bank. Kept it for a rainy day like this." Cathy's mother replied, "Ma man has got more than enough tae pay for it all. So don't worry, you won't have tae spend a penny." Cathy gave a broad smile towards her mother and asked an important question, "Where are we gonnae stay wi' our baby, ma?"

Her mother was quick to reply, "Your father has sorted it all out. He knows a guy in the Corporation Housing Department. He gave him a bung tae get ye a flat just along the corridor. The auld woman who lived there has just died and it's immaculate, a perfect home for you, Johnny and the baby." Cathy looked pleased, "Ah widnae want ma baby being brought up in a dirty slum wi' aw those rats running about."

So, over the tea and sandwiches, the matter had been resolved in an old fashioned Gorbals way. "Any questions Johnny?" her mother asked. "Nah, missus , it sounds great tae me. One thing though, ah'll have tae get a proper job now what ah'm settling down." She replied, "Don't worry about that son. Ma man says you can join his firm." Johnny felt a tight knot in his stomach but pretended he was agreeable to such employment prospects

But he thought he did not really want to be an enforcer, a hardman and thug for Cathy's father.

It was a tempting prospect but there was a chance if he took up such an offer he might spend a lot of time in jail. It was a matter he would have to consider carefully. For a few minutes he had an epiphany, he visualised the wedding and the 50 guests who would turn up. All the usual Gorbals suspects. In his mind he clearly saw Malky as his best man. So that was it, sorted. He would ask Malky when he saw him next. Of course, Malky, being a bit of a show off would be delighted. Right up his street. He was made for such a role! Johnny left the women in good cheer. He walked along the corridor to the lift and there were two teenagers standing there, one was writing obscene graffiti with an ink marker on the wall. He shouted, "Hey, what the hell are you doing? Fuck off somewhere else, ya wankers."

He did not recognise the boys, they must have been from outside the area and visiting relatives in the flats. One of the boys, aged about 15, pulled out an open razor and waved it towards him. He shouted, "Who the fuck are you? We can dae what we want, so you fuck off or you'll get this!"

Johnny lunged at him kicking him swiftly in the balls. He then head butted the other young guy. Johnny picked up the open razor and stuck it inside his pocket. He shouted to the injured teenagers, "If ah see you again ah'll fucking kill you….ah'll slash you to fuck. Cumbie ya bass!"

The lift took him down to ground level. He saw a large black car parked nearby. Inside was Cathy's father Bobby and two men. Bobby beckoned him over and said through an open window, "Jump inside son." He got into the car and there was a solemn look about the men. Bobby said, "So how did your meeting go Johnny? You still going ahead with the wedding and all that jazz?"

"Aye Bobby, too right, Ah' m really looking forward tae marrying Cathy and being your son in law."

Suddenly the solemn mood lifted and everyone seemed jovial. Cathy's' father laughed, "Just the answer ah wanted tae hear son. Because if it went the other way, we were all prepared, weren't we boys?"

The two men, one with a broken nose and another with a scar, said in unison, "That's right boss!" The guy with the broken nose suddenly produced a shotgun.

Cathy's father said, "You could say it's a shotgun wedding. You would have been shot if you gave the wrong answer."

The whole thing was absurd. But then again what was not absurd about living in the Gorbals? Even Albert Einstein would have been hard pressed to work that one out.

Chapter 43

RAVE ON

The course of love never runs smoothly, neither does the preparations for marriage. Johnny's priorities were (a) get a best man (b) get a suit (c) get a job. Getting a best man was a mere formality and when he asked his best pal, Malky, he leapt in the air with joy, "Oh ya beauty, ye," he shouted. He was a natural public performer and was not afraid to give speeches, especially at weddings and funerals. He was also a passable singer, his favourite being Buddy Holly's Rave On. With Malky on board, Johnny had really knocked it off. In Malky he also had a natural raconteur and comedian. He was a man of many talents, a man of many traits, but unfortunately, a master of none.

Johnny really could not have wished for a better best man than good old dependable Malky, "the salt of the earth" to many people. As he walked over the Jamaica Bridge to the town, to look at wedding suits, Malky put a pertinent question to his pal. "Dae ye really love this bird Cathy? I heard ye had a wee thing going wi' that other bird, Lorraine. In ma book Lorraine is a real cracker, but ah suppose Cathy is as well. How did you make your mind up between the two?"
Johnny had to be careful with his reply. His pal did not know about Lorraine being pregnant but was aware that Cathy was up the stick. He put on his most convincing voice that made him sound extremely frank,

343

"Malky, you know ah'm a bit of ladies' man. Always have been, always will be. But when Cathy told me she was pregnant, ah had tae give Lorraine the heave-ho, the big elbow. She's a smashing looking bird and ah think you should have a go at winchin' her."

Malky turned red in a state of nervous embarrassment, "Dae you really think ah've got a chance wi' Lorraine?" Johnny laughed, "Of course you have, Malky boy. You've got a lot of assets. Maybe not in money, but you're not bad looking, you've got gear, patter and you can sing. A lot of women would love to be on your arm." Malky chuckled, his confidence had just been boosted. "Well it would make a change fae all the polis being on ma arm!"

"Getting a bird like Lorraine might just settle you down."

Malky contemplated the words for a few moments, "So, when dae ye think ah should make the first move?" "After the wedding. Being a best man involves a lot of preparation and thinking. After that, you can do your Romeo stuff." They walked around the city centre and checked out a few tailors. They found one near St Enoch Square and bought two black suits, shoes, ties and hankies. When they tried their suits on, they looked in the mirror and admired themselves. Malky quipped, "We look like a couple of New York gangsters!" Johnny smiled," We are gangsters, Malky boy, Incredible Gorbals gangsters!"

Johnny paid for the gear in cash and decided to go to Paddy's Market for some boiled ham ribs and then they would do a pub crawl. Paddy's Market was very busy but they found a couple of spare seats in a wee café, tucked between a sneezing old age pensioner and down-and-out type who reeked of booze and pish. The ham and ribs were delicious. "Just what the doctor ordered!" Malky declared. As they were about to finish the meal, Johnny noticed two youths enter the other side of the café. They were dressed immaculately in handmade shirts, Levi Sta Prest trousers and Doc Marten boots. But they were certainly not the younger members of the Cumbie, they had Tongs written all over them. Johnny felt his heart pounding. One of the young guys he recognised. But from where? He said to Malky, "Those two bampots there, have you seen them before?"

Malky squinted his eyes and looked towards them. "Yeah, they're the young Tongs, we fought them a while ago." He was sure he recognised one of them, a guy of about 17, with an arrogant gangster air about him. The waitress, a fat woman in her late 60s, had a fag hanging out of her mouth and went over to the youths, "Can ah help ye, boys?" "Aye" said the youth, "Two big plates of soup and mince and tatties." "Certainly dear," she replied, "By the way, where are you two fae?" The youth smiled and replied in a comical voice, "The Gallowgate. Tongs ya bass!" The waitress laughed and hurried off to fetch her order.

It was then that it dawned on Johnny, the teenager was the guy who had thrown the razor blade potato at him during the Glasgow Green skirmish. Johnny said to the waitress, "Two teas, doll." He looked at his pal and said, "Back in a tick, Malky." In the lane outside there was a man selling fruit and veg. "The cheapest fruit and veg in Glesga," he was chanting. He said to Johnny, "Can ah get ye something son?" Johnny picked up a large potato and said," Just this." The fruit and veg seller looked bemused, "Just wan tottie? You're no' exactly planning a banquet, are ye son?" Johnny laughed and much to the man's surprise handed him a pound note and said, "Keep the change." The man was dumbfounded and thanked him for his generosity. Across the lane there was another fellow, clad in what looked like rags, selling razor blades, "The best dig in the grave (shave) you will ever have," he was shouting.

Johnny bought a packet of razor blades and stood in a dark doorway in the lane. He inserted two blades into the potato and then threw the rest of the packet away. He walked back into the café where Malky was sipping his tea. Johnny sat down. Malky said, "Where are we off to after this?" "We'll have our first pint in The Old Ship Bank pub. There's always a good wee sing song and then we'll head over tae the Gorbals," Johnny replied. The warmth of the tea made him feel more optimistic about life. They chatted about inane things for a few minutes, the usual stuff, Celtic and Rangers and Jock Stein.

The two young gangsters had not noticed Johnny and Malky but if they did they did not show it.

Both of the youths were laughing loudly. One said to his pal, "Got tae see ma granny after this before the auld bastard dies. She's got a dodgy ticker. Three heart attacks and two fits, but still going strong. The auld cow had got some constitution." His pal joked back, "Ah bet ye she has another heart attack when she sees your dial."
They laughed loudly and left after paying the waitress. Johnny said to Malky, "Right, man, let's move. Ah've got a wee bit of business tae finish." Malky shrugged his shoulders and looked bemused, he could never predict Johnny's behaviour.

They walked behind the Tong boys as they headed out of Paddy's Market in the direction of Glasgow Cross. Johnny pulled the potato out of his pocket and threw it full force at the youth who had put him in hospital. Thud! Bang on!

He gave out a loud shriek and fell to the pavement with the potato stuck in his back. His granny would not be seeing him that day. Malky was shocked at the sudden move but said nothing. They went into a side door to the The Old Ship Bank pub. Malky ordered two lagers, he was shaking slightly. Johnny sat at table watching the singers on the small stage. Malky said to Johnny, "What the fuck was that all about?"

Johnny gulped back his pint, "Oh, nothing, just a wee score ah had tae settle." More booze flowed, more 'Mick Jaggers' went down their necks. All their troubles seemed to disappear in a sea of alcohol.
Malky took to the stage singing his favourite… Rave On. "Rave on it's a crazy feeling…" It seemed a perfect end to a rather imperfect day. In a sense they were both raving mad.

Chapter 44

SAWMILLS

While in the midst of his wedding preparations, Malky turned up with what he thought was good news. He had landed a labouring job with South Side Sawmills. He encouraged Johnny to join him. Johnny was well aware of the sawmills, as a lot of his classmates from his old school worked there. The money was not that bad by Gorbals standards and the job did not involve using much brainpower. It was basically 9-5 shovelling sawdust and humping wood about. Malky had just finished his first week and was enthusiastic about his workplace. "What's it like?" Johnny asked. Malky laughed, it was the laugh of a madman, "Ach it's no' the greatest job in the world but it's a doddle. A bit of heavy labour now and again and a bit of sweeping up sawdust but its steady and the money is there at the end of the week. It's nice tae have a pay-packet every Friday, better than being on the fucking dole signing on wi' aw the losers."

Johnny was sceptical, "Are the people you work wi' any good or are they a bunch of wankers?" Malky got straight to the point, "It's like being back at school, the only thing is you have to clock on. If you go even a second over your card goes from black to red, then they deduct your wages for being a late timekeeper."

Johnny showed a flicker of interest, perhaps the sawmills would provide him with a way out of becoming an enforcer for Cathy's father. It was a job he was not frightened of doing, but a career he did not relish. He may have considered himself a gangster but professional gangsters like Bobby were a different breed. They seemed to live in a different world, both psychologically and physically.

Their psychology was – get the money by any means and that physically meant they would beat the shit out of anybody who got in their way. When Johnny meditated on becoming a lowly labourer it had a certain sort of appeal. It was a proper working-class job with enough money to keep a family, not in an ostentatious fashion, but a Gorbals fashion. This meant he would have to work hard and live frugally. He looked at Malky earnestly, "Come tae think of it, ah widnae mind joining you. It sounds like an adventure, maybe a good laugh."

Malky was pleased at his friend's decision, "Yeah, the boys will be over the moon when you join the workforce. You'll be a like a breath of fresh air in that place." Johnny was sceptical about the observation but said, "So, how can ah go about getting a start then?" His pal was quick off the mark, "Ah've already had a word wi' the "midget", Alex Johnstone. Remember him, that wee bachle who was at school wi us?" Johnny tried to recall and it suddenly came to him, "What, that fucking dwarf? He was a real teacher's pet."

Malky nodded his head, "Aye, well he's now a boss and has a bit of clout in the sawmills. He said he'll get ye a start, nae bother, when ye want."

Malky shook his pal's hand as he left. Johnny sat down in the kitchen and thought about where his life was going. He felt deflated. So this was his destiny, married to Cathy, living in the high flats, providing for an unwanted baby by working his bollocks off on low pay as a labourer in the sawmills. Suddenly his young brother Joseph appeared, just back from school in a perky mood, "Hey, Johnny, guess what the teacher told me today?"

"What's that?"

"Well, he said he had a look at ma exam results and reckons ah'm gonnae be a lawyer in the future."

Johnny felt more depressed, "Right enough, you've got the brains for it. But what sort of lawyer you gonnae be?

Joseph gave a childish laugh, "What do you think? A criminal lawyer. I'll defend aw the big crooks in the High Court and earn plenty of dosh doing it. Ah could be the Gorbals answer tae Perry Mason!" Johnny thought about his own future job prospects and felt even more depressed. He said to Joseph, "So, does that mean if ah ever get intae trouble in the future, you'd defend me for nothing?" The surprising thing was he was serious about the question.

Joseph laughed in a mocking way. He knew instinctively that his big brother was on a losing streak, he could read him like a book.

"Defend you for nothing? You've got tae be joking. Family is family and business is business. Ah'll go into law for the money, no' friendship or family."

"Oh aye, and what are ye gonnae dae when ye get aw this money?"

Joseph almost mocked him, "Ah'll have a big car, a pretty bird, a nice house and go on holiday tae places like the Caribbean."
"What, is Saltcoats no good enough for you?

Joseph became even more cocky, "Ah widnae piss on that place if it was on fire!"

Johnny felt his temper rise, "Look, get tae fuck oot o' here otherwise ah'll kick your arse all over the Gorbals. Ah'm sick tae death of your lawyer patter, so beat it!"
Joseph gave a mocking laugh before leaving the kitchen. But in a way, he was frightened of Johnny's temper. He had seen him many times in action and had no doubt about his brother's violent capabilities.

Johnny sat about and brooded. Perhaps he should run away and fuck them all. Fuck marrying Cathy! Fuck the sawmills! Fuck the Gorbals! But he had to get a grip, had to regain his composure.

He heard the front door open and his father walked in. He was his usual chirpy and exuberant self, "So, how's

the condemned man? No' long before you get the
biggest life sentence a man can have. Marriage."
Johnny sort of cheered up when he heard this patter,
"No bad, da. Ah'm still preparing. We've got the suits,
and the chapel and reception are being arranged." His
father looked pleased, "Good, son, ah honestly think
settling down will be the making of you. You'll enjoy
settling down instead of running about wi' that Cumbie
gang."

Johnny nodded his head in meek agreement, "So,
what's the news about the boats? You got any chance
of a job yet?"

"Ah went up tae the union guy this morning. He said
we're taking the case tae a tribunal and reckons ah've
got a good chance of winning ma job back. What about
you? Thought about work yet now that you're due to
be a married man?"
Johnny gulped. He struggled with the words coming
out of his mouth, "Malky has had a word wi' the gaffer
at the sawmills. He went tae school wi' me, more or
less said ah could start as a labourer anytime."

His father nodded his head and smiled, "The sawmills?
That's no' a bad wee number and it'll suit you with a
young family." His father went over to a cupboard in
the corner, pulled out a bottle of Eldorado wine and
placed two glasses on the table. He poured the
Gorbals elixir into the glasses and said. "You're looking
a wee bit down in the dumps son. Let's have a bevvy."

After a few sips Johnny instantly felt better. His father turned on more patter to cheer him up, "They say that getting married is the triumph of hope overcoming experience. Ah hated it at first but once you have weans like yourself come along, it changes things for the better."

"But da, ah don't know if ah'm the marrying type." Johnny said. His father smiled in agreement, "Ah didnae know either. Like you, ah was a man about town, wild and as game as fuck. But when ah met your mother everything changed for the better. Ah dropped ma wild ways, so marrying was good for me."

"Dae you think it'll be good for me?"

"Oh aye, but it's like serving an apprenticeship. Time makes it more worthwhile."

"But ah'll have tae give up leading the Cumbie and work in the sawmills, it's doing ma head in."

His father talked in a soft voice, "It's time ye gave up the Cumbie anyway, let another younger guy take over. Stay in the sawmills until you get fed up and look for another number. It's as easy as that son."

The wine and his father's advice rejuvenated Johnny's spirits. Perhaps his fate was not so bad after all. The strong wine made his father more loquacious, more mischievous, it always did, "How do you know when your wife has died?"

"Dunno."

"Well the sex is the same but the dishes keep mounting up in the sink."

Johnny felt bevvied and headed to his bed for a kip. There was a drunken man outside in the street singing, "Love and marriage, go together like a horse and carriage…"

He put his head on the pillow and had a dream that he and Cathy were in a field of red poppies as the sun shone brightly down. In the background, Lorraine stood with a breadknife in her hand watching their every move

Chapter 45

WEDDING

The wedding wasn't a grand affair but by Gorbals standards it was quite a do. Johnny arrived early with his best man, Malky, who was sporting a black eye. The night before they had got into an argument and followed a guy into the toilets of the Mally Arms and gave him a kicking. The guy was no mug though and managed to kick Johnny in his wedding tackle before hitting the deck. He grappled with Malky, punching him in the face, thus the black eye. As Johnny walked to the chapel, his testicles hurt but he hoped they would be in full operational order when it came to his honeymoon, five days in a caravan on the Ayrshire coast. Bobby McGee often used the caravan as a hideout for himself and his cronies. It was not a bad habitat, two rooms, a kitchen and a small toilet. Indeed, its facilities were far superior to many of the tenement flats in the Gorbals.

Johnny stood in front of the altar with his best man. They scrubbed up well for a couple of low life Gorbals gangsters. Johnny scanned the wedding congregation, many familiar faces on his side but there were a few dubious people sporting scars, presumably associates of Cathy's father. The priest came over and shook Johnny and Malky's hands, "Now, are you sure you've got the ring?" he said in his thick Irish brogue. Malky looked nervous for a few moments, fumbled in his jacket pockets and eventually pulled out the gold wedding ring. Beads of sweat fell from Johnny's head, "Thank goodness for that Malky, for a minute ah thought you'd lost it." Malky was dismissive, "Nah, nae problem, it fell intae the lining of ma jacket. Murphy's Law, man!"

The bride arrived looking radiant. Cathy was wearing a cream coloured wedding dress, perhaps suggesting that this was not a virginal affair. There were a couple of old ladies nearby nudging each other and whispering as Cathy and her bump headed to the altar. Even in the 1970s a pregnant bride was still a wee bit of a scandal. And what do old ladies like? A scandal, of course. Cathy was accompanied by her father who was sharply dressed in a black wedding suit, complete with carnation, the other thing was he seemed to be dripping in gold. Most of his fingers had gold rings on them. Perhaps this was to signify that he was a Gorbals man of means. And perhaps, also to signify that the rings could be used as knuckle dusters if need be.

The bride approached the altar and stood beside Johnny. There was no doubt about it, they were a very good looking couple. The wedding service went smoothly enough but at one point, Johnny became paranoid and imagined Lorraine barging in at any moment, like a scene from The Graduate movie, and try to steal him away. But it was all in his imagination, everything went to plan. Johnny was partly hung over from the night before and his balls still ached, so the

wedding became a bit of a blur. Afterwards all he could
remember was Malky fetching the ring and the priest
saying, "You may kiss the bride."
Afterwards, they were ferried to the Star Bar. In the taxi
Cathy gave Johnny a kiss saying, "This is the best day
of ma life. Husband and wife at last!" She patted her
stomach and added, "There's nae doubt we are in love
and this here proves it." Johnny was lost for words,
merely smiled and nodded his head. A further wave of
paranoia swept over him. Was he really in love? Did he
really want to become a father? Maybe a good bevvy
at the reception in the pub and a patter with Malky
would make his paranoia disappear. When they got to
the lounge of the Star Bar, the place was jam packed.
Although there had only been about 50 or so at the
wedding, gate crashers and hangers on had boosted
the number to 100.

There was a buffet laid on, sausage rolls, sandwiches
and crisps. Cathy's father had hired the whole pub for
the night and there was a free bar. No wonder there
were so many gate crashers. In the Gorbals there was
nothing that people loved more than a free bevvy.
There was a man in the centre of the lounge with an
electric guitar and amp. Johnny and Cathy had the first
dance, Engelbert Humperdinck's Ten Guitars, "I have a
band of men and all they do is play for me..." After the
dance Johnny sat down at a table with both sets of
parents. Bobby McGee silenced the guitar player and
made a speech. It was actually quite good, "Ladies
and gentlemen, I am the proudest man in the world

today. My lovely daughter Cathy has married the man of her dreams. Johnny is a bit of lad, mind you, but he's got a heart of gold. What I like about him is he has a reputation in the Gorbals for being fearless. There is no doubt about it, he is a game guy who I know would defend my daughter to the death. He is just the man Cathy needs. She has had many suitors before but they were all weak willed characters. Johnny comes from a different mould."

He lifted his glass and said, "To Cathy and Johnny, all the best for the future." Johnny felt a bit embarrassed at such adulation, he had never been praised so much before. He was used to people running him down or even attempting to stab or slash him. This was a new ball game and he liked it. Praise beats violence any day, he thought. Cathy was joined by her two bridesmaids, Maggie and Fanny. They wore nice dresses but there was no disguising the fact that they were, in local parlance, "as rough as fuck."

Maggie, a dark haired lady of 23, seemed to never have a fag out of her mouth. She also sported a Glasgow Celtic tattoo on her left arm with the declaration "Up the Tims, fuck the Huns." "Smashing wedding, Cathy. Better than the one ah had wi' that chancer who left me," she said. Her pal, Fanny, a blonde in her 20s, agreed, "Aye, a good wee do, hen, when ah get hitched ah want it tae be just like this."

Next up was Malky with his best man's speech. He seemed half cut and he was. To ease his nerves, he had swiftly sunk six pints of Tennent's lager before and it did the trick, it certainly boosted his confidence, "Ladies and gentlemen what a great day! Ma best pal Johnny getting married tae the beautiful Cathy. Days can't get any better than this. Ah've known Johnny for years and he is the best pal any guy could hope for. He can be a wee bit wild at times, take last night, that's how ah got this back eye!" The pub crowd laughed uproariously and Johnny went red with embarrassment.

Malky continued, "But, seriously, he has had found a lovely woman in Cathy and I am sure they will have a long and happy marriage." He paused for a moment and raised his pint, "Here's to Cathy and Johnny!" The crowd joined in on the toast.

But Malky was the kind of guy who did not know when to stop. He continued, "By the way, it's time guys like me and Johnny settled down and ah'm ready, willing and able!" The pub crowd laughed and some of the prettier young birds smiled and nodded their heads in agreement, perhaps signifying they might well take up his dubious romantic offer.

As the guitarist belted out the tunes, the pub began to bounce. There were people dancing all over the place, even on the tables. There was also a queue of people outside trying to get in to the free bar. It was like watching camels line up at a Sahara oasis.

But Bobby McGee had premeditated this and placed some of his henchmen at the front door to repel any unwanted gate crashers. Johnny's father danced with Cathy's mother and Bobby McGee danced with Johnny's mother. Cathy and Johnny also got up to dance several times. It was noticeable though that both Fanny and Maggie were making a play for Malky.

But during the course of the night, it looked like Fanny was leading the way, no doubt with Malky's romantic offer still ringing in her ears.

One of the door men came over to Johnny and whispered in his ear, "There's a drunk guy outside, says he want tae talk to you." Johnny replied, "Tell him tae fuck off. Who is it anyway? What does he look like?"
"An old guy in his 60s, says he's a pal of yours."

"What's his name?" Johnny asked.

"I don't know but the old fucker is stinking of fish."

Johnny sort of panicked, this was his worst nightmare. But being who he was, he had to confront the situation. He went outside and Lorraine's father was slightly unsteady on his feet and reeking of fish and alcohol. The aroma made Johnny feel sick but he disguised it with bravado. "How's it gaun? Ah heard ye wanted tae talk tae me."

"Aye, too right," the fish porter replied, "Are enjoying your fucking wedding do?"

"Aye of course I am. You don't get married every do you?"

The fish porter's face filled with drunken anger, "Well, you'd better tell that tae ma Lorraine. When she heard you were getting hitched she swallowed a bottle of sleeping pills. She's lucky she didnae die. She's lying in hospital now. And dae ye know what else?"
"Nah""

"She's lost the baby, all because of you, ya selfish bastard."

He then pulled out what appeared to be a fish cutter's knife and lunged towards Johnny. But he was too drunk and Johnny was too quick and wrestled him to the ground kicking the knife away.
He shouted to one of the doormen. "Get rid of this mad fucker. This is aw ah need on ma wedding day." He went back inside the pub, visibly shaken. He downed a double whisky and sat down, "What's the matter wi you, son?" his mother asked, "You look as white as sheet, like you've seen a ghost." He replied, "You're right, maw, ah've just seen a ghost fae the past that ah didnae want tae see."

The wedding reception continued and got more raucous. There were a few punch ups but nothing of major significance.

Johnny and Cathy decided to leave in a taxi and headed back to the house in the high flats. Outside, the defeated fish porter had well gone. Before they jumped into the taxi, Johnny noticed Malky and Fanny kissing passionately at the street corner, definitely in pre humping mode.

"Look at those two!" Johnny said to Cathy in the taxi. "Aye" she replied, "Love's young dream!" They kissed and laughed as the taxi pulled away to their destination and their married future.

Chapter 46

BAWS

Johnny awoke with a slight hangover and an ache in his balls. He had still not recovered from his testicles being whacked in the Mally Arms. The throbbing in his balls meant the marriage had not been consummated. Cathy did not really care about that. In her pregnant state she was more than happy to be in Johnny's arms in a state of married bliss. He felt quite content as well. But the events of the night before and the confrontation with the fish porter left him slightly perturbed. How the hell was he going to deal with the Lorraine overdose situation?

He would have at least a few days to think it over. Cathy's parents had given them the use of the flat for a couple of days while they stayed with relatives in Govanhill. It gave the lovebirds some quality time together. Things were progressing with the empty flat just along the corridor. Bobby McGee told Johnny he had bunged somebody in the Corporation's Housing Department "a hundred quid" to ensure the newly married couple had the accommodation they required. Johnny left Cathy sleeping and leapt out of bed. He looked out of the window and admired the view of the rest of the Gorbals and the River Clyde. His balls were still throbbing and he went into the kitchen to search for some painkillers to dull the pain. Perhaps the kick in the testicles had knocked some sense into him, a warning that life was short and not exactly pain free.

Suddenly there was loud banging on the front door. "Who the hell is that, Johnny? Cathy shouted from the bedroom. It was then he heard a voice shouting, "Johnny and Cathy, it's me, Malky. I've got a wee present for you." Johnny was bemused. He opened the door and looked at Malky, and he had obviously not been home from the night before.
He looked crumpled and dishevelled and reeked of last night's booze. His black eye also seemed to have got darker overnight. It was a comical sight. Johnny thought Malky would not be out of place in an old Laurel and Hardy movie. He was clutching a large bunch of flowers, "Got you these," he said, "Just to thank you and Cathy for making me best man." Johnny beckoned his best man in for a cup of tea. Malky grimaced, "Nah, Johnny, have ye no' got anything stronger? Johnny went into the living room and poured his pal "a large dram" from Bobby McGee's crystal decanter. Malky's hands were trembling, the symptoms of his night long bender. He knocked back the whisky and said, "Ah, that's better." Johnny poured him another and they sat down to talk. "So, how did it go?

He asked in a mischievous tone. Malky pretended he did not know what his pal was talking about. Johnny knew he was taking the piss but carried on with the façade anyway, "How did ye get on wi' Fanny? Did you have Fanny's fanny?" Malky spat out his mouthful of whisky, "What do you think? She's a smashing lassie and very passionate, if ye know what ah mean. In fact, ah now think we are an item!"

"An item! Surely you can do better than that. You and wee Fanny wi' the big fanny!" Johnny joked. His pal looked temporarily irked, "So what dae you suggest, Johnny boy?"

Well, ah think Lorraine is your woman. She's ten times better looking than Fanny and you never know she might end up giving you her fanny as well!" It was an absurd conversation but Malky knew his old pal was making an important point, a point that might take his life in a different direction. "So, should ah bomb out Fanny and take the chance that Lorraine might look twice at me?"

"Aye, that's the battle plan, Malky. Look, Fanny's a nice wee ride, that's aw, but she's no marriage material. Lorraine is, she'd suit you down to the ground."
Malky sipped more whisky and looked more confused than ever. In fact, he suddenly looked a little frightened. The prospect of courting the beautiful Lorraine was a daunting task. It might be difficult, in comparison Fanny was easy meat in more ways than one.
"Awright Johnny what dae ye think ma battle plan should be?"
"Lorraine has no' been well and is in a hospital ward at the Royal Infirmary"
Malky looked worried, "What the hell is the matter wi' her?"

Johnny whispered, "Woman's problems, if ye know what ah a mean." Malky looked more confused than ever, "Oh aye, woman's problems. Ah've heard of that but naebody knows what the fuck it is. A lot of women get it. In fact, ma auld man had women problems on and off for years. Ever since he married ma mother, she's a big problem!"
Johnny laughed like a schoolboy he was always amazed that his pal could come up with a funny gag for almost every situation, good or bad.
"Right, Malky, what ah want ye tae do is take this bunch of flowers away with you and go up to the hospital and give them to Lorraine. She's be feeling vulnerable at the moment and when you turn up wi' a bunch of flowers, she'll fall for you, hook, line and sinker."
Malky contemplated the ideas and nodded his head, "Ah suppose you're right Johnny, she might swallow the bait. Ah like Fanny, but when you compare her to Lorraine there's nae contest."

Malky left the flat clutching the bunch of flowers. He looked like a man on a mission. With those second-hand flowers he would try to win the heart of Lorraine and it could be well worth the gamble.
After his pal left, the throbbing in Johnny's balls had subsided to such an extent that he now felt like making love to his wife.

He went back to bed, Cathy was amorous and waiting for him with loving arms, "What did Malky want?" she enquired. "Nothing really, doll. He was asking me if ah wanted tae come on a celebratory pub crawl." She looked annoyed, "Oh aye and what did you say?" "Ah told him the days of me and him going out on the razzle were over. After all, ah'm a married man now with a baby on the way. It's time to grow up." Cathy kissed him passionately, she believed his bullshit patter, "Ah'm so glad tae hear that. You have grown up at last." They made passionate love and feel asleep.

A few days later they were on their honeymoon on the Ayrshire coast. The caravan was ideal and the weather was fine, great for a young couple in love. Johnny found the fresh air invigorating and it seemed to give him a new lease of life. The future was rosy after all. At one point the Gorbals and its shabby environment had almost stubbed out any positivity he had about life. But now it was coming back gradually, perhaps he and Cathy could escape the Gorbals forever and live by the seaside. Now that would be a Utopian existence, better than the dystopian existence he had experienced over the years in the Gorbals.

After five glorious sun-drenched days they were back. Bobby McGee greeted them with a big smile on his face and handed them the keys to their new flat. They got inside and discovered Cathy's father had paid for it to be newly decorated and furnished. It really did look like home sweet home. A few days later Cathy and her mother went up the town to do some shopping to buy a cot and baby clothes etc. Bobby McGee took it as a chance to have a man to man talk with his new son in law. He dispensed two large whiskies from his decanter and said, "Here's to you and Cathy, ah'm really made up that you've tied the knot."

Johnny raised his glass. Suddenly Bobby McGee's face changed from being the friendly father-in-law to aggressive gangster. He gritted his teeth in a semi violent way, "Now that the fun and games are over ah want you tae join the firm. Come and work for me, the money is good and as ah told ye, it can get a wee bit dangerous at times. But you're a big enough boy to handle all that shite." Johnny had been taken aback how suddenly Bobby had changed. It was like watching Jekyll and Hyde but he had been aware that Bobby McGee had a reputation for being a highly mercurial character, a psychopath in some cases. "So, what exactly do ye want me to dae?" Johnny asked.

Suddenly Bobby looked friendlier, his moods were changing faster than the weather. "Well a bit of money lending and collecting, and a bit of sorting people out, mostly cheeky bastards who owe me dosh."
To be an enforcer was an interesting offer but Johnny had a gut feeling it would not be a good move for him. He had to use his cunning to get out of it. He was aware any refusal might be taken as an insult to Bobby and might even damage the friendly relationship they had, "Bobby, ah've got tae be honest. Ah would love tae work for you, but no' yet. We've got a baby on the way and if ah get lifted by the polis it could upset the

applecart. Ah don't want the baby to grow up while ah'm behind bars in Barlinnie!"

Bobby mellowed when he heard this, "Ah suppose you're right, son. Ah didnae think about that. Ok, we'll wait after the baby is born and ah'm a grandfather, then we can make our minds up, agreed?"

"Agreed, Bobby." They shook hand on the matter. It was a close shave but Johnny had got out of it intact. Bobby asked, "So what are you gonnae do meantime? What you gonnae work at?"

"Ma pal has promised me a job at the South Side sawmills, twenty quid a week, it's no' a lot of money and it's hard work. But I'll take it in the meantime until after the baby is born."

"Aye ok," Bobby said, "But that sawmills is a bastard of a place.
They'll work you to the bone for a pittance. But if that's what you want to do son, ah'll no' stand in your way."

Cathy and her mother arrived back from their shopping trip with large bags. Cathy said, "We've bought lovely clothes for the wean." She pulled out a tiny baby suit and handed it to Bobby. He examined it carefully, "Ah feel proud to be a grandfather. The baby will want for nothing as long ah'm alive. Is that no' right Johnny?"

Johnny agreed, "You'll be a great grandfather." But in some ways is was an insincere reply, he knew in his heart he was not dealing with a nice grandpaw but a violent psychopath who would have no hesitation in killing him if he got on his wrong side. The next day he was walking along Crown Street and saw Malky approaching, "Hey Johnny," Malky shouted,"Your plan wi' the flowers worked. She fell for it big time. Lorraine says she gets out of hospital in the next few days. Then she'll be ma bird."

Johnny laughed, feeling relieved the Lorraine problem had been solved. She would no longer be a burden to him, neither would the fish porter. "But what about Fanny? Johnny asked his pal. Malky shrugged shoulders is a dismissive way, "Fanny? She can fuck off." The two of them made off along Crown Street both looking like contented men who had found love in their lives.

Chapter 47

MIDGET

And so, it came to pass. Johnny took up the job at the sawmills. He did not even have to go for an interview. The foreman, nicknamed "the midget" had passed on a message via Malky that he "could start "Monday 8am sharp." Johnny brought some overalls and working boots and arrived at the sawmills at the appointed time. There were a few minor formalities to go through. He had his name, date of birth and national insurance number registered with the personnel department and given his clocking in card with his name and workforce number on it. He felt sick inside knowing he was being inducted into some sort of working class slavery. Had he made the right move, or was it a giant mistake?

He cheered up when he went into the warehouse as there were many familiar faces there. A lot of the young guys he knew from school or being involved with the Cumbie gang. Indeed, when some of the guys saw him they gasped in awe. But others looked disappointed. What was the leader of the Cumbie gang doing here? Surely this was too low esteem for a gangster like him? But they were aware of his fearsome reputation and said nothing. A few came up to shake his hand and welcomed him aboard. He was then introduced to the midget foreman. The midget smiled broadly when he saw Johnny. He shook his hand firmly. In fact, Johnny was quite annoyed at how strong the midget's grip was. It hurt his fingers.

But from past experience, Johnny found that most small men had strong grips to make up for their lack of stature. "Good to have you on board Johnny boy," the midget said as the other guys looked on.

Johnny had the suspicion that the midget was putting on a show in front of the other workforce to give the illusion that they were old pals from school. But this was not the case, he could recall beating up the midget several times as school. In fact, his mother, who also looked like a midget, had gone to the school and complained about him beating up her boy. The result was six of the belt, which left his hands stinging for days. But it was all different now. They were no longer boys but grown men who worked together. The past had been consigned to the past. Johnny still detested the midget but put on an old pals act. "Aye great tae see you. Just like the auld days! How's your wee maw doing?" The midget smiled, "Ach, she's no changed, still mad about the bingo. She won the snowball of a hundred quid a few weeks ago and was over the moon. She goes to the bingo every night to squander her winnings and maybe win another snowball."

Alex showed Johnny around the sawmills. Row upon row of piles of wood and plasterboards. "Once you get used to it, it's quite simple. Your job will be shovelling sawdust, carrying wood from one section to another and to the vans outside. We deliver all over Scotland so the vans need filling up most of the day."

"Sounds simple" Johnny said.

"Aye, but it still takes a wee while to get intae the routine but there's one thing ah've got tae warn you about."

"What's that?"

"Late timekeeping. You've got tae clock in by eight every morning. The general manager Mr McDonald hates late timekeepers. If you are late your card goes fae black to red so he knows straight away who the punctual guys are and who the late timekeepers are."

Johnny felt irked, he had been right, working class slavery!

"Oh aye, who is this Mr McDonald?"

"You'll see him soon enough. He's in his office now but he usually wanders about here several times a day to see if everything is running smoothly. And if it isnae, you'll soon hear about it, ah can tell you!"

Johnny had never met McDonald but hated him already, he could feel his violent streak being turned on. "Where's Malky?" he asked. The midget replied, "He's out delivering wi' the vans. You'll no see much of your pal for a while."

Johnny felt a bit deflated. He had envisaged him and Malky having a laugh on the shop floor but so far it was not to be. The midget gave him a guided tour of the sawmills showing him such essential places as the toilets, which had a terrible stench about them and looked as though they belonged to a third world country. Nearby, there was a little hut they called "the tea room." It was where the men went with their flasks of tea and sandwiches.

He was given his first job, sweeping sawdust into piles and then shovelling it into bags. After a few hours working away he found it pretty soul destroying, but prided himself as being a working man, grafting to put bread on the table for his family. Lunchtime came and Johnny headed for the toilets. They were stinking worse than Lorraine's fish porter father. He went inside one of the cubicles and sat on the pan. He did not want to go to the toilet but decided it would be a great place to meditate for a few minutes, despite the stink. The smell from the pan was almost unbearable. There was a large turd there that had not been flushed away.

He flushed and flushed, pulling the chain above violently. But still the turd refused to move. Someone had left a rolled up newspaper and he battered the obstinate sewage with it. Eventually it disintegrated and after another flush of the chain it went on its way into the sewer.

He then heard two men coming into the toilet. He knew one of the voices, it was the midget and another guy.

They had come in for a pish. Johnny sat down on the pan and listened in on the conversation.

"Ah see big Johnny fae the Cumbie has joined us," the guy said. Alex replied, "Aye, what a come down. One minute he's the Gorbals top gang leader, now he's shovelling sawdust into bags." The other guy laughed and said, "This'll bring him back down to earth. He's no' a big-time gangster anymore, just a labourer like us. What made you give him the job?"

As the midget concluded his piss he replied, "Ah had nae choice. Ah don't really like the bastard. He bullied me at school. But when his best pal Malky asked me to gi' his pal a start, ah had to. If ah had turned him down it would have got out that ah had turned down Johnny, the leader of the Cumbie, for a job. Ma card would have been marked. Ah don't like hospital food, that's why he's working here today."

The other man giggled, "Ah don't blame you, ah widnae fuck wi' that mad bastard. He probably willnae last here long anyway, fingers crossed."
Alex said," Ah hope so, aye. Fingers crossed. "

They both left the stinking toilets unaware that Johnny had heard every word of their rather denigrating conversation. Beads of sweat fell from Johnny's head but they were not the result of hard work, or the stench of the toilet, but the result of his fear and paranoia. He threw some cold water on his face from the manky sink and wandered over to the tea hut.

He had forgotten to take his flask and sandwiches with
him to work, a typical rookie's mistake. When he got to
the hut there were about a dozen men eating their
sandwiches and drinking their tea from their flasks.
All the men looked around as he entered the hut.
Some had welcoming smiles on their faces as if to say,
"Welcome, pal!"

Other had grimaces on their faces as if to say, "Fuck
off, pal!" But he was unperturbed. If half of them loved
him and the other half hated him, he could live with
that. The midget was sitting at a table in the centre and
gave him a warm welcome, "Hey, it's Johnny boy! Sit
down and have a cup o' tea and ham sandwich wi'
me." "Two-faced bastard", Johnny thought but he
decided to play the game of being all pals at the
palace. He said in a humble voice, "Thanks, pal, a cup
of tea and a sandwich would go down very well." He
sat beside the midget and listened to the general
conversation. It was the usual guff about Celtic and
Rangers and horseracing. In many ways the tone and
topics of this working class conversation made him feel
demeaned.

Also, the fact that the midget could be nice to his face
but secretly ran him down, depressed him. He could
feel his anger rise and decided to get back to work.
There was a mountain of sawdust and plies of bags to
be filled. He laboured hard over the next few hours.

But as soon as one pile of sawdust disappeared
another sprang up, Working class slavery shite!
A few other labourers did come over to have a quick
chat with him, but they were also busy doing other
menial jobs. All this shovelling would keep him fit, no
chance of him getting fat. As he filled his umpteenth
bag of sawdust he began to sneeze uncontrollably.

The sawdust, like some people there, had got up his
nose. In fact, he could even taste it in his mouth as if
he had eaten a tree trunk. One of the other workers
gave him a mask to stop him sneezing and it seemed
to work after a few minutes.

Johnny had only been in the job for a few hours but
now he hated everything about the place, including the
sawdust and the two faced foreman. It was just when
he was thinking this when he heard a voice shouting in
his direction. "Hey, you in the mask wi' the sawdust.
Can ah have a wee word?" He took his mask off and
turned round to see a tall grey haired man in his late
50s facing him. He looked the typical office type, white
shirt, dark tie and highly polished shoes. He knew
straight away it was the manager Mr McDonald.
"Aye, what is it?" he said still holding his shovel.
"Look you're doing this job all wrong. The sawdust
should be placed over there in that corner and then put
into bags. You're new, aren't you?" McDonald said.
"Aye, just started this morning, pal."

"Ah'm no' your pal. My name is Mr McDonald and I am the boss around here, so don't forget it," he said in a tone that suggested he was the master and Johnny his servile slave. He continued, "Furthermore, make sure the sawdust is cleared and put into bags before the shift ends."

McDonald walked off with his haughty head in the air. Johnny felt like going after him and giving him a Glasgow kiss, a head-butt that might knock the haughtiness out of him. But he let his anger subside and carried on shovelling the sawdust into a corner as demanded by McDonald. He managed to bag up the remaining sawdust before clocking out at 4.05 pm and headed home feeling exhausted.

Cathy was waiting for him with a big smile, looking pleased and excited about her man's first day at work. "Ah've got your tea ready. How did your first day go?"

He put on a brave face, "No' bad, but hard physical work takes a bit of getting used to. It's no' for the faint hearted, Cathy." She laughed the way that women do when they are proud of their men, "Don't worry, you'll soon get used tae it. You've got a job for life there!" He nodded his head and gave a weak smile but said nothing. Feeling exhausted after an honest day's labour he lay in bed thinking about the phrase, "Only fools and horses work." He reflected how true it was.

Chapter 48

FACADE

For the next four weeks he kept up the facade and pretence of being a hard-working family man. At least it kept Cathy happy. She boasted to neighbours that the wild man she had married had finally settled down with had put his nose to the grindstone. But the stress of working such an obnoxious environment left Johnny at times having minor panic fits, which were the result of feeling nervous and anxious. He knew he was a square peg in a round hole and had utter contempt for his fellow employees. He met an older guy in his late 50s who had been working in the saw mills since he was 15, more than 35 years, man and boy. He wasn't the sharpest tool in the box and had a resigned look about him.

He told Johnny in the tea hut, "Ah came here straight after school. Ma father said it was a job for life, and he was right. The pay packets might no' be big but they're regular." Johnny instantly felt depressed. A whole life in the sawmills, doing the same mundane tasks, day after day. A life that had gone down the drain. Was he destined to end up like this? The very idea sent a shudder down his spine. Subconsciously, he knew he had to get the hell out of it. He could not walk out on the job as this would disappoint his young pregnant wife. No, getting the sack was the only option.

It was another case of slowly, slowly catch the money.
He was late for work almost every day with red time
marks all over his clocking in card. He was late by only
a few minutes day in day out but he knew that an
accumulation of red marks would mean he would get
called into the office for a warning by McDonald.
But much to his dismay, McDonald had been off for a
couple of weeks to have "a piles operation." So the big
boss had not been around to give him a warning about
his timekeeping. Through various conversations with
his fellow labourers in the tea hut he learned that
McDonald was an educated man and had gone to the
posh fee-paying Hutchie grammar school. He had then
studied business at Glasgow University. From then on,
he joined the Scots Guards as an officer and even had
a few medals for fighting in the Korean War. He was
reckoned to be a "hard but fair" man who treated his
workers as if they were privates in the army. Johnny
felt a deep contempt for McDonald with his posh lower
middle class accent.

Sure, he had fought a few battles in Korea but so had
Johnny in the Gorbals. He also heard through the
grapevine that McDonald was a big shot in the Orange
Lodge and a member of the Masons to boot. He
detested such people being members of a sectarian
movement and secret society. And those fucking
secret handshakes! It did not impress him, in fact it
made him feel repulsed. Another thing that got on
Johnny's wick was the fact that every time he went into

the toilet there was a large turd there that had not been flushed away.

He decided to find out who the culprit was. He was shifting wood near the toilets when he saw a guy called "Big Tam" go in. He had disliked the fellow from day one. Big Tam thought of himself as being a cut above the other labourers. In some ways he was. He was a forklift driver who had been there 20 years. He was an obnoxious looking fellow weighing almost 20 stone but his weight did not stop him operating his forklift truck. Johnny had been warned though to be careful what he said to Big Tam as he was known as being a workplace grass and often told tales to McDonald resulting in a few people getting the sack. He and McDonald were connected in more way than one. He was a member of the same Masonic lodge. Tam would be the ideal guy to pick on if he wanted the sack.

After Big Tam left the toilet cubicle Johnny went to check and sure enough there was a large turd there. The evidence was overwhelming, Big Tam was the mystery defecator. Johnny approached the forklift and shouted to the fat man, "Hey, ya fucking dirty bastard. Dae ye no' flush he lavvy after you've done the business?" Big Tam looked angry at such foul mouthed insolence, "What the fuck has it got to dae wi' you? A can shite where ah want." Johnny leapt at him and threw him from his forklift. He punched Big Tam heavily in the face causing his nose to bleed. The other labourers rushed forward to break them up. The midget looked as white as a sheet and took Johnny to one side, "That was no' a wise move. He's a big pal of McDonald and when he gets back there will be hell tae pay." Johnny shrugged his shoulders, "Who gives a fuck? The shitey bastard deserved it." He went back to work shovelling sawdust. From then on Big Tam kept out of his way. So did the midget who feared he could be the next recipient of Johnny's temper. But although he was still shovelling sawdust Johnny was pleased he had laid the foundations for his sacking.

It was Friday night and he and Cathy went to the Horseshoe Bar in Crown Street. The place was quite busy and when they sat down with their drinks they did look like a handsome couple. Johnny was in a three-piece suit, shirt and tie. Cathy was wearing a figure-hugging red dress and despite her pregnancy looked glamorous. A guy Johnny barely knew came over, slapped him on the back and said, "How's it going pal?" He then said to Cathy, "You look sexy in that dress doll." The guy was being insolent and he knew it. Johnny realised his change in status from being a gangster to a labourer had repercussions. People no longer respected him as before. Something had to be done about this.
He saw the guy go into the Gents and followed him in. The fellow was aged about 30 and also smartly dressed. Johnny grabbed him by the lapels, "Don't ever fucking slap me on the back and call me pal

again." He pulled out an open razor and held it to the guy's throat. "Also, don't ever talk tae ma wife like that again, if you do ah'll fucking throttle you and rip you." He let go of the man's throat knowing he had got the message. The man spluttered, "Ok, Johnny… ok." After that the weekend went well but he could still detect from some people that his status had been diminished. He said nothing to anyone, including Cathy. The weekend flew in and soon it was Monday morning. He was back in his overalls shovelling sawdust into bags. Suddenly, he heard McDonald's voice shouting to other labourers, "You there. Aye you! Shift those plaster boards to the other side." He shouted to another labourer, "You! Stop standing about scratching your balls. Get back to work, that's what you're paid for." The two men were frightened of getting the sack and said nothing, carrying on with their menial tasks.

It was obvious McDonald was in a bad mood. Perhaps the removal of his piles had left him with a sore arse. He moved towards Johnny and shouted, "You there, aye you wi' the sawdust. Tidy that area up, it looks a mess." Johnny put his shovel down, "Ma name is not you, fucking understand that ya tube, ye." McDonald was taken aback with such cheek. Johnny could see the fear on his face. A war hero be fuck, he wasn't in the same league as Johnny when it came to a fight. McDonald moved off towards his office. But Johnny was aware he had obviously not been told about the assault on Big Tam, yet.

It was only a matter of time and the clock was ticking. Just before lunchtime the midget came up to him with a worried look on his face, "McDonald wants to see you in his office. It's no' looking good Johnny." He replied, "Ah don't give a flying fuck." He went into the office and McDonald was sitting at his desk looking at Johnny's clocking in card with all the red marks. He was shaking his head. "Sit down, young man," he said in a voice that sounded like an officer talking to a private. He sat down facing McDonald, "What dae ye want me for, big shot?" McDonald was yet again taken aback by another insolent remark. In all his years at the sawmills and in the army he had never been talked to like this. "Since you started you have been continually late and aggressive, not only to me but other staff members." Johnny smiled, "So what?"

McDonald continued, "I have also been told you assaulted our forklift driver, Tam, when I was off." Johnny leered at him, "Too right, that orange, shitey, fat bastard deserved it." McDonald shook his head and tut-tutted, "Well you have given me no choice but to terminate your employment here." He handed Johnny a light pay packet, "Here's what we owe you for today and I wish you all the best for the future." They did not shake hands and Johnny left clutching the pay packet saying, "Thank fuck for that!" Still in his overalls and working boots, he headed back to the Gorbals. He did not want to give the game away by going back to the house and meeting Cathy, who would be upset at his sacking. Instead he went into the Mally Arms and found his pals Alex and Chris there. They were flush with cash. Alex told him they had pick-pocketed a drunk Irish labourer the night before who had a few quid in his donkey jacket. Johnny was glad to be with is old pals. Birds of a feather flock together!

He told them about his exploits at the sawmills. Chris said, "You're well out of there, let the slaves dae that work. You were made for bigger and better things." Alex chimed in, "Ah'll tell you what Johnny, dae you want me tae break into the sawmills tonight and set the whole fucking place on fire?"

Johnny laughed knowing the offer was genuine. If he wanted, Alex would burn the place to the ground with hundreds of people losing their jobs. Alex continued, "Wi' aw that wood it'll be the biggest fucking fire Glasgow has ever seen!" A cheered up Johnny bought Alex and Chris a round of drinks from his final, meagre pay-packet saying, "Nah let it be, fuck them. They are not even worth the price of a match. Keep your matches for your birthday cake."

Chapter 49

DECEIT

He arrived back at the house smelling heavily of
booze. Cathy looked at him as he was slightly swaying,
"Have you been drinking?" she said. "Aye" he replied
with a drunken smile on his face, "They were having a
leaving do for one of the boys, he's retired after 35
years at the sawmills." Cathy smiled, "You could do
that Johnny and one day if you are lucky you'll have a
leaving do like him." "Silly cow", he thought, but kept
up the pretence, "Forget about 35 years, ah want tae
dae 40 years, love the place." "Oh ah'm glad tae hear
that," Cathy said as she put his tea on the table. But
Johnny awoke in the morning with a sense of dread.
How was he going to tell her that he had been sacked
for punching the shitey forklift driver? He decided in a
flash not to. He put his overalls on as usual and had
his sandwiches and flask in hand. Before he left he
concealed some gear in a bag, a shirt, jacket, trousers
and shoes.
He kissed Cathy on the cheek saying cheerily, "Ah feel
like one of the seven dwarves "Hi ho, it's off to work I
go!" Cathy laughed saying, "You are a mad bastard
Johnny but I love you." He left the house feeling
ecstatic and was, as his missus had called him "a mad
bastard". Everyone in the Gorbals knew he was a mad
bastard. But at least his wife loved him for it. He went
into the toilets at Gorbals Cross, took off his overalls,
and changed into his street gear. He made a quick exit

over the bridge to the town where he could hide away safely until 4pm when his shift officially ended.

He was not short of money and went into his bank to delve into his secret savings, which even Cathy did not know about. His savings had been depleted, what with the marriage and the baby on the way. A cot, pram and baby clothes were not cheap and Cathy always insisted on the best. Also, the Lorraine pay off had dented his financial situation.
But he had stashed a few hundred quid away to play about with, enough to kill time until the baby was born. He dared not tell Cathy about his sacking, he feared the shock would give her a miscarriage. One thing he did was avoid pubs. It was too tempting to go and get drunk. No, he would spend his time on cultural pursuits visiting places like the Kelvingrove Museum, and taking the subway to places like Partick and Hillhead to wander around. He was lingering in a café in Partick when The Beatles came on the jukebox singing 'Revolution' He loved the line, "You can count me out…in!" That's the way he felt, it was a contradiction. At the moment he was out of work but pretending to be in.

One thing slightly niggled him though. Every Friday he handed his pay packet to Cathy who would put it on the kitchen table. Cathy would take her housekeeping money and he would be handed his pocket money. It was a ritual thousands of working men did all over Glasgow. As he was walking through Partick he saw a stationery shop and printers. He went inside and there was a poofy looking guy serving behind the counter with dyed blonde hair. He said to Johnny, "Good afternoon, sir. How can I help you?" Johnny felt embarrassed, the guy looked half woman, half man with his flowery shirt and dyed hair.

"Ah wonder if you have any pay packets?" The poofy fellow laughed, "We sure do. How many would you want? "Oh, about a dozen," Johnny said. He placed them on the counter and Johnny paid him the money.

The poof looked at him with a smile that was that was almost dazzling. "Oh, I suppose you are another one of those guys?" he said. "What dae you mean?" Johnny said. He was straight to the point, "Well we get a few customers who buy pay packets to give to their wives pretending they have lower wages." Johnny was relieved, at least he was not alone in his dilemma. The poof cheered him up by saying in the campest voice Johnny had ever heard, "She'll never notice the difference, and these pay packets are used by all the big firms in Glasgow. You'd have to be Sherlock Holmes to detect they were not genuine pay packets." He left the shop feeling bucked up and amused by the shop assistant's camp patter. For some reason the gay patter always seemed to cheer him up.

He walked back to the Gorbals toilets and changed back into his overalls. He knew the toilet attendant well, a wee ex-soldier in his early 60s called Billy. The toilet attendant had a small cubicle and had agreed to store Johnny's overalls for him. In exchange, Johnny gave him a half bottle of Eldorado wine for storage expenses. He got back to the house at 4.30pm. Cathy was there with his tea on the table as usual, "How did it go today?" she asked. He replied in the most convincing voice he could muster, "Oh, hard work as usual. Shovelling sawdust intae bags and then humping plaster boards all over the sawmills." She smiled, "I am so proud of you. You used tae be a wildman causing trouble all over then place. But now you are a hard-working man who has finally settled down. Even the neighbours are amazed how much you have changed."

He went with the flow, "Yeah, you can't beat being a hard working fella like me and have a beautiful looking wife like you." She blushed as Johnny ate his dinner, "Ah've just been thinking that when you have been there a few years they might make you a foreman and a few years after that, manager. Would that no' be great Johnny? You a foreman and even manager of the sawmills?"

He nodded and gave a false smile, "Aye, chance would be a fine thing. Ah'd like to be foreman and even manager one day. That would be a dream come true!" She looked ecstatic, "Oh ah'm so happy you have settled down. Wi' the baby on it's way we'll be one big happy family." "Yeah, one big happy family," he replied, then murmured under his breath, "Silly moo!"

Over the next few days he kept up this charade, leaving every morning in his overalls, changing at Gorbals Cross toilets then went up the town. When Friday came he took £20 from the bank. He put it into a pay packet and placed it on the kitchen table as usual. Cathy suspected nothing but surely it would not be long before she heard he had got "the Dan Mac" (the sack) from his job?

One morning he was walking through St Enoch's Square when he bumped into Alex who was as mercurial as usual. "Where you off tae, Johnny?" "Oh, just having a wander to kill a few hours, to pass the time away." Alex said with a mischievous grin, "Fancy going tae the pictures for free?" It sounded like a plan and Johnny decided to go along with it, "What cinema shows movies at this time in the morning?" he said. Alex replied, "Follow me and ah'll show you." They walked towards Renfield Street where the ABC Cinema was. It had started showing mostly children's cartoons from early morning.

Alex led Johnny into a lane at the side of the cinema. He pulled out a small screwdriver and forced the door open. The next minute they were sitting in the darkness watching Micky Mouse and Donald Duck cartoons. The surprising thing was they were the only customers there. But no-one came in and asked them for their tickets. As Johnny watched Donald Duck and Micky Mouse in action he amusingly thought that many of the cartoon characters resembled the numpties he had worked with in the sawmills.

When Popeye came on, his rival Bluto, reminded him of Big Tam the forklift driver, Donald Duck was like the foreman midget and Micky Mouse had certain characteristics that reminded him of McDonald. They left the cinema gigging like schoolboys. Alex said he was going into Lewis's department store as his mother needed some new tea towels "to do the dirty dishes." But Johnny had to get back to the Gorbals, and change into his overalls. It was just after 4pm when he had changed and was walking along Gorbals Street when he spotted the midget foreman and Big Tam. Both had frightened looks on their faces when they saw Johnny coming towards them. But he decided to be diplomatic, even to Big Tam.

"How's it going boys? Just finished work?" "Aye Johnny," the midget said. Big Tam merely grumbled either through hate or fear, perhaps a combination of both. Johnny decided to be cocky, "Are ye no' missing me?" Both of them looked nervous, perceiving this might be a precursor to violence. "Of course we are Johnny," the midget said, "Just a pity it turned out the way it did." Johnny gave a smile and shrugged his shoulders, "Ach, well that's the way it goes. Ah honestly couldnae stand it. Besides, you never see an eagle flying wi' pigeons dae you?"

The midget said, "You're completely right, you never ever see an eagle flying wi' pigeons!" Johnny put his hand out and the midget shook it warmly. Much to his surprise, Big Tam did also.

He concluded the interaction by saying, "Sorry about everything, it's just that that ah'm no' a sawdust kinda guy." They made off in the opposite direction and the two men reflected that they had been lucky to have found Johnny in an agreeable mood. When he got to the high flats in Queen Elizabeth Square, Bobby McGee and his two henchmen were waiting for him in a car.

Bobby said, "Where the fuck have you been? We've been looking for you everywhere, jump in." Johnny got in the car and said, "What's happening?" Bobby replied, "Cathy's been rushed to hospital, she's had contractions. A good job her mother was wi' her." They sped off in the direction of the Southern General Hospital in Govan.

On their way there Bobby said, "We went tae the sawmills and somebody told us you got the sack for thumping some fat orange bastard. Is that right?" Johnny nodded his head, "Aye that and other things." Bobby laughed, "Served the fat fucker right, that's good. Fuck that dump, that's for losers, no' winners like us."

"Too right, Bobby, it was full of imbeciles," Johnny said.

Bobby agreed, "The good news is you can come and work for me. You won't have tae shovel sawdust and carry planks, plus the money will be a lot better. Shake hands on it, son!" They shook hands on the dubious employment offer. When they got to the hospital, Cathy's mother was waiting in the corridor with an anxious look on her face. Bobby McGee and Johnny walked towards her, McGee said to his wife, "What's the news?" She replied, "The doctor says she's ready tae give birth any time now. So really it's a waiting game."

Bobby was in high spirits, "Well I am chuffed. It's no' every day you become a grandfather. And you Johnny, becoming a father, it proves you've grown up at last!" They waited for over an hour then a white-coated doctor appeared. He looked at them smiling and said, "Cathy has just given birth to a healthy baby boy. Six pounds, two ounces."

They were led into a maternity ward where Cathy was lying in a bed looking exhausted but happy, clutching the baby. Bobby looked closely at the baby and exclaimed in excitement, "Johnny, the wee man looks just like you!" Johnny had to agree.

Bobby asked his daughter, "What are ye gonnae call the baby?" She was in a tired mood and replied softly, "Oh, ah don't know, I'll let Johnny decide. We've discussed dozens of names."

Johnny felt a mellow mood overcome him. It was a sentimental feeling he had never experienced before, "We'll call him Johnny after me and give him the middle name, Robert, after your father," he said to Cathy. And so, it was to be. Johnny Robert McGrath had entered the world in the loving arms of a Gorbals family.

Chapter 50

BUSINESS

While Cathy was in the maternity ward, Johnny was free to drop his pretence of being a slave at the sawmills. No longer did he have to put on his hated overalls and change at the Gorbals toilets. Anyway, he had a new job offer with Bobby McGee but he was still curious as to what was involved. In the event, McGee arranged for a meeting with Johnny in his flat while the coast was clear.

His wife was spending most of her time at the hospital, at least for a few days until Cathy came home with the baby. Bobby led Johnny into his flat and offered him a large whisky from his decanter. They both sat down to discuss business. McGee was straight to the point, "Before you start working wi' me ah've got to explain what I do. But it's pretty confidential, understand?" Johnny nodded his head rather nervously, "Yeah Bobby I understand, my lips are sealed."

"Good," Bobby continued, "This is the score, I am in the insurance and banking business. I also have sidelines like having a window cleaning firm." "Sounds great" said Johnny, "Can you elaborate?"
"Right, here goes," Bobby said, "First of all, the insurance business. For a sum, depending on the size of the business, we protect people from any trouble. So, for example, you have a pub, for a couple of quid a

week we make sure there is no trouble there. And if there is, we sort out the troublemakers. So it's a good insurance policy for the landlord and gives him peace of mind that he has back up. The banking side is a wee bit different. We loan money to people starting at two bob, twenty pence in the pound. And the punter pays it back the next week. So, say you borrow a fiver, then next week you pay six quid, simple."
"But what happens if they don't pay?" Johnny asked rather naively. "Well, the interest then goes to four bob in the pound, forty pence, so the fiver goes up to seven quid."

"And what happens if they don't pay that?" Johnny asked. McGee was straight to the point with a scowl on his face, "Simple, they might get a slap on the face or a kick in the balls, depending on the circumstances. Bur we're no' like the big banks, we don't take your house from you. A good slap or kicking is usually enough tae ensure the dosh is paid back pronto. Ah'm no' like Arthur, Glasgow's Godfather, he's been known to crucify people, nail them to walls and floor if they don't cough up.

"On the gambling side we take bets from the punters and provide better odds than the official bookies. But reputation is important. We always pay out no matter how big or small the win is. One punter won £500 from me last week and we paid up straight away. The guy is a gambling degenerate, so I know I'll get ma money back eventually, and more. The takings are good for all bookies, official and unofficial ones like me. I mean have you ever seen a bookie on a bike?"

"No," Johnny laughed.

"Right, so that's the core of the business, banking, betting and insurance. But ah've just started a window cleaning business as well."

"Window cleaning?" Johnny asked in a bemused tone.

"We operate in posh areas like Milngavie, Giffnock, Shawlands and Hillhead where people have big houses with lots of valuables. My window cleaners clock what time they come and go and note the routine. Armed wi' the information, a separate mob of guys are employed tae burgle the places, simple!"

Johnny was really impressed. So this was what real gangsters did. It certainly was more exciting and far more lucrative than shovelling sawdust into bags.

"So, what's ma job?" he asked Bobby.

"Well now you are part of the family, you will be my right-hand man, enforcer and consiglieri."

"Consiglieri, what the fuck does that mean?"

"It's an old Mafia term, it means you give me advice when I can't make my mind up. The consiglieri is the guy the big boss consults when he needs steering in the right direction."

 And the hours?"

"The pay is a basic fifty quid plus bonuses, and the hours vary depending on what other wee jobs you have to dae. But ah'll tell you what, you won't have tae clock in like the sawmills!" Bobby laughed.

"What am I gonnae tell Cathy about leaving the sawmills"

"Don't worry about that, her mother told her you left there to join the family firm. Cathy doesn't know what ah do exactly. But she does have a faint idea ah'm in the banking, betting and insurance business."

"Sounds impressive Bobby. So you make a right few bob from this?"

Bobby smiled and rose from his chair, "You could say that. Come on and ah'll show you something." He led Johnny into another room and opened a safe in the wall which was hidden behind a painting. Inside the safe there were piles of £10 and £20 notes. "This is some of my ill-gotten gains," Bobby joked. Johnny was certainly impressed with what he had told him. And glimpses of his father in laws' dodgy wealth reinforced the idea that he should also be a professional gangster. It was a no-brainer.

Suddenly the phone rang. Bobby picked it up, "Hello? Oh, hello Arthur. What, ye want me up there now? No problem, ah'll be up straight away." He looked at Johnny, "Right we're off to see the big man."
Outside, one of Bobby's henchmen was waiting in a car. He drove them to a pub, owned by Arthur, in the Provanhill area of Glasgow. When they went into the pub, Arthur, looking every inch a businessman in a smart suit, was seated with a gang of his enforcers.

They were well-built men who, although friendly, were slightly intimidating. "Who is this?" Arthur said looking at Johnny. Bobby replied, "This is Johnny, my son in law, great guy, one of the boys and very dependable. He keeps his mouth shut when he has to."

"Good to hear it," Arthur replied and shook Johnny's hand while continuing to address his gang, "Right boys, if you can leave us for a while, ah've got to have a confidential meeting wi' Bobby and his pal." They nodded and left. Arthur put a diagram on the pub table, "This is a job ah've been planning for a while. Clydesdale Bank just off Sauchiehall Street. Ah've got a mole inside who tells me there will be thirty grand in the tills this Friday. I need two men to go in and take it. One will have a shotgun, the other a starting pistol. I will arrange for somebody to cut the alarm and telephone lines, before they go in.
"Ah've also lined up a getaway driver. I need another fit young guy wi' brains, for back up, tae enter the bank. Johnny, you look like you fit the bill."

Johnny felt nervous but nodded his head and said, "Aye, no problem, Arthur." They went over the plan in more detail. The robbery would take place at just before 3pm on Friday. Johnny and the other guy would wear stockings on their heads. Friday came along and Johnny and his accomplice, called Billy, who he had only met a couple of hours before the heist, entered the bank. Billy, brandishing a shotgun, shouted to the customers, "Get on the fucking floor!"

Johnny, shaking with fear and adrenaline, fired the starting pistol into the air. They handed two large bags to a teller who filled them up with notes. No alarm bells went off and they rushed outside to the car to make their getaway. No hitches, everything went according to plan. Johnny got back to the Gorbals and met Bobby in his flat. They turned on the radio, "A Glasgow bank was raided today by two armed men, wearing stockings over their faces. It is believed they got away with £25,000." Later they went back to Arthur's pub and the money, in bundles of banknotes, was shared out. When they got home, Bobby put his slice of cash in his wall safe, all in used, untraceable notes. Johnny had his £5,000 in two plastic bags which he hid under the floorboards in his flat. He had a quick wash and headed out for a walk around the Gorbals.

"Five thousand quid, for a few minutes work! He loved being a gangster. It was certainly better and more lucrative than shovelling sawdust into bags. As he was walking towards Gorbals Cross he saw wee Alex coming towards him with a big smile on his face.
"Where you been?" Johnny said.
"Up in the magistrates courts."
"What for?"
"Robbery and theft."
"Robbery and theft? Why, what happened?"
Alex gave a mad laugh, "After I left you the other day I went intae Lewis's department store and decided to steal a few tea towels and a packet of Brillo pads for ma mother. I also stole a woman's purse."

"So, you got caught Alex?"

"Yeah, they've got new hidden cameras in the store tae catch shoplifters like me. Ah was arrested and taken tae the police cells and then court. They adjourned the case until this morning for social work reports."

"And?"

"Well, a social worker, who knows me well, told the court something like I was 'a well known mental detective'. Ah think she meant that ah look like that Columbo guy on the telly. Wi' ma black hair and raincoat, ah'm a dead ringer for him. Anyway they let me go saying that they had taken into consideration that ah looked like a mental detective."

Wee Alex was serious. Johnny felt tears of laughter coming down his cheeks, he had never laughed so much in his life.

"Ah'll tell you what though," Alex said, "Crime does not pay!"

He agreed, "You're right pal, crime definitely does not pay, even if you are a well-known mental detective!"

Chapter 51

SWIMMING

Johnny was informed by Bobby that they were to have a forward planning meeting at the Rogano Restaurant "up the toon" with big Arthur. He told Johnny, "He was well impressed how you handled the bank job. Arthur wants to have a wee chat about further business opportunities. The Rogano is a smashing place, full of toffs, but, ah suppose because we have a few bob as well, we are the new toffs!" Johnny agreed, nodding his head rather nervously. He had been summoned to a top restaurant by the Godfather himself, this was indeed an honour. Bobby told him to look smart as Arthur liked people who were smart and clean.

He had got the message but the planned meeting put him on edge. Did this mean Arthur wanted him to do more bank jobs? It was a prospect he did not relish. He had just bought a smashing looking pin-striped suit which made him look every inch the provincial businessman, that was the smart part covered.

As for being clean, he headed to the Gorbals baths for a swim and hot shower. The admission price was pittance and you could swim as much as you wanted and stand under the hot showers for ages. Upstairs, they had baths which were used mostly by Irish labourers to get clean after grafting on the building sites. Johnny took his swimming trunks and towel along. He had been doing this since he was a schoolboy and often stood under the hot showers and talked to older Gorbals guys who had fascinating stories to tell. There were small changing rooms around the pool, where the swimmers changed. He was a good swimmer and decided to do 50 lengths. After his swim he went into the shower room and was surprised to see Malky there with hot water cascading over him.

He looked as though he had lost a bit of weight, his beer belly had been reduced considerably. Johnny shouted to him, "Malky ya bastard ye. You've lost a bit of weight, ye must be shagging too much." Malky laughed, "Maybe! So, how's it going? Ah see you didnae last too long in that sweat shop they call the sawmills." Johnny laughed, "Aye, Malky, it wisnae for me aw that shovelling sawdust shite. So how come you're no' at work?" Malky grimaced, "Back strain, was lifting a pile of planks out of a van when ma back went. The doctor has given me a sick note for a week off."

"A week's pay for a holiday, that's no' bad Malky!" Of course, there was an elephant in the room. None of them had mentioned Lorraine yet. For a few minutes there was an uncomfortable silence. Malky believed Johnny did not want to talk about Lorraine and Johnny believed Malky did not want to talk about Lorraine, so there was a sort of stalemate for a few minutes. But Johnny broke the silence, "So, how's things wi' you and Lorraine?" "Glad you asked," Malky replied with a sigh of relief, "We're going very strong but ah didnae want tae mention it after what she told me about you and her."

Johnny felt a knot develop in his stomach and covered up his nervousness by saying, "So what exactly did she tell you?" Malky shrugged as the hot water hit his shoulders, "She told me you wanted to marry her but she rejected you and you married Cathy on the rebound. All the worry about rejecting you put her in hospital with 'woman's trouble' but she's all right now. Is it true Johnny she rejected your offer to marry?" Johnny had to be diplomatic and bend the truth, "Yeah, it's true Malky, ma heart was broken when she turned me down. But you are the lucky man who got her instead, what a beautiful bird she is."

Malky cheered up on hearing Johnny's false patter, "Ah'm sorry it didnae work out for you, but Cathy's a good catch and you were right tae marry her." Johnny agreed, "Too right, Malky, Lorraine wisnae for me anyway. You're the best man for her, in fact the best man won!"

Malky smiled and nodded in agreement, "Ah'm glad you said that. Can ah tell you a wee secret?" "What's that Malky?"

"We're thinking of getting engaged, we've been up the toon looking for rings. There's just one thing that bothers me, her father stinks of fish, the smell follows him about everywhere. At times, it can be unbearable. It gets so bad he smells like a rat has crawled up his arse and died."

With this humorous yet slightly worrying remark Johnny left his pal in the showers and got dressed. When he glanced in a mirror he looked like the successful businessman, come gangster, he had always wanted to be.

He walked into a fish and chip shop in the city centre and could feel people were looking at him. What was this prosperous looking businessman doing in a dump like this? Clothes maketh the man! Even the pretty little waitress, who must have been about 17, brought him a cup of tea in a servile manner.

As she placed the tea on the table she said, "There you are, sir. If you fancy something to eat we have very nice cod and chips, sauce provided free." Johnny smiled and kept up his pretence of being a visiting businessman. He even changed his voice to make it sound more respectable. He said to the waitress, "No thanks, I'm eating at the Rogano Restaurant later." The young waitress blushed, "The Rogano? Ah've never been inside, far too posh for people like me, but for businessmen like you, ideal." He felt so bucked up he left her a pound tip. He liked this gangster, businessman role, it was as if he had been born for it.

He got to the Rogano at the appointed time of 7.30pm. The guy at the door, a Uriah Heep type character with a moustache, greeted him with the servility he had expected, "Good evening, sir, nice to see you again," he said in a foreign accent, probably French.

Johnny was amused that the guy had said it was nice to see him again as he had never been there before. But he knew it was all part of the posh patter syndrome.

When he walked inside there was not only the smell of fancy food but also the place reeked of money. Bobby was already there in small dimly-lit alcove opposite the bar. He was sitting in what in the Gorbals was known as "the gangsters' seat." He had a wall behind him and was clocking everyone coming through the front door. "Sit down and enjoy," Bobby said. There was a large bottle of champagne on the table in an ice bucket with three glasses.

Big Arthur arrived about 15 minutes later and had an aura about him. Bobby gave a toast, "To our various ventures!" They talked about inane things for about half an hour, because this was how business was done. Inanity before the financial reality of business.

To impress Arthur, Bobby told a feeble joke, "Daddy bull and his boy were at the top of a hill when they spotted a herd of cows below. The son said to daddy, 'Why don't we run down and fuck a couple of them?' Daddy bull says, 'No, we'll walk down and fuck them all'."

Big Arthur laughed perhaps realising that this was some kind of metaphor for how they did business. He spoke in a low voice, "You guys have impressed me. That bank job went well, as easy as spreading margarine. That's what I like, nobody got caught, that's the main thing. When I was younger, I did time in jail, but that's for idiots. Long may our business adventures continue." They all gave a toast. The night proceeded well and much to Johnny's relief there was no mention of another bank job. They headed into the dining room where a table was waiting for them. Johnny was handed a menu by the waiter but all the dishes were gobbledegook to him. Most of them had French titles. Arthur and Bobby had been many times before and knew what they wanted to order.

Johnny was slightly intimidated by the place with its elaborate menu and prices. The food titles baffled him and when asked by the French waiter what he'd like to order as a starter and main course, he bluffed it saying, "What do you recommend?" The waiter suggested as a starter, Moules Marinere and for the main course, Lobster Thermidor. He had no idea what they were, he was used to mince and tatties in the house and a fish supper from the local chippy.

This was a different ball game, food fit for a king, or a Glasgow gangster. The food was also very expensive, you wouldn't see may sawmills labourers in here, not unless they won the pools. The dishes came and were excellent, perhaps the best Johnny had ever tasted. More champagne was ordered and he began to feel slightly drunk. Arthur said at one point, "You pair are good operators, I'm quite prepared for you two guys to have a slice of the cake."

As he was getting drunker Johnny said to Arthur, "Can you do me a favour?"

"What's that son?"

"Ma wife has just had a baby boy, Johnny Robert McGrath. Will you be his godfather?"

Arthur smiled, "Of course I will, no bother son."

He then got up and left leaving Bobby and Johnny to pay the hefty bill. Bobby said, "Worth every fucking penny. We've now got the godfather of Glasgow as godfather to your son and my grandson. Brilliant move, Johnny, even I wouldn't have thought of that."

They left the restaurant staggering arm in arm looking every inch two well dressed, yet inebriated gangsters.

Chapter 52

APPRENTICE

Now that Johnny had been made Bobby's right hand man and consigliere he had to learn the ropes fast. After all, the banking, betting and insurance game needed skills and experience to run them. Bobby had no doubt that Johnny had the acumen and talent to run such an operation, but like an apprentice he would have to serve his time, learn and make a lot of mistakes along the way. It was clear Bobby was very fond of Johnny, indeed treated him like the son he never had. Or, to put it succinctly, for a short period of time he did have a son, briefly years before, but his wife had a miscarriage and he was lost forever. Cathy came along 18 months later.

As part of his induction into the workings of the Glasgow underworld, Bobby gave his protégé yet another "wee insight" into how things were run. "It's simple," he said, "We deal in money, ready cash which is untraceable." On the banking side he learnt that the attraction to punters was the fact they did not have to put any security up front. People were taken at face value. The majority were happy with the rates of interest and surprised how easy it was to get a loan of a few quid. The majority paid up on time but Johnny had to sort out those who tried to take him and Bobby for mugs. Johnny was quite good at giving a good slap, Glasgow kiss, or a "kick in the baws" to those who deserved it. His biggest problem was dealing with "the alkies", the guys who spent all their money on booze. But after a good slap, they usually sobered up enough to find the repayments.

All sorts of people had all sorts of excuses not to pay on time, but the psychology was fuck that, pay up or pay the price! On the betting side Johnny had fewer problems. The secret was to beat the official bookie odds. If the bookies offered 7-1 on a horse he would offer 8-1.

The important thing was to keep up the reputation of being generous, the word would spread and more punters would be attracted. He paid out a few big wins but in the end always won the money back, usually within a short period of time. On the insurance side Johnny had to beat up a few troublemakers. He even dealt with a gang of young guys who were going around with spray paint cans and vandalising properties. They were forced to scrub the graffiti off the walls with wire brushes. Also, a few shoplifters had their hands stood on by Johnny's Doc Marten boots. The businesses were grateful as they knew they were being well protected. There was also a bit of bootlegging, selling knocked off booze and tobacco smuggling, offering the cheapest fags and rolled tobacco in Glasgow.

Another unusual side-line was dealing in stolen works of art. Some collectors would order via the firm, a certain work of art they wanted and Johnny would try to provide it by hook or crook. In just a few months he had a great knowledge of all sides of the business.

Instead of shovelling sawdust into bags, he was now shovelling money into them.

At that point there was another side-line rearing its head: drugs. Up till then, Bobby and his team refused to deal in Charlie (cocaine) hash (marijuana) and even heroin. But times were changing and there was more and more demand for all sorts of drugs including amphetamine pills. Big Arthur and other gangsters were leading the way so it was only a matter of time before Bobby and his team followed suit. Being part of a money-making machine meant that Johnny had to have a low profile role. He was told to keep signing on the dole and remain in his council flat. Bobby had enough money to buy a mansion in leafy Bearsden but a low profile in his council flat meant there was less chance of him being noticed by the authorities. The message was… keep under the radar.

They were so busy that Bobby arranged for Johnny to have two henchmen, Archie and Kenny Boy. Archie was to be Johnny's driver and enforcer, and Kenny Boy was the other, jack of all trades, enforcer. Bobby told Johnny to delegate, and never to get his hands dirty "let them soil their hands for you." Johnny and Bobby met the men in a car outside the high flats. Both of the enforcers were very well dressed, Archie in a dark blue suit and Kenny in a black Crombie coat. When Johnny jumped into the back of the Ford Zephyr, he recognised Archie straight away. He was a thick set man, in his 30s, weighing about 16 stone. He had the look of an ex-boxer about him, big bent nose and thick black hair. Johnny had seen Archie a few times in the Portland Dancehall chatting up the birds. He was a fine dancer and for a big man, pretty nimble on his feet. He also recognised Kenny Boy. He was a thin guy in his late 20s with a mop of fair hair.

He was reading a copy of the racing paper Sporting Life. Johnny had heard he had been a wizard at school in mathematics. Presumably he was the guy who calculated the betting odds for the punters. Bobby introduced Johnny to the two men, "Right boys, as you may know, this is ma new deputy. You do what he says, but go easy on him, he's new to the job." He left the car and told Johnny to take over. Johnny said to his new enforcers, "So, what are we up to today boys?"

Archie replied, "Four pubs, three shops for insurance money. On the loan side, six punters who are overdue with repayments, and a further three who want a loan of a few bob. On the betting side, about a dozen guys who want to place bets and to collect their winnings."

Johnny was chauffeured round the Gorbals and nearby areas as his two men went into pubs and clubs to collect and dole out money. He barely had to do a thing. After every visit he was usually handed a pile of notes which he registered in a black book of accounts that Bobby had provided. He stored the cash inside a metal box which his boss had also given him. At the end of the day, he had collected more than £500 and paid out £50 in loans and winning bets. He was amazed at how easy it was to make money, especially

from a so-called impoverished place like the Gorbals, but as the English said, "Where there's muck, there's brass."
At the end of the day's trading, Archie sat at the steering wheel and said, "Where next boss?" Kenny was silent as he was still studying the odds in the paper.

"Crown Street, ah think ah'll call in and see ma wee maw," Johnny said. The car stopped outside the tenement close. He jumped out saying, "Back in a jiffy, boys." He put the key in the latch and went inside his parent's flat. His mother looked as though she had been crying. "What's the matter, maw?" He said. She looked shattered, "Ach, it's just one of those days, everything seems to be getting me down."

"Like what?"

"Two boys have been beating up your wee brother and some union guy has banned your father from ever working again on the boats."
He went into the "wee room" next door and found his brother Joseph looking depressed. He had bruises on his forehead and two black eyes. Johnny said angrily,

"Who did it?" but Joseph was reluctant to spill the beans, he was no grass. "Look, if you don't tell me who did it I'll be up to your school in the morning and ask every fucker, including your headmaster, who was behind your beating." Joseph reluctantly told him the two boy's names. Johnny knew that after school they hung around the Queens Park Café in Victoria Road. He ran down the tenement stairs determined to settle the score. He, Archie and Kenny walked into the café and ordered three cones. Johnny saw the two boys, aged about 15, straight away, laughing and tucking into two dishes of ice cream. He felt like going over and punching them straight away. But then Bobby's words came back to haunt him, "Don't get your hands dirty, delegate." He said in a low voice to his men, "See those two young wankers there? They're bullies who have been beating up ma wee bother. When they've come out, give them a slap." They headed to the car with their ice creams and waited for about 15 minutes until the boys appeared.

Archie said, "Let me handle this!" He walked up to the boys and shouted, "Ah hear you've been taking a liberty, battering wee Joseph." The boys looked ashen-faced with fright. Archie grabbed their two heads and banged them together. Both of them fell to pavement, crying like babies. Archie shouted to them again, "Fuck wi' wee Joseph and you're fucking wi' us." He jumped back behind the wheel and made off. Johnny and Kenny Boy could not stop laughing at the whole scenario. It had looked like a scene from a Three Stooges movie. Johnny told Archie to drop him back at the family tenement and finish for the day. They would take the money to Bobby in the high flats.

When he got back in his family house both Joseph and his mother were sitting gloomily in the kitchen. "Hey, you two, cheer up, it might never happen," he shouted, "By the way, those two boys who beat Joseph up won't be doing it again, ah can promise you that!"
Both mother and son cheered up, "What did you say to them?" Joseph asked. "I said nothing, but ah got one of ma men tae knock some sense into them." He exited the flat leaving them in far better spirits than when he had found them.
He adored being a gangster, it made him love life even more. It was an incredible feeling.

Chapter 53

ARCHIBALD

A few days later Johnny was busy working with Archie and Kenny and had been impressed with their variety of talents. Archie was everything an enforcer should be, tough, smart and had a very quick wit. Once when a punter had refused to pay his arrears, Archie went to his flat and hung him by the legs out of a three story tenement window. The guy ended up pleading upside down, "Please don't drop me, don't let me fall, ah'll get your money straight away." Of course, Archie had no intention of killing the fellow but merely intended to put the frighteners on him. On another occasion, another punter tried to "act fly" when asked for his overdue payment. He kept calling him "Archibald" which was the one thing he hated. It was his real name and he had been taunted for years at school about it with other pupils taunting him by chanting, "Archibald, Archibald, when you're auld you're gonnae be bald, Archibald!" The taunts had not come true, he had a full head of hair but the memories in the school playground still haunted him.

The punter had taunted him by saying, "Archibald, you'll get your money ok, Archibald?" He flipped and head butted the man on the nose, breaking it in several places. He met up with the debtor a few days later who paid up in full saying, "Sorry about the misunderstanding Archie." Johnny believed that if the

fellow had called him Archibald again he would have
killed him on the spot. Kenny was a different kettle of
fish. Unlike Archie he had a slow-burning fuse and
seemed to calculate his every move. When Archie
suggested breaking someone's legs for missing
several payments, Kenny had replied, "No' a good
idea, Archie. If the guy cannae walk he cannae work,
which means we'll get fuck all at the end of the day.
Let me have a word wi' him."

He saw the debtor in a pub and explained that Archie
planned to break his legs but had talked him out of it.
The guy eventually paid up in full a few days later. One
the betting side, Kenny lived up to his reputation as a
whiz kid with figures. He could calculate the odds on
any bet within a few seconds. And he was usually
never wrong in his predictions. He was also quite good
in fights and carried an old policeman's truncheon and
if need be would "batter some sense" into any punter
who tried to take him for a fool. Johnny reflected that
with these two enforcers by his side, and the backing
of Bobby McGee and even big Arthur, he could do no
wrong.
He had sent them on errands to collect money one day
and sat in the Sou' Wester pub on Eglinton Street and
reflected on things. Everything was going well, the
money was flowing in and he enjoyed the job. But had
Bobby been right in refusing to deal in drugs when
there were such big profits to be made? He had heard
through the grapevine that a Scouser from Liverpool
had arrived in Glasgow and started a drug dealing

business. He had been told the guy was called Tony Shaw, in his early 30s, and had based himself near Bridgeton Cross, where he had a garage that was a store for cocaine and marijuana. Johnny was just thinking about this when three strangers entered the bar.

They all had one thing in common. Strong Liverpool accents which stood out like a sore thumb in the Gorbals. One of the guys, thin with brown hair, was in his early 30s and the other two guys were in their late 40s. They were comparatively well dressed in suits. But the suits looked cheap and certainly not in the same class as the ones Johnny and his men wore. He presumed the young Scouser was Tony Shaw and his two Liverpool cronies were his enforcers.

Tony ordered three pints and looked in Johnny's direction. He came over to the table and said, "You must be Johnny McGrath. I've heard a lot about you." They shook hands and Tony sat down, leaving his pals standing at the bar. "Johnny, I know you are one of Bobby's men. Can you not get him to change his mind?"
"About what?"
"About dealing in Charlie and hash. If you and your mob joined up with us we'd make a good team. Plenty of dosh and it's easy money."
Johnny decided to play it cool, "I know ah've tried tae explain to Bobby but he's old school and looks down on the drug trade."

Tony looked slightly miffed, "Can he not see the profit potential? Business is booming and with your crew on board we could make a fortune." Johnny said he would have another word with Bobby and Tony Shaw scribbled out his address on a piece of paper, his small warehouse just off Bridgeton Cross. He and his two henchmen then left the pub in a good mood believing that Johnny would influence Bobby and go into business with them.

But when he got back to Bobby's flat and told him of the offer, he flew into a furious rage, "No way we are getting involved with those Scouse bastards, we'll end up doing 15 years each in jail. The judges are very strict on that. Money lending, betting and protection insurance you might get a slap on the wrist. But drugs? They'll lock you up and throw away the key, Johnny. Think of a plan to run those bastards out of town. "

He said he'd see what he could do and left Bobby's flat with a thumping headache. Cathy was out with the baby and her mother so he decided to head to his family home in Crown Street.
When he got there his mother and father were sitting having a cup of tea and looked dejected. His father explained, "I thought I was gonnae be back on the boats but this union official called Angus McTavish has put the blocks on it. Ah've never liked him and he hates me. We had a big argument and he said ah'll never work on the boats again." During the course of

the conversation, which lasted for half an hour, Johnny learnt that Angus McTavish was in his late 50s and was known for "going by the book" and punishing heavily any union men who broke the rules. When he heard Johnny's father had been caught fiddling tips he came down on him like a ton of bricks. Johnny asked his father to describe Angus. He said, "He's a big fat bastard, 6'2" with red hair and a beard to match, typical guy from the Highlands."

Johnny's first instinct was to find out if Angus had any weak points, an Achilles Heel, that he could focus on. Turned out, he had. He was "a ladies man" who hung around with prostitutes most nights in Betty's Bar in the Broomielaw, not far from the union's offices.

He bade his father farewell saying, "Don't worry, your luck will change soon, I can guarantee that. You'll be back on the boats before you know it." He met up with Archie and Kenny and they drove to Betty's Bar. It was about 9pm and the place was busy with drinkers, mostly seamen, and prostitutes.

They sat in the corner of the bar and monitored the situation. Sure enough the man they recognised as Angus was at a table looking very drunk, accompanied by two sleazy looking women. He was singing The Wild Rover in an out of tune voice, "Ah've been a wild rover." About 20 minutes later Angus got up and staggered out of the door. Johnny and his men got into the car outside and drove a few hundred yards to pull up beside Angus.

Johnny and Kenny bundled him into the car and sped off with Archie at the steering wheel. Angus was shouting, "Who the fuck are you guys? Where the fuck are you taking me?" Kenny hit him on the back of the head with his truncheon and knocked him unconscious. They drove for about 20 minutes and found themselves in a wood on the outskirts of Glasgow. Angus suddenly woke up and stared into the darkness of the wood. "Where the fuck am I?" he shouted. Archie pulled out a revolver, Johnny was not sure if it was real or a starting pistol. He told Angus to get out of the car. Still pointing the gun, Archie handed the union man a shovel and said," "Start digging a hole ye bastard, deep enough and wide enough for your fat body tae fit in." Angus began digging but began to sober up and burst out crying. He shouted, "Please don't kill me boys. Please, ah beg you, ah'll do anything. Ah've got a wife and kids in Oban, ah don't want tae die, please boys." Angus looked a pathetic sight, no longer was he the powerful union man. He knew his life could be ended at any minute.

Johnny came forward through the darkness, "Do you recall Jo Jo McGrath, the seaman who was caught fiddling?"

Angus began shaking violently, "Of course ah do."

Johnny growled, "Well, make sure he gets the go ahead to go back to work on the boats."

"But he's broken all the rules!"
Johnny shouted back, "It's either he gets his job back
by next week or pick up that fucking shovel and start
digging your own grave, ya fat wanker."
Angus was ashen white and trembling with fear, "Ok!
Ok! I get the message boys. He'll get the go-ahead to
start work on the boats again."

They bundled Angus into the car, put the shovel in the
boot and sped off back to Glasgow. Angus was told
that he would be "a dead man walking" if he told
anyone about the kidnap. They left him at a bus stop
near the Broomielaw and drove off laughing. Archie
said, "Ah think that big Highland bastard got the
message." Johnny laughed, "Aye, it's no' every day
you get the chance tae dig your own grave. Fat balloon
deserved it."
A few days later, Johnny was lying in bed with Cathy
by his side, and the baby in a cot nearby, when
suddenly there was loud knocking on the door. It was
only 7am. The baby began to cry loudly. Cathy said,
"Who the hell is that at this time in the morning?"
Johnny looked through a spy hole in the door, two
policemen stood outside. He opened the door. One of
the policemen said, "Johnny McGrath?"
"Aye, who's asking?"
"Glasgow police, we want to interview you about
allegations of assault." Johnny got ready and was
taken in handcuffs to police headquarters, near
Glasgow Cross. He was put in a police cell thinking,

"That Angus bastard has grassed me up. We should have just buried him." About an hour later the cell door opened and two policemen took him into an interview room. They were joined by a CID guy in his late 40s. He said to Johnny, "We believe you were behind a serious assault, can you tell me anything about it?" Of course he would tell them nothing, the grass seaman deserved everything he had got. "Tell you what?"

"Well, last week two schoolboys were assaulted outside a café in Victoria Road and say you and your pals were behind it."
In a way Johnny was relieved to hear this. "Ah did go into the Queens Park Café last week and there were a couple of cheeky schoolboys there. They gave a guy, who I do not know, a bit of lip. He ended up banging their heads together outside the café. But it's nothing to dae wi' me."

"So, you don't know who this guy is?"

"Nah never seen him before in ma life. He was a stranger from out of town."

The CID guy seemed unconvinced, he looked him straight in the eye, "The problem we've got, Johnny, is one of the assaulted boys is the head of CID's son. He wants the guy caught and locked up a.s.a.p." He replied, "Look, ah've got some info for you that might please your boss far better than catching the guy who battered his boy."

The CID guy raised his eyebrows, "Oh aye, what would this information be?"

"About a big drugs cache in Glasgow."
The CID guy smiled, he was definitely interested Johnny handed him a piece of paper with Tony Shaw's name and the address of the Bridgeton warehouse. The CID guy looked at it with an incredulous grin on his face. He said, "You're right this is very important information, far bigger than the slapping of two daft boys."
Johnny was free to go. The next day he went back to his father's house. He found his parents and brother in high spirits. His father exclaimed, "They've given me ma job back. Ah've been reinstated, it's a miracle!" Johnny replied, "Good for you da! I knew your luck would change for the better." That night, he picked up a copy of the Evening Times and the front page headline declared: **BIG DRUGS HAUL IN BRIDGETON. THREE LIVERPOOL MEN ARRESTED.**

Johnny was learning all the time. Being a gangster meant you had to make the right move at the right moment… perhaps he should take up playing chess.

Chapter 54

NARCOTICS

Johnny had a tinge of guilt as he had never grassed up anyone before and for a brief time, it gnawed at his conscience. In fact, he felt like he was cracking up more than Humpty Dumpty. But when he told Bobby, his boss was delighted, "Look, you've saved us a lot of money, time and hassle. If you hadn't done that we would have had to put a posse together, all on good money to run those Scousers out of town. It was a good move to tell the polis. In fact, ah heard big Arthur does it all the time."

Bobby emphasised that what Johnny had done was "a tactical move" to get their rivals out of town. But there was awareness that times were changing. They had noticed that a lot of Asian men were going about in big fancy cars buying investment properties in Glasgow. They had no doubts that drug money was behind this. They had been reliably informed that the Asians were importing hashish and heroin from Pakistan. It was certainly more lucrative than running a corner shop selling milk and bread. The tide was definitely turning in the direction of narcotics. But it was a matter of convincing Bobby to change with the times otherwise they would be left behind. The business they ran, betting, banking and insurance was lucrative enough but much of it was a drop in the ocean to what they could earn from selling drugs.

Meanwhile, Johnny had proved to be an effective second in command. With Archie and Kenny by his side they were certainly a formidable force, feared and respected by many. Johnny had decided that he and his men would have at least one day off, a Sunday. It gave them a chance to unwind and for Johnny to be a family man.

Cathy was a good wife and mother and Johnny, at least on a Sunday, made a big effort to be a good husband and father. When he was not in gangster mode on his day off, he made the conscious decision to dress down. He could be seen with his family in places like the Glasgow Green, usually dressed in a black t-shirt with black jeans to match. The dress style signified that he was not on duty and did not want to be approached on any business matters. But come Monday, the flashy suit was back on and it was business as usual.

One day, he, Archie and Kenny, were sitting in Cha Pa Pa's chippy in Crown Street when they were approached by a fat, prosperous-looking man dressed in a three piece suit. He said to Johnny, "Is it all right to have a wee word?" He was invited to join them. They instantly knew the guy, he was a legit bookmaker who had betting shops all over Glasgow and the rest of Scotland. "I've got a problem that I want you to sort out," he said. Johnny replied, "Oh aye, what's the problem man?" The bookie shuffled nervously on his feet, "A gang of chancers have been going at the demands for money. They say if I don't cough up they're are gonnae wreck my shops and put me out of business."

Johnny asked their names but they were a bunch of nobodies who were not in the same league as his mob.

They could be got rid of as easily as swatting a fly but he pretended to the bookie the situation was far worse than it was, "That's a heavy mob you are talking about. You're right, they could put you out of business unless something is done straight away." The bookie, who had a fat, ruddy face began to sweat profusely, "So, what can you do for me son?" Johnny kept up the pretence of the threatening guys being a danger, but they were in fact a bunch of mugs. He said, "Those guys will need to get sorted out, but it'll take manpower and money, so it'll no' be cheap."

The fat bookmaker looked relieved, "I don't really care how much it costs as long as I get them out of my hair."

"How many shops you got?" Johnny asked.

"Twenty in Glasgow and the rest of Scotland"

Johnny smirked, "No problem, pal. If you take out an insurance policy with us, we'll protect you straight away. But we'll need a payment up front."

"How much?" the bookie said nervously.

Johnny thought he'd push his luck, he knew the bookie was desperate, "Two grand up front and you pay a premium every month for our protection." The bookie suddenly looked relieved as if a heavy weight had been lifted from his shoulders. "Oh, that sounds reasonable. Can you come with me to the bank?" Johnny and his boys went outside where a red Rolls Royce was waiting, an incongruous sight in the Gorbals. The bookie had a chauffeur who drove them to a bank in the city centre. Archie went inside with the bookie to withdraw the money. They came back with £2,000 in crisp banknotes. They were dropped back in the Gorbals. Archie said, "That fat bookie bastard must have some dough tae afford a red Rolls Royce and a chauffeur. Ah think he got us cheap!"

"Nah," Kenny replied, "He'll be making substantial payments every month, so the odds are well in our favour. Easy money!"

Archie laughed, "Too right, ah've given the bookies planty of dosh over the years, its time we got it back!"

They soon found out where the main instigator of the gang who had threatened the bookie lived, a tenement in Cumberland Street. The guy, Dom Donnelly, aged 23, really was a nobody but had delusions of grandeur.

He lived in a fantasy world thinking he was a top notch mobster. But when faced with real gangsters like Johnny and his boys he shat himself. Archie said to him in a menacing voice, "We hear you've been causing a bit of bother wi' a bookmaker pal of ours."

Donnelly was frightened and began to stutter, "N... n... no b...b... boys it's aw a b... b... bit of a mis... misund... misundertanding."

Kenny grabbed him by the throat and held a razor to his face, "It fucking better be otherwise you'll be getting this."

Donnelly began shaking uncontrollably, "Oh... nae t... t... trouble, boys. Ah'll no, no be, be b... bothering him again."

They left it at that, Donnelly had got the message. They told Johnny who had been waiting in the car outside, "That wanker pissed in his pants when he saw us. We'll no' be having any bother from him again."

Johnny smiled in the back seat, "Thought so, that tube is a Walter Mitty but we'll keep up the pretence to the bookie that Donnelly is a real threat and we'll get him to pay plenty of protection money." Both Archie and Kenny had been increasingly impressed with Johnny's Machiavellian skills and nodded in agreement.

"Aye, we'll screw the bastard for a right few bob," Archie said in a tone that sounded more comical than aggressive.

They parked the car and went for a walk through the Gorbals, or rather what was left of it. Every day, tenements were being pulled down all over the place. The Gorbals was definitely disintegrating like a prehistoric monster. As one tenement was being pulled down in Thistle Street, Archie said to Johnny, "Would you look at that! Ma mother was born and brought up in that tenement and now it's a pile of rubble. Same wi' ma father's old tenement, it's as if they are trying to wipe us off the face of the Earth."

Johnny shrugged his shoulders, "Maybe, Archie, but while a lot of buildings are still standing and there are people about who need our services, we carry on regardless."

On his way back to his house in the high flats, Johnny bumped into wee Alex. He was standing at a corner in Ballater Street with another guy smoking a large joint. He was surprised. He knew Alex liked a good bevvy but had never seen him smoke drugs before. "Hey Johnny boy, fancy a smoke?" Alex shouted. He turned down the offer, "Nah, Alex, ah don't touch the Bob Hope. When did you start on the wacky backy?" Alex laughed, blew out a fume of smoke and said, "A couple of months ago. It gi's you a better hit than the wine or lager and can work out cheaper than buying a carry oot. Try some, for fuck's sake."

Johnny once again turned down the offer of the joint and walked away, thinking that perhaps it was a sign of the times. Drugs looked like they were on the way to replacing alcohol. It had become the in thing.

When he got back to Bobby's flat, he told him of the lucrative protection deal he had done with the bookie. Bobby was impressed, "Good work, son, this will be excellent business for us. A right few bob. Is there any other news?"

Johnny told him about his interaction with the drug smoking Alex. Bobby looked slightly worried and pondered the situation, "Maybe you're right, maybe times are changing. Big Arthur has been in contact saying the drug floodgates have opened and we've got to be involved. I hate drugs, but the public gets what the public wants."

Johnny nodded his head in agreement, "It sure is a sign of the changing times when somebody like wee Alex is smoking a joint. Usually he'd be stoned on a bottle of Eldorado wine."

Bobby replied, "Aye, you're right. Cannabis is as easy to buy now as cheap wine. Maybe it's time we changed our policy. Ah know big Arthur has." Johnny was taken by surprise at Bobby's change of attitude to drugs. But the gangster business was like any other business, it was all about supply and demand. If people wanted drugs it was their duty to supply them, it was as simple as that.

Chapter 55

CONTROL

Over the next few weeks Bobby and Johnny formulated a battle plan and had numerous conversations about the drug business. "The way I see it," Johnny said, "Smoking the marijuana is less harmful than going on an alcoholic binge. What ah noticed about wee Alex was with the bevvy he usually wants tae fight but the hash made him the complete opposite." Bobby said, "I'll tell you what, if they invented alcohol today it would be banned as a dangerous substance. Ah mean, how many people do you know who have ended up in Barlinnie because of the drink? Plenty. Barlinnie is full of bevvy merchants." "What do you think of cocaine?" Johnny asked. Bobby smiled and gave a mocking laugh, "Cocaine? All those posh young guys love putting it up their noses. It gives them confidence in their high flying jobs, but they can fucking afford it."
Both of them came to the conclusion that they would stay clear of heroin and as Bobby said, "All those dirty bastards injecting themselves with needles! Nah, we'll steer clear of that palaver. Let Arthur and all the other bampots on the street deal in that. There's enough money in cocaine and cannabis to keep us going." So far, their drug dealing had been confined to just talk. Big Arthur had built up his drug connections but Bobby wanted to construct his own set-up, being careful he

would not step on the godfather's toes. He would also guarantee Arthur a cut of his turnover.

Because of this, Arthur agreed not to stand in his way. But during one phone call between them, they were convinced their phones were being tapped. Any phone calls from then on had to be in code. If Arthur rang Bobby and said, "Fancy a fish supper?" it meant he wanted a meeting. It sounded banal but it worked. If they were being monitored and recorded by the police they couldn't exactly be prosecuted for fancying a fish supper, could they? The best thing to do though was phone each other from and to telephone boxes at an agreed time. Bobby and Johnny embarked on setting up their drug supply network. Bobby told Johnny, "Ah've got this pal in Marbella, Spain, and he's doing well out of the Charlie and hash game. His name is Patrick and ah trust him completely, he'll no' rip us off either. We went to school together and we're auld pals going back to when we were in short trousers. By the way, have you got a passport Johnny?"

Johnny said no, as he had never been on holiday abroad before. The furthest he had been was a caravan in Costa Del Troon on the Ayrshire coast. Bobby had had a passport for the past five years. Indeed, he loved going on holiday to places like Marbella, Majorca and Menorca, so he was pretty familiar with the Spanish way of life.

His childhood friend Pat had also taken to the Spanish lifestyle and from the proceeds of his drug business he set up a swanky restaurant in Marbella, which was frequented by the jet set – millionaire businessmen, film stars and footballers. Pat, a squat man in his 50s, had a fast line in patter and prided himself that he had come a long way from his upbringing in a crumbling Gorbals tenement. Bobby summed up his pal, "When Pat went over tae Spain he didnae have a pot tae pish in, now he's a millionaire." Spurred on by this, Johnny set about getting his passport.

As he cruised about the Gorbals with Archie and Kenny he could feel he was going up in the world. The banking, betting and insurance business was good but in his mind, he was now set to be an international businessman with connections on the Costa del Sol.

He obtained a passport and showed it to Bobby. He laughed when he saw Johnny's picture, "Ah'll tell you what it disnae dae you justice, you look like an ugly bastard!" They then got down to serious business. Bobby arranged for them to fly from Glasgow Airport to Malaga where they would be picked up and driven to Marbella. But Johnny was given strict instructions not to tell anyone about their trip, not even Cathy. He would tell her he was going to the Ayrshire coast with her father to "examine business opportunities." Besides, Bobby was aware that if their trip to Marbella leaked out it might lead to the ears of the police who would be highly suspicious. They flew off to Malaga the next week. Johnny had never flown before but loved every minute of the flight, it felt so glamorous. He was now experiencing the big time and savoured every moment. He was dying to celebrate his elevation in status by having a drink on the plane but Bobby cautioned against it, "We'll do that when we finish the deal. Meanwhile, we'll have tae be as sharp as fuck, and sober, to get our supply chain and network on the move. It's all about preparation- failure to prepare is preparing to fail."

When they arrived in Malaga it was baking hot. Johnny had never experienced heat like it. He had grown up feeling cold in the damp tenements of the Gorbals and had often yearned for heat. But this heat was almost unbearable. Waiting for them at the airport was Pat. At first Johnny thought he was an Asian man. But when he opened his mouth, with a thick Gorbals accent, he realised it was Pat with a deep golden suntan.

He greeted them warmly and led them to a yellow Porsche parked outside. He drove them along the coast to Marbella. Johnny was overawed not only by the brilliant sunshine but the scenery and wealth that seemed to abound along the coast – flash cars, big boats, fancy restaurants and hotels, this was a world away from the Gorbals.
Pat had indeed done well for himself. As he drove he turned on the patter, "Ah don't know how the fuck you can cope living in Glasgow. It's always cold and raining there. Here it's like paradise, that's why ah love it."
Bobby and Johnny could not disagree.

At one point they were suffering from such an inferiority complex they were lost for words. If this was paradise, what was the Gorbals? Hell? Pat had a villa on the outskirts of Marbella with large gardens and terrific sea views. "Welcome to ma wee tenement in the sun!" He joked.

After they had unpacked and settled in, Pat took them to his restaurant called "Velvet", in Puerto Banus. It was jam packed, full of beautiful people – glamorous models, businessmen and stars. Many of them were drinking champagne. The wealth on display in the Rogano in Glasgow was nothing compared to this. It almost took Johnny's breath away.

They had a fine four course dinner and some wine (but not enough to get drunk) and Monte Cristo cigars, and although Johnny did not smoke normally, he enjoyed puffing away. This was the life, man, definitely the big time. In fact it was incredible. They got back to Pat's villa and straight to business. Pat said, "Right then boys it's all about setting you up a network which I can take care of. First of all, hash. I can ship it in from Morocco, just over the water. From here, we can ship it, usually disguised in big freight boats to the west coast of Scotland. All's you've got to do is arrange for it to be picked up by a couple of your guys who will then take it to Glasgow.

The cocaine comes via Amsterdam. We can also ship this into Scotland as well or we can use small light aircraft to fly it there, usually to a small airport. But flying in the stuff can be a bit more expensive. Shipping is more popular and no' as dear. Up to you."

Johnny was amazed at how simple it all seemed. Why had they not thought of this before? Instead of beating the fuck out of some numpty in the Gorbals who owed a few quid they now had a chance to make some real money mingling with the jet set of Marbella. But his boss, Bobby, was less of a dreamer and more pragmatic about the situation. Unlike Johnny, he had experienced the baking hot sun before and witnessed the antics of the so called jet-set. It was not really his scene. They could keep the sun, boats and flash cars, to him the Gorbals was still the best place in the world to live. He said to Pat, "Aw this glamorous bullshit disnae impress me. Ah admire what you have achieved and you're a great pal but we're no' here to mess about wi' the jet set, but to make money. So, Pat, what do you need up front?"

Pat was quick to reply, "Ten grand up front. And another ten grand when you receive the first shipment." Johnny thought the figures were insane but Bobby replied, "No bother, ah'll sort it out by next week through your man in Glasgow. He'll get the first ten grand by Monday." The three of them shook hands on the deal. Bobby told Johnny he had cash hidden away "for a rainy day" and there was no problem making the initial payments. They stayed for three days and enjoyed themselves. Pat took them on a guided tour of the Costa del Sol, places like Estapona, Torremolinos and even Gibraltar.

Johnny was amazed that this little piece of Britain, with its English pubs and policemen, existed.

They also went for "a wee cruise" on Pat's 25ft boat, drinking champagne for the duration of the two hour trip. On their final night, Pat laid on a party for them at his restaurant. There was booze and a buffet for about 50 glamorous and influential people. At the end of the night Johnny and Bobby were in the company of two beautiful Swedish blondes. Johnny had the suspicion that they were two high class hookers that had been laid on for them.

They headed back to the villa, taking each blonde back to their individual rooms. In the morning Bobby looked pleased with himself, like the cat who had got the cream. He knew Johnny had slept with the other blonde saying, "For fuck's sake, if this ever gets back to our women there will be blue murder. But remember what happens on tour, stays on tour."

When Johnny arrived back at his flat in the Gorbals, Cathy gave him a suspicious look. "That's some tan you've got fae Troon."

"Aye," Johnny replied, "It's always sunny on the Ayrshire coast. You cannae beat it. Give me Troon any day over places like Spain. There's no place like Scotland."

Chapter 56

BAWHEID

The wheels had been set in motion. Now they had to restructure the organisation so that everything was running as smoothly as possible. Johnny was made head of distribution, which meant he would co-ordinate the shipments of drugs coming in and to distribute them accordingly. Archie was made head of transport, arranging for men and vehicles to pick the gear up. Kenny was put in charge of accountancy, calculating mark ups and profits, which he was very good at.

Because Johnny, Archie and Kenny had all been promoted, new men were drafted in. Bobby's cousin Joe, a guy in his 50s, became Johnny's driver and a young guy called Jake took over Kenny's role as the guy fixing the odds on the betting side. Bobby had drawn up the system on a piece of paper. It was like a pyramid and he was at the top. Johnny was underneath him, with Archie and Kenny reporting directly to them. The other guys made up the pyramid right down to the street dealers and low-level enforcers who made sure the money flowed in from the punters. Bobby's organisation more or less controlled the south side of the city and adjacent areas. Big Arthur had the largest slice of the cake, concentrating on the rest of Glasgow's drug trade but of course, had a cut of the south side profits also.

From the very first shipment, the money began to pour in. It was proving to be true, selling drugs was a far more profitable business than the other scams they had been involved in. Bobby had also drafted in a dodgy accountant called Percy, a grey-haired man in his 60s, who talked in a posh accent. With his pin striped suit and posh accent, Percy certainly looked like an accountant or bank manager.

But he had a dark past and had served time for defrauding several elderly clients out of their life savings. As the cash flowed in, Johnny and Bobby were puzzled what to do with it all. The problem was they could not exactly go out and be seen spending large amounts of ready cash, otherwise the police would be on their trail. But Percy was the sort of guy who had all the answers to such a dilemma. At a meeting, he told Johnny and his cohorts, "We have a great deal of what some would say was 'dirty money' coming in. The dilemma is what to do with this dirty money. And it's a simple matter of laundering it. We must set up legitimate businesses as a front for the money and the cash can be laundered through them."

"What sort of businesses are we talking about?" Johnny asked Percy.
"Oh, things like pubs, cafes and even taxis. All deal in ready cash and the dirty money can be disguised in the turnover and profits."

Bobby was delighted by the suggestion, "It's something that the Mafia have been doing for years in America.

So, if it's good enough for them, it's good enough for us." Percy was put in charge of acquisitions and sussing out what businesses to buy to launder the money. There were several such meetings a week and Johnny began to have a migraine after every one of them. He had been in riotous gang fights, had shovelled sawdust into bags but had never experienced stress like this. Big money brought along with it a variety of big problems. After one such meeting, he went for a walk through the Gorbals. It was the same old faces doing the same old things but he noticed many people looked at him in awe. He was now a big shot in the Glasgow underworld, a wee star in a big picture or a big star in a wee picture, depending how you looked at it.

In Gorbals Street, he bumped into wee Alex and a few other guys. All of them were smoking a joint which they passed between them. What surprised him was Alex's appearance had changed. He had got rid of his short back and sides and grown his hair long. He had also taken to wearing brightly coloured Paisley shirts which gave him a psychedelic look. Alex gave Johnny a puff of his joint. Normally he would have refused, but this time, because of his business migraine, he took up the offer. Alex said to him, "Go on, Johnny boy, inhale deeply and you'll feel top of the pops!"
Johnny did inhale deeply and instantly his headache disappeared. Alex said, "Told you, a few puffs has put you right. This is good gear." Johnny knew it was good gear as he had shipped in the stuff from Spain. A few

more puffs, and inhaling deeply, he looked at Alex and began to giggle like a schoolboy, "You look like a fucking hippy," he said. He began to giggle even more when Alex told him he was now listening to Bob Dylan and began to sing in an out of tune voice, "Hey Mr Tambourine Man…" It all seemed ludicrous. Once Alex had been tipped to become one of Glasgow's most violent gangsters but now he had metamorphosed into a Gorbals hippy. Perhaps drugs were a good thing, self-medication that turned you from being a psychopath into a peace loving beatnik.

When he was thinking this, Johnny suddenly felt anxious. A wave of paranoia came over him when he saw two men staring at them from across the road. At first glance, they looked like workmen in shabby overalls but at second glance, Johnny noticed their hands did not look right. They were white and soft looking. In fact, they looked like the hands of policemen.

Were these two fellows undercover policemen spying on them? He said to Alex, "Do you know those two guys over there?" Alex glanced over, "Nah, never seen them before in ma life." Johnny said, "Ah think those two wankers are undercover polis. So, watch yourself and don't let them catch you smoking a joint or you'll end up doing time." Alex gave a mad laugh, "Ach, you're just getting paranoid, Johnny, that's what hash does tae some people." Johnny bade his pal farewell but the image of the "two workers" with soft hands stayed in his mind. Definitely the polis. He walked back in the direction of his house in the high flats when he bumped into his old pal Malky, who had phoned in sick to take a day off from the sawmills. "Fancy a quick pint?" Malky said.

Johnny's mouth felt dry after smoking the marijuana and he quickly agreed. They ended up in a nearby pub. It was just like the old times but of course the gulf in their status was clear. Malky was still a lowly labourer in the sawmills, while Johnny was a high flying gangster. For about half an hour they had banter about the old days but then Johnny asked about Lorraine. Malky looked a bit disillusioned but masked the fact by giving a weak smile, "Oh, she wants tae get married as soon as possible. Ah suppose it's tae get away fae her stinking-of-fish father.

"So, when dae you think you're gonnae tie the knot?" Johnny asked.

"As soon as we can. That's why ah've taken the day off work on the sick. Ah'm meeting Lorraine up the toon and we're gonnae look again at rings, they won't be cheap!" Johnny looked genuinely pleased to hear about the engagement, "Ah'm made up for you, Malky. Lovely lassie, Lorraine. Like Cathy, she'll make a great wife. Cheers!" They raised their pints to celebrate the union. Before he left the pub, Johnny asked his old pal, "Have you noticed a lot of strangers in the Gorbals, some of them pretending to be workmen?"

"Aye" Malky replied, "Nae doubt about it, Glasgow is getting flooded with drugs and the chief constable told the papers a few weeks ago he was going to hammer the dealers by putting more undercover polis on the streets."

So that was it, problem solved! The news must have come out when he and Bobby were away in Spain. He headed for Bobby's flat. The door was answered by Archie. They went into the kitchen and Bobby was sniffing cocaine with a straw from the table. He shouted to Johnny, "Come away in and have some of this gear. Fucking magic!" Johnny was handed a straw and sniffed a line. Suddenly he felt extremely confident and energetic with some of the white powder still stuck to his nose, "Just been for a wee walk and there are a lot of strangers on the streets. A pal tells me they're undercover polis out to catch drug dealers."

Bobby replied in an over confident voice which had been fuelled by the Charlie, "Ah, don't worry about them. They're no' out to get us. They'll nab those low life druggie bastards on the streets."

Johnny was unsure about the remark, perhaps his boss was being too confident. But he did not argue and maybe he was being too paranoid. Archie said, "The boss is right. The polis will no' be messing wi' us. They'll take the easy route and jail the bampots who deal on the streets for pennies."

Bobby snorted another line of cocaine and shouted to Johnny, "Follow me and ah'll show you a right Aladdin's Cave." He walked into the next room and opened his safe. It was full of banknotes, packets of cocaine and some cannabis.

He declared, "This drug game has taken us up to a new league, Johnny boy." But Johnny had serious doubts. It was clear the cocaine had given Bobby a sense of invincibility. An invincibility that could become a weakness in the wrong hands.

Chapter 57

FUTURE

The drugs game was going far better than predicted. Bobby and the boys had acquired several businesses like pubs and cafes and even a small taxi firm to launder the money that was coming in. Many of the businesses had not actually been bought but merely "taken over." For example, one pub landlord agreed to front the money laundering by increasing his turnover five-fold. His takings of £300 a week jumped to £1500 a week. Other pub landlords and café owners followed suit for a fee, usually five to ten per cent of the increased turnover. They also had the advantage of protection by Bobby's mob. The guy responsible for laundering the most money was the bookie who had originally asked for protection. He was laundering anything between 5-10 grand a month.

The bookie was pleased with his cut of the dodgy profits and made the drug money disappear like a magician with a rabbit in a hat. Johnny and Bobby were invited to the bookie's mansion in the leafy Bearsden area for "a bite to eat" and a talk about business. Archie chauffeured them there and when they arrived they were very impressed with the set up. He had a five bedroom detached house which even had chandeliers inside with gaudy paintings. The bookie lived there alone after his wife of 30 years had left him for another business guy. But he was not a bitter man, he had house staff to look after him, a cook a cleaner, and a secretary. If he wanted sex, he had a little black book of expensive hookers to hand.

He handed Johnny and Bobby two big cigars as they sat in front of a huge log fire in his living room. On the mantelpiece was a photo of his wife with a dart stuck in it.
As the bookie puffed away on his cigar he poured the boys two large brandies and pontificated on the situation, "This money laundering lark is working quite well for us, do you no' think?" He began to laugh, "My 20-odd shops have certainly seen a higher turnover since ah got involved wi' you guys." They then went into the dining room where there was a buffet laid on with smoked salmon, and even caviar. They boys were impressed as they filled their plates and drank champagne. But although it was luxurious, the atmosphere felt a bit stiff. Bobby said to the bookie, "You certainly enjoy your wealth. You can explain it away wi' your bookie shops but we're caught in a sort of stalemate. We still live in council flats and drive old cars."
"Why's that?" the bookie said, "You've got the dough, so enjoy it."

"We'd love to," said Johnny sipping his Moet & Chandon, "But as soon as we're seen to be loaded, the polis will be on us a like a ton of bricks."

Bobby nodded his head, "Aye, sometimes ah just want tae shout out 'I'm fucking loaded' but that would give the game away. So far it's a case of being low profile. The jails are full of gangsters like us who decided tae go high profile with their wealth and appeared in newspapers and all that palaver. Ah suppose it's a case of all Glaswegians love bragging about what they've done." It was all getting a bit too serious for Johnny, he could feel a headache coming on and decided to tell a bragging joke to lighten up the meeting.

"There was a wee Glasgow guy shipwrecked and stuck on an island for a year wi' nae company, when suddenly he sees a big blonde on a raft. He dives into the ocean and saves her. They begin shagging all the time but after a while he gets fed up and says, 'Can you put ma shirt and trousers on?' She agrees and then the wee guy says, 'Can you put my hat on? And will you let me draw a moustache on you and call you Bob?' She agrees again. He then tells her to go for a walk along the beach. A few minutes later he runs up to her and shouts, 'Hey Bob, you want to see this big blonde ah've been shagging!'"

Bobby gave out a loud laugh, "That's exactly how ah feel. Ah'm dying to tell everybody how successful we are but we've got tae keep our mouths shut. That's if we want tae avoid doing time." The night went well and the bookie was quite intoxicated when he said to Johnny, "I know you admire my red Rolls Royce, come outside and have a look at it again." They went into the long driveway and Johnny looked at it with admiring eyes. The bookie handed him the keys and said, "Start up the engine." He did and it had a lovely purring noise. He said, "I have ordered a new Rolls so I want to give it to you." Johnny was dumbfounded and said, "It's very kind of you to offer me your Rolls Royce, but how the fuck would ah be able tae explain it away? We've told you already we've got to keep a low profile." "Simple," the bookie said, "Tell anyone who asks, you won it in a bet with me or I loaned you it. And if anyone asks further questions, including the police, ah'll back it up." Johnny could obviously not take up the offer of the free Rolls Royce straight away, but Archie could pick it up and store it in one of the many garages he had access to all over Glasgow. They left the bookie in good spirits and when they got back to the Gorbals, Bobby was in the mood to celebrate further, "Right, we'll have a few lines of Charlie to celebrate you becoming a Rolls Royce owner!"

They had four lines of coke and Bobby sniffed the majority. It was obvious he had an addictive personality. Having such a condition was dangerous in his position. But things got worse. Bobby pulled out a joint and began to smoke it. Johnny knew from previous experience that Bobby, had at times, been excessive with the bevvy, but now it had transferred to drugs. They seemed to have a grip on him, something that the bevvy had never achieved. In the morning,

Johnny was lying in bed with Cathy quite peacefully when he heard loud banging on the door. He looked at the clock, it was only 7.15 am. He got up and went to the door while Cathy was still asleep. He opened the door and it was her mother who had obviously been crying. She said to Johnny, "Come quick son, ah cannae wake Bobby up, he's comatose." Johnny rushed into their flat and Bobby was lying in his bed barely breathing. He checked his pulse, it was beating slowly and faintly. He shouted to Bobby, "Wake up, boss. Wake the fuck up!" But there was no movement. He said to Bobby's wife, "Quick, phone an ambulance!" The ambulance arrived 20 minutes later. The medics walked into Bobby's bedroom and checked his pulse, "He's still breathing,"one of them said, "But barely. We'll have to get him to hospital straight away."

Shortly after he said this his wife began to shout, "What's the matter wi' ma Bobby? Is it a heart attack?" The medic shook his head, "No missus, it looks like a drug overdose to me." She wailed, "A drug overdose? My Bobby disnae touch drugs." Of course, she had been unaware that when she was out Bobby regularly put excessive amounts of Charlie up his nose and often delved into his marijuana supply.

They took the barely-breathing Bobby away on a stretcher. To Johnny, this was a warning. He would never touch drugs again. Drugs were a good earner but it was a mistake to start abusing the stock. Bobby had broken the golden rule and suffered the consequences. Back in the kitchen, Bobby's wife said to him, "What the hell are we gonnae tell Cathy?" He came to the conclusion it was better for both of them to say nothing. If Cathy asked where her father was, she would be told he had gone away at the last minute on another "business trip to Troon." Later that morning, he went for a walk and noticed more strangers in the vicinity. When he stared at them, they seemed to turn their heads away. Was he being spied on? Were the strangers yet more undercover policemen? It was a dilemma that had to be thought about carefully. Meanwhile, he had to ensure that his boss had survived his ordeal. Would Bobby learn from his mistakes? Or would he get worse and become even more of a liability to them all?

Chapter 58

RECOVERY

With Bobby being invalidated by his own stupidity, Johnny took control. Over time, he had mastered the art of delegating and thinking through complicated situations. All sides of the business were doing well. The drugs were pulling in big money and the insurance, banking and betting were also prospering. Johnny had a rival in the organisation. It was not the other guys, who like him had trained on the streets of the Gorbals, but middle class Percy, who controlled the financial planning side of the organisation. There was no doubt about it, Percy was a very good accountant but on the other hand he could not punch his way out of a wet paper bag. Indeed, it was highly possible that Percy had never been in a fight in his life but Johnny had to admit he was good with money. As a dodgy accountant, Percy was perfect but he had as much chance of becoming a gangster as a one-legged man winning an arse kicking competition.

Nevertheless, Johnny considered him a good thief, and a man with a briefcase and a posh accent can be more dangerous than a guy with a razor and a guttural dialect. Johnny decided to visit his boss in the Royal Infirmary. He had been told Bobby was in a ward associated with drug addicts. When he got to the hospital ward, he was surprised to see Bobby sitting up in his bed, and who was sitting beside him? Percy, of course. Johnny hated the accountant bastard on sight and had an overwhelming feeling that he wanted to chib him there and then. But he held up a pretence of being friendly, "So, how's it gaun boss?"

He was armed with the usual bunch of grapes and bottle of Lucozade. Bobby looked pale and drawn, it was obvious the heavy drug abuse had taken it out of him. He was certainly not the man he used to be, but he was still the boss, that's all that mattered. "Aye, no' bad, Johnny boy," he replied from his bed, "Took too much Charlie and hash. An overdose, or so they tell me. Nearly copped ma whack. Ah'll have tae rest for a wee while." Percy nodded his head in agreement and said in his posh voice, "I think boss, the thing is you have to learn. It's ok for us to sell drugs to the common man but you should make it a rule that no-one in the organisation, including yourself, should take them as well."

Bobby looked annoyed at the mild telling off but then grinned, "You're right. Ah mean, if you ran a pub it would be a mistake to start drinking all the stock." Percy laughed at the remark, and as he did so, bared his teeth. They looked brown and yellow. They were the worst teeth Johnny had ever seen in a man. In fact, they reminded him of a row of condemned Gorbals tenements. Ironically, he had never noticed Percy's teeth before because in his job as accountant, he had never been seen to smile or laugh. Johnny thought, "What an ugly bastard. no wonder he never laughs wi'

those gnashers." He also had his suspicions about
Percy. The accountant knew where he and Bobby lived
but they did not know where Percy resided. He had
been vague about his address saying it was "a
bungalow" in the leafy area of Milngavie. Bobby took a
sip of his Lucozade, ate some grapes, and suddenly
announced, "Right boys, ah've been daft wi' this
addiction but it's business as usual. Johnny will run
things for a few weeks and you, Percy, make sure
there are no problems wi' the money flow." Percy
suggested a few modifications to the running of the
organisation.
It was agreed Johnny would be at the helm and Percy
would be his number two. Archie was doing well in
charge of transportation and Kenny was also
performing well as the guy who calculated the buy and
sell prices of drugs. Johnny had brought in several
young men, on a part time basis, to be his drivers and
enforcers.

Percy suggested that they needed "two full time
appointments" who would be gophers or a jack of all
trades. The stipulation was they had to be men they
knew and trusted. The last thing they needed was a
grass or as Percy put it in his posh accent, "An
informer who might spill the beans to the
constabulary." Johnny nodded his head in agreement.
Percy was preaching to the converted. He knew of
several young men who would jump at the chance to
join them but they would have to prove themselves
first. When Percy mentioned the informer part, he

immediately felt suspicious. What if Percy was secretly an informer? He knew enough to put them away for years.

But he had implicated himself to such an extent that he might be in danger of imprisonment if the police found out about his dodgy accountant dealings. Johnny had read about guys like Percy before. There was always a danger of employing posh guys like him as they could turn traitor at the turn of a coin. Sure, it happened all the time to the Mafia in America. Their biggest mistake was to bring in an outsider, who no-one really knew, to become accountants adding up all the money. Those bastards could not be trusted as had been proved by the Costra Nostra traitors.

Johnny, in the past, had no problems with Bobby's judgement, but the drugs seemed to have dulled his perception. The boss trusted Percy implicitly whereas Johnny felt he could not trust him as far as he could throw him.

"Ok, Bobby," Johnny said, "Ah'll take over for a while. Long enough for you to recuperate and Percy can do all the money stuff. How long dae you think you'll be out of the game for?"

Bobby thought for a moment and sighed, "About a month or so. My missus wants me tae go into rehab. It's no' cheap, going private is expensive but it'll be worth the money tae get off the drugs. Ah mean, look at the poor bastards here, there's no way they could afford to go private."

Johnny looked round the ward and he was right. There were about twenty beds filled with drug addicts. They were a pathetic, miserable sight. Some of them lay in bed with their arms showing syringe marks. They were obviously heroin addicts. Although Johnny and Bobby dealt in drugs, they kept to the stipulation that they would not deal in heroin. But it was now widely available in Glasgow and as easy to get as a bottle of Irn Bru. Bobby glanced around the ward, "Look at those smack heads and ah'm in here wi' them! Mind you, ah've always had an addictive personality, it's in the genes. Ma mother was addicted to her fags and bingo and ma father, booze and the horses. And now, ah'm addicted to cocaine and hash. What's your addiction, Percy? "

Percy was quick to reply, "Money! I love money. Love making it and love counting it. At times, I might even spend it. Money makes the world go round."
"Aye too right, Percy," Bobby agreed, "Ah've been poor and ah've been rich, so ah know which ah prefer. Right, Johnny boy, what's your addiction?"
Johnny smiled, "Jelly babies."
"Fuck off. Jelly babies?"
"When ah was at school, there wisnae a day went by when ah didnae have a packet of jelly babies. Ah was addicted tae them. Ah even used tae go out stealing packets from the corner shops. A big polis caught me and ah ended up in court for stealing a packet of jelly babies from the Co-op. The magistrate warned me if ah was ever caught stealing jelly babies again ah'd be

sent tae an approved school. So ah had tae stop and my addiction ended."

Bobby was mildly amused but mystified at the same time, "For fuck's sake, ah didnae know ah employed a jelly baby addict. That's worse than being a heroin addict. So, do you ever get an urge now?" Johnny went along with the humorous tone of the conversation because he realised that sometimes it was good to take the mickey out of yourself. "Oh aye, but now ah stick tae liquorice allsorts and they are no' as addictive. But there are times when ah'd give ma right arm for a jelly baby."

The absurd comic dialogue brought colour back into Bobby's cheeks and as the Sunday Post used to say, "Laughter is the best medicine." Bobby would go into private rehab for a few weeks, speculating that he might even bump into someone with a jelly baby addiction.

As Johnny got up to leave the ward a voice shouted, "Hey, Johnny boy, what's the score man?" He looked at one of the beds and it was wee Alex. "What the fuck are you doing here, Alex?" Alex shrugged his shoulders, "Well, ah was intae cannabis big time and a bit of Charlie when ah could afford it. But Morty said 'the big h' would give me a better high. So, ah started trying it and he was right. There's nae bigger hit than heroin." Johnny tut-tutted, he had seen this Morty fellow about. A filthy-looking bastard, in his 30s, who dealt in bad batches of heroin. He was the product of a mongrel family and had never held down a proper job.

But when heroin came flooding into Glasgow, he grabbed the opportunity with both hands.

Through the grapevine, Johnny heard Morty was responsible for at least two deaths in the Gorbals after he had sold a dodgy batch of heroin. Now it had almost finished off wee Alex, Johnny felt the anger rise inside him.
"Keep the fuck away fae that Morty wanker. If you don't you'll be pushing up the daisies before your time. The stuff he sells is shite, deadly shite." For once Alex listened to the voice of reason and agreed with his pal. Johnny went outside where his part time driver Andy was waiting. He was a young guy in his early 20s who was desperate to make a name for himself and maybe land a full time enforcer job.
"Where to, boss? He asked.
"Let's go for a wee run through the Gorbals." When they got to Thistle Street, Johnny saw Morty standing at a street corner talking to two young guys in their teens. He handed them a small packet and money was exchanged. "Stop here!" Johnny said, "Now go into that shop and buy me a bottle of Irn Bru and a packet of jelly babies."

The driver did so. Johnny pointed to Morty, "Now go over and hit that low life bastard over the head wi' the Irn Bru bottle."

Andy did what he was told, walked over and hit Morty full force on the head with it. Morty gave a squeal of pain, sounding like a pig, and his head gushed with blood as he lay on the pavement. Johnny stood above him, bit the head off a jelly baby and then threw the rest of the packet over Morty. "Now this is a warning to you. Keep away from the young guys like Alex wi' that shite heroin of yours. Otherwise you'll end up lifeless like these fucking jelly babies." Morty gave a groan as he lay in a pool of blood on the pavement.

As Johnny was chauffeured away, he reflected on the day and his conversation with Bobby. He had been taking the piss. He was not really addicted to jelly babies… he was addicted to violence.

Chapter 59

PURRING

While Bobby was away recuperating, the organisation was purring along nicely. Johnny loved being at the helm and ensured all sides of the business were under his control. He had a re-jig of staff as there were a couple of young enforcers who were not pulling their weight. The two of them, "Bawheid Billy" and "Sly Stevie" had been sent out on various errands to collect money but had often returned with only small amounts or nothing at all. Johnny had a meeting with them in the back of his car. "Why the fuck is it that every time we send you two guys out to pull in a couple of quid you come back wi' a couple of pennies?" he said to them. Bawheid and his pal looked flustered by the accusation. He replied, "Well, boss, money is tight at the moment and we've been lucky tae pull in what we did." His pal Stevie was equally apologetic, "Aye, boss, sometimes trying ta get dough out of those bastards is like trying tae pull teeth."

Johnny listened carefully but he could detect a degree of laziness, "You two wankers are getting too soft, people are taking the piss. For example, the Irish labourer, Mick, who owes us thirty quid. He should have weighed us in with at least a tenner last week. But you let him off wi' a fiver." Bawheid put on an apologetic tone, "But boss, he says he hisnae got any money tae spare and a fiver was all that he could afford." Stevie agreed, "He told us his pay packet was light because he hurt his back on the building site and could only work for a couple of days." Johnny had a feeling he was dealing with a couple of soft numpties, "Is that so? Why the fuck are ma spies telling me he's out getting pished in the pub every night? He's got the dough all right, but he's taking you two for mugs."

The two enforcers remained silent during their bollocking. Bawheid broke the silence by saying, "What do you want us tae do?" Johnny sort of growled, "Go to the pub where the bastard drinks and when he comes outside give him a good slap, that will knock some sense intae him. But make sure you don't put him in hospital, then he'll be out of work and have no money. Give the idiot a good fright and he'll soon be paying us the full amount. Now, fuck off and do it. If you don't, I'll get another couple of young gang guys who will." Both enforcers left the car looking slightly shaken. Archie had been at the driving wheel and said after they left, "That was the right thing to say to those two. They should never have given that Irish navvy an excuse not to pay."

Johnny agreed. In any organisation the employees needed a bollocking now and again if they were not pulling their weight. His mind then turned to Percy. He said to Archie, "What do you think of our accountant, Percy. Do you think we can trust him?" Archie sneered, "Nah there's something about him that is no' right, wi' his yellow teeth and crumpled suit. Ah think he's a good accountant but he's a cunning bastard and he'd stab you in the back as soon as look at you. He's aw nice, nice, nice. Too nice for ma liking."

Johnny nodded his head in agreement and if it was up to him, he would have sacked Percy there and then. But he was Bobby's appointment and he had to stay for the meantime. He felt compelled to hire new staff. He brought in Goo Goo as an enforcer and driver.

Goo Goo had been pestering him for a while "tae get a slice of the action." As a result, Johnny sent him on several money collecting jobs in which he excelled. Goo Goo, scar and all, was still leading his section of the Cumbie gang but saw his job as a part time enforcer as a step up the gangsters ladder. Johnny liked the guy as they were from the same mould. Goo Goo in turn looked up to him as a sort of hero, who he wanted to emulate. He would also do almost anything his boss asked of him. A few days before, Johnny picked up Goo Goo in a car and drove him to a café in Eglinton Street. He pointed out of the window, "See that Italian bastard in there who owns the café? He's stopped paying his protection money.

Thinks we're mugs. Go in and wreck the fucking place." Goo Goo said nothing and walked into the café and took a seat at a table. The Italian owner said to him, "Yes son, can I help you?" He ordered double egg and chips and a cup of tea. When they were placed on the table he picked up his knife and fork and tucked in.

464

The next minute he shouted to the Italian, "These fucking eggs are off and the tea tastes like pish."

The Italian was intimidated but did not show it, "It's your mouth that's off, get out ma café." Goo Goo picked up his plate and threw it through the café window smashing it to pieces, then threw the cup of tea over the Italian shouting, "Your food is crap. Your tea is pishwater and your cafe is a shitehole. He then proceeded to wreck the place overturning tables and chairs, smashing plates and throwing cutlery about. It was a scene of devastation. Before he left, he unzipped his fly and pished all over the floor. The Italian had been too shocked to intervene. He stood there frozen like a statue. The next day the Italian came to Johnny, turning on the humble patter, "Look, ah'm sorry about changing my insurance subscription with you. When I think of it, it was well worth a fiver a week. Will you take me back?" Johnny replied, "Aye certainly but because you've messed me about you are up to six pounds a week." The Italian was quick to shake hands on the deal.

Johnny thought of Goo Goo as some sort of lucky omen. He had learnt at a history lesson in school that when Napoleon was suggested a general who could go into battle he would ask, "Is he lucky?" Apart from his one-off scar, Goo Goo had been lucky in numerous gang fights and seemed to have the magic touch when it came to extracting money from people. One evening he was in the house when the phone rang. It was Pat from Marbella, "Hi Johnny, how's ma pal Bobby doing? He's no' been picking up his phone."

"He's gone away for a wee while, Pat, he's gone intae rehab for some treatment and it's no' cheap, ah can tell you," Johnny replied. Pat laughed, "Tell him when he gets better to get his fat arse over here to Spain for a wee holiday. A blast of sunshine will do him the world of good. Apart from that, one o' ma pals, Frankie, wants to see you. He needs a wee favour."

"No problem," Johnny said, "I look forward to meeting him." The phone conversation was cut short. They could not discuss too much over the phone as the police may have been listening in.

A few days later, he got a message from one of Pat's cousins to meet Frankie in the Turf Bar. He went into the pub and Frankie was instantly recognisable with his deep Marbella tan. They sat in a small room opposite the bar. He was a sharp suited guy in his 40s. He said to Johnny, "Let me get straight to the point, fuck all that small talk patter. We've got an order to get a Picasso, which one of our customers will pay big money for in Spain." Johnny was shocked and amused at the same time, "How the fuck are we gonnae get a Picasso? Steal it from a museum?"

"Nah, easier than that," Frankie said, "There's a big-time lawyer who lives in Balloch and has a private collection of art. He's got the Picasso we want. Our art collector will pay big bucks for it, even if it's stolen." He gave Johnny the wealthy lawyer's address, a large mansion overlooking Loch Lomond, "We know he and his family will be out next Tuesday night. So that's the time to strike. Have you got a man capable of doing the job?" Johnny put on his most confident voice, "Aye, nae problem, know just the guy." They went over a few details and the Picasso plan went into motion. Goo Goo and his pal were handed the job. They would disable the alarms with wire cutters, smash a window at the back of the house and make off with the painting. Goo Goo said to Johnny, "For fuck's sake, ah've done a lot of things but ah've never stolen a Picasso before."

On the Tuesday night, they set off and a few hours later they were back in Glasgow with the Picasso in the boot of their car. It was an odd-looking painting portraying a freakish looking woman with several eyes. Johnny headed up to Goo Goo's flat and went into the living room. He was surprised to see the Picasso "worth at least five million quid" hanging on the wall. The men opened cans of Tennent's lager to toast their success. Goo Goo raised his can for a toast, "Here's tae Pablo Picasso. I bet he never realised one of his paintings would end up in a Gorbals tenement!" Frankie turned up a few hours later and arranged for the painting to be dispatched to Marbella. "Good work, boys," he said, "We'll make art lovers out of you yet!" After he left, Johnny and the boys were in a state of elation, toasting their success with even more cans of lager. "So, what's my next job Johnny?" Goo Goo said.

Johnny replied, "Ah've got an easy one for you, Goo Goo."

"Oh aye, easier than stealing a Picasso?"

"What we want you to do is go to the Tower of London and steal the Crown Jewels."

Goo Goo spat out a mouthful of beer, "Ok, as long as ah don't have tae shake hands wi' the Queen as well... ah'm no' a Hun, ah'm a Celtic supporter!"

Chapter 60

QUIET

When not working, as stated before, Johnny enjoyed being a family man. It was an alternative role to being a gangster. Off with the suit, on with the black t-shirt, jeans and he would even wear a flat cap and sunglasses, so he would not be easily recognised. He, Cathy and his son, would have "wee days out" to places like the People's Palace in the Glasgow Green, the Kelvingrove Art Museum and even as stroll through Paddy's Market, watching all the characters. Cathy loved being with her man, as when he changed down, Johnny also changed his personality. No longer was he the tough-talking Glasgow wise guy but a fellow who mostly stayed quiet and seemed to be meditating most of the time.

When they stopped in the People's Palace they had tea in the Winter Gardens and Cathy said, "What's the future, Johnny? Surely to god we're no' gonnae be stuck in the Gorbals for the rest of our lives? You've got the money now to live anywhere we want so we don't have to be in the high flats anymore." He took into consideration what she was suggesting but merely said, "Cathy, doll, ah've got a battle plan for our future lined up but ah'm no gonnae tell you yet. You'll have to wait, but it's all good, ah can tell you!"

Cathy had taken a part-time job as a barmaid in a local pub, only 15 hours a week and her mother looked after the boy. She loved her "wee job" and it gave her a sense of independence and some pocket money she could call her own. Besides, it got her out of the house for a few hours every day. She certainly did not need the money but she liked dealing with the regulars when she was serving them. One customer, a drunk guy in his late 50s, had called her "a silly fucking cow" after she poured too big a head on his pint of Guinness.

She went home crying and told Johnny. The man was never seen again. He seemed to have dropped off the face of the earth.

On the money front, Johnny had been careful. He had been told all the Asians were placing their money in a Pakistani/Indian bank where they did not ask questions about where the cash came from. It was an ideal place to deposit his ill-gotten gains. When Johnny went to see the Asian bank manager, called Abdul, a fellow in his 40s, he was amused by it all. Abdul spoke in very stilted English. He sat down in the bank's office, made a cup of Darjeeling tea, and said, "Mr McGrath, we welcome your good business. We are a very good bank, your money safe here. No questions asked, put in as much as you want and take out as much as you wish. Your bank account is a secret with us."

As a result, Johnny deposited thousands, safe in the knowledge that his account was hidden away from the British authorities. He knew a lot of people took the piss out of the Asians. But he knew another thing. They were not stupid with money, that's why so many "invested" their cash with this bank. The Asian fellow who ran the local corner shop, who the locals called "John the darkie", told Johnny, "You put your money in a British bank and the UK authorities can look at it. With the Asian bank they know fuck all." He took the shopkeeper at his word. After all, he was the only Asian businessmen he knew who drove a Mercedes.

As Archie said, "The Asians come fae little villages in Pakistan and India and live in real poverty, where people are dying of starvation. It makes the poverty in the Gorbals look like paradise. That's why they are careful wi' their dough and where they put it."

Johnny nodded his head in agreement and smiled when he thought of the eccentric Asian bank manager who had a large unsightly wart on his nose. It was certainly not the kind of thing you would see in the Bank of Scotland. Also, you would never find dodgy untraceable accounts there.

He reckoned a lot of the Asian businessmen were crafty bastards, ducking and diving all the time. They succeeded, despite racist attitudes towards them. Archie told him a joke that summed up the racist attitudes they faced: "A guy dies and goes to the gates of Heaven. St Peter said, 'You can only get in here if you are a good speller. Spell cat.'

The guy replies, 'C-a-t.'

'You're in.'

Another guy turns up. St Peter says, 'Spell dog.'

'D-o-g.'

'You're in.'

An Asian guy turns up, wearing a turban. St Peter says, 'Spell… Engelbert Humperdinck.'

Suited and booted and back to work on Monday, Johnny held court with Goo Goo in the lounge of the Mally Arms. He had decided to use it as an informal office so his clients and pals could drop in and see him, usually between one and three in the afternoon. He was still awaiting news from Billy and his cohort Stevie. He wondered whether they had got the money from the Irish labourer Mick.

He didn't have to wait long. Both of them walked into the lounge looking rather sheepish. Billy had a black eye and Stevie had a plaster on his forehead. Goo Goo looked at them and gave a wry grin, "What the fuck happened to you two?"

Billy found it hard to get the words out of his mouth and left it to sly Stevie to explain the score, "Well, we went into the Seaforth bar on Friday night as we knew Irish Mick would just have been paid. The problem was he was drinking wi' a mob of his navvy pals. When we asked him for the money he knocked back a large Bushmills whiskey and shouted, 'You're getting nothing, so fuck off.' We were then set about by him and his pals and we got a bit of a hiding."

Johnny looked incredulous, "Got a hiding fae a bunch of fucking navvies? Where the hell is the money? Ah'm getting fed up wi aw these hard luck stories." Goo Goo agreed, "Why did you put yourself in that position? You should have waited and banged on his front door in the morning when he had sobered up wi' a hangover." Johnny was extremely angry with his so called enforcers, "You two have a lot to learn, you're a couple of fucking amateurs. Get tae fuck out of ma sight before ah chib the two of you. You useless wankers." They did as they were told and left as sheepishly as they had come in. Just as they were leaving, wee Alex appeared and his drug overdose had certainly not cured his drug addiction. He looked as high as a kite. He said to Johnny and Goo Goo, "Those two bampots couldnae get money out of a piggy bank. That Irish Mick knows they are a couple of mugs, that's why he's bumped you for the money." Goo Goo said, "So what would you do, Alex?"

Alex got straight to the point, "Simple. Set fire tae him. I'll do it. When he staggers out of the pub drunk, ah'll pour lighter fuel over him and strike a match. Poof! He'll be a Donegal ball of flames!" He looked at Johnny, "Do you want me to do it?" Johnny deliberated for a moment, "Nah, Alex, it's a very kind offer but ah think we can do it without setting fire to our customers." He looked at Goo Goo, "You got any suggestions, wee man?"

oo Goo laughed, "If Alex sets fire to Irish Mick we'll never get our money back. Leave it to me." Goo Goo then left the pub looking like a man on a mission. Johnny bought Alex a pint of Tennent's lager.

Alex said, "How's Bobby doing?"

"No' bad Alex, he's gone into rehab to kick the drugs and all that shite. What about you, you still partaking?" Alex shrugged his shoulders, "Just a wee bit, no' as bad as before. A wee bit of hash, a wee bit of Charlie, no heroin anymore. Besides, that Morty fella has disappeared from the scene after you sorted him out. Fucking jelly babies, man!" They both laughed at the ludicrousness of it all. The next day at about the same time, Goo Goo turned up at the Mally pub and put three tenners on the table in front of Johnny.
"What the fuck!" Johnny exclaimed, "Did you get this from Irish Mick?" Goo Goo nodded his head, "Yeah, ah got two of ma Cumbie pals to knock on his door this morning. His missus answered it wearing a green dressing gown. She shouted for him and he came to the door reeking of last night's booze. Ah stuck the nut on him and he fell inside. Ah broke his nose ah think. A few minutes later, his missus was bawling her eyes out and handed over the cash. So, there it is. There's nae pain without gain, is there Johnny?"

"Too right," Johnny replied, "At least we didnae have to set fire to him!"

Goo Goo smiled, "Ah don't know, maybe Alex was right. A wee fire might have warmed us up in this cold weather!"

Chapter 61

RETURN

Bobby was back. Bobby was back with a vengeance. When he went into the lounge of the Mally one afternoon, he looked like a changed man. A month away had done him the world of good. He had lost nearly two stone in weight as a result of the no booze and drugs regime in rehab. He had also been encouraged to work out as much as possible. So apart from the gym he went for long walks every day, and the weight just fell off him. Three weeks of "fucking torture" then a week with his old pal Pat in Marbella. The sun had given him a glow and with his new image he looked every inch the successful businessman. He had lost the fat, seedy gangster look and adopted a more sophisticated image.

"So, how did it go?" Johnny asked surprised to see him looking so well. He looked ten years younger at least.

"It was hard going. I had a craving for cocaine and booze but after a week, the urges went after a bit of cold turkey. Then they had me like a rabbit eating lettuce all the time. Ah'll tell you what, while ah was in there, ah would have killed for a black pudding supper." So how did he feel now that he was back in the Gorbals? "Yeah, it's good to be back. Marbella did the trick, didnae touch the booze though. Pat thought ah was boring. But fuck him, ah've had enough cocaine and booze tae last me a lifetime, maybe two lifetimes."

Johnny noticed straight away that his pal and boss was ten times sharper and leaner than when he had been on the drugs, he had got his mojo back. The spell in rehab, like the time he had spent in Borstal years before, had given him a short, sharp shock. Johnny informed him that things were going well with considerable profits being made. He said sales of Charlie and hash were "going through the roof" but was unsure of how much they were making as it was all in the hands of Percy. Bobby listened carefully but his newly acquired sharp mind could detect a major flaw in the feedback, "Have we got a copy of the drug account books?" he asked. Johnny replied, "Nah, Percy keeps the accounts close to his chest, except to say that profit and turnover are exceptional." "Exceptional?" Bobby said, "Well ah want tae see how exceptional our business is." He looked at Goo Goo and said, "Hey young fella, go and find where Percy is and bring him here. We need a meeting straight away."

Goo Goo left the pub and headed into his car to where he believed Percy was, a nearby tenement flat which he used as his office. Bobby looked at Johnny and said, "What dae you think of that Percy fella? Can we trust him?" It was evident that the spell in rehab had certainly made Bobby more smart and streetwise. His intuition had come back thanks to his sobriety. Johnny was diplomatic, "Percy is his own man. He handles all the drug accounts but it widnae do any harm to look at the books." "Good idea," Bobby said, "That's exactly what ah was thinking." Bobby bought a large glass of Barr's ginger beer and took a gulp, "Ah, lovely stuff. Better than the booze and Charlie and it disnae fuck up your mind or land you in rehab or jail." They had a general chat about things, mostly family stuff and Bobby told him he was proud of his grandson and Cathy who had turned out to be a good, loving mother. Johnny felt the same and a mellowness came over him. If one thing made him feel soft was talk of his family. Family was everything, a great buzz to talk about. A far better buzz than taking cocaine or indulging in binge drinking. The mellowness also hit Bobby hard, "Johnny, you and I might be business partners but don't forget you are family and that's all that matters. Never mind the betting, the money lending, the protection rackets and the drugs. Nothing can compare to having a family." Johnny was lost for words, the sentiment had got to him. He agreed wholeheartedly with the sentiments.

The mellowness between the two men evaporated when Goo Goo and Percy entered the lounge bar. Bobby rose to meet Percy, shouting, "Hey, ya auld bastard. How's business been while ah was away? Fancy a wee drink tae celebrate ma new found freedom?"

Percy sat down and looked nervous as if he was
concealing something. Both Bobby and Johnny could
detect this straight away, but hid it well. Percy said
smiling with his yellow teeth, "I'll have a large brandy, if
I may." Bobby smirked, "Large brandy! Ah told you
Johnny, this man has class. He's a man of education,
no' like us two half educated slum Glaswegians!"He
went to the bar and brought the large brandy over,

"Got you the best Percy, old chap. Napoleon brandy,
strictly for the toffs!" Percy gave a weak smile and
sipped the brandy slowly. Bobby was in a mischievous
mood, "So Percy, old chap. How is the Charlie and
hash side of the business?" "Oh, very good. We are
turning over a significant profit up there with the other
sides of the business." Bobby gave him a slap on the
back. It was intended to look friendly but Johnny could
detect there was a hint of nastiness about it.

Percy continued, "I see the month away has done you
the world of good. It's great to see you back where you
should be – at the helm of it all."

Bobby smiled but was not taken in by the false flattery,
"Aye, a wee rest has put me back on the ball. Now,
you know what we want to see, Percy?

"What's that, boss?" Percy said nervously.

"The books, the fucking books which show how much
is coming in and going out." Percy suddenly put on a

show of bravado but Bobby and Johnny could detect it was bullshit bravado. They could see Percy's lips had begun to quiver. "Well, Bobby I don't keep books as such, just general figures. We must be careful that the police have no evidence about what we are doing." Bobby nodded his head in fake agreement "I understand all this Percy, old chap. But you've got to knock together some figures that ah can understand. As far as I am concerned two plus two equals four, it's as simple as that… old chap." Johnny was amused that Bobby was using the "old chap" patter as a form of intimidation. Suddenly, Percy looked peeved and rose from the table, "Look, boss, I've got to get back to work. I'll have some figures for you tomorrow. Thanks for the excellent brandy, it's my favourite." Bobby told Goo Goo to run Percy back to his tenement office.

After they left, Bobby said to Johnny, "Ah can detect a lie like a fart in a car. That guy is hiding something. What do you think?" "You might be right Bobby," Johnny said, "But we'll see tomorrow when he has the figures for us." The next day, Bobby, Johnny, Goo Goo and Archie assembled at Percy's office. He put a large black accounts ledger on the kitchen table saying, "There you are, here are the figures you were asking for. I was working all night on them."

Bobby opened the ledger and glanced at the figures, it was all gobbledegook to a slum boy like him. He scanned the 100 pages or so, jam packed with numbers, but to him it was merely a foreign language. As he glanced through the audit book, he put on a pretence saying, "Looks very impressive, Percy, old chap. You've obviously done a good job when I was away. Well done, old chap."

Percy was becoming increasingly irritated with the "old chap" patter but it had served its intended purpose. It had made him nervous and paranoid, thinking his boss had something on him. He put on a brave façade, "Thank you, boss, all in the line of duty. I think all these figures, and I am not being cheeky, will make no sense to a layman like you." Bobby felt slightly miffed at being called "a layman." He realised Percy was using the same psychology on him as he had with the "old chap" patter. Bobby picked up the audit book, "Percy, old chap, ah'm going to take this home with me."

The accountant looked agitated, "What for, boss?"

"Oh, just to put under ma pillow so ah'll have sweet dreams about how much money we are making."

Percy's lips began to quiver again but he grinned with his yellow teeth, "It's certainly an unusual request but I suppose there is no harm in you taking the book back home with you for the night. As long as I can have it back in the morning. I need it for the good of the business." Bobby laughed out loud, "No problemo, old chap. You'll have the book back, wi' all the complicated figures, first thing in the morning." He slapped Percy on the back and bade him farewell.

When they got into the car Bobby said to Johnny, "Ah don't understand all these accounts, who do you think we should get to have a look at them? It must be somebody good with figures." Johnny said the obvious candidate was Kenny, as he was a whiz kid with numbers as he had proved on the betting side.

Goo Goo was told to fetch Kenny, who arrived at Bobby's flat about an hour later. "Take a look at these accounts and tell me what they mean," Bobby told him.

Kenny sat down at a table and studied the accounts book for almost two hours while Bobby and Johnny waited in the living room. Clutching the book, Kenny walked into see them. Bobby said, "What's the verdict Kenny boy, good or bad?" "Bad," said Kenny, "That Percy is a fly bastard. Do you want to hear the good news or bad news first?" Bobby looked slightly angry but covered it well. Give us the good news first, Kenny boy."

"The good news is the accounts are very professionally done, hundreds of complicated figures, but the bad news is no matter how many figures there are, it's clear Percy has bumped you for ten grand, at least." Although they had suspected something, both Bobby and Johnny were taken aback. Bobby exclaimed, "What, you mean the posh fucker has robbed me?"

"Aye ten grand at least is missing, could be more, but he's hidden the figures in such a way that it's hard to detect." Bobby's face turned red with rage, "Ah knew that Percy bastard was up to no good. We'll have a meeting with him in the morning."

"Aye, too right," Johnny said, "Ye can't con a con man. Especially a Gorbals con man like you." He and his comrades made their excuses and left.

Tomorrow was another day, a day of vengeance.

Chapter 62

BOMBAY

The next day, Johnny was up early and decided to go for a run in the Glasgow Green. During times of stress, he found running to be a great antidote to facing life's problems. As his heart pounded, he could feel his worries drift away. Puffed out, he sat on a bench and contemplated the oncoming day. He had arranged to meet Bobby, Goo Goo and Archie at 11am. Kenny would also be present with the accounts book. The plan was that they were going to "ambush" Percy in his office. As Johnny sat in the Glasgow Green, he contemplated life. He saw birds in the trees chirping away in chorus and in some ways he envied them. They sat in their branches and flew through the air, not really worrying about where their food came from every day. And through all sorts of weather, come rain or shine, they survived. They were enviable creatures.

He pondered the Percy situation. There was no doubt he was going to get beaten up, but he would take no part in the beating. He had calculated that punishing Percy would be a bad idea as the accountant knew too much about the organisation. Any beating may send him into the arms of the police, and he could testify with enough evidence to have them all sent down for years. No, the best idea was to let the others inflict the beating, but he would have no hand in it. Besides, he believed that if he showed Percy some degree of mercy, the accountant might in turn exclude him from any revelations to the police. It was a gamble, but a gamble well worth taking. Sitting on the bench, he had a deep think about Percy. He wasn't that bad a guy, even with his dreadful yellow teeth. At times the accountant had even made him laugh out loud, with some of the comments he made.

For example, when Johnny asked Percy what he did after work he replied in his posh voice, "Oh, there's nothing better than going home, sitting in front of the television, and having a good ham shank."

Johnny had asked him, "Do you have a ham shank every night?" Percy had replied, "Not every night but a good ham shank remains my favourite." Percy of course, with his posh upbringing, had no idea that a ham shank was Gorbals slang, for a wank, or rather masturbation. The conversation, with its double entendres highly amused Johnny and the boys. Of course, Percy was a crook just like the rest of them. They were all birds of feather. Percy had robbed Bobby but what did the boss expect? He would have done the same if the roles had been reversed. Percy fiddling the books was just a case of a thief stealing from another thief. If Johnny had his way, he would have just got a slap on the wrist, a stern talking to, and let him carry on from there.

But Bobby was a different kettle of fish. He had taken the fiddling personally and was out for vengeance. Percy was destined to suffer at his hands and Bobby did not have the common sense to see a beating could turn the accountant into a grass. Johnny continued running through the park and passed people, ordinary people, on their way to work. Mothers with babies in their prams, youngsters on their way to school. And how he envied them! There was something about being ordinary that attracted him. The bullshit of being a gangster was a travesty compared to the ordinary lives of these poor people. People who worked hard every day of their lives and ended up with fuck all at the end of it. But they did not know any other way, they were happy with their existences. Subconsciously, Johnny wished he could feel the same way. He had money, power and a family but real happiness was one thing that had evaded him. Oh, for the life of a working man! Not necessarily shovelling sawdust but a decent job with half decent pay. A job that did not involve violence and deception. But being a gangster meant he had to deal with violence and deception almost every minute of the day. He was fed up to the teeth with it.

He jogged round to his flat, got dressed into his gangster gear and met up with Bobby and the boys. They were in a car waiting for him. When he jumped into the vehicle, he could feel the air of violence and intimidation straight away. Bobby sort of snarled and said, "Right we're gonnae sort this Percy bastard out once and for all. Nobody gets away with ripping me off. Kenny has been up all night looking at the ledger again. Kenny, tell Johnny what you found at second glance." Kenny looked tired with bloodshot eyes, "A second glance at Percy's bullshit book shows he's ripped of Bobby for a lot more than ten grand but the figures are still hard to decipher."

486

Archie sneered, "Dirty robbing wanker. I knew he was no good all along. What do you think Johnny?" He replied, "It seems to me that he saw his chance to make some real cash and took it." Bobby raised a baseball bat, "Ah'll show him no' tae rob me ever again. This is gonnae go over his nut." Johnny smiled but knew Bobby was making a big mistake. A baseball bat "over the nut" was not exactly the best solution to the problem. But he kept his counsel. Better to say nothing and go with the flow.

To be a winner in the gangster game, you had to go with the flow or perish. They walked into his office and Percy was sitting at a table looking studious and was quite chirpy, "Good morning, boys. Have you brought my account book back? Kenny placed the ledger on the table. Percy said, "Everything to your satisfaction, boss?" He did not see that Bobby had a baseball bat behind his back. Bobby replied, "Not really, old chap. You've been fiddling the fuck out of me, haven't you… old chap?"

Percy's face drained of blood, "What do you mean, boss? The accounts are in perfect order. The figures may seem complicated to a layman like you but in the accountancy game that's how it is." Suddenly, Bobby whacked Percy in the mouth with the baseball bat and most of his yellow teeth were shattered. He fell to the ground with blood gushing from his mouth.

For a few moments, Johnny reflected that Bobby had done Percy a favour by knocking out all those dreadful teeth. Bobby began to batter into the accountant as he lay on the floor until his screams became unbearable. Johnny shouted to Bobby, "For fuck's sake don't kill the guy. We'll try to get the money back." By this time Percy was lying in a pool of blood groaning. Bobby shouted to him, "Where's ma fucking ten grand, you stole ya bastard ye?" Percy groaned and mumbled, "In my house, I was just looking after it for you." Johnny and Goo Goo were instructed to take Percy back to his house and recover the money. They bundled Percy into a car and Goo Goo handed him a towel to stem the flow of blood from his mouth. They drove to the leafy suburb of Milngavie and found Percy's house, a small detached bungalow.

They went inside and Johnny was almost apologetic, "Sorry about that, Percy, Bobby was gonnae kill you but luckily I stopped him in the nick of time. Now where's the money? Show us and we'll be on our way and your nightmare will be over." Percy went into a back bedroom and mumbled, "It's under the bed, in two suitcases." Johnny pulled out the suitcases and they were full of banknotes. He placed all the notes on the bed and began to count them. It was quite easy to do because Percy had arranged them in £500 bundles all with rubber bands round them. As the counting was concluded Johnny declared, "Twelve thousand five hundred pounds." He put ten grand into a bag and left £2,500 on the bed. Goo Goo took the bag to the car and Johnny was left alone with the bloodied and battered Percy. He said, "Bobby was out of order battering you like that. Ah'm leaving you two and a half grand so you can get yourself a new set of teeth.

They'll look a lot better than the ones you lost. Ah'll tell Bobby we only found ten grand."

Percy nodded, still with the towel pressed against his bloody mouth. Johnny gave him a firm handshake, "Sorry it ended up like this. Ah still think you are a good guy and a great accountant. That's why ah saved your life." He left the bungalow and went into the car. He was aware that what he had said to Percy might just save his bacon if the accountant turned grass.

As Goo Goo drove them away, Johnny said, "Poor bastard, at least we didnae kill him. Being an accountant, he probably thought his number was up!"

Chapter 63

STORM

Things were quiet for a while, too quiet. Johnny felt uneasy about it all and had an inkling that this was the lull before the storm. His instinct was related to his past experiences as a gang leader. When he was the leader of the Cumbie gang, there had been occasions, months on end, when everything was quiet but this was usually followed by extreme gang violence and warfare with opposing teams. He speculated what Percy's next move might be and was surprised he had not turned grass straight away. Meanwhile, he had to deal with business as usual. There were several incidents that required his immediate attention. (1) Moneylending. The loans were no problem, apart from a couple of so called "fly guys" who had refused to pay up. Johnny felt their behaviour was banal rather than overtly offensive. The first fellow, a guy in his 30s, had boasted to his pal in the pub that the enforcers "widnae get a penny" out of him

But his attitude ended one night when he was hit on the head with a hammer while standing at a bus stop in Crown Street. The blow put him into a coma for several days and when he emerged, heavily bandaged, he paid the outstanding amount straight away. The second fellow, from Nicholson Street, had built up a reputation as being a bit of a hard-drinking hardman and avoided paying his debt on numerous occasions. But one night his front door was set on fire. The next day, he coughed up.

(2) Insurance and protection. A Jewish wholesaler said he did not need cover but that changed when two masked men entered his store and made off with the contents of his till. He was quick to renew his subscription.

(3) Betting. A group of Irishmen had placed a big bet on a horse running at Ayr. They had £100 on the horse at 10-1, winning £1,000. Johnny just shrugged his shoulders, he knew he's get the money back after a while.

(4) The supplies from Marbella were constant and demand often exceeded supply. Kenny had drawn up a fresh set of account books which were far simpler to understand than Percy's version. Bobby would often keep the new ledger in his safe at home overnight, to ensure he knew where every penny was going. Through it all, Johnny was increasingly stressed. He often felt frustrated that he had to get others to carry out violent acts. He was a violent guy and missed it. To appease his violent tendencies, he ran more and swam 100 lengths a day at the Gorbals baths. The exercise made him calmer and all "the wankers" who showed him disrespect were easily dealt with. Like a Roman emperor he passed orders down through his command and his enemies were quickly put to the sword... or even a razor.

But it was not all deadly serious, he had his odd humorous moments. Hughie, an old guy in his 70s, came into the Mally Arms one afternoon and said he had a problem. He had won fifteen grand on the pools and asked Johnny to invest it for him, "Got the fucking jackpot, had six draws. All for ten bob!" He knew that Johnny would not rip him off as he was an old friend of the family. He also knew that if he invested in Johnny's organisation there would be a better rate of interest than the banks.

Johnny took the money gladly and told Hughie to tell no-one about the deal or about his pools win. Hughie would receive regular interest payments and of course have the backing of the organisation's enforcers if need be. The more money Johnny dealt with, the more throbbing headaches he got. His first instinct was to have a bevvy and get drunk, but common sense prevailed so pounding the pavements and going for a splash were good alternatives.

Swimming in the pool at the Gorbals baths seemed to disintegrate all of his tensions. The water not only cleansed his body but his soul as well. As he swam up and down the pool, he could feel his heart pumping the blood through his system. On his fifty second length he got to the deep end when a young man in his early 20s said, "Hello, Johnny boy!" At first, Johnny did not recognise the young man as he was wearing goggles. When he took them off, he recognised him straight away. It was Willie McKenzie from Thistle Street. A few year's back, Willie's mother had approached Johnny saying her son had been bullied at school and could he do something about it? She even offered him money, but he turned it down. In the event, he and his pals beat up the bullies so badly they even changed school.

The boy's mother said at the time, "Thanks for saving ma son, we owe you a big favour, which we hope to repay one day." Since then Johnny had heard Willie had done well at school and joined the police force hoping to be a detective. He had been a big fan of Kojak and Columbo on the telly. Johnny had to be careful. Why the fuck did a young copper want to talk to him, in all places, a swimming pool?

The young man said, "Glad ah bumped into you in the swimming pool. Now its ma turn to do you a favour." Johnny spat some swimming pool water out of his mouth and said, "And what would that be, Willie?" He was quick to the point, "A guy you used to employ called Percy has been singing like a canary up at police headquarters." Johnny felt a wave of shock go through his body, "What's he been saying? Has he been spilling the beans on me?" Willie shook his head, "All's ah know is he's implicated your boss Bobby involving a lot of things like drug deals. But as far I know, you are in the clear. Glad ah met you swimming, nobody will suspect ah gave you this information. Just tell Bobby tae be careful and cover his tracks." He then swam off, a favour repaid.

Johnny left the pool and quickly got dressed. He walked back to the high flats to warn Bobby. But when he got there, Bobby's wife told him he had gone out to meet a couple of his pals. He said that when Bobby did come back, he had to contact him straight away. Johnny got back to his own flat and had tea with Cathy and his son.

He waited all night for a knock on the door, but no knock came. He went to bed thinking he would alert Bobby in the morning. He fell soundly asleep with Cathy by his side. Everything would be sorted in the morning, or so he thought.

Chapter 64

HEAT

He was having terrible dreams. The giant machines were after him again, getting closer and closer, until he heard Cathy's voice saying, "Johnny, wake up! Wake up! She was looking out of the window and shouted, "The polis are raiding ma da's flat." He leapt from his bed and ran towards the front door, opened it, and looked outside the corridor. The place was swarming with police. His instinct was to go outside and head into Bobby's flat. But his head told him to keep well clear as any appearance could alert the police to his involvement with Bobby.

It was a Pandora's Box that he did not want to open. A Pandora's Box that had the potential to destroy them all. Then he heard Bobby's voice shouting from inside the flat, "Fuck off, ya bastards, get me ma lawyer." The police handcuffed Bobby and took him away. More worryingly, they had hired a safeblower to blow open his safe. Johnny heard a small explosion and also heard one of the CID guys inside shout, "Perfect, drugs and money. The bastard will no' be seeing the light of day for years."

Johnny looked out of his window onto the street and saw policemen loading bags containing bundles of money, cocaine and hash into their van. He also saw one carrying a black ledger, the new drug accounts book. Bobby had been stupid. He had stored the money and some drugs (from his addiction days) in the safe, believing no-one would find his cache. He had made the classic mistake of underestimating the police. Sure, the jails were full of people who had made the same error. Storing the drugs together with the money and having the accounts ledger beside them was utter insanity. The police would have no problem convicting him

Suddenly, Johnny had a revelation? Why had the police not raided his flat? He put it down to the fact that he had saved Percy's life and given him a few grand to fix his teeth and survive. His kindness had been repaid. Not only had Bobby underestimated the police, but Percy as well.

Cathy and her mother were crying and almost hysterical. How would Bobby get out of this? Worryingly, in recent years, High Court judges had been handing out stiff jail sentences of between ten to fifteen years to drug dealers like Bobby. It sent a shiver down his spine. Bobby's wife wiped away the tears and said to Johnny, "What do you think he'll get son?" He put on a brave façade, "It's no' easy to say but Bobby's usually a lucky guy and can talk his way out of anything. Maybe he's got a good alibi up his sleeve."

But, in reality, Johnny was unconvinced. As sure as eggs is eggs, Bobby was definitely going down for a long time. He consoled the two women for a while and then went out for a walk. It was the usual Gorbals cast. Old women with their shopping, guys in their bunnets standing at street corners, a few jakes staggering about and the odd scabby dog roaming the streets for

morsels. He heard a voice coming from a nearby
tenement close, "Hey man, over here." It was Goo Goo
being all secretive. Johnny walked into the close and
Goo Goo said "Fuck's sake, what happened? Ah heard
Bobby got lifted big time." Johnny shrugged his
shoulders in a dismissive, way. "The silly fucker had
drugs, money and even the account book in his safe.
He'll have to be a bigger magician than Harry Houdini
tae get off wi' this one." Goo Goo replied, "The boys
want tae see you. They're in a motor round the corner."

He walked round the block and climbed into the car.
Both Archie and Kenny had worried looks on their
faces. "What's the score, boss?" Archie asked.

"The score is Bobby has been done big time but as far
as ah know the grass accountant left us out of the
plotline. So, until ah know more we'll lie low for a while
then business as usual."

Kenny looked nervous and said, "How long do we lie
low for?"

"Until after the verdict but we'll still be doing business
in a quiet way, more low profile than before," Johnny
said.

Later that night they were taken aback when they saw
the headline in the Daily Record: **GLASGOW
BUSINESSMAN IN MAJOR DRUG BUST.** The report
said, "Police arrested Gorbals businessman Bobby
McGee at his south side flat after a tip off he had drugs
in a safe at his home. A police spokesman said, 'We
received significant information that the arrested man

was a major drug dealer. We found a substantial amount of drugs and money in a safe in his flat. He has been charged with numerous serious offences and will be appearing in court in the morning.' Beside the article there was a large picture of Bobby smiling. Archie said, "Look at that fucking picture. Ah'll bet he's no' smiling now." Kenny agreed, "If he gets found guilty, he'll no' be smiling for years."

Johnny felt depressed but did not show it, "We'll see what happens, boys. Meanwhile, I'm in charge while that silly fucker languishes in Barlinnie." He walked in the direction of his house but he had only gone a couple of yards when a car pulled up beside him, "Jump in," an Irish voice shouted. It was the IRA guy, big John. When he got into the car John said to him, "How could Bobby be so stupid? The polis will make mincemeat of him. Ah've got a bit of advice for you."

"What's that? Johnny said. The Irishman was straight to the point, "We know Bobby will never talk but make no mistake about it they'll be aiming for you next. My advice is to get the hell out of here for a while."

Although Johnny was sure Percy would not grass him up, he was aware that when the police compiled their evidence his name would be sure to crop up.

He lay in bed that night and contemplated his future. He had to get away from the Gorbals and formulated a plan. He would phone Pat in Marbella and tell him to obtain a property for him, preferably a villa with a swimming pool. He had enough hidden money to choke a dozen donkeys.

He would go to the Asian bank to see the manager and have the money transferred to Pat in Marbella. As for the organisation, Archie would be promoted to boss in Glasgow and Kenny his number two. But nothing could be done until Bobby's trial was over. A few weeks later he received a letter from Barlinnie prison with a visitor's pass to see Bobby. When he got to Barlinnie and walked into the visitors' room, it had a dozen or so inmates sitting at tables. He looked round and could not see Bobby. But when he glanced around the room again he saw an old looking man sitting at a corner table. The old man shouted, "Johnny boy, over here!" Johnny was shocked at his appearance. The arrest and incarceration had put years on his boss. He seemed to have turned grey and wrinkled overnight. He put on a brave face, "So how's it going, Bobby?" His boss sighed, "No' too good. Ah was a daft bastard and now ah'm paying for it. No' slept a wink since the arrest and the food here isnae helping, it's fucking terrible. It's not exactly the Rogano."

"So, what's your lawyer saying?"

"First of all, never plead guilty. He says our defence will be the polis planted the drugs, money and account book to frame me"

At this, Bobby's hand began to shake uncontrollably. It was embarrassing. So this is what crime did to you, turned you into a nervous old man with trembling hands. After that, they talked about generalities, the family, even Celtic and Rangers. But there was a futility about it all. A big prison guard hovering nearby did not help the situation.

Johnny wished his boss well and said, "Chin- up Bobby, everything will be ok in the end." When he left Barlinnie, he felt a great sense of relief. Half an hour in that place seemed like a lifetime – but what about doing 10-15 years in jail? It was unbearable to think about it. The old saying was right, crime definitely did not pay, especially when you got caught. The next, day he went to a pal's house and phoned Marbella. It was a contrast to his interaction with Bobby.

Pat said, "Terrible carry on with Bobby. The daft bastard should have settled here in Marbella instead of Barlinnie."

"That's what ah was thinking," Johnny said, "Look out for a villa for me and my family, swimming pool and all that. Ah'll arrange the funds to be sent to you." There was laughter from Pat, "You're in luck, Johnny boy, an old Hollywood director has just put his villa up for a greatly reduced price, for a quick sale. Six bedrooms and a massive swimming pool, bigger than the Gorbals baths! Ah know him well, ah'll get you a good price. The guy is a fucking cocaine and gambling degenerate."

Johnny was aware he was laying the foundations for his exit from the Gorbals. The next day, he went to see the Asian bank manager and told him he wanted to transfer all of his funds to an account in Marbella. Before the manager had been over friendly but when he learned of Johnny's plans his mood changed dramatically. "But Mr McGrath, it is quite a large sum of money, are you sure you want to transfer it all?"

"No," Johnny replied, "Leave a tenner in so we might use the account in the future." The Asian bank manager looked dismayed but readily agreed to the proposal. At this point, Johnny had an instinctive feeling that Abdul was not trustworthy but he told Johnny in a soothing voice, "All the funds will be in the Marbella account by next week, apart from the ten pounds."

He left the bank feeling gratified that he had achieved something. And what did the Chinese proverb say? "The journey of a thousand miles starts with one step." Meanwhile, he contemplated the forthcoming trial. Perhaps with the cunning of his solicitor, Bobby would get off. Perhaps not. Life in the Gorbals was always like that, a two sided coin. Heads you win, tails you lose. Fate and a jury would decide which way the coin would fall.

Chapter 65

BOBBY

During the run up to the trial, the organisation was still running effectively but on a more laid back level. A couple of chancers had not paid their money on time, believing Bobby and his mob were all washed up. Johnny would wait until after the trial. Beating up the two jokers might attract attention to his men and that is the last thing he wanted. On the gambling front, smaller bets and payouts were encouraged to avoid punters going round boasting they had a big win. The protection and insurance side did have minor setbacks with some clients. Some believed, with Bobby in jail, the organisation was in freefall. There were other minor irritations but it wasn't anything Johnny couldn't handle. Once the trial was over, the organisation would bounce back like a rubber ball, a giant rubber ball that would crush all those that stood in its way. One thing that did annoy Johnny was the fact that his money had still not been transferred to Marbella.

He sniffed a rat when he called round to the Asian bank and was told that the manager "was in Bombay" on urgent business and would see him when he came back. It sounded like a load of bollocks but Johnny decided to bide his time. The truth would come out at the end of the day. Meanwhile, old Hughie was quite content with his weekly interest payments from the windfall he had invested. Johnny would personally drop off his money every week, in a brown envelope, at a local bar in Gorbals Street. Hughie played cards with his pals there and Johnny rather liked sitting down with them to hear the old patter and stories. They were all elderly men who led single, solitary lives and dominoes took away any loneliness they might have had. While playing a game, Hughie made a strange request to Johnny, "Ah wonder if you could do me a favour son? When ah get back to ma flat ah can feel a bit lonely. Can you get ma a pet?"

"What sort of pet, a cat or a dog?"

"Nah, son ah've always wanted a parrot. Something that ah can talk to and it can talk back. Cats and dogs cannae do that. Do ye think you can get me a parrot that can talk?"

It was an unusual request but a bemused Johnny replied "Sure thing, Hughie. Ah'll put out some feelers and see what I can do."

Johnny promptly left the pub and instructed Goo Goo to find him "a talking parrot, fast," for one of his best customers. Goo Goo looked dumbfounded but replied he'd try his best. In many ways, the search for a talking parrot, by hook or by crook, brought some humour into their lives, especially with the seriousness of the Bobby court case on the horizon.

The next matter to deal with was the elusive Asian bank manager. Was he still in Bombay "on business" or was it all a concocted story? Johnny told Goo Goo to wait outside the bank from 8am every morning to see if the manager was going in. "How will ah know him?" Goo Goo enquired.

Johnny replied, "Simple. An ugly-looking Asian bastard wi' a big wart on his nose." For a week or so there were no developments on the parrot and bank manager front. But one day, Goo Goo walked into the Mally Arms carrying a bird cage with a parrot inside. "Where the fuck did you get that thing?" Johnny asked. Goo Goo laughed, "An amusement arcade in Jamaica Street called Treasure Island. As a publicity stunt, they had this parrot near the entrance and it talks like fuck. It fact it talks like a pirate!"

The next minute the parrot squeaked, "Pieces of eight, pieces of eight." Johnny could not believe it, "Fucking hell, Goo Goo, a pirate parrot! Take it round to old Hughie's place straight away."

The next morning, Johnny and Goo Goo turned up at the bank. At first, they were told the manager was "very busy" but when they insisted in an aggressive manner on seeing him, they were ushered into his office. On seeing them, the manager gave a large false smile, "Lovely to see you again. Sorry I've been away on business in India. What can I do for you?" Johnny was angry at the insolence, "Where's ma fucking money? Nothing has appeared in Marbella." "

"Ah sorry, Mr McGrath," he replied with yet another false grin, "There was a technical problem transferring the money. But it should be sorted out within the next couple of weeks." Johnny could tell straight away he was lying. He pulled out an open razor and placed it on the desk before the manager. "I know you guys eat Halal meat which means you slash the throat of the animal before it dies. Well if ah don't get ma fucking money back straight away ah'm, gonnae slit your fucking throat. And then you'll be Scotland's first Halal meat manager."

The Asian looked frightened and Goo Goo put two large canvas bags on the table, "Put all ma fucking money in there and we'll be on our way," Johnny said.

"But Mr McGrath, it is a large sum of money."

Johnny shouted and waved his razor wildly, "Put it in the fucking bag now, otherwise your throat is getting slashed." Two Indian flunkeys appeared and were ordered by the frightened bank manager to load "thousands of pounds" in bundles into the bags. After they did so, Johnny said, "Thanks, Abdul. It wasn't that hard was it? Did you remember to leave a tenner in the account?"

"Yes sir, I did."

"Good man," Johnny said, "Nice to do business wi' you."

They left the bank with the two loaded bags of money. Johnny had an arrangement with Pat who said he would instruct "a courier to take the dosh to Marbella." On the house front, Johnny had been informed the Hollywood director had agreed to sell his villa at a greatly reduced price, especially after he had snorted a great deal of cocaine provided by Pat. The next day, Johnny was astounded when he looked at the front page of the Glasgow Evening Times. There was a picture of a frail looking Bobby with the headline: "Gorbals businessman pleads not guilty to drug charges." The other story on the front page had a picture of a scrawny looking parrot with the headline: "Valuable pirate parrot stolen from arcade." Johnny had a humorous thought, thinking who looked worse, Bobby or the parrot.

Bobby's trial was scheduled to take place in a month's time at the High Court. Johnny was advised not to visit him again in Barlinnie, as the police might be watching, trying to work out who his accomplices were. On the day of the trial, Bobby appeared in the dock looking a shadow of his former self. A long line of policemen gave evidence about raiding his flat and finding drugs, money and the account ledger in his safe. But the star witness was Percy. As he stood in the witness box swearing "to tell the truth, the whole truth and nothing but the truth," it was clear to Johnny he was being very economical with the truth. He left out a load of facts including who his main enforcers were. Percy told the court, "It was Bobby McGee who employed me. He threatened my life if I did not work for him. For fear of death I worked for him as an accountant doing the books and making out the drug transactions." As grasses go, unfortunately for Bobby, he was very good and very articulate,

As he watched from the public gallery above, Johnny was impressed with Percy's new teeth. Now, instead of looking like a row of condemned buildings, he had a new set of expensive gnashers, which in turn impressed the jury.

In the event it was an open and shut case for Bobby. The jury found him guilty of all charges. He stood in the dock and trembled as the judge said to him, "Robert McGee you are a very evil man who once controlled the Glasgow drug business. As a result, you have made a lot of money but ruined many lives. Therefore, I have no hesitation in sending you to prison for 12 years." On hearing this Bobby fainted in the dock and had to be carried downstairs to the cells by several ushers and policemen.

His wife began to wail loudly in the public gallery shouting, "Oh Bobby, ma Bobby, it just isnae fair."

Johnny got out of the court as quick as he could and headed over the Albert Bridge to the Gorbals. He went into Hughie's flat in Thistle Street and the parrot was sitting quite happily on his perch in the cage squawking, "Piece of eight, pieces of eight." Over and over again. Hughie made Johnny a cup of tea and said, "It never stops talking but I enjoy it. It's just a pity that a creature like that has got to spend its life in a cage."

Johnny sipped his tea, "I know a guy who is in exactly the same position."

CHAPTER 66

PRISON

With Bobby locked up for the foreseeable future, Johnny decided to steer the organisation in the right direction. He called a meeting with Archie, Kenny and Goo Goo and explained his battle plan. He was going to run things from Marbella. Archie was to run the Glasgow side with Kenny his right hand man. Goo Goo would be in charge of all the enforcers. The first thing they did was sort out the couple of jokers who had refused to pay up when Bobby was awaiting trial. Both men received a beating and after that, the cash appeared. The Jewish businessman suddenly changed his mind and re-started paying his protection money. Johnny laughed at this, "Say what you like about the Jews but they certainly know how to play the game. When the guy thought Bobby's trial would weaken us, we couldnae get a penny out of him. But now he's glad to pay us right on the nail. Shrewd operators, the Jews." In his private life, Johnny also had a few problems. Since the trial Bobby's wife had cried non-stop every day and for a while Cathy was the same. But she bucked up after a while telling Johnny, "Ma father got himself into this mess, now he can get himself out of it."

She had visited her father in prison, but it had made her ill. There was something about the prison system that made her nauseous. She vowed from then on she would prefer to write to her father rather than visit him. Her mother was a different matter. She went and visited her husband as much as she could. She vowed to do so until his eventual release date in the years to come.

On a visit to Johnny and Cathy she said, "You want to get the hell out of the Gorbals. It could be Johnny next, as you never know what the polis are up to. They might even frame Johnny because of his involvement wi' Bobby."

When she left, Cathy said to Johnny, "What are we gonnae do?" We've got a young boy and ah don't want to see him grow up while you are inside."

Johnny reassured her that would not be the case, "Look darlin', don't worry, ah've thought up a wee plan to get us out of here." "Awright," she replied,"But make it sooner, rather than later." The police had nailed Bobby, and Johnny heard they were now setting their sights higher, namely big Arthur and John the Irishman. Word got about that Percy had supplied them with names of individuals who he had dealt with on an occasional basis. To put it simply, he knew where the skeletons were buried. But he was playing a dangerous game. These individuals were far more dangerous than the crooked accountant perceived.

Johnny felt for a time that at least he had fallen off the police radar as they concentrated on catching bigger fish. In fact, his confidence had increased to such an extent that he had picked up the gifted red Rolls Royce and had Goo Goo chauffeur him about Glasgow but they would avoid being sighted in the Gorbals. Johnny would be in the back wearing a flat cap and sunglasses so as not to attract attention to himself. And if the police got a sniff of this he would merely say, he had "borrowed it" from the wealthy bookie. When they stopped at traffic lights in Renfield Street in the city centre, a car pulled up alongside and Arthur was in the back. He signalled to Johnny to follow his car. They followed it to the outskirts of Glasgow and stopped in a side street. Arthur climbed out of the back of his car and said to Johnny, "Nice to see you've gone up in the world young man. Shame about Bobby being grassed up by that accountant guy. Ah hear he's been talking again to the polis. Do you know by any chance where he lives?"

Johnny said he did, and wrote Percy's address on a piece of paper and handed it to big Arthur. Arthur gave a weak smile and merely said, "Thank's son, much appreciated."

Later that day, around lunchtime, on the outskirts of Govanhill, they spotted Malky on his way back to work in the sawmills. He had the look of a defeated man. The Rolls Royce pulled up beside him and Johnny shouted, "Climb in, Malky boy, and we'll take you to work in style. He did so and Johnny said, "No' seen you for a while, how's Lorraine doing?" Malky sort of growled and replied, "Fucking terrible, she's a nutcase, a manic depressive. She tried to slash her wrists the other week there. But we managed to save her. Marrying that cow is the worst thing I ever did. She's a waste of time and so is her stinking father."

The Rolls stopped outside the sawmills and Johnny noticed all the familiar faces going back to work after their lunch break. He saw the manager McDonald who had sacked him and shouted, "Hey, any chance of getting ma job back? Ah miss shovelling aw that sawdust!" The manager gave a humourless nod and headed back inside the sawmills. Malky said to Johnny, "Same auld bastards doing the same auld jobs wi' the same auld patter. You're well out of all this crap, Johnny." He felt sorry for his pal and patted him on the back before he headed for his shift. Later that day, he went to his pal's house and phoned Pat in Marbella, "So, any news for me Pat?" On a crackling line Pat replied, "Plenty of news, Johnny. Ah've got you the villa for a knock down price. The money has all been paid, so it's all yours. It's here ready and waiting for you to move in. By the way, bring some sun cream wi' you. It's fucking roasting over here."

When an elated Johnny got back to his flat there was a letter waiting for him. It was from Bobby in Barlinnie, "Hi Johnny, I understand why you and Cathy have not been up to see me. Your best bet is to get you, Cathy and the boy out of the Gorbals for good and start a new life somewhere else. Do you know where I mean? In the past I made a few mistakes and now I am paying for it. Mind, we all make mistakes, that's why they put rubbers on top of pencils! So, take care and hopefully one day, me and my missus will be able to join you, Cathy and my grandson. Best wishes, Bobby."

Johnny thought long and hard about the letter. Although Bobby was a defeated man, he had preserved his Gorbals sense of humour. Cathy read the letter and had tears in her eyes, "So, what are we gonnae do Johnny? How the hell are we gonnae get out of the Gorbals? Ah don't want our boy growing up here." Johnny kissed her on the cheek and said, "Don't worry, ah've been setting the wheels in motion. We are moving to Marbella in Spain."

Cathy gasped, "Spain? But we cannae speak Spanish!" Johnny laughed, "You don't have to speak Spanish, everybody I know speaks English and the weather is fantastic. So, start packing you bags, we're off soon." Over the next week, he had several meetings with Archie, Kenny and Goo Goo. They readily agreed to his re-structuring of the organisation. It meant promotions for all of them and of course more money. Johnny would keep in contact by phone daily while residing in Marbella

He arranged for Goo Goo to pick up him, Cathy and the boy and drive them to Glasgow Airport where he had booked a flight to take them to Malaga. As they waited in the airport lounge, he picked up a copy of the Daily Record. The front page headline was **DRUG ACCOUNTANT FOUND BLASTED TO DEATH.** The story said Percy had been "assassinated" with a shotgun as he tended his garden in Milngavie.

The flight took a couple of hours and when they arrived in Malaga the sun was blazing. They went out of the airport and Pat was there to meet them in his Porsche. "Welcome to paradise," Pat shouted to them, "Aye," Cathy said, "It's better than that shithole they call the Gorbals. Ah never want to go back there again."

Johnny and Patrick laughed. They thought the comments were a bit over the top as they still had a great affection for the place, even with all its drawbacks.

The next day, Johnny lay on a sunbed beside the pool at his villa. He sipped on a glass of chilled white wine. He thought of his life and adventures in the Gorbals. It might even make a good book and a title came into his head, *"The Incredible Rise of a Gorbals Gangster."*

THE END

Printed in Great Britain
by Amazon

86400964R00292